Jacaranda Ridge

Angela Moran

ISBN: 978-99959-0-491-3
eISBN: 978-2-9199613-1-3

Contact: Jacaranda.Ridge@pt.lu
Website: jacaranda-ridge.net

Cover Portrait: "Jacaranda tree imported into the second dimension" by Angela Moran. © Angela Moran, 5 May 2020.

This book is dedicated to the memory of my grandparents:
Madeline from Westmeath,
Jack from Clare,
Tom from Wicklow,
and Molly, from a county that we lost.

About the Author

Angela Moran was born in Sydney in 1965 to Australian parents of Irish descent. She has worked as a journalist, a lecturer, and a lawyer and lives by the Moselle River.

Glossary

Clarification of words used in the Irish and /or Australian versions of the English language appear in footnotes.

Contents

PART I – REBELLION (1915–1916)

Attack 2
Rising 14
Storm 29
Shelter 71

PART II – ALLEGIANCES (1922–1923)

Education 120
Assassination 167
Capitulation 190
Redemption 231

PART III – HOLY DAYS (1928–1929)

Aspirations 248
Strategies 272
Instigation 308
Crucifixion 341

Part I - Rebellion
(1915–1916)

CHAPTER 1
ATTACK
November 1915

The back screen door yawned open as Nell pushed it through the parched dry air. One hand rested on the battered iron handle while the other lay across a tangle of wet washing, all gathered up in a basket and balanced at her hip.

There, at the veranda, by the pulse of the midday sun, she realized.

"It's that tree."

Nell let the door bang behind her, dropped the wicker basket, then ran toward the tool shed. There was a good half day of sunlight left. If she could get the tree chopped down and bag its flowers in burlap, then Eamon might sleep through a night. The hissing and sucking that was stealing his infant breath might vanish and bring a healthy child back.

The lower branches, thought Nell, as she rifled through the farm tools. *Take down the lower branches then cull it by the trunk, just like the men on O'Doherty's run.*[1]

Nell had used Rory's axe before but only to chop up logs for the winter fire. A job like this couldn't be much different, even in the heat. But it had to be finished by dusk.

The tree was like a feature work in an otherwise featureless gallery. Purple flowers spattered throughout its close-to-black branches, then spilled into bottomless blue. The tree had kept the name it bore when imported into Australia—*Jacaranda*—

---

[1] Farm.

2

and brandished the grandeur of age. Normally, no one would touch it, no one would come near it. But on this day in late spring, about a month before Christmas, Nell charged ahead, unflinching.

Her skin crept with sweat and her heart beat hard as she lifted the axe to attack. The nightly pain of hearing Eamon cry, and the terror that he might not, propelled each strike of metal on bark, as did watching and waiting for Eamon's rhythmless breath to texture out into safety.

It all had to stop, tonight, and this bloody Jacaranda tree had been the cause of it all along.

* * * * *

The heavy steel bit lay across the old nag's gums. She was railing hard against it, and her distress upset Rory as well.

The plan had been to retire her at the beginning of the year—to end a life of service she had begun with Rory's father. But at the moment, that wasn't affordable, and watching the old horse struggle weighted Rory with guilt.

He pulled over to the side of the road at Dead Dog Hill and sighed. He had already set the bit as freely as he could, so there was nothing more to be done.

"It won't be long now, old girl," said Rory, as he stroked her head and watered her. "The only journey you'll be making soon will be from one end of a paddock to the other."

The nag drank thirstily.

During their journey to the butter factory, where they shaved their way through khaki hills, Rory thought of the future: new horse, more children, and a farm that was finally in profit and doing more than providing a roof and enough to live off. Meanwhile, all around him, lean, long dead trees punctured an enormous shell of sky, pushing giant splinters against its shimmer.

Rory knew he was getting ahead of himself. The first thing to be done was to cure Eamon's breathing. He felt his own throat tighten. He had to stay strong for Nell. Just a tiny sign of improvement would carry them both to calm. Why was their baby battling, barely coping with the days and living even more desperately through the nights?

Rory arrived at the butter factory and tried to cast his worries aside.

"How are things with you, Mick?" he was able to ask cheerfully.

The manager, dressed in white from trousers to apron and shirt sleeves, walked toward him.

"Can't complain," replied Mick.

"The summer's starting already for us," said Rory. "The cream can is full this morning. It must be the lushness in the grass."

Mick smiled at Rory's sarcasm. Rory lifted the can from his cart into Mick's hands.

"I'm glad to hear it," said Mick. "I'm still using all you fellas can supply, war or no war. And they said we'd never be able to dairy this far west."

"Well, they were wrong, weren't they?" said Rory. "And you don't need a big population of fit young men to find people who want to eat butter and cream. Doesn't matter that most of 'em are off fightin' the Hun.[2]"

"Too right," said Mick.

---

[2] Pejorative term for Germans used throughout the British Empire in World War I.

Mick placed the can on the ground and straightened his back.

"Speaking of fit, young men," he said, "how's that baby boy of yours? I heard he was doing it tough—something to do with his breathin'?"

Rory was still standing on the milk cart. He pushed back his hat to the top of his brow and looked above Mick's balding head. They were all well meaninged, the townsfolk, but he couldn't see how chatter and talk would bring his family relief.

"He's getting there. He's just having a few problems adjusting to earthly livin'."

"Sorry to hear that," said Mick. "I wish there was something we could offer to help out you and Nell, but we never had worries like that with our kids. Dead lucky, we were. A round of measles and one of mumps, and that was about it."

"We appreciate you thinking of us. I'd better get on. Be late home for lunch."

"All right, Rory. I've added thruppence³ to the price. Take it. The quality of your cream is standout."

"Thanks, Mick," said Rory. "That's kind."

Rory climbed into the sulky⁴ and took the reins. The nag commenced the journey home. Viewed from a deep blue mountain to the west, and at a distance, Rory and his cart crept across the countryside like a giant queen ant parading royally on a path, as if it were made for them alone.

Rory reached home and frowned. Normally, at lunchtime, he was greeted by the smell of a freshly slaughtered chicken, duck, or cow sizzling on his young wife's stove. But today, he couldn't smell anything.

---

³ Three pennies.
⁴ Small and low-slung carriage pulled by a horse.

Rory tied his horse to the post on the shady side of their house. Once inside, he headed down the corridor to the kitchen. It was empty. Rory tracked back and checked all three rooms of their modest family home.

There was no sign of Nell. But mercifully, he found Eamon sleeping by the slip of a breeze near a bedroom window. That left only the scrap of a backyard and the chicken pen as places he might find his wife.

From the rear veranda, he saw her. She had her back toward him as she stood in front of the Jacaranda tree. An arc of purple blooms encircled Nell from above as she chopped at its lowest branch.

"Nell, love, what are you doing?" Rory called out.

He may as well have been talking to the birds. Somehow, she hadn't heard him.

Rory broke into a jog. When he reached Nell, he grabbed her shoulders and turned her to face him. Nell saw it was Rory, released the axe, and let it fall a foot away.

"Love, what *are* you doing?" cried Rory.

"It's Eamon's breathing," sobbed Nell.

She hung her arms around Rory's neck.

"What?"

"It's getting worse because of this tree. Look at the way its flowers have been dropping everywhere. It's the seeds getting caught in his tiny little lungs."

Rory pulled Nell close so that their warm bodies met. He let his cheekbone slide to settle on the crown of her head while she cried.

* * * * *

Father John O'Kelly, aged sixty-three, was resting in bed. His head lay on a well-plumped pillow, a plinth for a living bust. He sat up, ran his hand wearily through waves of chalk-white hair, and dropped his feet to the floor.

He walked to the back veranda, down the stairs, then through the garden to the lavatory. The toughness of the grass on his broad calloused feet and the dazzle of midday light completed his awakening.

Praise the Lord, thought O'Kelly. *I've a fever no more and am freed from a sick bed. I've God's work to be getting on with.*

Back in the kitchen, O'Kelly made tea and settled at the table. He reached across it and wrapped his hand around the last of the week's damper.[5] He opened its paper covering then watched its edges crumble as he pushed the butter knife through it. His was to be a humble meal of doughy bread and hot black tea. It was a pleasure that had stayed with him since the commencement of settlement and the cruder days of camp food. He thought its simplicity to be holy and its continuity in his life a comfort.

The parish was peopled now by decent families. Many had taken their chances and traveled out west in only the last ten years. Back then, massive runs of Crown[6] land had been sold off into blocks big enough for families to farm. And by goodness, they had farmed them well. Few were very wealthy, but none were very poor. And they were living honest lives, in accordance with God's laws.

It had not been like that in the beginning. O'Kelly had taken the calling to spread the word of God, and in turn, God

---

[5] Heavy Australian bread originally cooked by travelers in the coals of a campfire, but later in ovens.

[6] Symbol of governance in British colonial rule.

had sent him to Australia, and to people he thought, perhaps, to be beyond the reach of our Lord.

"John, why on earth Australia?" his mother had pled, when she learned this was where he would take his calling.

"Because an ancient people are being met with and harmed by us."

"But can't you protect people closer to Ireland?"

"Mother, it's you and Father who gifted me the virtue of knowing the difference between wrong and right. A new country is being carved out of one of earth's most uncharted continents, and God calls me to see it built by His word."

Little did I know, thought O'Kelly, *that the complexities of a far-flung frontier would dictate recourse to subtle tactics.*

Before the Town emerged, before the peace, O'Kelly carried packs of damper when making forays into the bush. The young priest, dressed in black from his leather boots to the peak of a rakish hat, sat high on a horse that was as dark as his clothing. They eased their way through the brittle scrub like a steady, marching shadow. And the soil compacted beneath the animal's hooves, hardening it as it went.

He wasn't sure what he would do once he encountered Aboriginals—how he would spread the word of God to the most diffident of folk. But they would have to learn it and capitulate. The settlement was well under way, and if he couldn't bring in Australia's first people, they would be left to the mercy of the new-comers.

Back in the early days, a couple of decades before the turn of the century, he sometimes stumbled across them; groups of Aboriginal women housed in humpies[7] made of strips of

---

[7] Dwellings lived in by Aboriginal people.

deadened bush. It was there, so it was said, that they tended children, baked the meat of game already hunted, and talked and laughed until the men returned from the search for more to eat, whether scavenged from fledgling farms or killed at their hands in the wild.

But it was nearly impossible to get close to them. Often the camps were empty. Years later, O'Kelly realized that they had seen or heard him coming and fled, fearing the man dressed in black trampling his way through their country.

Yet, every now and then, they didn't run, and O'Kelly would watch them from a distance. In the Aboriginals, there was an absence of awkwardness; legs glided to walk, and arms floated to reach. Dusty soil powdered their bodies, so that they might have emerged from the earth itself. And their perfect jawlines had stirred in him, just faintly, the sin of envy, with teeth set in flawless rows. His own teeth met in places that they oughtn't, so that the hinges beneath his ears creaked a little and sometimes cracked.

He remembered the day he stumbled across a barely finished fire. He had tied his horse to a sapling, left his hat hanging on the saddle, and crept toward the embers. There was a humpy standing not fifty yards from it, but he could see no sign of life. *Still*, he'd thought, *there just might be some people there*. He waited and stared into the remains of the fire, until one of them came forward.

O'Kelly watched as she walked toward him. Perhaps, he wondered, she was pondering.

Is he a creature that has come from the earth, or has he surfaced from the river?

She swaggered, one light foot padding after the other, her breasts swinging gently in time. Before she reached the fire, she picked up a stick. She was going to prod the embers.

So, there he was, crouched on one side, she at a right angle to him, crouched on another. She kept looking at the charcoal sticks and burnt gray dust in the center. The bush did what it always did; its insects buzzed.

His eyes were blue and hers were brown. The white-skinned people were always clothed; the black-skinned often naked. His nose might have looked to her like an ungainly beak; theirs were generally flatter and broader. And what about his shoes? They were more or less the shape of the long stones by the river. Did she wonder how he managed to walk, or even think, perhaps, that his cumbersome feet caused him to be carried by horse?

"Good day," he said. "My name is Father John… John O'Kelly. What is your name?"

She turned the stick to push over a small smoldering lump.

"I have food. Would you take some if I were to fetch it? I am not going to hurt you. I am here to help—to guide you through the changes that the white men are bringing."

She continued playing with the fire, prodding it here, poking it there. She glanced behind her, back toward the humpy, then shuffled a few paces sideways so that she was directly opposite him.

"Please, wait there. I will bring you what I have. It's simple fare—damper, the white man's bread—but you are welcome to what I have."

He rose, carefully, and walked slowly toward his horse. His back was turned to her for less than a minute, but when he returned, she was gone.

10

There hadn't been a warning; she had made no sound in motion. She had simply vanished, retreated back into infinity.

At the presbytery kitchen table, John O'Kelly finished eating and got up.

Damper. It still made him think of her and what might have become of her.

* * * * *

Nell and Rory's side veranda was the better place to be when the air started cooling at day's end. Delicate netting split the outer house from the open bush like protective meshing. In safety, Nell and Rory succumbed to its hypnosis. The bush was no place to be outside of daylight hours. Nighttime was for sealing the capsule—settlers inside, all things native out.

Nell had just succeeded in getting Eamon to sleep. She reached for the enormous half-carved chicken in the middle of the table. It was surrounded by potatoes the size of campfire stones and a trail of plump green peas. Rory would be ready for his seconds.

"Not tonight, thanks love," said Rory, motioning her back with his fork. "I'm not so hungry. That bit of drama today might have put me off my food. You're a sight, all right, with an axe in your hand."

Nell returned to her seat, sheepishly. She picked up her knife and fork and said nothing.

Rory stared off to his left into the black of the night then turned back toward his wife.

"I'll ride into Town tomorrow. See Dr. Dunne and find out when he can come by."

"Don't see what good his coming by can bring," said Nell. "He listens to his chest, checks his linen, takes his temperature, and then leaves. He keeps saying it's just a bit of croup that will pass. I'd hate to see what an ailment that gets worse looks like if Eamon's is only passing."

"Love, if Dr. Dunne can't work out why his breathing is as it is, then we can't either," replied Rory. "But it's not likely to be the Jacaranda tree. The lad's growin'. It's been a battle of an early life, but he's growin', so we'll just have to keep on doing what we're doing. You know Eamon's in Father O'Kelly's prayers, and most likely the rest of the parish's. Mick was asking after him today."

Nell was a woman who knew her own mind. It was one of the reasons Rory married her. But when she got like this and dug in her heels, it was like trying to reverse the tides.

"Why us, Rory?" she asked. "Nobody in my family or yours has ever had anything like this. And as for paying Dr. Dunne, again, to tell us more about something he doesn't understand, what good'll that do?"

Rory rubbed his chin and tried to get past the day's events.

"Barry Walsh is due here Friday. He's comin' over with one of his lads to help re-fence the back paddock. Might ask 'em to stay for supper."

There was a silence that seemed to Rory as dense as the night enfolding them. Eventually, Nell looked up.

"I'll roast that bit of rump in the meat safe[8] then—the one the Noonans gave us—and bake a caramel tart."

Rory smiled.

"That'd be perfect, love," he said. "Just the thing."

---

[8] Pre-refrigeration cupboard for storing meat.

Outside, and within the shelter of night, the bush felt it safe to come alive. Wild dogs were free to howl, and light-footed animals with fur like matting scurried from burrow to burrow, while others leaped from tree to tree. As they did, small bats flocked across a deadened, inky sky. The dazzling light of an Australian day had been reduced to pockmarks, throwing peppered rays—the shards of distant stars. And in the darkness, the land lay and lived just as it had for thousands of years before measured in time.

* * * * *

CHAPTER 2
RISING
April 1916

The sulky carrying Nell, Rory, and Eamon Burke creaked its way across a roughed-out path. The journey wasn't short. It was ninety minutes into Town, and ninety minutes back. But they would never miss mass. It hadn't occurred to the Burkes to pray at home some Sundays and confine the journey to once or twice a month. Mass was mandatory for everyone, every Sunday, under the laws of God.

So it happened every week. Rory sat straight and high at the top of his sulky in his best cotton shirt, tie, and hat, with Nell in the back in a Sunday-best dress.

Nell let the countryside roll limply by. She had just completed her second year as a west-lands bride. Nell grew up on a coastal run called Ballycallan, a farm located a long way to the south. It was gouged from the riches of the mighty Australian rainforests and covered with lush, wet lawn. But out here, the land was bitten by the sun. The soil was thin and the grass, heat-battered. But the sky had remained constant and slung itself loftily over everything.

One-year-and-one-month-old Eamon lay in her sturdy arms, snuggled in a light woollen wrap. The change in the seasons from summer to autumn had improved his health. There was more traction in his breathing, and he wheezed only occasionally. But Nell wasn't taking any chances. By night, his crib sat close to her marital bed, and by day, he was seldom alone.

"Nell," called Rory over his shoulder, "do you think we should be upping our offering[9] to a shilling a week?"

Nell looked up.

"What? You mean double it from sixpence? Why would we want to do that?"

"It's just that I haven't raised it for ages—didn't even add a haypenny[10] when you came to the parish. We have to pay our share, Nell, and I'm not sure that we have been."

"What about the budget for the new horse? We can't put off buying a new one for much longer."

The nag snorted and shook her head, as if signaling agreement.

"We're almost there, love. With Mick's tips for our quality cream, we should have enough by summer."

"Can we make up our mind next week, once I've had a chance to look over our books? Are you sure we can afford it?"

"I've had a quick look, and I reckon we can. We're doin' all right, you know."

Nell searched for an excuse to stop.

"Rory," she said. "Can you pull over for a second? I think Eamon's in need of a nappy[11] change."

"Didn't you change him just before we set out?"

"It doesn't matter, Rory. You can't predict the call of nature, and his bottom's gone warm."

Nell knew she would change Rory's mind if she could speak to him face to face. They didn't have the means to give the church any more—not yet, at any rate. It might be

---

[9] Money paid to the Catholic church every Sunday at mass, usually via an envelope dropped into a small tray passed around the congregation.

[10] Half a penny.

[11] Diaper.

too late if she waited until they reached the churchyard. The congregation could still be gathered there on their way into Sunday mass. She and Rory would have no privacy.

"False alarm," said Nell, after checking Eamon's nappy when they stopped.

She lifted Eamon from a shady rock.

"Must have been a rise in the air temperature."

Rory was standing by the nag, checking the reins and smoking. He dropped his cigarette and stubbed it out.

"Better get on then," he said. "Otherwise, we'll be late."

Nell lay Eamon on the seat of the sulky then turned toward Rory. She stopped him before he got back into the driving seat.

"Rory Burke, did you tie that tie with your thumbs this morning? Let me see if I can fix it."

The knot lay beneath the square of his chin. Nell undid it.

And at the same time, the advice of her father, given before she married Rory, filtered through Nell's mind.

"You can accept his hand, Nell," Hector McTiernan had said, once he'd relented and agreed to the marriage. "But I'm not lettin' it happen without conditions. For a start, you're to keep an eye on him. He's a solid man who'll treat you right, but it might be easy to put one over him,[12] and he could just be the sort of cove[13] to hang himself on his own good nature."

"Rory," said Nell gently, as she threaded a new knot. "About the offering. Have you thought about where we might be if we had an unexpected expense? Take Dr. Dunne. We can't be sure we're not going to need him for Eamon, or even a physician from the Port Town."

---

[12] To trick or fool someone.

[13] Nineteenth century and early twentieth century word for *guy*.

"I thought you weren't that keen on spending money on Dr. Dunne?"

"If he has another turn, we won't have a choice, and Dr. Dunne's the only route we have toward getting Eamon a physician. The truth is that we're not the O'Dohertys, and I can't see the point in trying to pretend to the church that we are."

Nell sensed the tightening in Rory's lips as if they were her own. She had been insensitive—too direct. She should have known better and taken a more measured approach, but a stop by the road before they reached the church was the only way to have a quiet talk.

"That's better," said Nell, patting Rory's tie. "We had better get on."

Eventually, the low-built church came into view. Several layers of glossy paint blended and smoothed the lines separating each tranche of wood set horizontally across its walls. The building glowed like fondant, stamping its place on the land. Its neatly mowed lawn ended as abruptly as the cutting marking it out, leaving the bushland towering around it.

The Burkes' tardy arrival meant that the churchyard was empty, save for Marcus Moloney, the postmaster, who was sprinting across it toward the sacristy after charging down presbytery hill. There lived Father O'Kelly. Nell wondered why Marcus was running.

The commotionless yard meant she had another chance at persuading Rory not to increase their offering. But she needn't have worried.

"You know what, Nell," said Rory. "You're right. The church can wait a while, and Father O'Kelly will understand. Gotta be sure we're clear of them medical bills before we start throwin' money away."

"Sorry, Rory, what was that?" asked Nell.

She stepped from the sulky with Eamon.

"The offering. I've changed my mind. Best to wait until we're further into the black.[14]"

Nell shuffled Eamon from her right hip to the left and walked by Rory's side.

"Whatever you think is the right thing, Rory," she said calmly. "Whatever my husband thinks."

* * * * *

Father O'Kelly was in the sacristy, praying and preparing. Every Sunday, he asked the Lord to help him—to maintain the peace of the parish and protect their men at war, along with the Aboriginal people who had survived settlement and who had to be accepted.

He remembered well how this last theme was received when he introduced it to his preaching. In the early days, he gave a series of sermons about respecting Aboriginal people and their ways.

And Roddy O'Doherty had asked to see him in private.

"Father, you seem to have misunderstood," he said, low-voiced and unswerving. "Aboriginal welfare is a matter for the colonial authorities. And I speak for all the parishioners when I say we expect closer adherence to Jesus' teachings."

"This is what I do," replied O'Kelly, "when I preach obedience to the commandments."

"Too late for that out here," retorted O'Doherty, while checking the time on his gold pocket watch. "The group that

---

[14] To be in profit. The term is from traditional book-keeping with origins in the color of the ink employed to show money coming in.

falls short of obeying God's law is made up solely of blacks.[15] Direct that at us and you alienate your own."

And worse still, thought O'Kelly, *from what I saw once I reached this country, I risk goading the settlers toward violence out of insolence.*

Suddenly, there was a knock at the sacristy door. O'Kelly didn't reply. Then, another knock, and someone burst in. O'Kelly was kneeling with his back to him.

"Father, I'm sorry. I tried to catch you at the presbytery before you left to start mass. Father, I've a telegram—a telegram from Ireland. You must read it. The English are finished at home."

The postmaster snatched open his satchel to retrieve it.

O'Kelly turned and saw Marcus Moloney, wide-eyed and breathless.

"What is it, Marcus?" asked O'Kelly.

As he stood, his robe cascaded into a perfect white line, arresting an inch above the ground.

"Look, we have a Republic in Ireland. At last, we're out of the British Empire and have a Republic. I popped into the post office this morning. This came Friday night."

He thrust the telegram into O'Kelly's hand.

The priest held the message half a yard from his face.

Marc,   *28ᵗʰ April 1916*
Revolution in motion. Republic proclaimed Easter Monday. Heavy fighting. British troops invaded. GPO,[16] Four Courts, occupied by Republican soldiers. At last, we are free.
Conor

---

[15] Contemptuous and hateful term for *Aboriginal people*.
[16] General Post Office.

"Who is Conor, Marcus?"

"He's my brother, Father. He's in the Irish Republican Brotherhood. He wouldn't make this up."

"Hmm."

O'Kelly kept pace with developments at home through the press that came up from the south, as well as by reading their own Catholic newspaper. But this message hadn't convinced him. They were in the middle of a war! He placed his hand on the postmaster's shoulder and walked him to the door.

"Marcus, I must start mass. We will find out in due course what is happening at home."

"All right, Father."

The postmaster put his hat back on clumsily.

"But Conor wouldn't spend the money on a telegram if this wasn't happening."

"I've no doubt, Marcus," replied O'Kelly. "But let's just wait and see."

O'Kelly sat on a chair in the corner of the sacristy and reread the telegram. The postmaster was impulsive, all right. He'd even left without retrieving it. But O'Kelly couldn't dismiss the telegram's contents as a fraud. It wasn't sent from the GPO allegedly under siege. From everything he'd read, the Republicans were unmoved by the emergency of the war with the Germans and were determined to fight on. But had they gathered up a head of steam to trigger insurrection?

* * * * *

A shilling was stashed in Rory's right pocket, while the offering envelope, containing sixpence, lay in his left. It was yet to be sealed. He sat on a pew by Nell and Eamon as they waited for their priest.

It had been niggling at Rory for a fair while now—the enduring absence of an increase in the offering on the part of the Burke family. But he knew that Nell would resist it, so he decided to spring the idea on her, slip it past her at the very last minute during their journey to the church. He would swap the coins if she agreed.

I hadn't backed her to pour cold water on it as quickly as she did, thought Rory, and it hurt his pride a little that she had. But Nell was right. Rainy-day money was still needed for Eamon until they could be sure he was in the clear. His wife had provided the pushback he needed to reach the right decision.

Nell and Rory's neighbors were seated on the pews in front of them. Dave Noonan and his pregnant wife Charlotte exchanged radiant smiles. Dave and Rory had grown up together and both of them married their wives in January of 1914. Rory made a mental note to get some counsel from Dave when they next shared a beer. How did he approach Charlotte when he wanted to change her mind, and did he ever relent when she wouldn't?

At first, Rory couldn't fathom it—why a girl like Nell was interested in a cove like him. Now aged twenty-seven, he was four years older than she. Rory's property, Jacaranda Ridge, was comprised of too little land for him to have been a serious prospect for marriage to Nell McTiernan. But once Rory was sure she was as keen as he was, he moved hell and high water to win her. Nell's da[17] Hector was no pushover, and Rory had to prove to him that he would see his daughter right.

Meanwhile, Nell felt a tap on her shoulder and turned behind her. Thellie Walsh handed over a piece of cloth that

---

[17] Irish word for *Dad.*

21

had fallen onto the back of the pew. She was with her husband Barry and four of their sons. Thellie and Barry Walsh lived three miles from the Burkes and were the parents of six lads and one daughter. She was grown up, married, and living in another parish, and two of their sons were overseas fighting for the British Empire.

Nell whispered, "Thank you," dabbed Eamon's mouth with the cloth just handed to her, and turned back toward the altar. As she did, she thanked the Lord that Rory was turning twenty-eight later in the year. He had reached an age at which he wasn't expected to run off and join the war. What's more, he worked in the production of food.

Appearances, thought Nell, as she surveyed the congregation. *Keeping them up is even more important out here than it was down Port Town way.*

The congregation of two hundred or so in their little Town church were as groomed as anyone needed to be to go to somebody's wedding. Yet, the church itself was spartan. It had plain glass windows, not stained ones. A statue of Jesus was positioned by the pulpit, and a six foot cross hung above it; that was all. But the church of Father John O'Kelly drew in worshippers from the most distant farms to the west.

What would the parishioners have made of me, wondered Nell, *if they'd seen me attacking that tree?* As Eamon slept, she worried herself. *Whatever possessed me to think that its flowers were the source of his breathing troubles?*

Then, she remembered: a couple of months of sleepless nights on the unfamiliar land of Jacaranda Ridge, and a rasp that only got worse. The land she was trying to learn to love had wrapped her in terror, then tightened it with string. She called it the choke of the lonely. *Thank you, merciful Lord*, prayed Nell, *for the apparent lifting of the cross of an unwell child.*

Nell looked at Rory and studied his ruddy face. It was long while hers was round. Her eyes were blue and his, brown. His light tan hair was as straight as the walls, while her thick black mane fell in waves. His skin was roughed to tan by the sun, and hers was milky, somehow spared it. She was talkative, he was reserved. And she'd been born into money and prospects, while Rory knew nothing but struggle.

But despite all that, Nell knew. Her father was wrong to worry about their pairing. Theirs was a love sprung from the magic of opposites, and a fine western family would be built from it.

The organist began playing a hymn. Their priest would shortly be with them.

* * * * *

Father O'Kelly recited the first part of the mass but was only partly present. His sermon occupied the workings of his mind as he struggled to make a decision. What *had* happened at home? Had the IRB[18] really moved on British rule? Did he need to change what he had planned to preach, to instead announce that Ireland had rebelled? Would it survive if it had, and what would it mean for the Irish out here?

With each thick hand spread the width of a banister, O'Kelly ascended the pulpit. All his parishioners were there, but with fewer men than women on account of the war. He thought again for a moment, then decided. If there really had been an upheaval at home, it was to be discussed within the authority of the church and not outside it.

---

[18] Irish Republican Brotherhood, predecessor to the Irish Republican Army (IRA).

"I was to preach today on the arrest of the apostles after the rising of Christ, of their flogging for defiance of unholy orders not to speak in the name of Jesus. Every day in the temple, and elsewhere, they did not cease to teach and proclaim Jesus as the Messiah, and despite the orders of the Council of Jerusalem, their defiance led to arrest, imprisonment, and further persecution. Yet, they did not waiver."

O'Kelly paused.

"It reminds us of the freedom we enjoy, here in Australia and all across the British Empire. Our freedom to live by the teachings of our Lord, to speak his name, and worship him here and in churches throughout the Empire. It reminds us of the struggles of the apostles, and the power of the word of God that has won out wherever and whenever there has been movement to stamp it out."

All of this was standard fare. Then, he altered the tone of his sermon.

"But there is another struggle to speak of today, one which calls for temperance, and with respect to which we must offer prayers for peace and the end to violence."

O'Kelly stopped, thought, then spoke again.

"There has been sudden news from Ireland."

A whisper ran through O'Kelly's flock. This was a departure from their priest's devotion to the teachings of scripture. Whenever he strayed, it was important.

"A telegram has been sent to our postmaster, carrying word of a rising in Dublin and the proclamation of a Republic in Ireland. There is apparently heavy fighting, and British troops are in conflict with the rebels."

He heard the worshippers gasp and saw many of them turn toward Marcus Moloney.

"We will find out in due course what has happened at home. At the moment, we have only a telegram. I am traveling south to visit the bishop within the next few weeks and will certainly seek his counsel. In the meantime, we shall all offer prayers for the restoration of peace in Ireland."

* * * * *

After mass, everyone milled on the churchyard lawn. Marcus had the congregation enthralled. They gathered around him. Rory huddled toward the rear of the men, but close enough so he could hear. Nell was in the outer circle with the women but toward the front of them. She rocked Eamon a little and listened intently. Father O'Kelly was still inside the church.

"I knew this day would come. By God, I knew it," said Marcus. "I just wish it had come earlier, and I'd have never made the voyage to this godforsaken country."

"Don't be daft," said Barry Walsh. "Declaring a Republic while we are at war with the Hun is madness."

"And I've got sons as well serving in the Irish brigades, and fightin' the Germans as we speak," another man added. "What's going to happen to them?"

"They're to make their choice, that's what they can bloody well do," retorted Marcus. "They can throw down their guns and go home, or fight for the English and their so-called British Empire and go and live there after the war, even if the Huns win."

"Fair enough, I say," said Dave Noonan. "The English have ground us into the dirt for centuries. No reason now for an Irish lad to be fightin' their fights for 'em."

For Nell and Rory, this was all as unsettling as the rumble of summer thunder.

Rory's thoughts shot to his parents. How he wished they were alive to hear this.

If only God had let Ma see me wed, thought Rory, *rather than take her with pneumonia in the autumn of 1912.*

But his da, Sean, had passed away only last year. When Rory was a boy, Sean would curse from the depths of exhaustion, collapsed in a homemade rocking chair in their rickety family shack at the base of a hill on Jacaranda Ridge.

"Why did it have to be so hard to own land in Ireland? The Crown's a gentle giant here, but the land itself is a flamin' tyrant."

It had fought Sean every inch of the way. Just about every act of settlement was met by the land with the defiance of the landlords at home.

"At least this country is ours, lad," Sean would say. "At least it's ours. And if we've lost Ireland in order to take her, then by God she'll pay us our due."

And Rory recalled his mother Hannah fretting—fretting and grieving. There were six children all told, Rory the eldest and five little sisters, the youngest two being twins.

The voyage out from Ireland lay dimly in his memory. Rory remembered the eternal lapping of sea on the side of a ship, but little else. He was barely aged five when they sailed. But he could recall the birth in Australia of the youngest of his sisters, and his mother struggling to rear her children.

"Rory, would you fetch me this? Rory, would you bring me that? I don't think you should hold her that way—better this way," Hannah would say. But she was never sure herself.

"Why did I have to fall in love with a man determined to better himself?" Hannah confided to Rory when he was older.

From the periphery, Nell looked on to the brewing affray[19] with an inherited sense of relief. Her da would dance a jig if all Moloney was saying were true. It was English rule that had driven him and her ma from Ireland in the first place.

Before the voyage, Hector McTiernan had been a blacksmith in a manor house by the River Nore. It was the home of Anglican gentry, and his sweetheart Violet was one of its servants. Between the two of them, they learned a lot about farming land and wanted one of their own.

"My wife was to be a lady in her own stately home," Hector explained to Nell many years later. "And never again a servant in someone else's."

So, Nell's parents married and then set off, before they were blessed with children, to the far-flung reaches of the British Empire. In Australia, everyone said, there was plentiful, quality, and empty land.

After the voyage, Hector earned a steady income as a blacksmith. It came by the grace of a country building itself off the back of horses. In time, he also secured a lush run of land, not far from the coast but well north of the City. Hector called his run Ballycallan, after the parish of his birth in County Kilkenny.

Nell, Violet, and Nell's four brothers, all of them older than she, did much of the work in running the farm. Hector was often occupied with blacksmithing.

But Nell loved the land and worked as well as the best of the boys.

Perhaps, thought Nell, in Father O'Kelly's churchyard, *a better life might have unfolded for my family if we had all stayed*

---

[19] Intense physical tussle.

in Ireland? Is everything that stood in our way back home in the process of dissolving?

"Our lads should turn their guns on the English military and end the bloody war," cried Marcus. "Then, they can make their way out to Australia and deal with the bastards out here."

O'Kelly appeared, suddenly, white-robed and agitated. He assumed, by the simple force of presence, the place that had been occupied by Marcus. The postmaster melted into the crowd, and Father O'Kelly became its focus.

Rory kicked the ground as O'Kelly bellowed. Nell held Eamon closer.

"Enough," cried O'Kelly. "That's enough. Any talk of violence or disrespect for the Empire has no place in the precincts of this church. You're to stop, you hear me? This talk is to stop at once."

Discord was flattened to silence.

The congregation dispersed, at the behumbled pace of the chastised. The bush throbbed on, the insects buzzed, and the midday sun shone high.

* * * * *

CHAPTER 3

STORM

October 1916

Before going to Australia, Sean Burke had not known that a house could be made of wood. A house, after all, was solid. A house was but four walls of stone, wedged tightly into grass-padded hills and boxing out the elements. Assaults from the sky were warded off, in a house, by a roof of flattened slate that deftly caught the rain then trickled it to the ground.

The curvaceous hills of Ireland were dotted from sea to sea by the protective vista of the house. They were strewn across the countryside like naked dice. A house was the marker of humans on the island of Ireland and their means of securing safety.

And in the west of Kerry, mile after mile of low granite walls checkered the landscape, because jagged stones were piled along the boundaries of the farmers' lots. Once in Australia, Sean had vowed, their lots too would be marked out by walls like these, but a great deal longer. They would form giant squares to be walked around in the course of hours, not minutes.

In the cities of Australia, stones had been cut and houses built in the likeness of those at home. But out in the west, there were no stonecutters and even fewer stones, leaving the settlers to build cruder shelters. And fencing was a matter of threading scraps of beaten wire through splintery strips of wood. They lightly scratched across the land rather than scoring it in grids. In this new land, a house was still a house, and a fence still a fence, but through a lean continuum of function.

So, this is how it was, on a mid-spring morning, that Rory came to amble away from a place he called his house. With a hoe resting on his shoulder, he sang as he went, in the way that Hannah had when her spirits so allowed.

The palm trees wave on high above the fertile shore,
Adieu the hills of Kerry I ne'er will see no more.
Oh why did I leave my home, why did I cross the sea,
And leave the small birds singing around you, sweet Tralee.

Rory wandered by the iron obelisk that was the Jacaranda Ridge windmill. It was capped at the top with a circle of steel that flickered as it turned. For Nell and Rory, it pumped water from the underground bores; but when Rory was a boy, it had served an additional purpose.

Sean would lash a trespassing black man to its tinny frame and give him a thrashin' a he'd never forget for thieving their chooks[20] or stealing a heifer.[21] It frightened Rory, when he was a lad, to hear an Aboriginal's scream while his father roared. Rory would bury his face in Hannah's skirts and hide from Sean when he returned to the shack, bespeckled with blood.

Rory reached the open field at the perimeter of Jacaranda Ridge and immediately got to work. As his hoe cut the land, strips of hardy couch grass snapped in half, opening up rich, dark dirt. Thank God Dave had handed over these thirty acres. They yielded paddocks that were as green as could be. It was better to use it for growing something than for grazing cattle.

---

[20] Chickens.

[21] Cow that has not borne a calf or which has borne only one calf.

Rory wasn't sure yet what he would sow, but the soil was good and a profit certain.

It had all been planned on a winter night by the fire at Dave Noonan's farmhouse, not long before his engagement to Nell and Dave's to Charlotte. Rory remembered.

"Mate," said Rory. "I just can't see Nell's old man agreeing to her hand with a cove with a run of less than two hundred acres. I've only a hundred and fifty-five. Makes me nowhere near the runnin'."

"Take thirty acres from the northern end of my plot," said Dave. "We can move the fence and you can consider it yours. Just pay me off by the month. That way, when ole Hector comes up to inspect Jacaranda Ridge, he'll see you've a run with prospects and that's big enough to keep his daughter."

"Dave, I couldn't ask you to do that for me. It would be like takin' charity."

"No, it isn't mate. I said you can pay me off. But let's make it a long-haul venture so your finances don't get drained. A shilling sixpence a month over fifteen years pulls us up at around thirteen pounds. A fair price for land my grandfather got from squattin',[22] so we're apples.[23]"

As Rory worked on, the mist of a dewy morning hovered over the oblong-shaped paddock. On three sides, it was made of wire interspersed with squares of wood. On the fourth side, it was closed by a sharply rising mountain, blued by a blanket of scrub born of an underground spring.

From up there, Rory looked like a tiny, hatted, long-legged figurine, wrapped in a flannel from the waist up and in moleskin trousers from the waist down. As he inched his way

---

[22] Practice of occupying land with a view to eventual ownership.
[23] To be fine.

across a plain made luscious by a wet winter, his hoe swung like an arresting pendulum, repeatedly stopping as it hit the ground. Native birds flew high, running splits through the sky and filling it with song.

The soil tilled loosely, but with a grip to the ground that cheered him. It reminded Rory of Sean's lament of the seasonal moods of Australian earth.

"Lad, it's as dry as the coastline of west Kerry in summer but rich like peat in winter."

Rory couldn't picture it any other way. Could soil really be so dense as to turn all year round in the way that Sean had said? Could it ever be so turgid as to take the scorch of the sun in its stride? Sometimes, Rory wondered if it were all true, if Ireland was exactly as his parents had said, or if it had been warped in their memories by time.

But there were no two ways about it. This was a good bit of land. Rory finished tilling and started the walk back home. When he reached the windmill, he remembered how right Sean had been. The blackfellas[24] were lazy and let all this land go to waste. A thrashing' was never pretty. But whatever else could Sean have been expected to do with 'em?

* * * * *

The horsehair brush pushed across the floorboards, sluicing out the finest grains of dirt and dust. Nell washed them every second Tuesday afternoon, from one end of the house to the other. First, they were swept thoroughly, then scrubbed wall to wall with boiling water and a dash of white vinegar.

---

[24] An informal term used widely in Australian English for Aboriginal people. It is a fusion of "black" and "fellow".

It was a task Nell had grown up with. As the only girl among five McTiernan children, she shared with her mother Violet the job of cleaning their enormous homestead[25] floor.

With the job half-done, Nell stopped, sat on her haunches, and put the brush in its bucket. Would she and Rory ever have a homestead, or would they remain forever in this house? Would she ever regret the decision she made? Marry into the landed gentry, as her parents had wished, and live a life of tea parties and charity functions, or head out west to the next frontier, on the arm of an up-and-coming farmer? For Nell, there hadn't been a choice. She wanted to remain a woman of the land, and she wanted to marry Rory.

"Why is your run called 'Jacaranda Ridge'?" Nell had asked Rory on a summer night when the two of them were courting.

"Because there are three ridges within twenty miles to the south of the Town. Ours stands out for the Jacaranda tree not far from the road at the bottom of the run. It was there when Da chose the land and grew into a beaudy.[26] So everyone started to call his farm 'Jacaranda Ridge'."

Nell walked to the veranda railing and looked across to the first of their low hilltops. It rose lethargically from a tired-looking plain. *A homestead right there,* thought Nell, *would fit us well.* Close enough to the road and with a view of all they had from a wraparound veranda. But it was a dream that remained, for the moment, as distant from her and Rory as Ballycallan to the south.

---

[25] Opulent homes built on large runs owned by the wealthy.

[26] An excellent and impressive incidence of something. More or less a noun for "great".

Nell returned to the bucket, squatted, then pulled the brush from its water. She lost her balance, momentarily, and tipped some of the water across the floor.

"Argh," she cried, as she snatched the bucket before it lost all its contents. "Keep your feet on the ground, Nell Burke. Look where your daydreaming lands you."

And there was no rush. This was a house that was already becoming a home, that held between its walls the beginnings of their family tale. There, on the side veranda, as she scrubbed the floor one Tuesday afternoon just a year and a half ago, her waters had broken, forewarning the imminent birth of Eamon Lawrence Burke.

The morning of that very same day, Rory had crossed a line into the affairs of women. He'd asked whether she should be cleaning the floorboards with the baby so close to due.

"You don't risk forcing or breaking something, do you, love?" he had probed tentatively.

"Don't be daft, Rory," Nell replied. "The baby will come when it's ready. I'm more concerned that we welcome him or her into a clean and ready home."

But Nell still wondered if Rory was right, and if she had scrubbed baby Eamon into an early birth.

Nell picked up the horsehair brush. With it, she pushed the water spilled on the veranda across the floorboards. What a day it had been, the day Eamon was born. Rory had come home and found her laying on a sheepskin birth rug on their bed. He had then fled the house, snatched a bridle, and rode bareback on the three-mile journey to the Walshes'. He had to beat the night, beat the baby, and ferry Thellie Walsh back to their home in time to help his wife give birth.

Then, he waited in the kitchen until just before midnight. Nell knew that Rory would have struggled not to weep and would have prayed all the while through her screams. He would have fretted and worried that Thellie, as experienced a midwife as she was, might strike a problem that needed Dr. Dunne. His horse was saddled, a lamp was ready, and Rory was prepared to ride through the night.

But the noise Nell made was broken by another—the first fitful cries of Rory Burke's son.

Nell finished cleaning the last of the floorboards then wiped her brow. The days were getting warmer. She tipped the remains of the dirty water off the edge of the open veranda. Pattering liquid falling on soil moistened a row of seeds she had planted to grow beans. Everything was still. The sounds of the day had relented, and the noises of the night were yet to start.

Nell looked up. The aqua hills of the horizon kept a cloudless, implacable sky from the pale green plane stretched ahead.

There was only one imperfection, thought Nell, as she carried the empty bucket to the washroom, *in that early autumn night of March 1915.* She wished she could have seen Rory's face when Thellie said it was a boy.

* * * * *

Rory scaled the low wooden steps of his back veranda in the late afternoon, returning from a trip into Town. With the Jacaranda tree behind him and Nell's kitchen ahead, he mused over how far they had come. He and Nell were in their very own room. Eamon now slept in one for himself and for any brothers that might come along, and there was a spare room now that Sean had passed on, ready for Eamon's sisters. The shack that all eight Burkes had squeezed into when Rory was a boy still lay at the bottom of a hill a couple of hundred yards away—a relic reminder of their success.

On the top stair, Rory lamented that he had never told Nell the truth—the truth about the top thirty acres of Jacaranda Ridge he'd worked on that morning. Nell still didn't know that he stored part of the cream payments at the back of the drawer in which he kept his nails in the workshop, then passed them on to Dave once a month as repayment. But whenever his holy duty to be truthful to his wife began to well up, the promise made to Dave just before marriage to Nell intercepted.

"Mate, that's an arrangement to be kept between you and me. Turns out I've had the same drama with Charlotte's family as you've had with Nell over the size of my land holding— but worse for a whole heap of reasons. She and Nell will get friendly in no time. If Nell gets wind you don't quite own those top paddocks, she'll more than likely tell Charlotte, then I'll have somethin' to answer for. There's no harm done in keepin' it between ourselves. The land is yours. Just keep slippin' me the repayments and we'll be jake.[27]"

"Dave, if things were that tight, why did you sell it? I was gonna tell Nell straight after the weddin'."

"Because you had your heart set on marrying her, and I had just enough land to keep Charlotte's father happy—at least on the property front—so I thought I may as well give it to ya. And now I've managed to persuade him to let me marry Charlotte, I just don't want the boat rocked, and for all of us to live happily ever after."

So, Rory had relented.

---

[27] To be fine.

"All right, Dave. I'll keep it to myself."

Rory walked into the kitchen and kissed Nell's cheek as she worked at the stove. Boned steak baked on a hot iron pan. The fire beneath it cracked and hissed.

"There'll be no potatoes with your steak tonight," said Nell. "They're becoming scarcer on account of the war. We'll have to start growing our own."

Rory sat at the kitchen table and poured himself a glass of water. The odd shortage didn't bother him. He was glad to be so far from all the fighting.

"Bumped into Marcus Moloney in the street this afternoon," said Rory. "Tells me his missus is pregnant—wasn't the happiest cove I've ever seen."

"How could he be unhappy?" said Nell. "It'll be their first, and he's getting on."

"Because it means that they're stayin'. He's still gettin' around like a bloke who's found a shilling and lost a pound. It's all over those executions in Dublin a few months back. He can't seem to get over it—his rebels in Ireland gettin' what was always gonna come to them, and their revolution gettin' crushed by the English."

Rory untied his laces.

"That was months ago," said Nell. "I couldn't believe it was ever going to last—a Republic, I mean—tossing off English rule as if it were a shawl. And he and Roisin have a good life here. Steady income and light work, he should be counting his blessings."

Nell turned the steak. In a way, she was relieved the rebellion in Ireland had failed. Her parents' journey hadn't been futile; the only way to a better life had been, after all, to take the voyage to Australia.

Nell changed the subject to concerns closer to home.

"I wrote a letter today to the twins, since we've not heard from them for a bit. It's on the shelf in our bedroom ready to send off to the City."

Rory regretted a little that letter writing, even to his sisters, was work done in families by women.

"I'll go have a read of it. Our boy asleep?" asked Rory.

He stripped to his singlet.[28] The house was amply warmed by Nell's stove.

"No, he's lying on our bed. He just woke up."

Rory wandered down the corridor. First, he sat at the edge of the bed to look at his son. Then he lay his long and lean body next to Eamon and held his hands above his face. The baby reached up, playfully grasping at his father's fingers while his legs kicked with excitement.

"Da, da, da."

How, thought Rory, could a man be any happier—a wife like Nell, a decent run of land, and his very own boy? Once the war was over, a mess of little girls and a brother or two for Eamon was the only way life could be made better.

Then, all of a sudden, Eamon was spluttering, and Rory heard a wheeze. He waited a few minutes, but it didn't stop. Rory darted back to the kitchen.

"Nell, love, he's wheezin' again. Come and take a look."

Nell looked up from her almost cooked steaks, disbelieving.

"Are you sure?" she said. "He's been as good as gold for the longest time since he was born—six months, at least."

"Nell, I'm not makin' it up. He's just slipped back into that horrible cough."

---

[28] Vest underwear.

Nell fought a gush of panic, the same flood of desperation that had unleashed her attack on the Jacaranda tree. But tonight, she wasn't alone. She was at home with Rory and anchored to reason.

"The wash cloths are drying by the bathtub," stammered Nell. "Fetch one and I'll scald it. There's boiling water on the stove."

Nell had read about a home cure for breathing difficulties. It had something to do with steam.

In the bedroom Nell held Eamon just below her bustline and bit her bottom lip. Rory was right. He was breathing in rasps.

"Rory," said Nell. "Wring that wash cloth out and suspend it over his face. The steam is supposed to help loosen his lungs."

Rory fished it out with a fork from a scalding pot of water. Then, with a steely squeeze by calloused hands, Rory wrung the wash cloth until it stopped dripping. Not a jot of scalding water was to touch his boy's soft skin.

Rory pulled at the cloth, tightly, so it hung like a tarpaulin from Eamon's chin to the top of his head. Nell and Rory listened. They lost themselves in each other's eyes, waiting and hoping for the relief and comfort of soft, smooth breathing.

* * * * *

Archibald Withers stood by a window that was as tall and slim as he. It was a slither of an opening onto the Town main street from atop its only bank.

Lack of foresight, mused Withers, was a clear and evident failing of his predecessor. A manager on his game knows very well that a full view of his realm is essential. If a man can get sight of what is happening on the street, it serves to keep him ahead. The narrow gap in the wall behind his desk wasn't sufficient for this to occur. The now deceased Mr. Harvey hadn't thought of this at all when he built the Town's first bank.

It was half past five. The sun was close to full retreat and the main street dulled to shadows. The bit of activity Withers was able to see was petering to nothing.

With ghost-white hands in the pockets of pinstriped trousers, Withers listed the changes to be made. The introduction of rigor in the bank's dealings with the settlers was priority number one. The opening of his door without prior appointment would be, from here on, discouraged. Delay in repayment of customer loans would be tolerated only rarely. And the buggers were to be encouraged to save, all of them. So financial support for building social clubs or, God forbid, another hotel was going to be refused.

That bit of distance will be maintained. Hotel at the western end of Town, bank at its eastern.

Withers turned from the window and caught his reflection in a face mirror attached to the wall. He'd used enough wax on a strip of black moustache to maintain its line to day's end. The gradual thinning of his coal-black hair was well disguised by oil, but the skin that covered his bony face was sadly starting to tan.

Blast, thought Withers, *I must be more careful and never go out unshielded by a hat.*

Interrupted by a knock at the door, he quickly took his place at his desk.

"Come in," called Withers, after clearing his throat.

He feigned reading a document.

The Reverend Ian Parker pushed the office door open, a large and square object protected by newspaper held tightly under his arm.

"Welcome, Reverend," said Withers. "I see my request was followed, and the side door to the bank left open when the bank closed at five o'clock. The only access it provides is up to my office, so leaving it ajar for a little while didn't pose a risk."

"Indeed, it was, Archie," said Reverend Parker. "And I have taken the liberty of locking it after me, so your bank is now firmly shut."

"Well done, Reverend," said Withers. "You have saved me a trip down the stairs."

Withers was smiling, but his blood was boiling. *Over familiarity,* he thought, *was the worst part of country living.* His vicar had called him "Archie" from day one, although Withers replied, always, with Parker's title.

"As you can see, I found the picture you asked for. It was right at the back of the cellar. Are you sure, Archie, this is what you want to do? I mean, dear Mr. Harvey, God rest his soul, took down the King's portrait for a reason. He had no wish to intimidate the settlers, which is why it ended up in storage. We are a close community, Archie. If you hang this picture on the wall above your desk, it will create a gulf between you and everyone."

Parker always managed to appear cheerful, even when he was disgruntled.

"But that is precisely my point, Reverend," replied Withers. "It's time for the pendulum to be pushed back. Lack of respect for the man in charge results in the same for his rules. I am duty bound to protect the bank and am wasting no time in pursuit of it. I've a man coming to hang the portrait of our King before business opens in the morning."

Parker leaned the painting on the side of Withers' desk.

"Very well, Archie," he said. "Banking's hardly my area of expertise. Now, you wanted to speak to me about the short list of candidates for the post of your personal clerk."

"Indeed, Reverend, please take a seat. This is something on which you *can* help me. The interviews took up most of the day."

Withers took a folder from a drawer in his desk, still wondering how much to say.

Parker and I enjoy all the harmony of an untuned instrument but, for this, I am dependent on his advice.

"Reverend, I was wondering if you would be able to shed light on something I found to be curious. I had as many candidates for my post among Catholic men as Protestants. Personal clerk to the manager of a bank requires the utmost in discretion. It somewhat surprised me that young Catholic men didn't hesitate to apply."

"Well," said Parker, "that gives you an insight into the sort of community we have built here. The Protestants and Catholics lead separate lives, but we are free from the shackles of hierarchy. Separate but equal, with neither harboring perceptions of superiority over the other."

"Oh really?" said Withers. "How enchanting."

"And peaceful, Archie. That's the gold standard here. There's not a hint of sectarian conflict."

Be that as it may, thought Withers, *hell will freeze over before this fine opportunity is given to a devotee of Rome.*

"That's all very well," said Withers. "But on this occasion, I regret to report I am unable to be bipartisan. One young man came in head and shoulders above the rest, and he has relatives here in the region."

"That's a shame in a way, Archie. But who might this young man be?"

"A fellow by the name of Richard Hall. He was taken on last year in the Port Town main branch as a teller. But my colleagues down there say he's management material and is wasted where he is."

"Ah," said Parker. "There are Halls out here. They are committed members of our Anglican community, and William Hall is one of the region's better farmers."

"That's the name he dropped," replied Withers. "An uncle of his, apparently."

"I've no reservations about the Halls," said Parker. "William is an excellent fellow."

Withers closed the folder and put it back in the drawer, happy to have had his way.

"Well, that's one decision you've helped me make, Reverend," he said. "Let's hope it's the first of many."

* * * * *

Nell and Rory had both grown up with the rat-a-tat-tat of beating rain on ribbed iron roofs. But that night, it roared. It was one of the nights for roaring rain; and in the clammy darkness, the crescendo shuddered to a new peak.

But neither of them saw it coming; they had failed to sense the swelling in the sky that forewarned of the cloudburst to follow.

"I can stay up with him through the night, Nell," shouted Rory, so as to be heard above the din. "You try and get some sleep."

"No, Rory, we're to take it in turns. Otherwise, you'll be exhausted tomorrow, and you'll need to go and get Dr. Dunne."

The bucketing rain pummeled the grass surrounding their house. The downpour opened the surface of the earth—first in pockmarks, then in sheets. The silt had little to do but run down the incline on which Sean Burke had chosen to build his house.

The waves of mud that rippled down the hill grew into miniature torrents. At the height of the storm, the mud rolled in muddy waves two inches high a piece, only tipping when reaching the road.

They needed that soil. It underpinned a series of posts that Sean had crafted from the thicker trees that yielded hard wood. They lifted up the house, bringing in the breeze. Sean had rammed the posts as deeply he could into the reluctant ground at Jacaranda Ridge and as far, he had thought, as a man need do to build an Australian house.

It had taken almost all of the night for the soil beneath the posts to succumb, to be dragged down to the gully by the road, to be liberated from the exotic toil of elevating a house.

By morning, stillness reigned. The scents of grass, bushland, and leaf had been driven away by the rain. The song of birds reclaiming the sky came in with a crystal dawn.

"Nell," said Rory, touching her shoulder. "I think he's sleeping more or less normally. Take a look. It's been like that for about an hour. There's a bit of a wheeze, but that's all."

It hadn't taken much to wake her. Nell was barely dozing. She sat up, rubbed her eyes, and looked in Eamon's crib.

"So it seems," said Nell. "Why do you think he's improved? And more importantly, why did it start?"

Nell leaned her head on Rory's shoulder and pulled a little at his arm. The west-lands weren't yet like home, and its mysteries still intimidated her.

"I've no idea, love," said Rory. "Maybe it was the steam. But for whatever reason, he seems to be headin' back to normal."

"You're still to fetch Dr. Dunne. I want him to check him over and hear what he thinks. Dunne's all we've got, and Eamon might have caught a flu."

Eamon slept on, and deeply. His parents didn't know it, but he was enjoying the ease of drawing in air stripped clean of pollens by rain.

Nell got up from the crib. Rory needed his breakfast before going into Town. There was the stove to fire, tea to make, and eggs to cook and serve on her home-baked bread. After seeing Rory off, she'd feed Eamon.

From her kitchen window, the Jacaranda tree sparkled. Droplets of rain speckled its stubborn foliage, its buds at the verge of bursting. There were a series of shallow cuts on the front lower branch where Nell had hit it with Rory's axe. Nell blushed a little at the reminder of what she had done.

It could be a tree of diamonds today, thought Nell, as she reached into her bread basket.

"Or, it could be a tree of poison," she muttered, breaking off a piece of bread.

That was the problem out here. They just didn't know about anything, and there was almost no one to ask, save for a neighbor like Charlotte or Thellie who might just be able to guess. Life was all about bumbling and struggling on a tough piece of country and praying that what they were doing would bring a return, before the land struck back at them.

As Nell and Rory ate their breakfast, there was not a creak, nor a movement, that might have hinted at the failing support of their four back stumps.

"Be careful on that road today," said Nell, as Rory bent to kiss her goodbye. "I don't want Dr. Dunne treating a broken bone as well as Eamon's condition."

"I'll have him back here by lunch, no fear," said Rory, reaching for his hat by the door.

* * * * *

You could put a wager[29] on it. They would be on the veranda by half past eight.

The lengthening days meant that Father O'Kelly could predict it to the minute. Everyone was being rolled from slumber, ever earlier, by an eagerly rising sun. It chivvied the birds along as much as the people, shifting daily routines toward the early beginnings and endings of the warm part of the year. And they were creatures of habit, waiting at the same time every day.

Father O'Kelly stepped onto his veranda with a plate of staling bread in one hand and a wide bowl of water in the other. The birds were gathered and eager.

They made for a menagerie. The yellow-crested whites, restless at the center, were the first to jump from the respectful limits of the railing and land on the table to claim their morning feed. The handsome laughing birds, white-bellied, long-nosed, and well-coiffed in auburn tints, glided in behind. The blackbirds were happy to linger on the drying railing, but once they were good and ready, they would barge to the front and shamelessly take what they knew to be theirs.

O'Kelly sat nearby on a wooden chair that hadn't been touched by the rain. The comfort of cushions and the nearby sofa was something yet to be earned. The day would soon be commencing, and there was more of God's work to be done.

---

[29] Nineteenth and early twentieth century term for a *bet*.

Now, there is a fight, thought O'Kelly, *that meets the proportions of what is at stake.* All the birds were hungry, all were thirsty; some were pushing and shoving, while others won out through cunning. All of this was a predictable part of the daily quest for nourishment.

Not so for the humans, lamented O'Kelly, *with the whole of Europe engulfed in carnage on the scale of the biblical famines. And for what? The folly of madmen who are driven by nothing but power.*

As for mother Ireland, there was little to do but pray— trapped, as she was, in the middle, unsure of which way to turn.

O'Kelly looked out from atop Presbytery Hill. Tranquility ebbed through everything near him, while there was nothing but war at a distance.

What he saw might have fallen from the breath of God, vistas of calm that rolled in low waves, beneath halo-bright sunshine that ran to the horizon. And if there ever were a gunshot, O'Kelly could be sure it would be for the purpose of bringing in food and not the taking of human life.

Except when it came to Aboriginal people.

He didn't know how many were still living off the land, but they were becoming ever more visible. They could be seen every other day, huddled in clusters just beyond the eastern end of the Town.

It was becoming a draw for them, and O'Kelly had begun to worry. The Aboriginals would be tolerated by the settlers, but only if they kept out of sight. They eked their living from the remaining swathes of uncleared bushland, stole food that wouldn't be missed, and collected government parcels from their so-called state Protector,[30] on the occasions it was offered.

O'Kelly leaned on the veranda railing. If Aboriginals dared to break these boundaries, there would be trouble, no doubt, from the whites.

If I can't tackle the wrongness of this head on, I will work toward keeping my parishioners humbled to the obedience of God's laws, so they understand them as universal.

The western end of the Town's long main street was clear from Presbytery Hill. There, in the space of a quarter of an hour, O'Kelly counted one, two, then three of the settlers. Two horse-drawn carriages and one man on horseback broke in from the bush into the precincts of the Town. All three raised dust in their wake as they left the scrubland behind. This trickle of life would swell by lunchtime: traveling salesmen here, customers buying merchandise there, townsfolk milling and going about their everyday business.

Another sulky flashed into view. Was that Mr. Rory Burke, pushing his aged horse, entering the Town in a hurry? Rory was a kindly man, not a cruel one. If he were to push a horse, it would be for good reason.

I hope this isn't about Eamon.

O'Kelly's attention returned to the birds. He raised a smile as the cockiest of the laughing ones fought the largest of the crows for the last of the tiny breadcrumbs. The minds of men were more complex, all right. But their sense of proportion was less balanced.

A solitary blackbird stared him down as he began clearing the table.

---

[30] Government official with responsibility in Australia in the nineteenth and early to mid-twentieth centuries for the welfare of Aboriginals.

"Shoo," said O'Kelly. "Shoo! I've the day to be getting on with."

He looked at his watch as the bird flew off. It cried out as if in victory. *My goodness*, thought O'Kelly. *Time has passed at speed.* It was almost nine o'clock. Time to go and visit the sick.

* * * * *

Nell put Eamon in his basket under the shade of the Jacaranda tree. She wanted to gather the eggs from her chook pen. Rory's insistence that the tree was benign, and the fact that it hadn't yet blossomed, afforded it the benefit of the doubt. And she didn't want to leave Eamon in the house out of her sight.

Some of her chickens were drinking from puddles in the mud as she went into the wire pen. They clucked and flew to its rear. Nell pulled at the drawer of each wooden hen box and was gladdened by what she saw. A dozen eggs would last them a week, with enough to serve Rory seconds.

Nell bent down to pick up her egg basket when a loud noise stopped her like a brake. From behind, there was a crack, then a crash, then the woody clatter of timber tumbling on timber. She turned, stood up straight and put her hand to her mouth.

"God in heaven," cried Nell, as she ran back toward her home.

The posts had slid away in the mud and taken with them a third of the house—the back veranda, the spare room, and Nell's kitchen. That part of the house was reduced to a shanty; broken wood and shattered windows lay in a jumble.

Nell walked, gingerly, by the crumpled veranda, slowly taking it in.

Meanwhile, the kookaburras broke into a chorus, and the yellow-crested whites flew low. The birds settled in the upper reaches of the Jacaranda tree, as if watching.

The posts supporting the back end of the Burke family house had slipped at the base and moved toward the front road. The roof had opened along an iron seam as the stumps gave way. A thick crack ran along the rear part of the side wall, exposing a wooden frame that had snapped when the house fell. And in the middle, amid hanging floorboards, Nell's stove had crashed. One end was jammed into the mud, while the other end hung at an angle from collapsed fragments of kitchen floor.

Nell moved in a little bit closer and crouched down. From there, she could see her kitchen table sunk into the mud along with the ceramic teapot her mother had given her when she and Rory married, and which usually took pride of place at the center of the table. It was tossed aside and nearly drowned in silt. Glimpses of pink porcelain peeked through the mud. Her pots and pans were littered toward the foreground, and four kitchen chairs, lacquered by Nell herself with varnish purchased by mail-order catalogue, leaned crookedly every which way, as if preparing to seat a dinner for warlocks.

With trembling hands, Nell went back to the Jacaranda tree and picked up Eamon's basket. She walked in a daze to the front of the house and waited for Rory on the bottom front step.

A little later, she ran to the road to meet him.

"Rory, the back of the house has fallen down!" she cried.

"What do you mean, it's fallen down?"

"It's fair fallen down! The stumps shifted in the mud, and it fell down while I was in the chicken pen."

"You'll have to show me. Jump in."

Walking along the back of his home, Rory was speechless with what he saw. The Burkes looked at each other, aghast. Wooden houses would sometimes collapse when beaten by wind, storms, and rain combined, but neither of them had seen damage like this in the wake of a downpour alone.

Nell rushed over to the side wall of the kitchen, while Rory paced up and down.

"Everything's ruined! What's left of the floor, the roof, and my curtains are on the ground. Everything's wrecked!" cried Nell.

Rory remained silent, preoccupied as he was with the structure of the house. How bad was the damage to the frame, and were they going to be able to live in the house at all? Rory sat down on a stump, with legs spread apart, looking at the ground.

What in the bloody hell are we going to do now?

* * * * *

Dr. Dermott Dunne was examining Eamon while a marital dispute unfolded, in the background, a few yards behind him. Nell and Rory were whispering in angry spurts, trying to hide a fight.

"Rory, did you and Sean talk to any tradesman before you built this house? I mean, it's just not normal for a house to fall down from a bit of rain."

"Nell, that wasn't just a bit of rain. And I told you, Da built it. I was just a lad. I helped fetch and carry things. I've no idea how he worked out how to put it up."

Nell's face flushed. That wasn't how she remembered it.

"Rory," she said, lowering her voice. "When we were courting, you said that you had built it with Sean. That the house was as sound as a pound, and that he'd taught you all he knew about carpentry."

Rory baulked at what he viewed as a challenge.

"I never said Da was a flamin' expert, did I?"

"Rory, Eamon would have been killed if he hadn't been ill last night. Ordinarily, I leave him in his basket in the kitchen when I go to fetch the eggs. Look at it! The house is a death trap."

"Nell, you can keep your melodrama to yourself," said Rory. "We never had a problem in this house; never in the eleven years me, Ma, Da, and my sisters lived in it as a family."

"Well, we've got a problem now, haven't we, and a visitor and all to share it with."

Crouching in the sketchy shade of a Jacaranda tree that had taken a beating in the storm, Dr. Dunne pulled at his stubby beard. Eamon gurgled, smiled, and kicked his feet in his basket.

As the doctor stood, Nell and Rory walked toward him, the irritation of one with the other, betrayed by their quickness of step.

"Well, Mr. and Mrs. Burke, what I see today is a perfectly healthy child. Can you please tell me, Mrs. Burke, exactly what happened?" said Dunne. "I mean, with respect to Eamon."

"Of course, Doctor. He'd been well for many months. Since autumn in fact. But last night, when Rory came home, it started up again—the wheezing, I mean—probably around half past five."

"Nell wasn't there when it started, Doctor," added Rory, hoping to persuade him. "It was just me in the bedroom with him. But what happened was as clear as still water and came on from one second to the next. He was as good as gold, but then began rasping."

"We were up with him half the night when he finally drifted off around two o'clock," explained Nell. "But we still took turns watching him and decided to fetch you come daylight, seeing as it's so long since he's had a turn. I was afraid he might have the flu."

Dr. Dunne looked around at the sodden farmland. An eerie quiet comforted all living things in recovery from the downpour. This was a respected couple. They weren't liars or frauds, and they needed a plausible answer.

"Are there any natives[31] still trying to live off Crown land out here?" asked Dunne.

He returned his stethoscope to his bag.

"Are there any what?" asked Nell.

"Black-skinned people. Natives. Has there been a recent sighting by any chance?"

"They've been long gone from my land," replied Rory. "I still come across them livin' in humpies every now and then, if I venture out into the bush. And I see them sometimes at the edges of Town. But they know not to cross onto Burke family land, or they'll be met with a hidin'."

"Well, Mr. Burke, they may not pass the boundary onto Burke family territory," said Dr. Dunne. "But that doesn't mean that you know what they are up to. Some still practice a black man's magic—pointing bones of God knows what dead creature at Christian white families and wishing the worst for them, including their children."

Nell scowled.

---

[31] Offensive term for indigenous people in usage throughout the British Empire in colonial times, including Australia.

"That would be the first I've heard of that, Dr. Dunne," she said. "My da employed black stockmen[32] on our family run down to the southeast. He made sure, all right, that they kept their distance from us, especially when we were kids, but I never heard a word of worry about witchcraft or spells. And he couldn't have navigated his way through the bush without the help of the black-trackers.[33]"

Rory was annoyed. Not because Nell had spoken, but because she didn't respect the local folklore.

"Nell, love," said Rory, clearing his throat. "I've told you, haven't I, about the way the blacks cursed the O'Doherty family when they came out here to settle the land? You remember, don't you, how old man O'Doherty arrived up here around fifty years back with a team of southern cattle and three strappin' sons? He offered the blackfellas work and wages, and what he got in return was stolen livestock and two dead sons—wretched themselves to death from bushland tucker[34] that the same pack of blacks had shown 'em how to eat."

The remaining son, Mr. Roddy O'Doherty, had more power and money than anyone in the west, and nobody questioned his stance on anything, especially when it came to Aboriginals.

And Rory knew it.

Nell brushed a fly from Eamon's face. This wasn't the moment for a row, in company, over the local Aboriginal people. She withdrew from the discussion by sitting on a rock.

"I'm glad you see things my way, Mr. Burke," said Dunne.

---

[32] Cowboys.

[33] Aboriginal guides in colonial Australia of bushland and countryside. Often used by police but also settlers.

[34] Food.

The doctor was relieved he had found an explanation that was acceptable—at least to the child's father.

"I would keep my eyes peeled if I were you. In all my experience in medicine, a child, and particularly an infant, is either ill or it isn't. A sporadic condition of the kind Eamon suffers might well find its cause beyond science."

Dr. Dunne walked toward his horse with Rory by his side.

"I'll keep that in mind, Doctor, and be on the lookout," said Rory. "Many thanks for the advice and for making the journey."

* * * * *

It was midafternoon the same day. Rory set out from Jacaranda Ridge to fetch a carpenter. When he was gone, Nell slipped beneath the back end of the house and dragged out the metal plate of her stove. They had to get on, and she needed to start thinking about dinner. There was fresh meat in the meat safe and some already salted in the meat room. She could easily cook it on the plate of the stove if suspended by stones over a fire.

There was a circle of seat-sized boulders not far from the Jacaranda tree. Its early spring buds had been sliced open by rain, spattering lilac across the rocks. It welcomed her like wet confetti. There they would sit.

Nell went to the nearby scrubland to gather kindling for the fire while Eamon dozed. *What more could a wife want?* she thought, as dry sticks collapsed beneath her wide and firm feet. *A crumpled house, no kitchen, and a child supposedly cursed by invisible Aboriginal people. You wouldn't read about it!* [35]

---

[35] A turn of events so unusual that it would be impossible to make up.

Nell bent to gather the dry-to-brittle sticks of scrub in the scoop of her arm. The day's events reminded her of the struggle she'd had in persuading her da to let her marry Rory.

"Rory is the only man that fits me, Da. He's no false charm, and he'll never keep a secret from me. Of that you can be sure."

"I'm more worried by whether he can keep you at all, Nell, and not whether he fits you."

Nell stepped on something hard and put down the kindling. It pressed on the sole of her foot, as if defying the ubiquitous dust. She looked to see what it was.

A horseshoe—rusted, buckled, and about to fall apart. But nonetheless, a horseshoe.

Nell hadn't held one since leaving Ballycallan. She clutched it like a long-lost lucky charm.

Growing up around horses had meant that life was never dull. There were always cups of tea and scones in the kitchen for the men who came to shoe their horses. Hector and Violet's home at Ballycallan was a community hub. Often, the men would come in sulkies and bring their children for the treat of a trip. Then games and laughter would begin.

"It's my turn to throw," someone would cry, after a horseshoe was pitched at a metal rod rammed into the dirt.

"No, it isn't, it's mine!" came a common refrain, and a contest would soon be on. Violet always had a prize for the winner.

And in the summer, there was swimming to be had in the meek little river at the back of Ballycallan. It was nothing like the surge of the River Nore as it gouged its way through County Kilkenny. But at least the river on Ballycallan was theirs, and the McTiernan children didn't know that a river could be anything different.

Nell returned to the campsite and sat on a rock. She looked at Eamon as he stirred, and the Jacaranda tree rustled in the breeze. *Will me and Rory be able to give you, my love, the same sort of childhood up here? Or will your grandfather turn out to be right and, in the end, we'll resettle on Ballycallan?*

Nell put the kindling in the fireplace and returned to the rock. Pillar-like legs rooted her feet to the earth as she recovered her resolve. Her da's forebodings were to be left where they belonged, which was right at the back of her mind. They would get through this, somehow, and prove her father wrong.

* * * * *

Rory was lucky. Billy Murphy was home when he went by, and the only man in the region who'd trained with professional carpenters had time to visit their farm. The house would be inspected before dusk.

"I'd be restumpin' the whole house, Rory," said Murphy.

"How did it happen?" asked Rory. "This house has been through the tail end of a cyclone[36] a couple of times and weathered everything ever thrown at it."

"Doesn't matter, Rory. It's the stumpin' that's all wrong. That was the heaviest rain that anyone can remember. It's washed away the soil, and these stumps were only sunk in two feet. They needed to be going down twice that far," said Murphy. "At least."

Murphy peered at the base of the first fallen stump. Rory crouched next to him.

---

[36] Weather system similar to a hurricane.

"And you need a long gully at the top of the hill at the back of the house to stop the erosion when it next rains."

"How much'll all that set us back?"

Murphy rubbed his chin.

"Have to jack up the house, stabilize it, and put in fresh posts. Then have to rebuild the back of the house, lower it onto the new stumps, then finish off with a new back roof. Won't be cheap. I'll do what I can, but we're going to have to hire modern machinery and manpower."

"Never mind the building," said Rory. "Dave Noonan and I can handle that. Can't manage the restumpin' though."

"Even then, we're talking pounds, Rory, and not shillings. It's a big job."

The two men stood up straight.

"We'll have to be doin' as much for ourselves as we can," said Rory.

"The good news is that the rest of the house is sound," said Murphy. "You can still sleep in the bedroom, seein' as it's built at the front veranda."

He wanted to finish with a little cheer.

"And as long as we don't get another storm like last night's, there's no reason why you won't be safe."

"Doesn't look like we've got much of a choice," said Rory.

He walked to the road and waved Billy Murphy goodbye, then plodded through the mud back up to Nell, an unlit kerosene lamp in one hand, his hat in the other. He sat down on the rock opposite her, not far from the Jacaranda tree. Nell took a pot, plates, knives, and forks from the burlap sack in which they had been delivered by Billy Murphy, along with some spuds and fresh green beans, all donated by his wife. Nell placed them on the flattest of the rocks.

"At least the rest of the house is safe, but it's gonna have to be fixed soon," said Rory.

"Of course it will have to be fixed soon," said Nell curtly.

She glanced toward the gifts from the Murphys.

"I've got to be able to get into my kitchen. We can't be relyin' on neighbors for food and pans."

Nell hadn't meant it harshly, but the day had shortened her temper.

"How much will the fixin' cost?" she asked.

She reached for a potato and started peeling.

"He's not sure. But we don't have enough in the bank. We'll have to get a loan."

Nell drew breath. Rory thought he knew what she was going to say and stopped her.

"No, Nell. We are not going to your parents."

Nell paused, momentarily, before replying. Going to her father was the last of the suggestions she was going to make. He might try to move them down south immediately if he knew about what had happened. But Nell understood that a bit of resistance would bind Rory to his stance.

"Rory, they won't mind. They've always earned a steady living, and there'll be savings. Why don't we just borrow from them?"

Nell picked up another potato.

"Because it's our farm and our problem, and it's for us to deal with. I can't take a handout, Nell. Not from anyone, and that includes Hector."

Rory's thoughts turned to the paddock he had begun ploughing the day before. Once it dried out, he would have to get back up there and start over.

"It wouldn't be a handout, Rory. They don't want to see us livin' in the remains of that shack over the hill."

Rory pulled a match from his pocket and lit the kerosene lamp, then the kindling, without speaking. The sun had all but departed, and the drum of the night had begun.

"It will be all right, Nell," said Rory. "Tomorrow, I'll head into Town and have a talk with Mr. Withers."

* * * * *

Rory set out at half past eight to be at the bank when it opened at ten. The rocking of the sulky and the huffing of his horse reminded him. Crisis or no crisis, his nag had to be retired; otherwise, she'd die in service. A new horse would wipe out their savings, so none of them could go toward the rebuild.

The rain had dusted off the brightly painted storefronts of the Town. Wedges of primary color were stenciled, loudly, across the grays, ochers, and dim greens of the land.

The bank was at the top end of the street. It was three stories of hardwood, balconied twice over and skirted with iron lace. As Rory walked up the stairs, he went through the questions Mr. Withers might ask. *Any other loans, Mr. Burke? Average annual yield of your farm, Mr. Burke? Repayments over what period were you thinking?* Rory made another decision. Better they were both there, both him and Nell, once the questions and planning started. He could turn to her if he got stuck.

"Can I help you?" asked Richard Hall, from behind a metal grid.

He finished his counting, looked up, and smiled.

"Good day," said Rory. "My wife and I would like to have a meeting with Mr. Withers in our home at Jacaranda Ridge. Is he still in the habit of making farm visits?"

"Don't see why not. He's just in. I'll go and check if he can see you for a moment now. Take a seat."

Richard was back within a minute.

"Go through, Mr. Burke."

He was motioned toward the office at the rear. Its high plaster ceiling and wood-paneled walls weren't daily features of Rory's world. And the portrait of the King above Withers' desk was among the first he had ever seen.

"Mr. Burke, how lovely to see you."

Archibald Withers extended a slim and ghostly hand. At twenty-nine, he was about a year older than Rory. But the banker, in demeanor, was a man aged closer to his forties.

He looks a bit more pressed than usual, thought Rory. The parting in the center of his skull was perfectly straight, and his lacquered black hair fairly gripped at his skull—not that Rory saw him that often. Withers wasn't a Catholic.

"Thanks for seeing me, Mr. Withers. I wanted to know if you were doing farm visits. My wife and I are looking for a loan and would like to talk it through."

"Please take a seat, Mr. Burke. I'm very pleased to see that you have had the foresight to ask for an appointment, rather than simply barging in."

Rory looked toward the ground and coughed.

"May I ask what the loan will be for? Expanding the farm, are we?"

Withers was tapping his pen on the leather padding of his desk.

"Not quite. We had some damage in the storm the night before last. The house needs restumping and the back end rebuilding."

Rory pulled on the brim of his hat.

"My goodness," said Mr. Withers. "I am sorry. I have all your records in my files. I could take them out and consider the position now."

Withers jumped at the prospect of unexpected profit, albeit projected, a supplement to his quarterly report.

Matters were moving too quickly. Rory stopped him.

"That's kind, Mr. Withers, but I would prefer my wife to be present if we are to talk more," said Rory. "We've a baby, and it's hard for her to leave the house."

Archibald Withers veiled his disgust. The occasions were rare in which he was constrained to involve women in the complex affairs of commerce. But he had caught a whiff of Burke's desperation and wanted to keep a deal within reach.

"Wise enough, Mr. Burke, albeit out of the ordinary," he said. "That will save you, I am sure, from explaining any agreement we might reach should Mrs. Burke ever concern herself with it. And you are in luck. My two o'clock appointment has canceled, so I can set out in the early afternoon and be at your home by half past three, if that's convenient. You are on the third ridge to the south, are you not?"

Withers had been in Town for only a few months, but knew fully well the location of Jacaranda Ridge, and all the other farms, along with the value of every property, credits out, and the overdraft limits of each farmer.

"Yes, sir, we are. We can offer you tea in the drawing room. It's in the part of the house that's sound, but the kitchen has collapsed, so we can offer little else by way of hospitality."

"My goodness, never mind that," replied Withers. "Tea is all I take at that time of day. I'll see you out at your farm."

* * * * *

The main street was filling up, sluggishly, with the current of morning commerce. A farmer pulled up in front of the saddlery on one side of the road as a woman entered the grocery store on the other. Her heavy skirt was further weighted by the tug of a blonde and fair-eyed child.

It was as Father O'Kelly preferred it. If he'd left his own shopping to later in the day, he'd have risked the disturbance of bustle.

Almost a dozen businesses, noted O'Kelly, as he wandered to the general store, had sprouted from a strip of land that had once been populated by tents. Clothing, farm tools, food, and medicine could be purchased within their walls and behind panes of glass, confirming the permanence of settlement.

O'Kelly was approaching their general store when he spotted Rory Burke. He was leaving the bank at the top of the street with his shoulders a little stooped. *Two trips into Town in two days*, thought O'Kelly, *a habit a little unusual for a man earning a living from farming.* He walked the ten yards between them.

"Good day, Mr. Burke, and what a lovely surprise to see you. I am a man of habits and run my errands every Thursday morning. But this is the first time, I believe, our paths have crossed at this time of the week."

"Good day," said Rory. "And indeed, you're right. I should be delivering cream."

"I thought as much," said Father O'Kelly. "Is everything all right?"

Rory leaned a little on the neck of his horse. He was ever reluctant to broadcast his woes and despised the talk that followed. But Father O'Kelly had asked a question, and to a priest, Rory had to reply.

"A little bit of drama, Father, I guess you could say. We had some damage to the house in the storm the night before last. Might need a bit of help from Mr. Withers to fund a few repairs."

Now there was a fellow, thought O'Kelly, *who had not made a good impression.*

"Oh dear," said Father O'Kelly. "I am sorry to hear that. You must have taken a heavy hit if you can't do the work yourself. You're one of the better amateur carpenters that we have in the region."

"That's kind of you, Father, and you're right, the repairs won't be minor. But we'll manage, as we do."

Rory fiddled with the rein that hung off his horse and squinted into the sharpening light. It drenched the open stretch of dusty land that the settlers called a street with an intensity nearing white light.

"And what about that son of yours? Are we well and truly out of the woods when it comes to problems with his breathing?"

Rory kicked a little at the sunburnt dirt, just as he had when he was a boy. For O'Kelly, that nervous right leg had been Rory Burke's giveaway since about the age of seven. He struck at the ground and lowered his head whenever he was in strife.[37]

"I'd like to say we're clear of that, but he's had a bit of a relapse. Just before the storm, that terrible wheeze came back. We've already had Dr. Dunne come by, but he still can't pinpoint what's wrong."

O'Kelly battled the reflex to scowl at the mention of the Town's only doctor. He had little faith in their man of medicine but would never, ever, show it. He had read in a City newspaper

---

[37] Trouble.

about new cures for respiratory ailments. But none of them seemed to be known to Dr. Dunne or were sold in the Town's new pharmacy.

"Oh dear. What a shame. And I was hoping you were through that," said O'Kelly. "Perhaps I can offer some help. When I next travel to the Port Town, I can drop in on an old friend who's a pharmacist. It would do no harm to ask him for guidance on the latest cures for poor breathing."

"That's kind of you, Father, it really is. Me and Nell welcome any suggestion on how Eamon might be helped."

Fatigue had settled into Rory Burke's face, drawn, tired, and anxious. He was as little forthcoming in manhood, mused O'Kelly, as he had been when he was a boy. Nonetheless, he betrayed himself. He was not able to disguise his feelings.

"Well, I must get on, Mr. Burke, or I will start to lose the day."

"Very well, Father," said Rory. "And thank you. I'll let Nell know you've been kind enough to seek out some help for Eamon."

* * * * *

Each thick heel clipped hard against the stairs as Withers left the bank after lunch. He looked toward the end of the street nearest to him. At the narrowing, where the road humbled back into a bush track at the eastern end of the Town, there was a gaggle of them jabbering.

The black men were clad in strips of dirty calico, so that shreds of smudged and creamy fabric lay tattily across their skin. Their chattering was as impenetrable to Withers as it was disconcerting. Their backs were turned to Withers, but they were open to each other.

"Blasted blacks."

They are going to have to be cleared off, thought Withers.

He resolved to raise it in Town Council and have a word with their Protector when he next passed through. He would not have native filth loitering within the limits of the Town.

Archibald Withers got into his sulky to set out for Jacaranda Ridge. He despised these forays into the bush. It took a large handkerchief to keep the sweat off his brow, and no matter how well ironed his collar, it would buckle in the heat. And all this had to be suffered through the monotony of the westlands' tepid hills.

At least it's still a little chilly, he thought, as he readied the reins to depart. *I shan't be disheveled when I reach their home.* But the bank was right. These farm visits were essential, and he had decided to keep making them, albeit at *his* convenience and not the farmers'. The visits kept up good relations, and he'd discovered already that the settlers could be difficult. It was all helping him meet his targets, so that a job in management in the City, or perhaps even one at home, drew nearer.

At Rory and Nell's, Withers was met with a pleasant surprise—tea served in quality china in a drawing room fully intact. He felt better. Indeed, comfortable, even though the household was Catholic. Decent couple, neat home—what was left of it—and his records showed that they were careful with what they had. And to his great relief, the wife was keeping quiet.

Rory stated his case.

"Jacaranda Ridge has been our farm for over two decades, Mr. Withers. My father purchased seventy acres with all he had, then cleared the rest from the scrub. It kept all eight of us when my parents were alive—Ma and Da, me, and my five sisters. The elder three of them are married now and live on farms in other parts of the state, and the younger two, the twins, work as nannies in the City. Jacaranda Ridge is all mine now, and Nell and I know we will work it up into profit."

Withers took a mental note of muddled social class. Money for china, but sisters in service. The Burkes were going to be hard to rank.

"I can see you have done well from cattle and cream. But that's rather a narrow base, Mr. Burke. How do you see the farm expanding in the future?"

"Well," said Rory, glancing toward Nell, "I've dedicated some of our larger paddocks to growing produce. We're about to turn them over to corn."

"Well, you won't be the first to do that," said Withers. "From what I've seen, corn does well out here. But what about after that? Have you turned your minds to what you might do with any profit this new venture might make?"

Rory hadn't thought that far ahead. He turned toward Nell. His trawl of her face for an answer netted nothing.

Then, he blurted something out.

"A piggery."

Nell winced.

"I'd like to add a piggery," stammered Rory. "We don't want to move the farm completely away from livestock. We will continue with dairy farming, but a piggery is the way I'd like to go."

Withers face broke into a sickly grin. A spontaneous response was always a giveaway. Typical Irish Catholics the

Burkes were after all. No sense of planning. No perception of the need to remain ever ready for the unforeseen. And now, they expected the bank to get them out of trouble.

"That's all very well, Mr. Burke, but may I see the figures for the budget you have compiled?"

Rory hadn't a clue what to say. So Nell broke taboo and entered into the discussion of finance.

"We've roughed them out, Mr. Withers, but they're not in any state to be presented to a commercial man. Can we give them a tidy and deliver them to you at the bank a little later?"

Rory breathed a sigh of relief, discreetly. Never was a man so lucky as to have a wife like Nell.

"Very well," Withers replied tetchily. "I'd be interested in seeing them. But sooner rather than later, if you wouldn't mind."

He ignored Nell and addressed Rory.

"In the meantime, we can fill out the loan agreement. You can sign here, Mr. Burke, and I will sign for the bank once I see those figures. That should expedite, I would say, a clear case of urgency."

Rory penciled in the form. Nell took a peek over his shoulder before it was inked in. She interrupted, again.

"Rory, you've marked the size of our run incorrectly. We've one hundred and eighty-five acres, not a hundred and fifty-five."

Rory's hand stopped abruptly, as if seized by the ghost of truth. *Bugger it*, he thought. He had missed a trick. He had wanted Nell present to help him deal with Withers but had forgotten the risk that entailed.

There are thirty acres on Jacaranda Ridge that technically belong to Dave!

Withers was arching an eyebrow, and Rory made a move to lower it.

"That's just my handwriting, love," said Rory. "That's an eight, not a five."

"Well then, you'd best close the loop in that marking. At the moment, it looks like a five."

Rory hadn't a choice. He altered the figure as she said.

Nell leaned back into the settee.

Rory remembered the first time Hector visited Jacaranda Ridge. His prospective father-in-law trooped around it like an officer in the army—stocky, eagle-eyed, and looking for fault. Rory and Dave had shifted the fence just the day before, extending the run of Rory's land by thirty acres.

"So one hundred and eighty-five acres you reckon this makes?" Hector had asked.

"That's right, Mr. McTiernan. More than enough land to rear a family, if not quite the two hundred you mentioned."

"I don't doubt that, Rory," replied Hector. "But the family it will be rearing will be part of mine."

Rory had found the mettle to stand firm.

"And I'll see to it that it's reared as one of the very best in the region."

Hector hadn't meant to be a mongrel, thought Rory, as he came to the end of the form. He was as tough as a nut, all right, but loved Nell as much as he. That was the only motive Rory ever saw in the grilling Hector gave him.

Withers took the agreement as signed by Rory. He then shut his briefcase with a snap.

"Mr. Withers, would you like to take a quick turn around our property? I can walk you to the outer boundaries and show you the state of the place."

"No, thank you, Mr. Burke," said Withers. "I am already familiar with the land out here and am expected, in any event, for dinner at the vicar's."

* * * * *

CHAPTER 4
SHELTER
December 1916

Nell was in a paddock in the top thirty acres, thrashing wads of straw onto a crude iron cross.

"Another of Rory's bright ideas," she muttered a little bitterly. Put up a couple of scarecrows and keep the birds from a freshly tilled field, even before anything has been sowed.

It was Friday, the first of December, and over a hundred degrees. As Nell yanked at the ties firming each of the scarecrow's arms, she looked up to see if Charlotte was making progress. She was walking toward Nell, halfway down the field, in the full stride characteristic of the western women. Her hoe rested across the back of her shoulders. Charlotte thrived on the work and the heat.

"My man's up and hatted," she said brightly, "and enough to frighten any bird—or other living thing, for that matter. I've tilled the upper three rows of this paddock as well. All good and ready to be sowed."

The sun gripped the back of Nell's neck.

"God bless you, Charlotte," she replied, wearily. "I don't know what I'd have done without you."

"Not a bit, Nell. And I know what you'd have done. You'd have coped."

"I can't say I'm sure of that myself," said Nell.

"Well, I am," replied Charlotte. "Anyway, we've earned a spell.[38] Come for a walk over to ours and sit by the pond

---

[38] Rest.

with me. Thellie's expecting to mind the little ones for at least another hour or so."

The pond at the Noonans' wasn't far away, just the other side of the boundary they shared with Jacaranda Ridge. The pond was really a dammed-up gully, sourced at its base by a natural bore. The surface of the water was pierced by the trunks of half a dozen burnt-out trees. Chalky gray and charred to black at their edges, they shot skyward from the water like bayonets, a military guard of sorts, honoring victories over bushfires past.

"Nell," said Charlotte, once they were settled at the pond's edge. "You and Rory have been half-camping for over a month. You know you are all welcome to come and stay with us. It would be a bit of a squeeze, but we have plenty of beds on our veranda. We would love the company."

"That's so kind of you to offer," replied Nell. "But Rory says we're not so far from being able to start the rebuild. And for the sake of everyone, I hope he's right."

Charlotte took a moment to choose her words. She looked across the pond, as if hoping to find them there.

"Nell," said Charlotte tentatively. "You and Rory have soldiered on magnificently, and I don't mean to pry, but what's the hold-up in getting the house repaired?"

Nell wiped a handkerchief across her sweat-drenched forehead.

She had known Charlotte now for almost three years. She was as solid as a person could be. And Charlotte understood the codes of the women of the land. Nothing said in confidence from one to another would ever be passed to their men.

"It's money, Charlotte. Billy Murphy has men on hand to do the work, but we've not enough in the bank to cover it, and Mr. Withers is yet to approve a loan.

Not that it's his fault. Rory hasn't yet gathered the figures that Mr. Withers has asked for, figures on costings for our future plans for the farm."

"The bank?" said Charlotte. "Nell, I know that both of Rory's parents are dead, but is there no one else in the family who could help see you through this?"

Nell was unsurprised by the question. She knew Charlotte had an inkling that she, just like her, was from a family of means.

"In theory," said Nell. "But it's a bit more complex than that."

And then, as if prized open by the extended hand of friendship, Nell poured out her story. She spoke of the cool autumn nights of her courtship with Rory, when they sat against the back of her community hall down south, talking through their dream of sharing the work on Jacaranda Ridge, their own family farm. How she had met Rory at the dances held half a dozen times a year down Port Town way, where tilley lamps hanging high blazed the evening into day. How Rory would ride like lightning for days to attend them, camping in the bush as he went. How he was older, quieter, and steadier than the rest.

And how her parents hadn't approved.

"Why ever not?" asked Charlotte. "He's a good provider, honest, and heaven knows a hard worker."

"My parents are well-to-do, Charlotte," said Nell. "They wanted me to marry a society man, and all I wanted was to keep working the land."

"Well, if that's the case, why on earth can't they give you a loan?"

Nell played with the hem of her skirt. She had shared half the story. She might as well tell the rest.

"Because I'm frightened my father will to try and wind us up and offer Rory a salaried job on his run, Ballycallan, just south of the Port Town. He consented to the marriage, in the end, but he keeps an eye on us—asks for an update on how we are progressing in almost every letter. If he were to find out about the problems with the house, and that we can't pay for them, he is just as likely to try and move us now."

"Oh dear," said Charlotte. "But can your father really do that, Nell? I mean, how could he force you out of land that Rory owns?"

"You don't know my da," said Nell. "He'll have all sorts of tricks up his sleeve. For a start, he's done something unusual and left a fifth of Ballycallan to me in his will. He's split it five ways among all his children, rather than in four in favor of only my brothers. Once Da dies, I'll be free to sell it and keep the profits. Da says it's to see that I'm rewarded for all the work I did when I was growing up. If I were ever to side with Rory and dig my heels in to stay here, he might change his mind over the will."

"That *is* unusual," said Charlotte, "a father leaving land to a daughter. But would he really be so mean as to threaten disinheritance? If he's put you in his will, he's put you in his will. Is he really likely to change his mind?"

"It would be more subtle than that. Da might just use it as leverage, as a way to get me round to his side if he were to offer Rory a job on his run as an employed farmer, which Rory would want to decline. But I've Eamon to think of now. That money could help set up his life."

Charlotte looked again toward the pond.

"You're right, Nell. That is a conundrum," she said. "And who wants to live a life as an outcast from family?"

"Exactly," said Nell. "So, we're to find our own way through this. Me and Rory, as man and wife."

Nell broke a silence that was lengthening into tension.

"Charlotte, Rory knows nothing at all about this. I mean, that my da has put me in his will. He's no idea that he still lives under the shadow of the great Hector McTiernan. I was going to tell him about the inheritance as soon as we married. Da barred me from telling any of my suitors when I was courting to keep away the gold diggers, and once we were wed, I realized that Rory might see it as an insult, a challenge to his ability to provide."

"So, do you never plan to tell him, Nell?"

"Of course I will—once we've established Jacaranda Ridge in healthy profit, and I've my da off our back. Then, I can be sure that his promise will stick and the will won't be changed."

A swan at full wingspan landed on the pond with an elegant web-footed glide. It shook off the drops of water trickling down its head and drifted toward the rushes.

"You would never breathe a word to Dave, would you, Charlotte?" said Nell. "If what I've told you ever got back to Rory, there would be no end of trouble. I'm supposed to be *his* wife, with no lingering link to my da."

"My goodness, Nell," said Charlotte. "That goes without saying. Everything shared by the side of this pond is for my ears alone. You're not to worry for a moment."

Charlotte stood up and brushed her skirt. Nell relaxed beneath the conviction that she had found a friend.

"Come along," said Charlotte. "I'll have Dave hitch the sulky so we can go and get the children. But first, you're to stop at ours for a cuppa[39] and a bit of sponge.[40]"

* * * * *

---

[39] Cup of tea.

[40] Light sweet cake served with whipped cream and icing.

A strip of bacon, two poached eggs, half a fried tomato, and black tea. Withers' breakfast rarely varied. If a day was to be run to the drill of precision, the place to commence was first thing.

Withers sliced the rasher, briskly, with a knife that was as sharp as he. Daylight filled his kitchen table as he squinted out the window. It was barely half past seven and the weather was already aggressing.

The sun, he lamented, *that hooligan sun had almost tipped the balance.*

Canada or Australia, Australia or Canada—he'd considered both before he left. Wholesale conquest of the native races was a virtue the colonies shared. In both, civilization progressed at a pace, while lesser races decayed. It was a cruel reality for young men like him, bred with the manners and grace of the class that ruled but forever consigned to its edge. The sole route open to social advancement lay in leaving to help build the Empire.

But while the weather was better, the colonies of Canada had failed to eject the French. If Archibald Withers were to serve the King, it would be under British rule and British ways, unblighted.

He stood for a moment at the open window to take in the fresh morning air. All of a sudden, on the far side of the street, the door to a dwelling flashed open.

"You bugger off back[41] to where you bloody well came from, you lazy black bastards!"

The shopkeeper held a shoe above his head as he charged out into the street.

"Filthy, dirty coons![42] Get off our street and go to hell!"

---

[41] A command to rapidly return to place of origin and stay there.

[42] Obscene term for *Aboriginal people*.

The shopkeeper threw the shoe with the force of a fired projectile. Withers didn't need to see its target. He knew at whom it was directed.

Withers sat down and continued his breakfast. He cut the tomato with vigor that the vegetable didn't need. Withers cursed the day he'd relented to management and agreed to leave the City.

"The black man has almost died out in the north, Mr. Withers. You'll likely never see them. That part of the state is in need of development, and we feel you're the perfect man."

He had commenced with polite resistance.

"It's just that I never dreamed, not for a moment, that if I came to the colony, I would ever work in the country, and near natives no less. I've barely set a foot into rural climbs in my life, be it here or back at home, and I would prefer it if I didn't have to."

"We all do country time in Australia," Withers' City manager had said. "And you should take it as a compliment that you will be head of a branch when you've been in the country for two years. It's an unexpected emergency, Mr. Withers, with the sudden death of Mr. Harvey. You'll be doing the bank a great service."

The equation Withers was charged with resolving wasn't complex. The failing properties were to be scooped up by the bank. Economic development was his only priority, not playing nursemaid to incompetent farmers. Flush them out, and he'd be out of the Town in no time, rewarded with a promotion. And Rory Burke and his meddling wife were the perfect place to start.

Withers crossed his knife across the scoop of his fork, then leaned back to enjoy his tea.

Five weeks, two days, and on a rough approximation, about sixteen hours had passed since he'd visited their farm. And not a sign of willingness to supply the figures he'd asked for had followed. They made it hard, the bloody Irish, for him to build a reputation for fairness.

"It's a majority Catholic community, Mr. Withers," his City manager had explained, "by about sixty to sixty-five percent. They tend to have bigger families than us, so their number will likely increase."

At the time, Withers bit his bottom lip to catch the curse there resting. A dominance of Catholics was a terrible base on which to ground a British community.

"Sir, is there no other branch in the precincts of the state in need of a manager?"

"No, there isn't, Mr. Withers. And I need you to mark these words. *All* our managers are community leaders, which means all men are to be treated equally in commerce, irrespective of denomination."

For Withers, fair play was only ever going to prosper on a gaming board uncorrupted. The likes of the Burkes had to be pushed back to the class to which they belonged, but discreetly, step by step.

Three flies shot through the open window and landed on Withers' plate. He snatched at a tea towel and dealt them their death with a single, steely blow.

"I won't be finishing you off like that, Mr. Burke," muttered Withers. "The Town's new banker is a gentleman."

* * * * *

Nell and Rory both learned about love in their own marital bed. How a caress could become a tingle, and then a torrent of pleasure. But as their marriage progressed, the bedroom also became a forum for hosting arguments.

Eamon lay in his crib not far from their bed, on account of his shaky breathing. It tempered his parents' rage. They lay on the bed as rigid as posts, neither touching the other, speaking in angry whispers.

"I told you, Nell, the figures are coming in the post. As soon as I get 'em, I'll write 'em up and give 'em to Mr. Withers, and we'll be out of the woods in no time."

"You said they were coming from Barry Walsh, then somehow through Billy Murphy and a pig farmer he knows toward the coast. Before we know it, it will be two months since the back of the house fell down, and we're getting absolutely nowhere."

"I'll be the first cove up this way to have a try at pig farming," shot back Rory. "Barry and Dave thought the butcher might know how to price pig meat for sale to abattoirs,[43] but he didn't. And Billy's mate Harry had sold up and moved on when I went by his pig farm to the east."

"Why are you so sure you'll get them in the post?"

"How many times do we have to go through this?" said Rory. He raised his voice, a little, and continued.

"Because Mick's brother-in-law is a bloody pig farmer, that's why. Mick's written to him. Saw the letter with my own eyes at the butter factory when I was delivering our cream. Mick's asked him to send me some viable figures for a pig farm. He'll probably send 'em by return post."

"Rory, don't speak loudly. You'll wake Eamon, and he's been coughing and hacking all day."

_____

[43] Slaughterhouses

"Well, if you'd have shown a bit of bloody tact with Dr. Dunne and played along with his theory about the curse of the blackfellas, we might get a bit more attention from him and the boy might not be ill. I've told you a hundred times, Nell. Out here, we all fall into step with what the O'Dohertys say, and the O'Dohertys reckon they were cursed."

"For God's sake, Rory, why are we talking about the O'Dohertys? There are no black people out here—not near our land anyway. And even if there were, they'd have nothing to do with Eamon's breathing. Dunne just hadn't a clue what was causing it and was grasping for a reason."

"Well, what he said isn't as half as barmy as you takin' an axe to the flamin' Jacaranda tree to stop the flowers blocking his lungs. And you were the one who's always said you were so glad my ma made da build the house in front of it so the kids might play there. Guess what, Nell? There are no flowers on the tree this year on account of the storm, and Eamon *still* strains to breathe."

Nell sat bolt upright in bed.

"By God, Rory Burke, you take up the habit of speaking to me like that, then you can cook and clean for yourself," snapped Nell. "You hear me? *I'm not havin' it!*"

Eamon woke with a cry. Nell jumped from the bed to cradle him.

"Look what you've done now!" she said.

The darkness held their hurt and rage in a balloon that just might burst. It lingered, briefly, but floated away once Eamon was sleeping again. Still, Nell rolled away from Rory, and Rory away from Nell.

* * * * *

"Richard, are you sure that it's a Wednesday afternoon that he goes to the hotel to drink?"

The Town main street was starting to calm, drained by the dimming sun. Withers and Richard looked without purpose into the window of the saddlery. Neither intended to buy the wares on offer, neither whip nor stirrups or the flash[44] silver spurs that had just arrived from the City. The saddlery was opposite the pub, so a strategic place to catch a sideways glance of who was entering it.

"I have done exactly as you asked of me when I first joined the bank," said Richard. "Every day, I either take a walk or otherwise find an excuse to be on the street just before four o'clock. I have a good idea now of the drinking habits of all the region's men. Every Wednesday at four and of a Saturday afternoon, Rory Burke goes to the Hotel Imperial, as clockwork as church on a Sunday."

"Well, it's a quarter past four and there's no sign of the bugger," hissed Withers. "We're beginning to look like loiterers."

"Not at all, sir, if I may say. We're just gentlemen interested in riding."

Withers turned, casually, toward the eastern end of the street. Rory Burke walked out onto it at midpoint, at the post office.

"Richard, you were right," said Withers. "Skedaddle. Our man is on his way."

"Yes, sir, Mr. Withers," replied Richard. "See you at the office in the morning."

---

[44] Fancy.

Withers was naturally brisk of step, but he did his best to amble. This encounter was to occur purely by chance, and his message transmitted in passing.

"Why, good day, Mr. Burke. What a pleasure to see you. What brings you to Town this late in the day?"

Rory's heart was already sinking, and it almost stopped on sight of the banker. If he'd seen him coming earlier, he'd have crossed the street. A chat with Withers was the last thing he needed after the news he'd just received.

"Well, good day, Mr. Withers," said Rory, tipping his hat. "I'm usually here late on a Wednesday. My wife permits me a couple of beers in the middle of the week. It's part of my regular habits."

"Well, no wonder our paths haven't crossed before. On Wednesdays, I usually work on until seven to be sure my desk is clear come Friday."

"Wise, if I may say, Mr. Withers," said Rory. "Forward planning is the mark of a gentleman."

What an absolute hypocrite, thought Withers, *from a man who couldn't plan a picnic.*

"Speaking of planning," said Withers, "am I to take it that you and your wife are no longer seeking a loan? I do hope so because the file I opened is shortly due to close."

Shadows stretched across the dusty street, to which Rory wished he could escape.

"To close, Mr. Withers?" asked Rory. "Are you about to lock us out?"

Withers smiled.

"Oh, Mr. Burke, you put it too highly," he said. "But nothing is open forever. Your application bears the date of my visit to your farm in October and can't stay live much longer. If I've received no figures come New Year, then I am afraid my offer will lapse. An emergency loan can only be granted across an arc of a couple of months."

"Says who?" asked Rory.

"Say my superiors in the City, to whom I have to answer."

Rory managed to curse so softly that it was audible to no one but him.

"Thank you, Mr. Withers," he said. "That's handy for me and Nell to know. We'll get a budget to you in no time."

Rory shot off to the Hotel Imperial and the refuge supplied by its high tiled walls. His seat at the bar would have been a haven against the dust, the dirt, and the heat if not for the haze of slow-burning tobacco. Cigarette smoke filled a spartan room to every crack and cranny.

Rory let the rabble wash around his worries. A ring of moisture encircled his glass then evaporated, as if mirroring his hopes. He gulped at the beer like his tired-out work horse at water, after a day in the field. There was nothing more to be done. He had to go to Hector.

Rory gripped at what was left of his beer so that the glass might break. Then he reread the letter he'd picked up at the post office. Perhaps he'd misunderstood it.

Dear Mr. Burke,   *25ᵗʰ November 1916*

My brother-in-law Michael has asked me to write to you with some quotations on starting a piggery. I have been in the business for many years and would like to be able to help out.

Unfortunately, the information you are seeking is more complex than it appears.

Much of the buying and selling of livestock in the pig trade takes place once a year at the Port Town Show, which happens, as you probably know, in the first weekend of June. As I am nearing retirement, I haven't participated in that market for over two years and have instead been concentrating my efforts on winding down my business. So, I am in no position to provide guidance for starting a piggery from scratch. I've no current figures for a market that is prone to fluctuation.

The best advice I can give is to suggest you attend the Port Town Show next June when the available livestock in the region will be traded. I would, of course, be more than willing to meet you there for a beer and introduce you around. Mick has spoken very highly of you, and I am always happy to lend a hand to our hardworking young farmers.

I hope this is of some help.

Yours faithfully,
Seamus Geelan

June, thought Rory. *June!* That would mean no rebuild before the onset of winter frost.

A sprightly Dave Noonan made for the bar and slapped Rory on the shoulder.

"You're a little late today, you old bugger. Popped in at four but you were nowhere to be seen."

"Oh, g'day, Dave," said Rory. "Went to the post office at four, then I had some readin' to do."

"What, more bad news? You been forgettin' to say your prayers or them mystery blackfellas out our way still pointin' the bone at ya? Freddy, give us a couple beers, will you? Make it schooners. Rory here's down on his luck."

"Do me a favor, mate, and don't shout about it," mumbled Rory. "Things can't get much worse."

"What's happening now?" asked Dave.

He pulled up a stool.

"Got a letter from Seamus Geelan, old Mick's brother-in-law. He can't give me figures for the piggery either. Says he hasn't been tradin' livestock for a couple of years and hasn't got a clue."

"Sorry to hear that, mate. Listen, can't we just make 'em up? The figures, I mean. If you can't find out how much it costs, then how can Withers? Would he ever know the difference?"

"I wouldn't mess around with a cove like Withers. We'd blow our goodwill with the bank for good if he ever found out I'd duped him."

"I suppose. Guess it's not worth the risk. So, where in the world does that leave ya?"

"No bloody idea. But I just ran into Withers. Reckons he can't carry his offer over past New Year. So, I gotta come up with them figures by Christmas."

Dave picked up his beer.

"Struthe. Sounds like you and Nell will be movin' back into that shack you grew up in with your sisters."

"No. I'm not going back there, not with Nell and Eamon."

"If it helps, I don't need that shilling and sixpence a month you slip me for the top thirty acres. We can put off them repayments until you're back on your feet."

"Thanks, mate, but sticking a finger in a bursting dike doesn't stop a flood. A shilling and a bit here and there makes no difference. We haven't got a choice. I'll have to ride down Port Town way and go cap in hand to Hector."

Dave put his hat on the bar.

"You know what, Rory? I didn't want to say so before, but it's not such a bad idea. Not a word to Nell, mind, but we've been to Charlotte's folks a couple of times for help. A bit of money out from my in-laws is nothing to 'em. And ole Hector probably expects you'll ask for a bob[45] or two at some stage."

Rory finished his beer in one long swallow, then reached for the schooner Dave had bought him.

"I hope you're right, mate," said Rory, "'cause there isn't any other way, and now I've gotta work out how to tell Nell."

Barry Walsh charged through flapping pub doors.

"Thought I'd find you here," sputtered Barry. "Mate, you'd better come up to the hospital. It's Eamon. I went by your place a little while back to pick up Thellie, and the boy was almost blue. I've left him and Nell with Matron at the hospital, and just been to fetch Dr. Dunne. He's on his way up there as well."

Rory's face fell into his hands. Could they at least have a reprieve over Eamon?

* * * * *

Thellie Walsh had taken command in the absence of Dr. Dunne. The Town's only midwife was the next best person for treating an infant's ailments.

"I am not going to lie to you, Nell. This is the worst case of croup I can remember. There's something not right, something irritating all of his air passages in a way I've not seen before."

Nell cradled Eamon and paced a ward of entirely white, from the walls, the roof, the bed cover and pillows, to the dresser and drawers in the corner. Blue sneaked in via a door to the veranda, with a glimpse of immaculate sky.

Nell was fighting waves of despair.

"Thellie, have you a clue at all on how to help him? I'm ready to listen to the barmiest suggestions. Any home remedy you've ever heard of, I'm willing to give a try."

---

[45] Slang word for *shilling*, which in turn is made up of twelve pence.

"Well, eucalyptus oil is best for colds, but I've not yet tried it for croup. Matron might add some drops to the wash cloths after they're soaked in boiling water. It might add a kick to the steaming."

"Should I go and speak to Matron?"

"No. I'll go, Nell. I'll find out first if they keep it."

"What do you mean?"

"Well, it's just that Dr. Dunne doesn't like it—anything to do with native cures. He says they're all based on superstition and not science. He'll only provide us with European medicines. That's all they're likely to have here for treating respiratory ailments."

Nell was about to blurt out that she felt that to be ridiculous, when Eamon stirred. She looked down at her son's little face. It had changed, thank God, from the edge of blue to a tired and more temperate red, but the tissue around his eyes was swollen.

"So, does that mean there'll be no eucalyptus kept in stock at all?" asked Nell.

"I don't know," said Thellie. "I'll go and ask Matron now."

Nell perched herself on the side of the bed, pulled Eamon closer, and looked out toward the garden. A bed of distressed red and white roses baked beneath the sun.

"Is that it, my boy?" she whispered. "Are you just like the flowers that suffer out here but thrive in your grandparents' garden? Would you be better off, my little love, in the gentler climes of the south?"

Three flustered men appeared in the doorway: Dr. Dunne, Rory behind him, followed by Barry Walsh.

"Good day, Mrs. Burke," said Dr. Dunne. "I came as soon as I could. I can see from here the little lad is ill. You were right to bring him to Town."

Rory pushed past Dr. Dunne to be at Nell's side. She smiled and kissed his cheek.

"Struuuthe," said Rory. "He's battlin', all right. When did all of this start?"

"Just after lunch," said Nell. "When the heat wave began rolling in."

"Have you steamed him yet?" asked Rory.

"Matron's preparing the wash cloths," said Nell.

Thellie bustled back in.

"Good day, Doctor. Good day, Rory," she said. "I'm glad Barry found you, Rory. Matron will be here in a minute to steam him. But the wash cloths will be soaked in boiling water only. She's no eucalyptus oil to hand."

"Pardon me?" asked Dr. Dunne.

"Oh goodness, Doctor," said Thellie. "You've managed to walk in at the middle of a conversation. Mrs. Burke happened to ask me about native cures, and I remembered the benefits of an oil."

Dunne scowled. The very use of the term *native* offended him, and the idea that some of their cures were "accepted" was appalling. He walked over to Nell, opened his black bag, and examined Eamon in silence. A few minutes later, he spoke.

"*My* prognosis," said Dr. Dunne, "is as follows. This child has croup. It is sporadic and severe. The best first step for breathing ailments is to make sure the patient's immediate environment is clean. Pristine clean. This boy is to stay at the hospital for at least the next few days, and his mother, of course, can stay with him. The hospital is relatively cool and spotless. And I am also disinclined, when he is in this state, to leave him anywhere near the bushland. The steaming can continue, but I see no point in adding eucalyptus oil. I will reassess his condition later."

Rory gulped and looked at Nell. A glint of a tear collected in her eye. There wasn't any way around it. A hospital bill would be added to their woes and, perhaps, the services of a physician.

* * * * *

Nell hadn't spent a night in Town, nor a night apart from Rory, since January of 1914. But she had taken it as a godsend—an evening alone to retreat and think about all that had passed since the wedding.

"Nell, Billy Murphy's due home first thing in the morning. He's offered to pop by and check if the house is still sound. But I could go by his place and rearrange things, so I can stay here with you and Eamon," said Rory. "Maybe I could sleep on the veranda?"

"Rory, there's not a chance in the world the Matron would allow that," replied Nell. "And we can't put off getting the house checked over. The nurse is here, and Dr. Dunne nearby. I can get Eamon through the night. He'll sleep in the crib just by me."

Nell lay in a bed in a room of her own for the first time since leaving her parents. At Ballycallan, she'd taken for granted the furnishings of the ward—a firm and expensive bed, her own enormous dresser, and fixed-to-the-wall gas lighting.

The noises made by the bush in the dark were duller here in Town. Foliage had been cut away from the hospital to accommodate a garden. Nell let the night draw her out to the veranda. She plopped herself into a deep wicker chair and rested her head in the palm of her hand.

"You always have to have things your way, don't you, Nell?" she whispered.

She remembered how they'd planned it, she and shy but somehow handsome Rory Burke of the far northwest. He'd already a house big enough for a family, but the trick lay in developing the land. They would stay in dairying short term, save every penny, then work out how to invest it. Crown land lay to the west of Jacaranda Ridge. The state government would eventually sell it, and they'd have enough saved to buy it.

It had all felt, at that distant time, like a sequence that had already unfolded. It wasn't a dream, but a life she simply had to run out to meet, catch with both hands, and claim. A brand-new family in the frontier lands; a fresh run worked with the man she loved, eased into the bands of profit.

And it hadn't occurred to me for a second, thought Nell, *that I might be careering toward a precipice on a farm called Jacaranda Ridge!*

Nell changed the hand on which she leaned her head. She had barely given a thought, back then, to all she was giving up.

Goodness knows her parents had tried. She'd been lectured at many a family dinner about the scale of the risk ahead.

"Before you were born, Nell," said Hector, on a temperate winter evening, "your mother and I were out on that land fourteen hours a day. It wasn't making any money—it was barely able to keep us. We got over the hump just after you were born. But that's what it takes, Nell, for a subsistence farm to be turned into a business. It's not an experience, I can frankly say, that I'd like to repeat myself."

Nell looked up. The sky was salted with the same brilliant stars she'd grown up with at Ballycallan. She might as well have been on her parents' veranda, taking a moment of quiet reflection before joining the merriment of their home.

"There are way fewer laughs out here, at least for the moment," muttered Nell.

"Are you sure this is what you want?" Violet had asked. "You will be rearing a family alone."

"I won't be alone, Ma," Nell had replied. "I'll write to you and Da once a week and get the advice I need by post. And there will be other women out in the west going through the same trials as me. We'll help each other as we go, the way that country folk do."

But now, Nell had to admit it. If Violet were teaching her the art of mothering, in the way she'd passed on keeping house, everything would have been much easier.

Eamon cried out. Nell ran inside, lifted him from the crib, and settled him in bed next to her. He was wheezing but breathing rhythmically. Nell studied his face beneath a pool of light afforded by the wall-mounted gas lamp. He was all Rory from the nose up, but with a mouth and jaw shape all hers. A lovely boy made up of both his parents, who had to be helped past a challenge.

"The truth is, you're the most important part now of all I have," whispered Nell. "And what's best for you will govern."

Nell stroked his head.

I have to go carefully, she thought. *I haven't another choice.*

Keeping Rory from knowledge of her eventual inheritance hadn't been solely to protect his pride. It was something retained from a comfortable childhood that she wasn't ready to release.

Nell breathed a sigh of reluctant relief. *I love you, Rory Burke, but that inheritance will have to remain a secret until its passage to Eamon is secure.*

* * * * *

Father John O'Kelly was climbing the stairs of the Town's only hospital. It was a quarter to four on a Sunday afternoon. He'd planned the timing of his visit. There would have been many a well-wisher before and after family Sunday lunch. But by now, the last of them would have likely gone home. O'Kelly wanted a few moments in private with Nell and Rory Burke.

He padded down the corridor, not wishing to stir a soul. He halted a few yards short of the ward where Mrs. Burke was staying. He heard something, then waited—five, ten, fifteen seconds. Marcus and Roisin Moloney were just about to leave.

"Come along, grumpy guts," said Roisin brightly. "It's time for us to give the Burkes some peace and quiet. And I need to make our dinner."

Poor Mr. Moloney, thought O'Kelly. He'd been so full of hope, back in April of this year, when he'd handed over that telegram. But he was yet to accept the grizzly end of Ireland's Easter Rising. It was more than time for Mr. Moloney to accept that the rebellion at home was over. *Help him, Lord*, O'Kelly prayed, *to embrace the blessings of his peaceful new life here in this beautiful land.*

"Why, good day, Mr. and Mrs. Moloney. Good day, Mr. and Mrs. Burke. And there I was thinking I'd be the last to come and find out how Eamon is fairing."

All four adults rose from their seats at the sight of their parish priest.

"Good day, Father," came the collective reply.

"I'll just go out to the veranda," added Rory, "and find you a decent seat."

"It's lovely to see you, Father," said Roisin. "But we were about to take our leave. My parents are due at home for dinner. We'll be eating light and early today out of respect for the habits of the elderly."

"Not at all, Mrs. Moloney. Please don't let me hold you up. And you, Mr. Moloney—you're keeping well, I trust?"

"I am, Father, I am," said Marcus quietly.

"Well, I am very pleased to hear it. And I hope you pass a most pleasant evening in the company of your family."

As the Moloneys left, he was buoyed by the sight of a picture-perfect family. Nell was lifting Eamon from his crib on the far side of the bed, and Rory joined her. He leaned over his young wife's shoulder to better see his son.

This is a loving couple sure enough, thought O'Kelly. *What a shame they are beset with troubles.*

"Well, I think it might be fair to say you're a family down on your luck," said O'Kelly.

Eamon stirred in his mother's arms.

"You could well say that we are, Father," said Nell.

"Tell me," said O'Kelly. "Before I move on to the trials of your boy, may I ask what is happening with your house? It mustn't be easy living out on the farm with half of it fallen away?"

Rory moved to a chair toward the end of the bed so he could better speak with his priest. He smoothed the wrinkles on the thighs of his pants before speaking.

"It's not a picnic, Father, I can tell you that," said Rory. "But Billy Murphy's just been by, and he says the house is still sound. We're hoping to get the repairs underway in no time. Should be started by Christmas."

"Well, there's some good news," said O'Kelly. "Better to have an unwell child housed in solid accommodation. Tell me, Mr. Burke. Is Mr. Murphy terribly busy? Some time has gone by since the storm."

Nell looked at Rory. He shot a glance back to her, making it clear she was to say nothing that might embarrass him, which meant no talk of money.

"No, Father," said Rory. "Billy's ready to help. We've had a bit of a problem with cash flow, which is about to be resolved."

O'Kelly assessed what was conveyed by the look Mr. Burke gave his wife. The door to discussion of the family's finances wasn't going to be opened.

O'Kelly let it lie.

I will reflect later at home at the presbytery, thought O'Kelly, *on how I might find out more.*

"May I move a little closer, Mrs. Burke, and take a look at your lovely son?"

"Of course, Father, but you're to stay there. I'll bring him over to you."

Eamon coughed, then kept wheezing, as Nell approached the priest.

"This struggle has gone on and off since he was six months old, Father," explained Nell. "He seemed to settle in the autumn and winter, but by the middle of October, it was back with a vengeance—the wheezing, I mean. And there's been only sporadic respite ever since."

"How old is he now, Mrs. Burke?" asked O'Kelly.

"He was born on the twentieth of March 1915, so he's one year and nine months old."

"And this is the worst he's been?"

"Yes, Father. It is."

"This poor boy really is suffering," said O'Kelly. "How many nights has he been hospitalized?"

"Tonight will be his fifth," said Nell. "And I'd like to be able to say that a restful sleep has been secured by both mother and child, but I can't. I've not had the courage to tell Dr. Dunne, but being in Town hasn't made much difference."

O'Kelly was unsurprised that Dr. Dunne's strategy hadn't worked. But he didn't comment. So much the better that he had made some inquiries with his old friend, the Port Town pharmacist. He opened his small black briefcase.

"Mrs. Burke," said O'Kelly, "on a recent trip down to the Port Town, I visited one of the largest of the pharmacies to be found outside of the City. I've known the owner for many years, and he gave me this elegant little bottle. It's elderberry oil from England. Apparently, it's all the rage over there for alleviating respiratory ailments. I was just wondering, Mrs. Burke, whether Dr. Dunne had prescribed anything of this kind?"

"I can't say he has, Father," said Nell. "But if a Port Town pharmacist gives it the nod, I don't see why we shouldn't try it."

"Too right, I say," added Rory.

"How do we use it Father?" asked Nell.

"Drops of it are simply placed on a handkerchief and the patient breathes them in."

The Matron entered. She was carrying a metal tray with two steaming wash cloths. She had missed the presence of their distinguished guest in a corner of the ward. She put the tray on the dresser.

"Right," she said. "Time for his late afternoon steaming."

The Matron turned around.

"Oh, my goodness, Father. I didn't see you there. Good day to you."

"And good day to you too, Matron," said Father O'Kelly. "Speaking of treating Eamon, I have just been sharing with Mr. and Mrs. Burke a suggestion from a Port Town pharmacist for a small addition to Eamon's handkerchiefs. Here. Take this."

The Matron read the label.

"Oil of the elderberry," she said. "I can't say that I've heard of this, Father. In any event, Dr. Dunne is averse to native medicines."

"Ah," said O'Kelly. "Then there will be no problem. The oil of the elderberry isn't native, Sister. It's come all the way from England and is a fashionable British cure."

O'Kelly noticed that Rory wished to speak. He guessed rightly that Rory was anxious to push the point so as to avoid paying a physician.

"Matron, I can't see the harm in giving this a try if it's come from Port Town pharmacist. It was very kind of you, Father— really very generous—to get a bottle of it for us," said Rory.

"All right," said the Matron. "But not tonight. I'll discuss it with the doctor in the morning."

Father O'Kelly picked up his briefcase, his mission fully accomplished.

"My goodness, look at the time. Matron, please give the doctor my very best," said O'Kelly. "I hope this has been of some help."

* * * * *

Rory Burke had slept alone for a fifth cauterized night. Reversion to the husk that was the life of a bachelor had left him out of sorts. But alone in a home beset by bad luck, his resolve had somehow returned. *Damn you, Archibald Withers,* he cursed, stretched across an unmade bed.

There wasn't a dint or a quirk in the banking records of either Sean or Rory Burke, not a blemish or a blotch to give Mr. Withers good reason to refuse him a loan. And now Eamon's health had multiplied his problems, and his duties as a man. He had to find a way to get the bank to step in and support his fledgling family.

So, later that Monday morning, Rory waited in the hallway to Withers' office, having made an appointment Friday. There, in a drafty corridor, he prepared to state his case.

"He was called out unexpectedly, Mr. Burke," said Richard, "to the farm of one of our customers. He should be back by noon, as planned, but he requested I ask you to wait."

I'll wait for you, Withers, until hell freezes over, thought Rory.

The minutes passed in chunks. Five, ten, then fifteen of them, slipped by with each glance at the clock. *Withers is a cunning bugger,* mused Rory, as he spun his hat in his hands. *He knows how to make a man stew.*

Rory rehearsed his strategy in his head. Show no weakness and conceal desperation; pleading for mercy would gain nothing. The only way through to a cove like Withers was to show what was in it for him.

Suddenly the banker turned the corner and strode down the corridor toward him.

"Why, Mr. Burke, how lovely to see you. And how glad I am that you are here. I am sorry to be so late."

Rory settled a leg that had begun to tremble, then stood.

"Not a problem, Mr. Withers," replied Rory. "We all have commitments to meet."

"Indeed, we do," said Withers. "Please come inside."

Rory studied Withers as he slid into position. Reed thin with confidence aplenty, the banker eased in behind his desk.

"Do take a seat, Mr. Burke. And I hope you're here to pass me the figures I need to get your loan approved. Figures for pig farming, I mean. Or perhaps the news is even better, and you've found the help you need elsewhere?"

Rory managed to smile.

"Not quite, Mr. Withers, sir. But I was hoping we might strike a deal."

"Oh really, Mr. Burke?" replied the banker. "So, you haven't the figures for the loan?"

Withers delighted in imminent conquest and commenced rocking in his chair.

"No, Mr. Withers, I don't. But that's for a very good reason."

"Well, do tell, Mr. Burke. But as you know I'm bound by the bank's procedures."

Rory coughed then sat up straighter.

"Well," said Rory, "I reckon I've come up with a way to persuade your bosses why I'm an exception to the rule. You see, the idea of farming pigs was something that struck me as an original thought—a market I might be able to pioneer, since it's not been tried in this region. I understand, Mr. Withers, that normally such ventures require planning. But it's so much easier said than done when a cove is the first to try something."

Rory watched Withers intently.

"Of course, I see your point, Mr. Burke. So, what is it that you propose?"

"Well, I imagine, sir," said Rory, "that the sole concern of you and the bank is that you don't blow your dough—that you can be sure me and Nell will meet the repayments, and that it won't all end in tears."

"Very astute, Mr. Burke, if I may say," said Withers dryly.

"Mr. Withers, I've had a look at our records, and neither me nor my father ever skipped a beat with the bank. You're probably not aware, Mr. Withers, being fairly new in Town, that Sean, my father, was among the bank's very first customers. He opened his account on this main street when the bank did its dealings from a tent."

"You're quite right, Mr. Burke. I have to confess that you have shared something that might, indeed, have escaped me."

I must sustain the impression of fairness, thought Withers, *if I'm to retain the community's respect.*

Rory sensed a chance.

"Good," said Rory. "So, this is what I suggest. Obviously, if we ever default, you will be entitled to Jacaranda Ridge. We are close, Mr. Withers—really very close—to turning it into a commercial venture. If the bank forwards us the loan, without the figures for my pig farm, I will share ten percent of the piggery profits for the first five years of trading. In addition, of course, to the repayments. And if there's nothing to share, and the piggery doesn't work, then you can surely call us in. Jacaranda Ridge will belong to the bank. That's how determined I am, Mr. Withers, to make our venture work."

Withers grimaced. Burke had thrown a spanner[46] in the works. A flat-out no would be repeated around Town, and there might be talk that the bank had been harsh. A tranche of time, albeit a brief one, was to pass before he could fell the axe.

"Mr. Burke," said Withers curtly, "the problem is as follows. The bank has procedures—procedures that are put in place so that unseemly acquisition of land for bad debts is a remote and

---

[46] Wrench. The phrase "to throw a spanner in the works" means to disrupt something unexpectedly.

final resort. By doing this blind, you are asking me to breach a cardinal practice of the bank. And I must say, I am loathe to do that. I need to know if pig farming is viable. It is as simple and as uncomplicated as that."

Rory shook his head.

"But you will never have to call us in, Mr. Withers. On that, you have my word."

"Your word is enough for me, Mr. Burke, but it isn't for the bank!"

An awkward pause came to an end as Withers folded his arms.

"Leave it with me, Mr. Burke," said Withers with a sigh. "I will revert in a couple of days."

* * * * *

"I have to say, Matron, this is a most remarkable improvement."

Dr. Dunne had been with Eamon for around thirty minutes. The child wasn't wheezing, and the Matron said he'd been well for two full days.

"What do you think has changed, Doctor?" asked the Matron.

"There would seem to be two things," said Dunne. "The mercury has now fallen below ninety degrees. This is a child that clearly suffers in the heat. The change in the weather has suited him."

Both doctor and nurse continued peering into little Eamon's crib. The baby smiled back at them and gurgled.

"And the second?" asked the Matron.

Dunne smiled.

"The elderberry oil supplied by Father O'Kelly might have helped him turn a corner. I have to confess, I have seen it mentioned in the *British Medical Journal*, but I was yet to follow it up. Father O'Kelly was right. It is indeed being praised at home for the treatment of respiratory ailments."

Eamon coughed, but for only a few seconds.

"He is not a hundred percent," said Dunne. "But he is certainly much better."

Nell and Rory waited on the veranda. They were hoping that this would be the last of the days on which Nell had to stay in Town. It was exactly a week since mother and son had been held for observation at the hospital.

Rory leaned against the veranda railing and drew slowly from a smoke. Nell knitted in the wicker chair while they waited.

"You reckon we're out of the woods, love?" asked Rory, tentatively.

Rory stubbed out his cigarette in a battered copper ashtray.

"God willing, we are," said Nell. "He's been back to normal more or less for two days, except for a little cough."

"Maybe that oil Father brought from the Port Town might be some sort of permanent cure?"

Nell kept knitting.

"I wouldn't say permanent, not yet anyway. But it looks like the end of medical bills for the moment."

Rory looked out across the garden. He did so without squinting, as the sun shone without a harsh edge. Even the bed of roses in front of him seemed to be breathing freely. No news from the bank for a couple of days meant he was ready to tell Nell that Withers might have relented.

"I had a meeting with Mr. Withers earlier this week," said Rory. "Reckon I've found a way to get that loan released."

Nell stopped knitting, abruptly.

"How's that?" she asked.

"I offered him somethin' out of our pig farming ventures. I figured that a cove like Withers is not moved so much by pity. His only interest is profit for the bank. So, I said I'd share with them ten percent over the course of the first five years. I pointed out that pork and bacon were both new ventures out here, so that's why we'd been a bit late with the figures. Once I gave him a reason why he'd not had 'em, he said he'd give my suggestion a think."

Nell looked past her husband into the garden behind him. Rory wondered why she'd gone quiet. He was doing his best as a husband and a man, but she didn't seem to be pleased.

"Well, that might just work," said Nell, quietly, before returning to her knitting.

Rory was about to probe his wife's thoughts when Dr. Dunne came on to the veranda.

"Mr. and Mrs. Burke, I'm bringing good news. You can take Eamon home today. Please come inside."

* * * * *

"Did he provide any further detail at all on what in the hell this is all about?"

Archibald Withers paced the length of his desk, propelled by sinewy limbs. He had fifteen more minutes to prepare a defense for a meeting of undisclosed aims.

It was a quarter past ten on Thursday morning. Richard took Withers through the day's commitments, as listed in his diary. Father O'Kelly had come by on Monday afternoon, seeking an appointment. Richard had made one for half past ten, on Thursday, telling him that was the best he could do. This wasn't true. Richard knew his boss would want to know more before meeting a Catholic priest in private.

"He didn't, sir," said Richard. "And I've dropped in a discreet query here and there with the few Roman Catholics I know. That drew nothing out of the ordinary. From what I can gather, there is nothing significant brewing in their community."

"And have you checked their bank accounts, Richard?"

"Indeed, both the accounts of the church and the private one held by Father O'Kelly. All are healthy, well in the black, and there have been no sudden cash movements out. So, we can exclude that he's liable to ask for a loan or raise a concern about impropriety."

Withers stopped pacing, put his hands on his hips, then took his place at his desk. Richard, seated opposite him, returned to checking the diary to be sure the briefing was complete.

"And don't forget you've a farm visit at three, a good hour's ride from Town."

Bugger the bloody farm visit, thought Withers. *I've got a priest to deal with first!*

"Is Mrs. Evans preparing the morning tea in the very best of our china?"

"Of course, sir," said Richard. "And she will bring Father O'Kelly to your office, rather than me, so she can ask about sugar and milk."

"Very well, Richard. You had better get out to the floor to greet him when he gets here."

Alone in his office, Withers checked his look in the face mirror on the wall. The bout of intemperance of the preceding minutes had disturbed the grooming of his hair. He parted it again, combed it, and put it back in position. Withers blew his nose, sat down, and set about reading some papers. It was important to be seen in control and at the helm when the priest was brought in to see him.

But, at the sound of a knock, he bounded toward the door.

"My goodness, Father O'Kelly, what a pleasure to see you. It has been far too long between meetings."

Father O'Kelly removed his hat and shook the banker's hand.

"Indeed, it has, Mr. Withers. Afternoon tea at the presbytery, I believe it was, in your first month of service."

"You are right, of course, and how remiss of me to be so slow about offering a return."

An experience I didn't want to repeat, thought Withers. *A tedious exchange about the role of the bank in ensuring community care revealed the priest was to be avoided.*

"Not at all, Mr. Withers. I am sure your time has been filled to brimming settling into a new command."

"Well, at least I can offer tea now. Mrs. Evans, can you see to that, please?"

"Yes, of course, sir, and with cake. Milk and sugar, Father O'Kelly?"

"Just milk, Mrs. Evans, thank you."

With small talk finished and morning tea delivered, Withers took the initiative.

Asking head on just might thwart him.

"Father, it's our pleasure that you are here, and I see that your accounts are in order. Would it be terribly blunt, or perhaps even rude, if I asked how I am able to help?"

"Of course not," replied O'Kelly. "It's just that I've an idea for a new avenue of business, and I wanted to seek your views."

"Well, I'm always interested in that Father. Please do go on."

O'Kelly looked at the portrait of their Imperial King hanging above Withers' head. It somehow made him falter.

Withers leaned back in his comfortable seat, pleased to see another of his strategies working.

"Before I go ahead and speak with the Bishop, I would first appreciate your thoughts. As you are aware, our finances are sound, and I want to see them put to good use."

"Well, that would hardly be the business of the bank," said Withers. "We are simply the guardians of your funds."

O'Kelly decided to share in one breathe the ruse he had constructed—a ruse to find out what Mr. Burke meant when he said he'd a problem with cash flow.

"For ordinary expenditure, I would say this were true, but that's not what I have in mind. Under my duties in providing pastoral care, I would like to set up a fund for farmers. A resource from which they might be able to borrow whenever hard times strike. It's a committee structure I have in mind. Farmers could apply to the fund for tide-over loans when beset by misfortune or trouble. I would set up a board, perhaps of three, comprised of me, the parish chairman, and you. Our farming community has nearly doubled in the course of the last ten years. And I don't see why the church shouldn't do its bit to provide support when it might be needed."

Archibald Withers cocked an eyebrow so high that it threatened to take flight from his forehead. This was a thought to be stopped before it birthed action. The bank was there to maintain its monopoly over finance across every sector.

"An interesting thought, if I may say, Father, but I fear it cannot work. The division between church, commerce, and Crown are the holy trinity, if you like, on which this great country is based. And I must confess this is the first I've heard that the three of them should be melded."

"And I agree, Mr. Withers, it's a novel idea, but I came seeking your views."

Withers stared, defiantly, into O'Kelly's eyes. They sparkled back in crystal blue.

"And I would add to this my doubts about need. The Catholic farmers in these parts do as well, if not better, than the Protestants. Are the problems so pressing that they merit intervention on the part of your church?"

Withers' voice was close to piercing.

"I wouldn't say there was mass demand," replied O'Kelly, quietly. "But there might be one or two."

There was a single name hanging between the two men.

Mr. Rory Burke.

But you haven't left open the tiniest crack, thought O'Kelly, *from which I might probe bank policy. If I spoke specifically of Mr. Burke, more harm would follow than good.*

Withers maneuvered to wrap up the meeting.

Father O'Kelly glanced again at the portrait of the King.

This banker doesn't want to help out.

"Father, I will reflect on your suggestions. But state management would be loathe, I fear, to let me move a mountain in my very first year in saddle. Let me show you to the door."

Once it was closed Withers took from his drawer pen and watermarked paper, teeth gritted and ears a-steaming.

You have pushed me, old man, into unleashing immediately Rory Burke's ejection.

* * * * *

Rory was keyed up. Nell wasn't. They had to find a solution, and it was down to her, as a dutiful wife, to try to calm him down.

"Rory," she said gently, "please would you come sit by me?"

The fire was spitting. Rory paced in a semi-circle at the far end of the campfire of their makeshift kitchen, not far from the Jacaranda tree. Eamon was lying in his crib next to Nell, dozing.

"Rory," said Nell again. "You'll be wearing out your boots before you know it, and we haven't the money to be buying any others. Please come sit."

Rory stopped, dropped his hands, and turned to his beckoning wife. She was bathed in the light of the dancing fire. It set her perfect skin aglow.

A few campsite swigs of whiskey had done nothing to quell the pain of rebuke. It had come, again, in writing.

Dear Mr. Burke,　　　　　　　　　　　*14ᵗʰ December 1916*

Due consideration has been given to your proposal, about sharing speculated profits from pig farming. I regret to repeat that the guidelines of the bank are as fixed as they are firm. Any other route would, quite frankly, be fiscally irresponsible and put the bank into disrepute. The absence of figures for commercial projects precludes the issue of a loan.

The bank wishes your family well.

Archibald Withers esq.

"Nell," said Rory, still standing by the fire. "What are we going to do?"

"I don't know, Rory. Not yet, anyway. But I can't see how stomping around the fire, or drowning your sorrows in whiskey, will help us out of this any sooner."

Rory sat on the stone next to Nell and rested his elbows on his knees. His hands cradled his head.

He looked up.

"Why don't I try heading down Port Town way?" said Rory. "Visit a few of the big abattoirs just to the south of it and start askin' a few questions about the wholesale price of pork meat. I can leave you and Eamon to stop with Dave and Charlotte and be back up home in no time."

"Rory, with the trip there and the journey home, you'll be gone for well over a week, so we'll lose that in cream income and more. Charlotte's door is always open to us, but I would prefer not to have to rely on it. And the countryfolk down there don't know you from Adam. I don't see why they'd be willing to help."

Rory snatched at a route toward Hector.

"Well, why don't I drop into Ballycallan?" he said casually. "Everyone knows Hector down there."

Nell sighed. She may have run out of diversions.

"What?" she said, tiredly.

Rory sprung to his feet, re-enlivened.

"Hector'll be able to point me in the right direction. Lemme know who I should be talkin' to about pig farming."

Nell's mind clambered to find a reply as the hum of the night flooded in. But the stammer of insects and the flight of the bats barely reached her ears.

Rory stood stock-still and stared into the fire. It was opening up again—something he called the cavern. Whenever they spoke of Hector, a crevasse emerged between he and his wife that he had never been able to fathom.

Then, Nell spoke softly.

"I don't think that's a good idea."

For Nell, the flush of everlasting love led her to an answer—the well of feeling that had gathered in drips, then later in waves, on the back veranda of her local dance hall as she got to know Rory Burke. And now his candor, determination, and commitment to family were anchoring her to the west-lands. This wasn't the moment for a return to the coast, to quit before they'd met the first of the hurdles to their dreams for Jacaranda Ridge.

Rory fought the surge in the back of his eyes that threatened to burst into tears. Why *had* a lady of prospects like Nell McTiernan wanted to marry a cove like him? How could a bloke like himself ever have hoped to make her happy? He wished his parents were alive. They were the only people he'd ever known to whom he felt close enough to ask. His sisters only knew him as their invincible big brother. If they could see him now, they would call their eyes liars.

Then, all of a sudden, Nell smiled. Not the brilliant grin of sudden relief, but one of cautious hope.

"Rory, I've another suggestion," she said. "Let's see what Father O'Kelly says. Why not go and see him in the morning, see if he has any ideas? He came up with a route for alleviating Eamon's coughing, so perhaps he can help with the figures? He's been up here for decades and knows all of the farmers all over this region and probably beyond. He might know someone who knows about pig farming. Let's do that before we go and trouble Da, talk to our own parish priest. But for now, will you come here and please kiss your son? He's drifting between sleeping and waking."

Rory dragged his ragged form toward his precious little family. His arms were as heavy as the thickening night, but he was still able to wrap them around his rock of a wife. They would work their way out of this all right, Rory swore it quietly on Sean's and Hannah's graves. He'd find a way to resolve their troubles and somehow take care of his own.

* * * * *

The third Saturday of every month was dedicated to book-keeping. December wasn't any different. Fountain pen, ink well, pencil, ruler, and eraser were all laid out at his desk. With its cardboard covers and meticulous math, the account book was more than a fiscal record. For Father O'Kelly, it rather told a story; it was a kind of community archive. Tending to its entries was among the tasks he counted as a blessing. Every figure was significant, and all notations mattered in telling the tale to the generations to follow of the parish he had founded.

One hand reached to open the ledger while the other adjusted his glasses. *Just half-glasses*, O'Kelly thought proudly, *only needed for reading.* The ledger was barely opened, his mind resting at the precipice of focus, when he heard a knock at the door.

A little odd for a visitor to pass this early, not long since breakfast and well before morning tea.

He hoped that it wasn't a distress call.

"Coming," called O'Kelly, as a second knock echoed through the hallway.

"Mr. Rory Burke," said O'Kelly, as sunlight surged into the dim. "It's always a pleasure to see you, but I fear the reason may not be pleasurable if you are passing at this hour."

Rory had barely taken off his hat when agitation betrayed his desperation.

"Good morning, Father," replied Rory. "I'm sorry to come by so early in the day, but Nell and I are in need of advice. We thought this would be the best place to find it."

"Of course, Mr. Burke. Do come in. In fact, you've saved me a trip. I was planning to call on you and Mrs. Burke next week to see how Eamon is fairing."

"Thank you, Father," said Rory.

He followed O'Kelly to the presbytery study and sat in a chair, opposite him, at his desk.

"Eamon has been doing much better in the last few days, thanks to the oil of the elderberry and the cool turn in weather. But that's not the reason I'm here."

"Well, that's good news. So, what can I do to help?"

It was a tried and true technique. O'Kelly had relied on it to reach his parishioners from the earliest days of his priesthood. Let them talk, tell their story fully, then guide them in finding their own answers.

Morose but verbose, Rory Burke rambled. Mr. Withers had given them nothing but grief over advancing his family a loan. He wanted pounds, shillings, and pence on how Jacaranda Ridge would be improved, particularly when it came to pig farming, and Rory couldn't provide figures. Withers had firmed his line this week by putting it into writing, and he and Nell received the letter yesterday. The bank needed figures now. Rory spoke of how he was loathe to go to his father-in-law for money, but that there seemed to be no other way.

For Father O'Kelly, it was clear why Withers had written.

You sensed I wanted to help the Burkes out, thought O'Kelly, *and so sought to speed their demise.*

"My goodness, what a time you've been having, Mr. Burke. What a terrible time. I wasn't aware that the bank was being difficult when it came to helping you over the house."

"We don't like to advertise our troubles, Father."

"How is Mrs. Burke coping?"

"You know Nell, Father. She's as solid as they come. Only thing that she frets over is Eamon."

"Well, that's understandable, Mr. Burke. But I can help at least with the figures."

I will not be out-foxed by a banker.

"How's that, Father?" queried Rory.

"Over in that cupboard is my record of our regional publications," said O'Kelly. "It's comprehensive. I've the newsletter of the Port Town Chamber of Commerce going back to its inception just over a decade ago, our Catholic press, and of course, the local paper. But by chance, I've a collection also of the livestock prices of every Port Town Show. I've made a point of keeping the *Show Annual* every year since 1900. The 1916 edition will surely feature this year's going rate for the selling and buying of pigs, and the price paid by the abattoirs for their meat."

Rory leaped like a man who had won at the races.

"My word, Father, that is wonderful news. Please don't get up. Let me fetch it."

It was all written up in just over an hour, under Father O'Kelly's elegant hand—a flawless budget for establishing a piggery. O'Kelly signed and dated the papers.

"He won't be able to argue with these figures, Mr. Burke."

And certainly not when signed by a priest.

"Father, I don't know how to thank you."

"Just a moment, Mr. Burke," said O'Kelly, as Rory leaned forward to take them. "I know how fastidious a Protestant banker can be. I've a smart white envelope here in my drawer. Let me slip the figures into it and address it to him, by hand."

Rory leaned back, humbled. What a man they had in Father John O'Kelly.

"There you are, Mr. Burke," said O'Kelly. "You can deliver it first thing Monday. But before you seal the envelope, you might pop in a note. Let Mr. Withers know the figures came from the Port Town *Show Annual* and that he's welcome to come and inspect them at the presbytery. It's always a pleasure to see him."

O'Kelly returned his pen to its place by the inkwell.

Withers won't dare show his face here, once he's worked out this is a retort.

The two men walked toward the presbytery door, Rory as if on air.

"Father," he said. "There's just one other matter that's been bothering me. May I ask your opinion before I leave?"

"Of course, Mr. Burke. Go on."

Stress and fatigue conspired to make Rory ask.

"It's Eamon's condition," said Rory. "Dr. Dunne says he might have been cursed by the blacks, last spring perhaps. He told us when we left the hospital that we're to bring him back into Town on the sight of a blackfella anywhere near our land. Would you have any ideas, Father? Would you have any clue if Dr. Dunne is right and the blackfellas might have cursed him? Nell thought it might be the flowers of the Jacaranda tree, but that makes no sense to me either."

O'Kelly stopped walking midstride.

Talk in the Town had already begun. The more Aboriginal people were seen, the more they would be accused, irrationally, and the greater the chance of trouble.

I will have to keep an eye on all of my parishioners, if a sensible man like this one believes nonsense.

"I've little knowledge, Mr. Burke, of Jacaranda trees," said O'Kelly curtly. "But I've some of the Aboriginal people. I've never seen them harm a living soul, and I have yet to see them engaging in the cursing of settlers either, and certainly not infants, even if white folklore is to the contrary."

Rory blushed.

"Thank you, Father," he replied. "You are right, of course. We'll keep Eamon on the straight and narrow with the help of modern medicines."

* * * * *

The rebuild commenced soon after. Peace was forged with the land.

Nell kept cooking on the fireplace by the Jacaranda tree for everyone: Billy Murphy and his two men, Dave Noonan when he stayed for dinner, and Rory. Sometimes, the visitors camped overnight, and sometimes they were joined by Charlotte, who would come by with a large pot of stew and damper, her girls toddling at her skirts. With them, the Noonans brought a small packet of feed for Rory's newly retired nag and some ribbon for the fence—a nod to the feast of Christmas.

The adults yarned[47] and swapped tall tales until late in the evening, as their world shriveled to a fire's glow.

From a distance, they were watched by ancient eyes. At dawn, the blanched morning departed as if the smoke of a fresh fire were burning through it, easing the day into life. The shuffle of waking feet tumbled through the muggy gray light, nudging it nether. A collection of limbs could soon be seen gathered in a circle near the flickering flames. Forearms lifted at the elbow as they ate and drank themselves into daylight.

Rory, Billy Murphy, and his support crew of two jacked up the house with iron supports, reckoned it level, then dug out

---

[47] Chatted.

each disused post. They piled them up a few yards past the Jacaranda tree.

"Firewood for a whole winter," said Rory, as they carried off the last of them.

"You'll be splitting that lot yourself," replied Murphy. "Or can I pitch in for a portion of it?"

"I can agree to that," said Rory.

He knew that it was more than they would use.

Dave Noonan and Rory commenced the rebuild by crafting wooden boards from the pile of disused posts. They restricted their raid on the apprehensive bushland to a pair of trees long enough to yield wood fit to replace the damaged frame. They chopped, hacked, and hammered for almost every minute granted by day, along with some afforded by lamplight.

The new posts crafted by Billy Murphy's team fell sturdily into the soil. The ground heaved with relief when the rebuilt house was lowered and eased onto them. It was anchored now in the familiar fashion of the bushland's trees; the burden was no longer intolerable.

Father O'Kelly came by Jacaranda Ridge on a heavy-with-heat Friday. The reconstruction of the family farmhouse would be all the talk after mass. It merited inspection, especially in light of his own contribution. And O'Kelly wanted to encourage the turn in his parishioners' interests toward community events and developments. All discussion of insurrection in Ireland had ceased and, at least for now, there was little chatter about Aboriginal people and the trouble they allegedly caused.

He was greeted by Nell.

"Mrs. Burke, I am astonished by the wonder of your outdoor kitchen. It fits perfectly among the rocks, and by the shelter of the Jacaranda tree."

"There's one blessing, Father," replied Nell. "One kitchen gone, collapsed into the earth, and another born regardless. I've said more than one Hail Mary of thanks."

"Well, Mrs. Burke, I've brought something along to add to those blessings. I've half a dozen fresh fish, caught from the river by some of the lads in Town. They were given to me just this morning. Surplus, I understand, from a bountiful catch. It occurred to me they might serve well as your evening meal."

"Father, you shouldn't have, but I can't say we don't need it. We'd have been feasting tonight on peas, carrots, and potatoes all on their own."

Rory abandoned his tools when he saw their priest.

"Father, kind of you to pass by," he said, bounding toward him. "As you can see, we're well into the rebuild."

"Indeed, Mr. Burke. It seems I will be passing by again in a short time for a fresh home blessing."

"Just after the holidays at this rate, Father," replied Rory. "But you're to pleasure us next time by staying for a meal, cooked in a proper kitchen and served on our dinner table."

"The pleasure, Mr. Burke, will be all mine."

Throughout construction Nell fetched and carried whatever the men needed, even though she might have fallen pregnant. She was keeping it to herself until completely certain she had baby joy to share but was happy that Eamon had stabilized. He slept reasonably well by day, although a little less so at night.

"New frame's solid, Rory," said Dave Noonan, one day toward the end of the rebuild. "Huey[48] can throw down whatever he likes. You won't be gettin' teared down again from what I can see, at least not from rain."

---

[48] Slang word for *God*.

"Too right," replied Rory.

"Hey Rory," said Dave, "I think I can see our Mr. Withers down by the roadside. He's parked his sulky and havin' a good look our way. Might even have binoculars, and it looks like he's got himself a flamin' chauffeur. Hang on. Maybe they saw me watchin'. Now it looks like he's movin' on."

Good riddance, thought Rory, ignoring what Dave had said.

"Nell, love, there's another tin of nails on the bench in my workshop. Can you bring 'em?" called Rory in their last hour of labor, hunkered high over an open ceiling.

"This new roof's as hard as a vicar's, missus," said Noonan. "I hope them nails are sharp-ended."

By the end of the month, the house made of wood stood on contended land, and the soil had relinquished its rebellion.

* * * * *

Part II - Allegiances
(1922–1923)

Chapter 5
Education
August 1922

Eamon Burke was seven years old, and his mother wished him to go to school.

For the first year of his education, Eamon was being taught at home. When Nell was a child, there was a school a half-mile walk away from Ballycallan. At Eamon's age, Nell, along with her brothers, had easels and chalkboards, books, and a playground. Most importantly, they had a trained teacher. Nell wanted at least that for all her children.

And now that the kiddies of the western end of the parish numbered more than ten, a case could be made to the church for funding a second school.

Nell was working in her laundry, which gave out onto the patchy grass around the Burke family yard. She pulled the plug out of the washtub and looked up to check on her children as the silty water drained away. Eamon was so good with the girls. It was Friday, and a particularly high sky of a day, with winter sun shining gently upon them. Eamon had his sisters arranged as he wished beneath the Jacaranda tree. Eighteen-month-old Polly was sitting upright in her basket, covered by a light blanket and waving a yellow ribbon, and Daisy, aged five, sat cross-legged next to her, clapping wildly, in stockings, skirt, and jumper.[49]

"Ta da! I said I'd make it," Eamon called out triumphantly from the end of one of the low branches.

---

[49] Sweater.

"When I'm grown up, I'll climb this tree to its top, no risk," he shouted.

By then, Daisy was jumping up and down.

"And I'll be climbin' behind ya."

Eamon won't be climbing anything in the spring or summer, thought Nell, *unless Dr. Dunne and the so-far-useless men of science find a cure for his breathing.*

But his illness remained only seasonal. Eamon was as well as could be in the winter and the autumn, and the girls showed no trace of his condition. For that, Nell counted her blessings.

She had to get him into a school. With Rory's help, maybe she could persuade the church to build one out their way? She pushed one of Rory's wringing wet shirts down the washboard, so that the dust and the dirt were squeezed free.

The problem with Rory was that he would not make a fuss. He would work himself to the bone, sure. But start anything, or speak up to move something along? That wasn't Rory's way.

Take the time in the week before Polly was born, when she wanted him to return a new saddle to the store in Town. Nell had found Rory in the workshop, preparing for the ride to fetch Thellie for the birth and cursing the saddler mercilessly. He had forgotten to hole either of the straps for hanging the stirrups. There was Rory with hammer in one hand, nail in the other, finishing the job himself.

"For goodness' sake, Rory, you should just return it. We've paid him good money," Nell had said.

"It isn't worth the bother, Nell, tellin' a local cove he's no good at his job. Next time we buy a saddle, we buy one down Port Town way and avoid any talk if we have to return it."

Away to the east of the washroom, the cattle drifted down the crest of a hill and toward the front of Jacaranda Ridge. Nell wondered if anything had happened. The time of the year had already begun when the magpies swooped on all that hailed beneath them, as if marking out their territory. The animals brought in from elsewhere reacted in much the same way as the people from elsewhere and moved on at the first swoop. Their cries of attack as they dived like black bullets were all the warning anyone needed.

Nell reached for another piece of sodden cloth. It was a good time to speak to Rory about the school. He was on his way to the bank to make one of their loan repayments. Rory came home walking a little taller whenever a payment was made, and ever more so as they neared the loan's end. And if the school were to be built by January, the start of Eamon's second year of primary education, and Daisy's first, she needed to move sooner rather than later.

It was a good time indeed to talk more about the future—the future of their children. Their loan from the bank would be paid out by November. They were back in the black and would feast to it that evening with a fresh cut of beef, potatoes and carrots from Nell's own vegetable patch, some freshly harvested beans, and Rory's favorite pud, a lemon meringue pie.

Nell looked up again and out the window, toward the rocks by the Jacaranda tree where she made a makeshift kitchen when the back of the house collapsed.

Once Jacaranda Ridge is embedded in profit, and we are completely in the clear, I'll tell Rory right there about the share of Ballycalan to be left to me by Da.

Nell hung the washboard back in its place on the laundry wall. First, she had to get moving on the school.

* * * * *

Rory walked toward Withers' office for a midafternoon appointment. He wasn't sure why the banker wanted to see him, but he welcomed the chance to deliver the check in person. It was the last but three of their repayments. Rory had counter-invited Withers out to Jacaranda Ridge so that Nell would be able to join them. But Withers declined. He was simply too busy.

So, Rory was keeping Nell in the dark until he found out what Withers wanted. She thought he was just dropping off a check.

Rory knocked on Withers' door. He ambled in at the command to enter.

Withers greeted Rory with a smile more stiff than warm.

"Mr. Burke, what a pleasure it is to see you. And my word, you appear to have dressed for the occasion."

"Good day, Mr. Withers. I'm wearing a new shirt, sir, and I felt it merited a tie, so I suppose you could call that dressing. Anyway, you've presented me with an opportunity to thank you for your kindness to my family."

"And what kindness would that be, Mr. Burke?"

"For lending us the money to get back on our feet. We are back in the black, and after today's repayment, there are only three to go."

Withers folded his arms.

"Great minds think alike," he replied. "That's exactly why I asked you to come in. Let me go and retrieve your file. Please take a seat."

In Withers' absence, Rory reflected on the trials and hopes of the preceding six years. Times had been good since the end of the war. He'd taken a chance and seen it pay off. After they had settled the bill for the rebuild of the house and purchased a new horse, their loan still wasn't quite spent. So, Rory paid Billy Murphy to help put up a piggery. It was soon occupied by a boar and a sow, purchased at the Port Town Show in June of 1917.

By the time Daisy was born, there was a litter of piglets. By the time Polly came along in the year before last, the pig heard numbered twenty. Income from cream, corn, and the production of pork had finally turned Jacaranda Ridge into a commercial venture.

Rory looked around, taking in the empty office. Between the bank and time spent at the homestead at Ballycallan, he was becoming accustomed to the decorations preferred by the moneyed classes: spotlessly clean floors, walls paneled with lacquered wood, and ceilings closed with plaster, pinned in the middle with a dome of electric light. All of it was starting to feel ordinary. They would have modern ceilings and electric light at Jacaranda Ridge one day, and soon. Before too long he, Rory Burke, would be a middle-class farmer.

Withers walked back in, the Burke family file open in his hands, his eyes scanning it.

"Mr. Burke," said Withers, as he eased into a chair behind his desk, "there seems to have been a misunderstanding between lender and borrower. I won't beat around the bush. I was wondering if you would be kind enough to take a look at line ten of the agreement signed with your own good hand back in October of 1916."

"Of course, Mr. Withers," said Rory. "I hope your records don't show that we ever missed a payment."

"Indeed not, Mr. Burke, not at all. Your credit record is perfect. There is something more fundamental, I am afraid, that needs to be clarified."

Withers spun the folder toward Rory and handed it to him across the desk.

"Please read line ten."

"Well, the question asks about the number of acres encompassed in our landholding, and the question has been answered—one hundred and eighty-five."

"Correct, Mr. Burke. And could I now trouble you to read line four of the agreement?"

"It asks for the full address of the property and the allotment number. I have provided it and stated that the allotment number is forty-seven."

"And you stand by this as a full and fair statement?" asked Withers.

Rory's head began to fog. Then he stammered.

"Well yes, sir, of course I do."

Withers pulled the file from Rory and snapped it shut.

"This is the problem with emergency loans. They never allow time enough for primary records to be checked."

Withers' hands rested in front of his mouth, the tip of each long finger touching its counterpart.

And Rory realized a day of reckoning had arrived.

"You see, Mr. Burke, I've just been down to the land registry office in the Port Town. I was there to check the boundaries of the Noonan family run on the map of the sector where you live. Someone is seeking a loan to pay for an easement over the eastern end of Noonan's land, on the side furthest from yours."

"Dave has mentioned something to that effect," said Rory. "That he was selling some sort of right of way."

"That is correct. But you see, Mr. Burke, once I looked at the maps, I noticed something odd. Your own Jacaranda Ridge, as recorded by the state land registry, stretches for only one hundred and fifty-five acres, and not the one hundred and eighty-five you marked for the loan."

Rory gulped. It would take all the smarts he could muster to get out of this.

"Well, that's easily explained, Mr. Withers. I farm thirty acres of what is technically Dave's land. But I bought it off him just before I was married."

"Is that so?" said Mr. Withers. "Well, if that is the case, I have two questions. Where is the contract of sale, and why does the transfer remain unregistered in our region of the state land registry?"

"There is a simple reason for that, sir. Dave and I are mates from childhood. The whole thing was done as a gentleman's agreement. Nothing was written down."

"Well then, surely you have a record of the purchase price paid from you to Mr. Noonan, or was the land a gift?"

"No, sir—not a gift," said Rory. "As you know, I don't take charity. I pay Mr. Noonan in cash, by way of monthly installments."

Withers scowled. Burke was as sloppy with money and records as the Irish Catholics came.

Rory's pulse began to quicken.

"So what does all this mean for us, Mr. Withers?"

Withers leaned forward.

"Quite simply, Mr. Burke, it means you have defrauded the bank. You do not own a holding of one hundred and eighty-five acres, but a holding of one hundred and fifty-five acres. You have lied to us, and I am going to have to manage this unhappy fact with my superiors in the City."

Rory looked up at the portrait of the King hanging above Withers' head, as if pleading for clemency.

"Mr. Withers, it never occurred to me that I wasn't doing the right thing."

Withers relaxed back into his chair.

"Well, I am afraid you haven't. One hundred and fifty-five acres is simply insufficient capital to support the sum we forwarded. But for your dishonesty, we never would have done so. Emergency loans are never extended to properties smaller than one hundred and eighty acres."

Rory managed to still his tongue before it moved to share his thoughts. The Rory of old would have been on his feet, protesting out loud and alleging unfairness. But marriage to Nell had taught him the virtue of temperance.

"And it's not a question, Mr. Burke, of you not having done the right thing," added Withers. "It's a question of you meeting your commitments and bearing the consequences for failing to do so."

"And what might they be?" asked Rory, his voice dropping to near whisper.

"Well, the bank might wish to enforce its rights under the law. That means prosecution for fraud, and damages. Civil damages, I mean, from you, Mr. Burke."

Rory turned white.

Withers witnessed his first step accomplished and so decided to move on to the second.

"Mr. Burke," said Withers sympathetically, "leave it with me for the moment. I will not yet contact the head office in the City, even though I am duty bound to do so. Perhaps something can be done. We should meet again in about a fortnight's time. In the meantime, hang on to today's repayment and keep what has happened strictly between us."

"Why don't you take the check?" mumbled Rory. "Our money's still as good as anyone's."

"Because for the moment, our agreement is suspended. If I accept a payment with knowledge of your deceit, that might be taken as a waiver."

Rory stood up, slowly.

"Best get on to the post office."

"Good day, Mr. Burke," said Withers. "I promise to do all I can."

* * * * *

Dusk was kept for the study of the New Testament, and dawn was set aside for the Old. Father O'Kelly turned the pages of the Gospel according to St. Luke, absorbing all its words.

"And he said to him also that had invited him: When thou makest a dinner or a supper, call not thy friends, nor thy brethren, nor thy kinsmen, nor thy neighbours who are rich; lest perhaps they also invite thee again, and a recompense be made to thee. But when thou makest a feast, call the poor, the maimed, the lame, and the blind. And thou shalt be blessed, because they have not herewith to make thee recompense: for recompense shall be made thee at the resurrection of the just."

The holy sheaths imparting God's words floated like autumnal leaves when turned from page to page. Docile winter wind flicked at a crest of O'Kelly's wavy white hair and caressed his sun-thickened skin.

Father O'Kelly breathed deeply, several seconds in, the same number out. From the open walls of his back veranda, the spirit of the Lord mixed with the elements of time; a shimmering stretch of fading sun, the crouching spirits of a pregnant night, and the ancient aroma of aged lands wafted their way toward him. He looked up and smiled.

In the bushland beside the presbytery, a scrabble of branches leaned to the left and meandered to the right, crossing and dashing through the muddle of scrub.

The trunk, he thought, *must lie beneath the earth, and its branches are pressing for light. Only in this Australian land could leaves hang comfortably off twisted masts, bent as if cowed by winds or dipping to honor the sun.*

If there were ever a tree on the island of Ireland that hadn't grown straight and toward the sky, O'Kelly had never seen one.

To the right, the bushland rustled. It captured his ear and turned his head. There was movement in the scrub—not the rhythmic crunch of bouncing marsupials, but the punch and slide of breaking sticks. *Dingos*[50] *or people,* thought O'Kelly, but the night was too young for the animals.

They broke from the scrub in a group of four. Within moments, it had doubled in size. Forms as black as peat and clad in grimy rags wandered toward him, calmly. Two tall boys straggled at the rear, while the sturdiest of the women led them. She halted ten feet from the base of the stairs, one thin infant bundled to her hip, the other gripping at a big-boned leg. She struck her chest and spoke.

"Got flour, Father? Any flour?"

"No, I don't, good lady," said O'Kelly. "But why is it that you need it?"

"Blackfellas hungry. No men, no food."

In the background, the others spoke to each other, low voiced, but in a language O'Kelly didn't understand.

It was as incomprehensible to O'Kelly this fading winter day as it had been decades before—a warble of low tones, a hum without pause, the tone of a bass tenor cast into speech.

---

[50] Dog-like Australian animal.

The Aboriginal people were lean by nature, but O'Kelly was shocked at the prevalence of skeleton. Prominent cheeks, ribbed chests, and protruding knees prompted O'Kelly to stand. He leaned across the railing, breaching the boundary between their world and his.

"Come, please, come inside. I've a freshly plucked chicken, with enough meat on it for us all to share. A sack of young potatoes and corn as well. It's good for the little ones."

He motioned them to enter.

"Please, please come. I can see you are hungry. There is nothing here to harm you."

The woman took a step backward.

Reticence hung between the Aboriginals and O'Kelly like a heavy winter curtain.

"Wait then," said O'Kelly. "Please wait. I'll go inside and fetch what I have."

O'Kelly prayed as he rushed to the kitchen. If he were more than a few seconds, they might turn their backs and drift. He snatched a sack, filled it with food, then hurried back.

They were sitting in a circle, some of them drawing in the dirt, when O'Kelly returned. The woman stood up gracefully.

O'Kelly walked to the bottom of the stairs. He purchased chicken only once a quarter. That evening, it was meant for his guest, but he decided he could make do without it.

"Here, this is for you. There is a chicken ready to cook on a fire and some vegetables. They can be eaten either warmed or raw. Please take it, and God bless."

He placed the sack about a foot in front of her.

O'Kelly retreated, then watched them from the edge of a dim bedroom window.

The woman opened the bag and peered inside, then slung it over her shoulder. She returned into the depths of the bush and the rest of them followed, wordlessly.

O'Kelly didn't take his eyes off them until they disappeared.

Where was their government Protector? He thought. *His food drops are becoming less frequent.*

There was only one thing for it. They had to be enticed into living on a mission.[51]

* * * * *

Wish, wish, I might have caught a fish.

The bank was closed, and the staff had all gone home. It had been a watershed week, and Withers needed a drink.

He removed the crystal decanter hidden in the sideboard and selected one of the glasses kept for the bank's best clients. The working men had the Hotel Imperial, a place to gather and talk. But the moneyed class of the far northwest were yet to found a club, or even a lounge bar, and they did their drinking in private.

Just as well, mused Withers. *This Friday night, I would have struggled to keep a brave face in company.*

He reread the correspondence from the head office in the City. It bittered Withers' week.

"We are delighted to confirm the permanence of your appointment as one of our rural managers," the letter read. "A fine achievement, and the Directors are unanimous in the regard they hold for your work."

Withers took a swig of whiskey before reading on.

---

[51] Institution established by churches in colonial times to feed and house indigenous people and convert them to Christianity.

"It is, however, simply out of the question to accede to your request for a transfer to the City. The bank has you on track for an excellent career in the regions, a specialty in and of itself, and it makes no sense to move you."

Withers tossed the letter to the far corner of his desk, not bothering to reread further.

"Rural banker," he muttered, as he swirled the ice around his glass. "Archibald Withers, *Rural Banker.*" He'd worked well, all right, with the yokels out west, but he'd never dreamed that he'd be stuck with them for life.

Withers swiveled his chair and stared out the window. Through the fading light, he could just make them out—*Christ, they are in a huddle beneath the paper bark tree that otherwise pretties the Town.*

If he was staying, the blacks were going.

He swiveled back toward his desk and put his feet upon it. With arms clasped behind his head, he resolved to work his way out of it. He would do *so* well that the head office in the south would have to return him to the City, it being a waste of talent to leave him where he was. The key lay in expanding rural industry and settling what was left of Crown land. More farms meant more profit for the bank, and higher standing for him. But the blacks still lived on the land he needed and were getting in the way.

Withers put his feet down and reached for his copy of the *Anglican Weekly.* He leafed through it with detachment, searching for allies. No chance he'd find them there. If the truth be known, his own Anglican church appalled him. It was made up of the "sanctity of life, save the native souls and teach them our ways" type of Christian, the "do unto others as you would have them do unto you" sort of moaner who was blind to the inferiority of the dark-skinned races.

And Parker was the worst of them, so the Anglicans would be kept at a distance.

That meant sticking to plan A. Bind in a man over whom he has power, limit his options, then tie it off with a cast-iron interest in the maintenance of secrecy—an experienced bushman who could locate with ease the black man's hideouts in the bush.

Enter, stage left, my precious little fish.

Rory Burke, with his thirty-acre fraud, was the stand-out perfect man.

The delicious thing about Burke was that he possessed *some* acumen—enough to produce figures for his piggery back in 1916, with the help of that bloody priest—but he was clueless on how to deploy the little ability he had.

"Ever tried standing up for yourself when utterly alone?" muttered Withers, raising a glass to thin lips.

Withers answered his own question before taking a sip.

"Of course, you haven't. And you can't."

Head Office wasn't likely to risk local goodwill over Burke's pathetic little fib. But Burke wasn't cluey enough to ever work that out.

Withers put down the empty glass with a flourish of self-satisfaction. Square the state government, keep the Anglicans at bay, and a perfect plan would be laid.

He opened his diary and inked in a note for nine o'clock on Monday.

Step two is to be executed before I next see Mr. Burke.

"Have Richard arrange when he visits the week after next a meeting with the government Protector."

* * * * *

The creak in the back screen door heralded Rory's arrival. He made for the washroom, hastily.

"Hello, love," said Rory, poking his head into the kitchen. "Better get these smart clothes off. Wouldn't want 'em to spoil."

Nell was preparing dinner at the stove. Polly was grabbing at her skirts, and Daisy was drawing at the table.

"Do I not get a kiss from my gentleman farmer before he withdraws to bathe?" asked Nell, cheekily.

"Too right," said Rory.

He kissed her quickly on the lips.

"You got to the bank all right?" asked Nell.

"Sure did," said Rory. "Here, I picked this up from the post office on my way home. It's to you from Hector."

Rory pulled the letter from the pocket of his shirt and darted off. Nell opened it, gasped a little, and covered her mouth as she read it. She folded it into her apron and kept cooking.

My goodness, wait until Rory hears this.

The mild evening drew them to dinner on the veranda, their first since the onset of winter. Polly had already been fed and was playing in her high chair with a toy. Daisy and Eamon were restless. A full day of play in the sunshine hadn't wearied them. Daisy flicked the little spheres of carrot on her plate onto Eamon's beside her, just for the sport of it. Rory responded as he always did with their children. Almost every intervention was a lesson.

"Girl, you'll be no lady like your ma if you keep that up," he said. "Son, give your sister back her dinner, and put some manners on it for her."

Eamon moved his plate to hers and tipped it so that every carrot was returned, aided by a prod with his knife.

"Thank you, Daisy," he said. "But I've enough to eat already."

Eamon looked to Rory for approval.

"Good boy," said Rory.

Eamon unfurled a gappy grin.

In the tunnel running between man and wife formed by their children's retreat into their meal, Rory drew breath to let Nell know that something had happened at the bank. The time for deception was over, and now he needed his wife. He wanted to say that once the kids were in bed, they needed a quiet word. Then he would tell her everything. That Withers had called him in to see him, that he'd tried to get their bank manager to meet them both at Jacaranda Ridge but failed, that they didn't actually own the paddocks in which they cultivated corn, and that the bank had just found out and were now threatening to ruin them.

But Nell spoke first, rushing to share all her father had said.

"By golly, Rory, God's showering blessings on us. You won't believe what Da's suggesting!"

Rory stopped cutting his steak.

"I probably won't, knowing Hector. What did he have to say?"

"First thing is that he's so pleased with how we've handled our dealings with the bank that he wants to nominate you to join the Pastoralists' Club, down Port Town way."

"Flamin' heck," said Rory. "They desperate for members or somethin'?"

"No, Rory, they're not," replied Nell, gently. "It's just Da's way of showing that you've earned your way. You belong with the commercial men now."

Rory frowned. Hector would take it no way but badly if he knew there was strife with the bank.

"And that's not all," added Nell.

She put down her knife and fork and dabbed her mouth with her napkin.

"I know you're reluctant to take any favor from Da, but he says he's had a bumper year and he wants to do something for his grandkids. He says that several Port Town companies will soon be going public—by offering share issues I mean."

"Lucky for Hector. He'll know where to buy, no risk."

"Rory it affects us. He says that if we start diverting half the amount that was going into the loan repayments to an account to buy shares for our children, he'll match it with funds from his estate. He wants to set up a trust for the kids. He'll start buying shares when they go on sale in the first quarter of next year, with the funds supplied by him and us together."

"What's ole Hector up to this time then? Doesn't he think we can provide for 'em?"

Rory resumed eating without looking at Nell.

"That's not it at all," said Nell. "He says he wants to do this for all his grandkids. Not just our three. He's setting it up for all five families, ours and my brothers'."

Eamon interrupted his parents.

"Mum, what's a trust?" he asked.

"It's sort of like a lolly[52] shop for grown-ups. Look, you've not yet eaten your greens. Finish them up first. Chat comes later."

Nell realized that her children were not quite young enough to be oblivious to talk about investments—at least, if they were involved. She changed the subject away from anything that would interest them.

"How did you get on in Town? Did you drop off the check?"

---

[52] Candy.

The contents of Hector's letter changed Rory's mind. He would tell Nell nothing, for the moment.

"Of course," said Rory. "I was in and out in no time."

"So, do you have a receipt for my records?" asked Nell.

Rory swallowed a piece of steak.

"Struthe. I forgot. I guess they'll send it in the post."

Nell was reaching for the salt. She stopped, suddenly.

"You forgot?"

"It's not a big deal, love. We get one by post when we send in the checks by post, so I'm sure they'll just send it out."

"But I've nothing for my records in the meantime," said Nell.

Rory collected some peas with his fork.

"So what? Everything is on file at the bank, love, and we've got the check stub. There's no drama here to be made."

Nell pierced a potato through to the plate. When it came to money, her husband needed a bit of an eye kept on him. She had told him a million times to sign everything in duplicate and bring documents straight home. The bank was like the pub; it was for the men only, and Nell could never go in and query what they were doing.

So, she was going to have to take Rory's word for it, and wait.

* * * * *

Father O'Kelly removed two steaks from a sizzling, spitting pan. With a metal egg-lifter, he placed one after the other onto the best of his porcelain plates. At the kitchen table, he added potatoes, greens, and butter. It melted into the glistening juice of each hunk of meat.

Roddy O'Doherty was waiting in the dining room. O'Kelly set off with the meals to join him, girded and ready to persuade.

They didn't meet that often. John O'Kelly held no favorites and valued all parishioners equally. But for Mr. O'Doherty, O'Kelly made an exception. Wealth and power had to be kept under surveillance, and work put in to control it.

So, Father O'Kelly adhered to a practice to protect his own position. All of their meetings were held at the presbytery, on O'Kelly's terms and O'Kelly's turf, and not on O'Doherty's vast run.

The dining table was only six feet long, and the room was dimly lit. Two men with values as far apart as Venus was from Mars were seated at each end.

Small talk is not the way through to this fellow, thought O'Kelly. *I'd better just start in.*

"I was to offer you chicken tonight, Mr. O'Doherty," said O'Kelly. "But an occasion arose to donate it to the poor, so I did."

"Really, Father?" said O'Doherty. "How did that come about?"

O'Doherty's stiff shirt collar encircled a neck made more of muscle than flesh. It was buttoned up tightly and closed with a red woolen tie which followed the curve of his fattier stomach, ending at the other side of its rise.

"A group of Aboriginal people appeared out of the scrubland at the back of the presbytery. They were almost starving, in a terrible state. So, I gave them the chicken I was going to roast and said prayers for them at dusk. It's a terrible shame, Mr. O'Doherty, that we can't persuade them to come and live on a Catholic mission. I'm frightened they'll die of starvation."

O'Doherty picked up his knife and fork at the same time as Father O'Kelly. But he gripped at his cutlery, prodded to anger, while O'Kelly cut gently at his steak.

"Oh really, Father?" he said calmly. "I was hoping to interest you in the new Catholic secondary school for boys in the Port Town. Everything's on schedule for a January opening. We should be planning, I think, to send some of our lads down to board."

O'Kelly chewed his food slowly. That was the heart of the whole wretched problem. The Aboriginal people had never been "us," which was why they were always excluded.

"That's good news, Mr. O'Doherty. That really is. I know that there are a couple of boys in our Town Catholic school with intellectual gifts meriting development. But I was wondering if I could probe your thoughts on a more immediate problem. What can we do about getting food to our local Aboriginal people? Their so-called Protector appears to have forgotten them. He's not visited these parts in months."

O'Doherty started to saw at his steak, then tossed morsels of it into his mouth. He would not look at his priest.

I know what has enraged him, thought O'Kelly. *I have dared to call them "people".*

"I can have a word with him, Father, when I'm next down Port Town way. I'll drop into his office and find out."

O'Doherty's face was like stone.

What are you thinking, Mr. O'Doherty? That the Aboriginals are not to get in the way of everything we are building?

O'Kelly suppressed a sigh. The wound afflicting the O'Doherty family wasn't ever likely to heal. The loss of two of their sons, Roddy's elder brothers, and supposedly at Aboriginal hands, left a wound that remained ever raw.

But if I could get him interested in Aboriginal welfare, thought O'Kelly, *it might commence a process of forgiveness.*

"Mr. O'Doherty," said O'Kelly gently. "I am a man of God, not of politics, and I fully understand that aside from the work of the missions the welfare of the Aboriginals is a matter for the state. But we must do what we can to encourage the government to do its duty to them—as Christians, I mean, and God's servants."

O'Kelly pushed past the resistance of his guest for reasons other than trying to soften him. He couldn't talk to the Protector himself without raising the ire of the Bishop. It would be viewed as interfering with the affairs of the state—the same state that funded their teachers. But if Mr. O'Doherty spoke to the Protector, progress might be made. He was the only man in the congregation with the standing to be able do it.

"Or I could, of course," added O'Kelly, "simply make this subject a topic for a sermon and call on the parishioners to help."

O'Doherty reached for a glass of water. He downed it in a single gulp as if chugging at a beer. Then he lowered his voice to signal arrival at the end of his shortening tether.

"All right, Father," he said. "I will take the time to see the Protector and will do my very best. But for now, could you pass me the pepper?"

O'Kelly obliged and launched into the subject most cherished by his guest: the Port Town school for boys.

* * * * *

After dinner, Nell put Polly, Eamon, and Daisy to bed. She read them a story, but a short one. Rory's evasive behavior during the family meal had unsettled her. She wanted to join him in the drawing room as soon as she could.

Rory was reading the newspaper. It was spread open across his face. Nell entered with a tray and a fresh pot of tea.

"So," said Nell, as she was pouring it. "What's the news of the world?"

Rory coughed.

"Black and Tans[53] finally done and dusted in Ireland. Civil war is still tearing the place apart. IRB still don't have the upper hand over the Free State. No sign it'll finish."

Nell handed Rory his tea, then sat in the armchair opposite his and stirred her own. Between the Black and Tans and the IRB, the Ireland her parents had left behind was gone. She was thankful for the life they had here. This great empty land that gave them all they needed, and where everyone lived in a peace with their neighbor that could never be assailed.

"Ma and Da will be beside themselves," said Nell. "They'll be wanting to get more of the family out here. There's no future for them in Ireland."

"Sounds like a good idea to me, love," replied Rory, still engrossed in the news.

"You all right, Rory?" asked Nell.

She reached for her needles and wool.

"I expected you to be a bit more chipper, with all the good news in from Ballycallan. And now the kids are in bed, what *do* you think of Da's idea about these shares?"

She started knitting.

"What was that, love?" said Rory, from behind the paper.

"The shares. Can we start sending Da some money so he can sort out some shares for the kids next year? The idea is that we send him a payment once a month after the loan is paid

---

[53] Special force unit of the British Government to quelle insurrection in Ireland.

out in November, then he buys the shares with an option he's organized."

"Of course, love," said Rory.

He peered at her from above the paper.

"As long as we leave the details to Hector. I'm a man of the land, not commerce."

Rory put the newspaper aside and reached for his tea. Nell watched him through her knitting. He wasn't fidgeting or squirming or showing any sign of distress. She relaxed a little. Rory was just being Rory—the man who never made a fuss.

It was the moment to press on with her plan.

"Rory," she said, "I've been thinking about something else. We need to start putting together a strategy for Daisy and Eamon's schooling."

"We need to talk to Father O'Kelly about getting Eamon the third-term books for year one," replied Rory.

"No, I mean, getting him to a school," said Nell.

Rory put the cup and saucer on the table to his side.

"Love, the school in Town is too far away," said Rory. "He's too little to ride at a gallop, and anyway, we couldn't send him alone with his condition—not in the hot months, at any rate."

"But we need to be seeing to getting a school out here, and a teacher. I counted them up, and there's almost a dozen kids aged under ten years within three miles of us," said Nell. "All of them are of our faith, and there's more on the way. Might be time for the church to be setting up another primary school. We've got the numbers now."

"Well, that's a matter for the church, love."

Rory hadn't quite cottoned on to what she was suggesting.

"Father O'Kelly will tell us if they decide there's a need for another one," he added.

Rory reached for his paper, but Nell caught his eye before he could return to reading it.

"I thought I would talk to him myself. I mean, we could stay after Mass one Sunday and just see if there are any plans for another school in the parish. It couldn't hurt to ask."

"I don't mind asking," replied Rory. "But as long as that's all we'd be doing. Father will see to it that they all get books, and your readin' and writin's as good as anyone's. He's learnt how to read at a pace with you. And he's already taken to the lessons I've given him on how to add up and subtract. That's all they need when they're little."

Rory clasped his hands across his stomach and looked at her.

Nell put down her needles and stared back at him.

"But I want more for our children," said Nell. "I want a proper school, if they can't have a governess like the families on the big runs farther west. I had a school with a proper teacher. That's the next best thing there is."

"We can talk to him, Nell," said Rory. "Maybe sometime after Mass, but there's no rush with it. I'm not turning it into a big deal. The church will see 'em right."

Rory smiled, walked over to his wife, and took her hand. The wall he'd constructed between them earlier that evening crumbled under the weight of feeling.

"I think it's time for this country gent and his lady wife to retire, isn't it?" said Rory, meshing his fingers with hers.

* * * * *

Rory Burke was up at the bails on a chilly Monday morning. He pulled on the teats of the best of his heifers and thought about Nell, Hannah, and Sean. Spears of milk surged with every squeeze, ramming the base of the metal bucket as if about to pierce it.

"Jacaranda Ridge will be all yours one day, lad. It will all be yours," Sean had said when Rory turned thirteen. "So now you're to come with me whenever I go onto the land. You'll be a man before we know it, and there's plenty for me to learn ya."

Rory kept milking and wondered. Had Sean ever done to Hannah as he had done to Nell on Friday; blurted out a lie over dinner while he was working out what to do and then gone ahead and made love to Hannah all the same?

Rory remembered how he hated leaving the comfort of his mother and the company of his sisters. But Hannah wouldn't hear a word of it when it came to challenging Sean.

"Rory, love, you'll have to go with your da now," Hannah had said. "You can't be stoppin' with me and your sisters all day in the shack, readin' books—well, not anymore. We'll read in the evening from here on in, by the fire and out loud, so your da can join in."

Rory never saw anything between Hannah and Sean but a solid wall of unity.

The bucket was brimming with milk. Rory poured its contents into an old wooden vat. From there, he would separate the thick white liquid into waste and cream.

What sort of life, thought Rory, *would I have had if I could have stayed at home with Hannah, kept reading, and become a man of letters?*

He was only a few months short of the goal his parents had chosen for him: Rory Burke, gentleman farmer. In November, he would be free of the bank.

But it might be going wrong.

Rory pushed the heifer out of the back of the bails and brought in another for milking. The grass was wet, the biting frost having melted. Birdsong wafted all the way from the blue of a mountain to the west. But Rory turned his back on all of it and returned to the task of milking.

A trust fund for his children! Hannah and Sean wouldn't have dreamt of it. Rory Burke, son of an illiterate Irishman, marries for love and winds up dining at the Port Town Pastoralists' Club!

Provided, of course, he could get himself free of the mess he'd ended up in with Withers.

What was it, he wondered, between him and Nell that stopped them from working as one in the same way as Hannah and Sean?

If they had, would the dodgy [54] thirty acres have ever been part of their marriage? As the milk tapped on the base of the old tin bucket, Rory realized that he and Nell shared another fault that hadn't afflicted his parents. They both leaped before they looked.

When Eamon was a baby, Nell had taken a bloomin' axe to the Jacaranda tree without asking him first if *he* thought it was harming his breathing. He'd told Mr. Withers he'd plans to become a pig farmer when they applied for that loan when it should have been talked through first with Nell.

And in Sean's marriage to Hannah, there hadn't been a Hector.

Nell and her father were as thick as thieves, two peas in a pod, and seemed to share everything. They even broke the convention of leaving the penning of family letters to wives.

---

[54] Dishonest to the point of being illegal.

Hector and Nell corresponded directly. Rory had never known a cove to be as proud of his daughter as Hector was of Nell.

If Nell told Hector that he'd lied from the beginning about the size of his run, and that the bank was calling him in, he'd need to find the Houdini in him to get out of that depth of strife.

Rory put his finger in the rich white liquid gathering in the bucket and tasted it. There was nothing wrong with the quality, but he was worried about price. The big dairy farms of the lush lands to the east were able to produce way more, and so sold their cream for less. He wasn't sure how long profit from cream would last. But the income from corn was steady, and they had windfalls each time they slaughtered a pig.

The crisp air of the open yard brightened Rory. He rounded up another of his herd. There might yet be a way out. Withers had given him two weeks.

All the Burkes were due at the Noonans' next Saturday afternoon. He'd let Nell and the children head off in advance while he tinkered in the workshop, then slip into the drawing room where the files were kept by Nell. In the solitude of an empty house, he could study the loan contract closely.

You never know, thought Rory, as he resumed milking. A clerical error on the size of his run might not matter when read within the letter of the agreement. *And I might just find the man in me to dare Mr. Withers to act.*

* * * * *

It was a Tuesday morning in the office at the bank run by Archibald Withers. By the miracle of electric light, the cleaning lady had come in to work the night before. The aroma of polish on his shiny office floor filled Withers' nostrils. A fresh, unsullied room was intoxicating. It was perfect for welcoming the Protector.

He was a portly man, who declined all offers of biscuits,[55] cake, and tea.

"Never on government time, Mr. Withers," he said, settling into a chair in front of the desk. "As pleasurable as it is to find a reason to meet, I must confine myself to the service of the state between nine o'clock in the morning and five o'clock in the afternoon."

"Of course," replied Withers. "Foolish of me to think otherwise."

The Protector's suit was square cut and khaki, his hat flattened at the top. The Protector brushed a mark off its brim as it rested in his lap. Withers commenced his inquiries.

"Protector, I wanted to see you so we could have a chat about the shed you keep on bank land, and to find out if we might, perhaps, be able to offer you more."

"Our office is very appreciative, Mr. Withers, of the assistance the bank has provided. And I am happy to confide that the rent you charge is below the costs we usually incur."

"That's the least we can do," said Withers. "But to start, I wanted to ask a few questions. First of all, why did you place it on the top of a hill, half a mile or so from the road? Hardly the most discreet of the locations we made available to your department."

Withers wanted it moved to the flats if the Protector could be so persuaded. He needed to look inside the shed himself.

"That's a good question, sir," replied the Protector. "But the answer is quite simple. The best security is visibility. We have all

---

[55] Cookies.

sorts of foodstuffs up there, and if it were to be hidden away in the bush, or put too close to a road, then the chances of theft would be greater. It's in departmental policy now to place the stores where they will be most visible but not necessarily easy to access."

Withers breathed in the scent of polish and reflected.

Checkmate one, he thought.

The stores will have to stay there. Up-ending state policy isn't feasible.

"Ah, I see," said Withers. "What clever thinking. No quality lock keeps a thief from goods if he knows he won't be seen. I, of course, have my keys, but I've never been up there myself. The fact is I'm an urban type, and I've never learned to ride in a saddle. No chance of getting a sulky up there, so I've not been able to get near it. Would it be intrusive if I were to ask exactly what you keep inside the shed?"

He peered at the Protector over his glasses.

"Not at all, Mr. Withers. We keep items of various kinds for distribution to the natives. Clothing, blankets, nonperishable foods—that sort of thing."

"And what sorts of food might that be?"

"Tinned meats, beans, and flour are the staples we distribute. I send a man up from down Port Town way when I can, and we leave it at the natives' camps."

"And does not the food get taken by animals?" asked Withers.

"No, sir, it doesn't. We leave an implement for opening the tins which the Aboriginal man is capable of using, so they remain sealed until eaten. As for the flour, it is kept in a bin in the shed, then bagged in burlap by whoever I send to deliver it. Flour is not a food that is ever eaten by animals. They are all herbivores and stick to grass and leaf. We tend to leave small sacks of flour under rocks to protect them from the elements but in places where the natives can see them. They simply take them away."

Withers was encouraged by what he heard. The blacks were as distant from the state Protector as they were from everyone else. If there were no relationship between them, there could never be any squealing.

"So, do you never speak to the natives?" asked Withers. "Never at all?"

"Elsewhere, certainly, Mr. Withers. Many have befriended my men. But the Aboriginals of the northwest are, to be frank, hostile. Their attitude complicates our efforts to help."

Withers pulled a handkerchief from the pocket of his trousers. He covered his mouth and coughed.

There, he thought, *lies the key. Could support from the Town in the distribution of supplies make the Protector's life a little easier?*

"I sympathize, Protector, and I asked to meet you today to find out if I can help. I know you cover an enormous area, but we don't see you here so often. Can I ask why that might be?"

"It's no mystery," replied the Protector. "We are a department of limited resources, so I spend my time where I can help the most. The same goes for the allocation of men to deliver the department's rations. They are active the most in parts of the state where what we do is working. Out here, we leave out food, but we can never be sure where it goes. The Aboriginals here simply will not speak to us."

At that Withers pounced.

"I see, but have you ever thought of decentralizing?"

The Protector frowned.

"What do you mean?"

"I mean, hiring men locally to deliver the food in storage."

"Indeed, I have," said the Protector. "In some of the regions, we leave distribution of the rations to local agents. But I have never been able to find an able bushman here who would be willing to help. In fact, I have mentioned this to Mr. Roddy O'Doherty, who I try to see when I am in the region. He has said to me that up this way, labor isn't easy to find, and that the black man has alienated the white."

Withers smiled, thinly. How he wished there were men like Roddy O'Doherty in his lily-livered Anglican church. It needed clever folk like Mr. O'Doherty who knew how to hide an agenda.

"Well, Protector, consider the search done," said Withers. "I am on friendly terms with the best of our bushmen. They are not always easy to persuade, but with a little charm and perhaps a carrot, I am sure I can find you the right one."

The Protector returned his hat to his head. He'd justified the time that he'd spent at the bank, and the meeting was coming to a close.

"That would be an enormous help, Mr. Withers. An able local bushman could do the job with ease, seeing it only entails delivery. When I get back to the Port Town, I'll post you a map of the Crown land here, with Aboriginal camps marked on it. It will be of some assistance in finding them."

"Very well," replied Withers. "That's likely a good idea. And I will be in touch once I have the right man."

* * * * *

The third Wednesday afternoon of every month, the women gathered on Nell's side veranda. She baked in the morning, saw Rory off back out onto the land after lunch, then welcomed her neighbors and friends. Thellie Walsh and Charlotte Noonan were regulars. The women usually numbered about half a dozen. They would bring their knitting, sewing, or some other craft, along with their children, who were supplied on arrival with Nell's homemade lemonade and a fairy cake topped with icing. Then, they dashed out to play on the long piece of land that ran by the side of the house within view of their mothers.

Nell couldn't help being drawn into her thoughts once she set foot in the kitchen. She waited for the kettle to boil while the women settled on the veranda, and stared out of the window into the rustling foliage of the Jacaranda tree. Over the course of the last fortnight, Rory was speaking less often. She feared he was being pulled away, by something.

He was even disinterested in the children.

Just the night before, in the drawing room, Nell told him about the progress Polly was making with her speech.

"I'm sure I'm not mistaken, Rory. Polly pointed up the hill today and said 'cow'. She'll be puttin' together sentences before we know it."

But Rory had grunted and kept reading.

It was as if the good fortune bestowed on them by her father and the promise of a trust fund with shares, had somehow driven him away.

Nell carried the tea tray to the veranda without help, even though it was heavy. She filled her friends' cups, then joined the circle of knitters and sewers with her own works in progress: dresses for her little girls and a jumper for Eamon for next winter. Nell's worries receded as she immersed herself in the company of friends. Thellie Walsh was in full flight, telling a tale about her canny teenage lads, the last of her children remaining at home, and the campaign they had run for a pay rise.

"Morris was in the paddock, stuck in mud and cow dung up to his knees. He was alternating between pushing at a heifer and pulling her tail, trying to get her moving. He fell clean on his backside while his brother Gary was watching from the fence. I heard him call out, 'Morris, you're doing that for tuppence haypenny a day!'"

The women laughed.

"And Barry was soon confronted with a delegation made up of his two youngest sons, both of them demanding a pay rise!"

"Young Gary has a head for figures then?" asked Charlotte.

"More so than his father, you can be sure of that!" replied Thellie.

They were all in fine form, so Nell made her move, easing the conversation toward the idea of a second school out here in the country.

"Was it you who taught them, Thell—both Maths and English?" asked Nell.

"And a bit of Biology on top of that," replied Thellie proudly.

"Were they quick learners, Thellie?" asked Charlotte.

"Quick enough. The hardest part was getting them to sit still long enough. All my boys wanted their lessons over and done with so that they could get out onto the land to work with Barry."

"That's the problem with schooling them at home," said Nell. "If they had a schoolhouse, it would be easier to divide the day between the three Rs and the farm."

Charlotte Noonan put her sewing in her lap.

"Why, Nell, I couldn't agree more. You can't beat four walls, discipline, and a good teacher to get them well educated. I certainly want that for my girls."

Charlotte had more learning than any of the women. She had grown up in the Port Town in a middle-class family and met Dave Noonan at the Port Town Show. Charlotte had relented, to her own surprise, to a courtship pursued against the friction of distance by a determined, western farmer. She had pictured herself in her early teens as a Port Town bride, married to a merchant or a man of the professions. But she had been taken by the honesty of Dave Noonan's feelings and the adventure of a life on the land.

"Look at all of these children," said Nell. "There are only five of us today with little ones, and there's nine of them out there playing. They're just about a schoolyard already."

"You offering your veranda, Nell, as a classroom?" one of the women asked.

"I wouldn't mind at all," replied Nell. "If we had a teacher who was willing to use it."

Thellie chuckled.

"You won't be taken up on that in a hurry. Aside from Father O'Kelly and Dr. Dunne, the last man of learning to set foot in these parts was the Bishop. That was ten years ago, when he opened the Catholic school in Town."

"Well, it's high time we were graced by the presence of another," replied Nell.

She passed around the biscuits. There wasn't a naysayer among them. It was time to talk to their priest.

* * * * *

"Mr. Burke, thank you for coming by. I am afraid the news isn't good. I've made some discreet inquiries and, ordinarily, the bank moves to enforce its rights in the event of the slightest incidence of fraud. We don't tolerate the thin edge of the wedge."

Archibald Withers paced a circle in the wide area behind his desk. One eyebrow was cocked, and his arms flapped, bent at the elbows with hands that gripped his meager, bony hips. He was working Rory Burke like the southern farmers worked sheep.

Rory settled into a chair at Withers' desk. He was in form and ready to argue.

"That's no surprise, Mr. Withers," replied Rory calmly. "But I've brought my copy of the contract with me and thought we might talk some things through."

Withers kept moving. A tried and tested blocking technique. Burke was to be shut out before he could take the initiative.

"By the way, Mr. Burke, you haven't mentioned the matter to Mrs. Burke, have you? After all, commerce is not the natural province of women."

Withers was picking up the pace, but Rory wasn't wavering.

"As it happens, Mr. Withers, I haven't."

"Splendid," said Withers. "Because I am able to propose something that might get you out of this. But it will require a measure of discretion."

"Oh, Mr. Withers, I am glad to hear that," replied Rory. "I was going to propose something myself."

Withers stopped pacing, faced Rory, and spread his legs into an inverted V of authority. His pupils barreled into Rory's, blocking him from saying anything.

"Mr. Burke, how much do you know about our local blacks?"

Rory squirmed.

"What do I know? As much as any of the other long-term locals, I suppose."

"And what might that be?"

He took a pace toward his seat at the desk.

"Well, that they're to be avoided because of disease. That they live like savages on land owned by the Crown—when they're not hangin' around the outskirts of Town, that is. That it's said that some of 'em practice black magic, cursin' good Christian folk, that they killed two of the O'Doherty boys early in the settlement of this region. And something I learnt from my da was that the only thing that they respect is a hidin'," said Rory, blandly.

"Now, that last thing you mention is most interesting, Mr. Burke. How is it that you know that?"

"Well, because there hasn't been a blackfella seen near our property in more than twenty years. That's because Sean, my da, would catch 'em, tie 'em to the windmill at Jacaranda Ridge, and flog 'em. He reckoned they eventually worked it out— what'd happen to them if they ever crossed over onto Burke family land."

Withers grabbed the back of his chair and slipped into it, swiftly. He *had* found his man.

"That is *fascinating*, Mr. Burke. And do you have any idea where they are camped now?"

"Some idea, Mr. Withers. I could probably find 'em pretty easily at any rate. I'm sorry, Mr. Withers, but can I ask, what does all of this have to do with the loan?"

Withers cleared his throat, as if preparing to make a speech.

"The blacks, Mr. Burke, are a dying race, and the age of the primitive races is done."

"I'm with you on that score, Mr. Withers. But the loan. That's what I'd like to talk about, sir."

Rory reached to open his satchel and retrieve his copy of the contract. There was nothing in it that said that an error made in the size of his run would lead to any consequences, and Rory wanted to argue it.

But Withers cut him off.

"Not necessary, Mr. Burke, not necessary," stammered Withers. "The two subjects are not unconnected. Indeed, they form a neat and convenient whole."

Rory let his satchel slip to the floor, with the contract remaining in it.

"It's simple, Mr. Burke. The bank would like to see the western lands opened up as soon as possible—the lands you mentioned that are still owned by the Crown. But the Crown is unlikely to release them if the buggers are still loitering on them. And as a member of the Town Council, I have real concerns in terms of community health. As you say, the blacks are filthy. I am not a man of medicine, but common sense tells me that there is a real risk that they are carrying disease."

"I can't disagree with what you're saying, Mr. Withers," said Rory. "But the loan, sir, I want to talk about the loan."

"Mr. Burke," continued Withers. "What I would like to do is simply accelerate a process—the process of their demise."

Rory scratched his head. He was about to decide his banker was mad when Withers blurted out what he wanted.

"There is a bin of flour in a shed on bank land near your own. The bank stores it as a favor to the Protector before its distribution to the blacks. But his men are visiting this area ever less frequently. It's not for me to question why, but I have promised the Protector a reliable man to bag it in sacks that are kept in the shed. They can then be dropped through the scrublands where the camps of the blacks are scattered."

Rory relaxed on a wave of relief.

"If that is what you are asking me to do, Mr. Withers, I can agree to it, no risk," said Rory. "So long as I don't have to have any contact with them and nobody knows it was me. I wouldn't want anyone to get the idea that I was supporting their lazy ways. And if I do this, will the bank take no action over the loan?"

Withers lowered his voice.

"Not quite, Mr. Burke. I can shoulder the blame with my superiors in the City for what might be called a mix-up over the size of Jacaranda Ridge. But we must agree on a small further step."

"And what might that be?" asked Rory.

"The flour requires a little treating, in the form of the addition of arsenic. I've a bottle myself for you to take to the shed; it's not so hard to come by in the City. Once the treated flour has been consumed, the blacks would, of course, then die off, quietly, with no one to be saddled with the blame. That would leave the bank in a far better position to secure release of Crown lands going to waste, and I could proceed to closing off your loan."

There was a pause that seemed as long to Withers as Parker's tedious Sunday sermons. He worried, momentarily, that Burke was learning the ways of the educated. He could have sworn that he was reflecting.

"I am not a man of the law," said Rory. "But I see nothing in what was signed in the contract to justify a punishment and trouble from your office in the City. It was a simple mistake,

Mr. Withers, a simple clerical mistake that surely a magistrate would forgive."

"You said it, Mr. Burke. You are no man of the law."

Withers jumped to his feet and barked.

"There *isn't* an alternative. Unless, of course, you wish to take this matter up with your solicitor. If that is the case, I will close our dealings, inform the state prosecutor, and see you in court."

Rory gasped, as if punched in the guts.

"And that's all. That's all I'd have to do?" asked Rory, eventually.

"What?" said Withers.

"Feed the blackfellas that flour and be done with it."

Withers sat back down in his seat and breathed.

"That's right, Mr. Burke," said Withers calmly. "Your loan done and dusted in barely more than an afternoon of work, once the last repayments are made. Open the sacks of flour, add the arsenic, then drop it off. Nobody would ever know."

Rory looked past Withers toward the window. Withers sensed he was close to ensnaring him but needed to make sure.

"Mr. Burke, I know it sounds a little extreme, but a little arsenic in a bushman's flour was a technique not uncommon in the century just past. And that's not so long ago. We will be assisting a natural process."

Rory concealed all feeling.

"It's a kind offer all right, Mr. Withers, sir. Very kind, indeed. May I give it a think for a bit?"

"Of course, Mr. Burke, of course," said Withers. "But you must remember this is a commercial matter to be shared between us alone, as gentlemen. It is for repetition to no one, no one at all—especially Mrs. Burke."

"Of course, Mr. Withers," mumbled Rory. "On that, you have my word."

* * * * *

Nell was one of the last to leave the church after Sunday Mass. She had been caught up inside, chatting.

From the top of its stairs, she saw the whole of the congregation. The women's hats showcased the vibrant colors and varied styles that were fashionable after the war. And there were nearly as many townsmen now, dressed in tailored suits in the style of the City, as the farmers in their best cotton shirts and moleskin trousers. They were a carnival, encircled as they were by a flamboyant fringe of bushland. It was shot through, brusquely, with smooth, tall, trees that rose like white rockets before bursting into sprays of leaves, suspended against the sky.

Nell could see Father O'Kelly walking through the crowd in his ghostly white robe. The time to chat with the congregation was as important as the Mass itself. How Nell admired him. He knew each family as well as he knew the scripture—how many children each had, how long the marriage had been and, to be sure, where any problems lay.

Nell descended the stairs to speak to him, Polly on her hip and Daisy held in hand. Rory was a good twenty yards away, standing in a chain of men configured in a semi-circle. Their heads were lowered, letting Nell know they would be gathered for a while. Either the civil unrest in Ireland or complaint about the distant federal government that was supposed to be their own, were her two best guesses at the subject of discussion.

O'Kelly was speaking with Marcus and Roisin Moloney. Their two boys played nearby as Nell approached.

"Father, my sister says the Republicans might have lost the battle of the Four Courts, but that's all. There'll be fighting all over the country if the Free State does not renounce the treaty," said Marcus.

The postmaster was muting his passion. He was in the presence of a priest.

"But Mr. Moloney," replied O'Kelly, "how could Ireland prosper if she were cast out on her own? And now we have descended into a war among ourselves out of a wish to secure exactly that."

O'Kelly seemed to Nell to have assumed the tone of a mildly annoyed schoolmaster. She didn't blame him. He was dealing with a man who had to be guided to temperance.

"But Father, we have forsaken the Catholics in the north. What lies ahead for them? What life?" said Marcus.

Father O'Kelly noticed Nell and her girls approaching and seized an opportunity for escape.

"Mrs. Burke, good day! These girls are more of a picture with each passing Sunday and the image of their mother," said O'Kelly.

"Thank you, Father," said Nell, "but it's their da they'd be taking after."

"Not at all," replied O'Kelly.

He stepped back to open the circle.

"They're a picture, all right," said Roisin.

She too was relieved by the turn toward levity.

"Nell, I hope we can have an extended word next Sunday," said Roisin. "I'm down to make a double sponge for the hospital fete, but mine never turn out nearly as light and fluffy as yours. Could I trouble you to talk me through your secrets?"

"It'd be no trouble at all," replied Nell.

"It's a shame we've guests for lunch today," said Marcus. "If we don't head home soon, there'll be no roast for any of us," he added dryly.

"Well," O'Kelly said, "we can't be having empty stomachs, certainly not on a Sunday."

When the Moloneys left, Nell found her courage.

"Father, I've been wanting to have a word with you about Eamon's schooling. He's seven now. We were wondering if we could have a look at the educational books for the third term of the year."

Nell and Father O'Kelly looked toward her fair-headed son. Eamon was perched on the backboard of Roddy O'Doherty's magnificent motor vehicle in a line with three other boys. They were swinging their legs and taking turns to jump off it.

"How has Eamon been of late, in body and in mind? Has he thrown any tantrums or given you backchat in the way he behaved last summer?"

"He hasn't, Father. He's as gentle as a lamb when he's able to breathe. No stomping off into his room whenever he loses a game or shouting when he can't have his way."

"And how does he cope now that spring is almost upon us?"

"No problems yet, Father, but the weather is still fairly cool. I've stocks of elderberry oil at the ready for when we come into the spring."

Nell pushed a hair from Polly's forehead. Her illicit use of eucalyptus oil would forever remain veiled.

"Good," said Father O'Kelly. "I've the books he needs in the presbytery parlor. Come with me and you can collect them."

Nell sat at O'Kelly's desk with Polly on her lap, and Daisy popped by her on a chair. Daisy pulled at a rag doll Nell had made for her fifth birthday. There was a cross high on the wall facing them and a picture of Jesus to the left, but nothing else decorating the study's humble wooden walls. Nell watched O'Kelly in profile in front of a bookcase, hand on chin, his red-brown forehead creased into a frown.

"Mrs. Burke, I can't seem to find either the book on the alphabet or part three of the first-year reader," he said, scanning the shelves. "I am losing track of what I have distributed."

He moved toward his desk to take a seat.

"I'll be meeting the Bishop in the Port Town shortly. I shall bring some more books back with me and, perhaps, we can talk again then. I am sorry."

Nell jiggled Polly on her lap.

"Thank you, Father, but I was wondering about something else. The children at the western end of the parish number around a dozen now. Would it be time to start thinking about another primary school, like the one we have here in Town?"

The tipping of O'Kelly's head was close to imperceptible. Women never spoke about matters requiring the support of the church in the absence of their men. This Port Town bride of Rory Burke was spirited, all right.

"That is certain—our numbers are growing. A teacher for the children would, of course, be funded by the government, but a new building would be another matter. A Catholic school has to be paid for by the church."

"But we could build it ourselves, Father," suggested Nell. "My Rory is not the only man who would help, I'm sure. And Billy Murphy is a properly trained carpenter. Perhaps we could manage if the church could provide the materials?"

Nell flinched. Father O'Kelly was slow to respond, and Nell knew why. She had spoken about matters connected to finance when her husband wasn't present.

"But would the men have time?" asked O'Kelly, tentatively.

"Well, we could call a meeting and find out. Father, it's just that I'd like the children out our way to have the same chance as those nearer Town. Who knows? Some of the country boys might be bright enough for the new secondary school in the Port Town. But we might never find out if they're left to be schooled by their parents."

Father O'Kelly looked at his watch. He knew she had a point but wanted to finish up.

"Well, let's not get ahead of ourselves. The first step is for me to have a word with the Bishop. I shall add these thoughts to my package of topics for my next talk with him in the Port Town."

Nell stood up gingerly, Polly in one arm and taking Daisy's hand with the other.

"Thank you, Father, and for all the children. By the grace of the church, they'll all be seen right, one way or the other."

"Indeed, they will," replied O'Kelly. "But there is to be no raising of hopes. The Bishop will do whatever he can, but there are others in need across the diocese, and he's many concerns to balance."

"Worry not, Father," said Nell. "We've no expectations at all."

* * * * *

Rory was trying to listen, but the conversation with Mr. Withers in the bank on Thursday was interfering. He was standing in the shadow of the church while the other men chatted in the light.

"You'd think they had enough of it. Wagin' war against the Hun, then they go and start wagin' one against each other," said Barry Walsh.

A murmur of approval followed.

"It's hard to understand, all right," said Billy Murphy. "The rest of the world is booming, and our mob at home are tearing at each other's throats. What's wrong with a Free State anyway? That's pretty much what we have here, isn't it?"

"Right on both counts," said Roddy O'Doherty, suddenly but quietly.

When Roddy spoke, they all listened, and closely. The richest man in the region was the most intelligent of men. Roddy let the silence linger, then continued.

"The stock market in America is surging. Even old Europe's pulled itself out of the pummeling it got during the War, and a Free State is a mighty fine way to run a government. Keeps the benefits of the Empire that the Yanks don't have, and we still run our own show. The Irish are splittin' hairs and shootin' themselves in the foot. While out here, we are building a great country."

"That's the way I see it as well," added Dr. Dunne.

Rory pulled out one of his roll-your-own smokes. War in Ireland didn't interest him even at the best of times, and much less so when he had his own problems to resolve. Withers had offered him a way out, but could he take it? Sean would give the blackfellas a hidin', but would he ever have gone so far as to consider taking their lives?

Rory drew on his cigarette. A lot of what Withers had said was true; they were a primitive race that was coming to an end. What's more, they were in the way and wasting promising farmland.

Dave Noonan noticed Rory drifting. He tried to pull him back into the group.

"Rory, are you planning to show cattle this year? I've spotted a few fine heifers that I would prefer to have on my side of the fence than yours."

"Might do, Dave," replied Rory. "Could be time to give you a run for your money."

On the quiet, Rory was cursing Dave. He loved him like the brother he never had, but he wouldn't be in the mess he had landed in now if Nell knew about those bloody thirty acres in the first place!

"I wouldn't get carried away just yet, mate. You might make me run, but the Noonan heifers have taken top honors for as long as anyone can remember," replied Dave, grinning.

"Might be time for a bit of variety then," said Rory.

Rory went back into his thoughts as the discussion moved on to cattle prices.

Killin'. What Withers was talking about was killin', something forbidden under the Lord's commandments. The black man was inferior to the white; there were no two ways about that. But they weren't bloody farm animals either.

Rory looked around the churchyard. A bit of sponge and a cuppa were starting to interest him, but the women hadn't even started preparing morning tea, and his wife was nowhere to be seen.

Rory was glad. He didn't even want to think about this while Nell was around. If he ever told her, it'd start a terrible row. If she'd defend the Aboriginals when their doctor said that they might have cursed their son, she'd stop him from letting poisoned flour anywhere near them, whatever the consequences.

And there was no point in sharing his woes with Dave—he knew how he'd react. He'd slap him on the shoulder, call him an old softie, and tell him to get Withers the hell off his back and make the bloody delivery.

The men bantered on, alternating discussion of world affairs with that of local commerce. Discouraged by neither distance nor dust, the rural lords of a self-made realm deliberated in the cadence of a class in charge. And one day soon, Rory Burke vowed, he'd step up and be able to join them.

* * * * *

CHAPTER 6
ASSASSINATION
September 1922

The three-day journey to the Port Town hadn't quickened. The road was wider and smoother than in times gone by. It was bordered now by lengthy openings of paddock. The wilderness had diminished. There were three towns to pass through rather than one, and a half-dozen travelers' pubs dotted between them. Back in the early days, O'Kelly would charge along the narrow track to the Port Town, rammed as it was through the virgin bush, on steed and saddle alone. Old age had consigned him to the more dignified pace of horse and sulky, which meant that the trip was just as long.

Travel by carriage ill-suited him. But it ensured his arrival in a state befitting a meeting with the Bishop.

The sandy soil of the west sustained only meager tangles of low-lying trees. They spiraled like twisted toffee, sometimes contorting sideways as if stretching out for life. They could barely be called trees at all. Even their trunks peeled away, in shades of brown, white, purple, and burnt red at the edges where the water ran out.

O'Kelly spent the second night away from home in the parish of Father Peter Reilly, to the southeast of his own. He was met with a warm handshake and a hot meal. Reilly was a younger man, with a congregation of over five hundred and a small convent of nuns to assist him. And he had recently opened a mission for the salvation of Aboriginals.

"Peter, how did you manage to bring them in? That's the part that I can't fathom," asked O'Kelly at dinner, over a piping hot stew.

"Now, there's a good question," said Reilly. "I can tell you, it wasn't easy. I didn't manage it through sweet talk, that's for sure. The terrible truth is that their situation became so desperate that the church was their only option."

"How did it come down to that?" asked O'Kelly.

"Close to all of the bushland in this area was turned over long ago to farming. Some of the Aboriginals had jobs on remote farms, but nothing like most of them. With naught to hunt, they were living off the Protector's food drops, but that wasn't enough. I started leaving food for them in a deserted barn a couple of miles from here, not far from where the Protector had tried to settle them. Before too long, a group of them were living there—squatting, I mean."

"And were they amenable to speaking with you?" asked O'Kelly.

"Eventually. At first, they would hide away when we arrived and come back for the food once they saw we were gone. But after a while, they'd be there every Wednesday afternoon, just waiting to be fed," said Reilly.

"So, where did you take it from there, Peter? Was it by providing beds and other support so the barn became their place?"

"More or less. As you know, eventually, the Bishop provided the funds to build a mission. But we had to put it way, way out in the bush. The parishioners started complaining about the church encouraging Aboriginal people to live near a white settlement, and the contact that came with it. But they moved into the mission easily enough once it was built. And we can accommodate more, John. So, if you were able to befriend your local Aboriginals, there'd be room for them down here."

"Thank you, Peter," said O'Kelly. "Things are a bit more complicated up our way. We suffer from lack of relationship with them—always have—and the prejudice against the Aboriginals is intense. I am ashamed to say that none of them have ever worked anywhere in my parish. There is a terrible myth that has passed into the Town folklore about the Aboriginal people having killed by cursing and poisoning two sons of the founder of the O'Doherty run, now the richest in the parish. I'll never get any of them off the land up our way by getting settlers to employ them, and the strategies I use to break down the prejudice have to be discreet, if I'm not to turn the white man against the black man any more than he already is."

"It's not *so* much better here," replied Riley. "I have no hope either of securing jobs for any of them within our town. I wanted one of the girls from the mission here in the presbytery to help Mrs. Hardcastle with the housework and to clean the church. All my testing of waters led to an outcome I hadn't envisaged—a congregation rebellion. I've come up with an idea though. Some of the farmers that live further away from the Town are still willing to have Aboriginals on their land and teach them a few skills, provided they aren't paid."

"That's problematic though, isn't it, Peter? Don't we draw the line at enslaving them?"

"John, if it's the only way I can edge the parishioners toward accepting them, then it's a route I'm inclined to pursue."

"And what about their government Protector? Is he active in the parish?" asked O'Kelly.

"My word, John, that's one thing I can be grateful for. He visits at least once a month. And now that the church has given them housing in the mission, he has guaranteed they will be fed and clothed. He is also working toward the provision of formal education—at the expense of the state, of course."

O'Kelly chased the last of the meatballs swimming in his stew. It was all too depressing. His parish was light-years away from all this. And his suspicions were correct. Up north, they were being neglected, and Mr. O'Doherty had done nothing effective, despite his promise to have a word with the Protector.

Better to move on to a topic on which progress might be made.

"Peter, I've another problem—one that I need to address if I'm to keep my parishioners happy. The families on the western runs would like the church to build a primary school out their way, to get the children off home learning. Have you any idea how the Bishop would receive a request for funding if I raised the subject tomorrow?"

Reilly took another spoonful of stew before replying.

"I'm not surprised you need another school, the way your area is growing. I've not seen the Bishop for a few months, so I can't tell you what sort of humor he'll be in. But he was in good spirits then. We'd just opened the mission, and he was pleased that we were keeping up with the efforts of the Protestants in saving Aboriginal souls. But that was before civil war had broken out in Ireland. That might well have put him out of sorts."

"Ah," said O'Kelly. "I'll look out for that. And I can't say I blame him. The fighting has to end. We can only be thankful that we are half a world away from it. Not that it's any comfort for those of us with family at home caught in the middle of it."

"Most my congregation do, and they are all worried sick," replied Reilly.

"It's much the same up my way."

O'Kelly was getting tired. If they entered into a discussion of the war at home, they might be there all night.

"Peter, it's been a long day. I was looking forward to an evening in the pleasure of your company by the parlor fire, but I fear the years are catching up with me. Would I be a most ungracious guest if I turned in early?"

"Not at all, John, not at all," said Reilly. "You've a ride all right ahead of you tomorrow, so sleep well."

* * * * *

Only their feet were wet.

There was an art to it—one at which both children excelled.

Eamon and Daisy crouched at the edges of the lapping little river, their tailbones almost touching the rippling water beneath them. They were on the lookout, their heads perched squarely over the stream. Daisy searched for pretty stones, Eamon for the flat ones. His was a quest for smooth projectiles to skip across breaks in the water's flow. Hers was a search for beauty.

The little girl hoped to gather a fistful of treasure, or perhaps even two. The early spring heat and the grip of her hand would dull the stones to pale. She planned to restore them in her mum's spent jam jars, plonking them in one by one, their color replenished by water.

Eamon savored the beginning of Spring. Once it got warmer and the sun shone with sting, his mother and father wouldn't allow him to go and play in the bush.

"Look at this one, Daisy. It's as flat as a penny. I'll bounce it across to the other side of the reach, no risk," said Eamon.

"How many skips before it'll stop?"

"I'd reckon four, maybe three."

"I bet next week's lollies you can't."

"You're on, Daisy. You're on."

Nell and Rory's children were well short of being spoiled, but they had a scheme of rewards. One pocket bag of general store lollies was given to Eamon and Daisy every Saturday, provided they said their prayers, made their beds, and played together without scrapping. A breach of any of the three golden rules resulted in one week's lolly forfeit but more if they gave any cheek.

Eamon rolled the thought of a double haul come Saturday morning through his tantalized mind. The sun had started dimming. The bunch of willow trees crowding the banks threw lengthening shadows across the river. Whichever spot was chosen, the skip would start in the daylight, then bounce to its end in the shade. Eamon laid the penny rock flat in his palm. It held three skips all right. All he needed to do was toss it clean and choose the right place on still water.

Eamon had taken two paces upstream when Daisy shouted, still ankle deep in water.

"Stop, Eamon! Stop! There's pickaninnies[56] heading to the side of the river."

"Where?" said Eamon, squinting at the shadows. "There's no one here but us."

"Yes, there is. They've just arrived. They're sitting on a boulder now, just before the bend."

---

[56] Belittling and contemptuous term used for indigenous people in colonial times, including in Australia.

She was right. He could just make them out; three black children who looked about his age, perhaps a little older. Six skinny legs dangled to the water's edge. One child dropped into the waterhole while the others clapped and whooped.

They were a fair way up the river, maybe half as long as the walk to the bails. But Eamon knew the rule and never defied his father when he laid down the law. His words rung in Eamon's ears.

"Son, what I'm about to tell you isn't ever likely to happen, but you're to remember it, all right? You're to head straight home if you ever come across any bloody blackfellas," Rory had said. "Do you hear me, lad? You're to have naught to do with them."

"Will they hurt us, Dad?" Eamon had asked.

"Not if you keep clear of 'em," said Rory. "They've their ways and we have ours, and you're not so much as to give 'em a glance."

The champion stone would keep.

"Daisy, we had better get home. We're not allowed to play with 'em, Dad says, and supper's not long off. I'll skip the stone tomorrow and win my prize then."

Daisy splashed out to dry land.

"Not before I race you, Eamon. I'm racing you, and I'll be touching the Jacaranda tree ahead of you."

Eamon looked back. There were three wet pickaninnies there for sure, now laughing in the sun. They could have the river for now. He'd another challenge to meet, and he ran off to catch up with his swift little sister.

* * * * *

"Mr. Withers, sir, it's just that I've been thinking—killin' blackfellas is against the law, just like killin' anyone. I'm an

173

honest man, Mr. Withers, and while I see the virtue in what you seek to achieve, I don't know how I could bring myself to knowingly take a life."

Time was up. Their next repayment was nearly due, and Rory had come to the bank to turn Withers down.

The banker closed the narrow pane of window behind him, then turned on his heel toward Rory.

"If you don't mind my reminding you, Mr. Burke, you have already broken the law by lying to the bank and securing an advantage for which you were otherwise ineligible! Mr. Burke, please do sit down. In any event, the question you ask about the legal foundations of killing is an excellent one. The bank would never let any of its customers come to grief with the law, and certainly not a prized one like your very good self."

Withers took his seat, grandly, and coughed to clear his throat. He would work this man into position if it took every drop of cunning in his soul.

"And I've taken a look at the Bible, as well," said Rory. "I'm not a man of the law, Mr. Withers, but I know my way around the word of our Lord. It looks pretty clear to me, sir. There's no defense against killin' a man—black, white, or brown."

Withers peered over the slivers that were his half-spectacles.

"If I may say, you fall into an error that is common to those with innate intelligence but who have been deprived of the benefits of formal education. You read the Bible too literally, Mr. Burke. What about war? Plenty of killing goes on during that. God commanded it in the defense of the Israelites. And as we've already discussed, the blacks are already dying out. It's an act of compassion if we end their misery and help them go in peace."

Rory shook his head.

"It's just that I've a concern about how this might be viewed in the eyes of our law—I mean, sir, the law of the state. Doesn't the law of crime usually mirror the Bible? I mean, what would happen if we got found out? We'd finish up in front of a Port Town magistrate and end up in jail ourselves."

Withers was delighting in Rory's simplicity.

"Again, you fall into the folly of following a literal line. Mr. Burke, the blacks aren't people under the law of the state. And nor are they citizens of this country. Goodness, they are not even counted as people under the national census! It is quite impossible Mr. Burke, quite impossible, to commit murder against a person who isn't a person. And in the utterly unlikely event we were ever found out, that would be our line of defense."

Rory scratched his head. He could see that getting caught was not very likely, but he had read about whitefellas[57] being hung for shooting Aboriginals dead. Withers wasn't telling the whole truth. But Rory wanted to get out of this without offending him.

"But seein' that this is a problem that isn't cut and dry, I would ordinarily talk to Father O'Kelly about it. If you don't mind my saying, sir, if you want the blackfellas dealt with in accordance with God's laws, shouldn't you be having a word with your Reverend Parker?"

Withers' face blanched to snow white. He recovered himself, tapped the fountain pen he was holding on his desk, and continued.

"Oh no, not at all, not at all," stammered Withers. "This is not a concern of the clergy. As we agreed, it's a commercial

---

[57] An informal term used widely in Australian English for European people. It is a fusion of "white" and "fellow."

matter—an arrangement to be made between the bank and yourself. We are merely concerned with tying off your loan quietly before the head office finds out about your fraud. I am afraid, Mr. Burke, the bank couldn't tolerate the involvement of men of religion. I would have to withdraw my offer entirely."

Rory looked Mr. Withers in the eye and was about to bid him good day, when the banker retook the initiative.

"Mr. Burke, as the guardian of your affairs, I've a question to ask, if it's not indelicate. My clerk Richard tells me that earlier in the week you opened a new bank account, entitled something like 'Burke children trust'. May I ask what that is for?"

Rory didn't want Withers to know about their financial plans. But unfortunately questions posed by bankers, like those of priests, had to be answered.

"It's for deposits I will start making for our children, sir, as soon as the loan is paid out. They will be going to their grandfather so he can set them up with a trust made up of shares in leading Port Town firms."

Withers feigned a gasp of dismay.

"Mr. Burke, I am afraid that I can't believe my ears—that a fine Christian fellow like you would jeopardize the future of his children for the sake of a gaggle of miserable blacks! This newfound prosperity will crumble abruptly unless we cleanse you of an act of fraud—a slap in the face to a national bank for its generosity and fairness to farmers."

Rory trembled a little, a dart having hit his heart. He took a moment, and then spoke.

"Sir," asked Rory quietly, "could I have a little more time to reflect?"

Withers tacked back; it was strategic to show compassion.

"Mr. Burke," he said, lowering his voice to match Rory's, "no one cares about the blacks, and it's not as if I am talking about shooting them. The nearest police office is a hundred miles away, and a magistrate even further. Their Protector will reach the truthful conclusion once they are found—death by natural causes. There is no risk entailed in this act of compassion. It is *just*, Mr. Burke. It is *just*."

"A little time, sir, that's all I ask," said Rory.

Withers dropped his pen to the table.

"Very well, Mr. Burke, very well. But I cannot hold out forever."

* * * * *

The last part of O'Kelly's journey was the easiest.

The bushland between the cultivated fields grew denser as the coast drew nearer, its foliage darker. The leaves were nearly white when he set out, and closer to black by its end. The flimsy clusters of leaf that struggled to draw water in O'Kelly's parish were transformed by the second day into thick, rich, and shiny plants with stalks that bent beneath the weight of their own moisture.

As O'Kelly drew closer to the Port Town, luscious trees broke the horizon. The brown hills of his parish were replaced, as the journey progressed, with dauntless green swells. And across the sky, reams of round clouds fell into line, one after the other, in step with the curve of the earth and dividing the dimensions above.

He entered a forest—a world of enormous trees with wide solid trunks in the likeness of those at home. Hardy vines wrapped around everything that grew high, and lush ferns lightened the dark with a pitch of glowing green. The gray stones that gathered in arid packs in the bushland were here smothered in moss. As the sun petered through and the moist air thickened, O'Kelly was transported to the vale of Glendalough. There, he had hurried over four decades before to meet the other novices for prayer. But the dream was short-lived. The forest arrested at the top of a hill. A swathe of sea the color of cobalt came into view—a shade of blue that had never been cast across the oceans of Ireland. And on this glorious segment of Australian shore sprawled the sparkle that was the Port Town.

As he descended toward it, O'Kelly thought through the content of his quarterly report. Two elderly in ill-health, three new births, two couples experiencing marital difficulties, Aboriginal people appearing at the presbytery in need of food, weekly offerings for Mass steady, more books required for the younger children, and one suggestion for a second parish primary school.

The trot through the Port Town was always a delight. Its grand avenues were studded with trees imported from abroad. They bore deciduous leaves and bright blooms, filtering the sun before it struck the bitumen[58] street. The homes were stylish in the fashion of those in the City, with manicured gardens and beds of rose, tulip, and daffodil. Some Port Town homes were now being built from sandstone blocks shipped in by sea. Others were made out of the very best hardwood, painted with layers of gloss in colors ranging from muted yellow to deep red.

The Bishop's home was the finest of them all. It was kept from the street by a high white fence. Its gate opened

---

[58] Asphalt.

onto a soft felt lawn that was graced at each end by a marble birdbath, crafted in Rome. Each was elevated to three feet tall by a gleaming-white stalk and adorned by an angel on the rim. Behind them, three blooming trees splashed snowy petals across the grass; under one lay a white garden bench on which the Bishop might read. And along each side of the house, from halfway down the lawn to the back garden, there were two wide hedges, both scooped to concave and shorn perfectly flat at the top.

O'Kelly tethered his horse to the post set aside for visitors. The enormous white house was stumped six feet high, built on an incline, and capped with a curve of iron ribbing that was painted the same color as the lawn. The roof was topped with a large Celtic cross in the style of those crafted in Glendalough a thousand years before, where the symbols of the local tribes were first melded with those of the followers of Christ.

O'Kelly pulled the brass knocker and let it fall. Soon after, the door eased open.

"Good afternoon, Father O'Kelly. I hope you've had a safe journey," said the housekeeper, as O'Kelly stepped inside.

"Indeed, Mrs. Redmond, I have. I fear I am a little early. The road was dry and firm throughout my journey down."

"Not at all," replied Mrs. Redmond. "Your room has been made up, and I've just now filled the basin in your bathroom with water. The Bishop will receive you in an hour."

They walked down the corridor to the rear of the house.

"Thank you, Mrs. Redmond. And what a fine job the gardener has done throughout the winter. His work has blossomed with the spring."

"Indeed, Father. There might not be a contest, but he's almost sure to be the best gardener living in the near north."

Alone in his room, O'Kelly finalized his strategy for securing his requests, electing to focus on the one he might win. He would ask for permission to speak, at least tentatively, with the men from the parish about the time and equipment they might contribute to building a schoolhouse. If the parish could supply the manpower, perhaps the diocese could meet the cost of materials and speak to the state about paying a salary for a teacher?

But on getting the Aboriginals into a mission, he didn't know where to start.

* * * * *

Nell was in the drawing room, perched at a rickety desk. She made a careful entry on every line of the ledger, noting with precision all outgoings incurred last quarter and every penny returned as income, first in pencil, then in ink once she checked everything twice over.

Book-keeping was as close to finance as a woman could get, and Nell updated their accounts once a quarter. There was no windfall income to write in this time, no sale of a pig for slaughter to note or profit from the harvest of corn. But income from cream was still trickling in, and their outgoings would be halved come November. Nell prepared a new entry with pride: "Deposits: children's trust account."

Usually, the task steadied her. Solid numbers committed to a page told her they were growing. But as she worked, her emotions bubbled. Her connection to Rory was loosening, and her influence over him waning.

Cagey, thought Nell, as she made her last entry. *That is the only way to describe him.*

Rory's remote demeanor had continued into the temperate beginnings of spring. Caginess dominated his behavior when it came to her, and he was often simply absent.

A game with Polly when he came off the land was followed by a turn with Eamon. He was giving their son an additional hour each day to help develop his math. A story with Daisy, or sometimes two, after their family meal meant less time to talk after dinner, and he often went striaght to bed.

And that bloody receipt from the August repayment still hadn't arrived.

Nell opened the filing drawer at the side of the desk to put away the ledger. Her fingers flicked across the cardboard dividers, then stopped. She looked once, then again. One of the files had been moved from its place—the one marked "Loan contract with bank."

Third from the back, that was where they kept it. But it had been misplaced toward the middle. She took out the file and opened it.

It was still there, all right, the paper commitment to a loan from the bank that had served to both save and enchain them. But why was it in the wrong place?

"Rory, are you keeping something from me?" muttered Nell. "If you're burdened by a secret, you should know by now that I *will* find out."

Nell had probed Rory twice about the missing receipt for August. She was met with an indignant block.

"Nell, I'll start chasin' the bank once a real problem surfaces, and a scrap of missing paper doesn't rate. It will probably come later with the one for September."

"Rory, I can't see how you'd be offending the bank by giving them a gentle reminder."

"And what would you know about dealin' with banks? It's not like going to the butcher's."

Polly cried out from her bassinet, and Nell went to her at the window. She picked her up, rocked her a little, then settled on the sofa.

It had to have been Rory who pulled that file out. But why?

He was away in Town on an errand to deposit their quarterly takings—a task he'd put off, but which he usually relished. Niggling doubt kicked around Nell's mind.

Was Rory avoiding the bank?

Daisy charged into the drawing room, armed with two forked sticks of dried-out scrub. She gripped them like battle staffs in her tiny, determined hands.

"Mum, Eamon says these are right for making Shanghais.[59] Can you keep them for Dad when he gets back?" asked Daisy, gleefully.

"Leave them on the back veranda, Daisy," said Nell gently, "and I'll see to it that your da has got them as soon as he's home."

Daisy fled the drawing room as quickly as she had flashed in. Nell returned a dozing Polly back to her bassinet and sunk into the sofa.

She stared at the ribbing of their crude tin ceiling. What on earth was Rory up to?

* * * * *

"My lord."

O'Kelly kissed the stone in the Bishop's golden ring.

---

[59] Sling-shots.

"Good afternoon, Father O'Kelly. Please take a seat on the lounge."

O'Kelly obeyed, and the Bishop took his rightful place in a large leather armchair. Clad in purple, he seeped regally into the all-red salon, from its chairs to its curtains and the delicately embossed paper patterning the walls.

O'Kelly was dressed in black from head to toe, save for a starch white collar. He was, in every sense, the loyal foot soldier reporting to the field marshal.

O'Kelly talked through his list, including a gentle query about their absent Protector and what was to be done, and ended with the question of the second parish school. When he finished, the Bishop said nothing. The monologue of the meeting had unsettled O'Kelly. It had been too easy, especially the part about funding a school. The Bishop normally dissected all he said with questions and comments.

Instead, he leaned toward the low mahogany table dividing them and pushed a newspaper lying on it to within O'Kelly's reach.

"This just arrived," the Bishop said. "Take a look."

O'Kelly picked up the newspaper.

"Michael Collins assassinated in Cork."

O'Kelly looked up, speechless. He set about reading the article.

"Dear God!"

With the newspaper placed back on the table the Bishop spoke, curtly.

"I'd dinner with the state governor the night before last. He asked if there were any danger of insurrection in the Catholic communities here if the civil war in Ireland carries on."

O'Kelly shook his head.

"Not that I can see in my parish, my lord. There is fervent interest—indeed, worry—especially among the newer immigrants. But for the most part, this is the limit of their interest in the war in Ireland. Almost all my parishioners are loyal to their church and the British Empire despite the troubles at home."

The Bishop pursed his lips.

"If Mr. de Valera has his way, and the Free State in Ireland fails, he will create a fine line on which we will be bound to walk. Should this Republic transpire, we will be part of an Empire in which our homeland is no longer embraced, and the pillars of our church in Ireland will be cast outside its realm. I am not convinced this loyalty to the British Empire, here, would necessarily sustain in such circumstances."

The Bishop removed his glasses and rubbed them.

O'Kelly did not agree but said so respectfully. There were pockets of Irish Republican support in Australia, but it would never be accompanied by action of any kind. Of that, he was sure.

"My lord, provided the Australian governmental authorities keep out of it, and everyone here is permitted to carry on profiting from their labors, there will be no cause for them to organize against the Crown," said O'Kelly. "What the Irish at home crave is opportunity and, here, they have it."

"I said something like that to the governor," replied the Bishop. "But it was plain he was seeking my assurance that there are no troubles brewing in our Irish communities that might ignite in the event of another declaration of a Republic at home."

"For my parish, I can give it, my lord."

184

The Bishop returned his spectacles to his face.

"Good. My word, it's dinner time. Come through to the dining room, and we will talk through your problems with schooling over a meal. The table will be laid."

* * * * *

An iron peg protruded from the back-veranda wall like the rusty ruins of a gargoyle. Rory Burke hung his hat on it and looked around for a seat.

It had been an easy decision to make in the end, thought Rory, as he picked up a low wooden stool. It was in a corner on the veranda where it didn't belong, where one of his children had left it. Rory returned it to its place by the back screen door, then sat and untied his laces.

He didn't buy what Withers was threatening.

Rory knew that it was serious, lying to a bank, but he and Nell had met every repayment. What's more, going around killin' blackfellas would drop him in something about a hundred times worse than a false declaration on a contract.

It was in the Bible. He didn't need to talk to Father O'Kelly. From the sixth commandment to Mark 10:19, Matthew 5:21, Luke 18:20, and the book of the Romans—it was all in the pocket Bible kept in his workshop. Murder was one of the mortal sins, and God held all committing it to account, in this life and the next.

The only way to play it was with a straight Christian bat[60] and take the consequence on the chin for a little bit of dishonesty. Rory wondered how the letter he left at the bank was received by Mr. Withers.

---

[60] To deal with people honestly and openly.

Dear Mr. Withers, 15th *September 1922*

I am sorry not to deliver this news in person, but I thought it best to move with speed rather than delay by seeking an appointment with you.

I wanted to thank you for your kindness and patience over the misunderstanding with respect to our loan. After considering your generous offer, I have reached the conclusion that it is best that I decline. My wife and I are ordinary folk, and it is best that we follow the ordinary path.

That being so, I will forward you by post our monthly loan repayments until it is cleared in November. To that end, I enclose the checks for August and September. I expect to receive receipts from the bank in due course, by post.

I accept whatever the consequences may be for the clerical error on the size of Jacaranda Ridge.

I remain, sir, your ever faithful,

Rory Edmund Burke

Rory sat in his socks, taking in the silhouette of their majestic Jacaranda tree. Night was falling. With the sudden turn in the weather to near midsummer heat, it would be bursting into purple before they knew it, and early. Perhaps that's where he'd tell all to Nell, by the cluster of rocks just to its right, where they had managed to work out, as man and wife, how to fund the rebuild of the house. He might tell her right there that the bank had threatened to make a big deal over a lie on the size of Jacaranda Ridge, but that he'd told Withers where to go.[61]

---

[61] To reject someone in such a way as entailing a wish to have no further discussion on the matter concerned.

Rory rolled the events of the last month or so through his wrung-out-to-exhausted-mind. The worst might never occur, and there was a chance Mr. Withers would retreat. The strategy was simple. Turn him down, take the consequences a step at a time, and hope the bugger was bluffing.

Rory stood up on two steady feet, stretched, and pondered.

More to the point, when should I tell her?

Perhaps he should wait—until the petals of the Jacaranda tree showered the sky in lavender, so that everything was lightened by its hue? Or, should he just get it over and done with? Tell Nell earlier, perhaps even tonight, within the walls of their family home?

He was sure of one thing. He'd forever be able to look his wife in the eye. If he'd gone off on a romp and started killin' blackfellas, he might never have done so again.

Rory pushed at the back screen door and ambled inside.

"Eamon, love, try not to cry. Please be brave. The water's almost boiled. We'll have your head under a hot towel in eucalyptus and steam in no time."

Nell was bustling down the corridor carrying Eamon, his skinny legs wrapped around her hips, his arms thrown around her firm neck.

"But Mum, it hurts," sobbed Eamon. "It hurts like a burn."

"I know, love, but you're not to fret. We'll have you breathin' easy again in no time. The water will be boiled, and I've a bottle of eucalyptus oil to hand."

Nell sat Eamon at the kitchen table and turned toward the stove. She barely noticed that Rory was home.

"Bit early for this, isn't it? When did it start?" asked Rory.

He slipped into his seat at the head of the table.

"A few hours back. It's the heat. He was playing with the girls in the yard and started wheezing. I made him lie down, but it's not done any good. You might have to fetch Dr. Dunne in the morning."

Nell pulled a little bottle out of her apron and added a few drops of its contents to the water.

"I thought he told you not to use eucalyptus and that we should stick with using the elderberry oil from England," said Rory.

"Well, he's got that wrong," said Nell. "And what Dr. Dunne doesn't know won't hurt him. We always used eucalyptus when I was a child for treating colds and flu. I use it for steaming in the privacy of home and leave the elderberry for spotting Eamon's hankies."

Nell moved the pot of boiling water to the table. She draped Eamon's head in a towel and positioned it over the pot.

"Take it nice and slow there, lad," said Rory. "Your ma will have this fixed in no time."

Rory watched his wife and his first-born child. His hands were clasped now behind his head, his legs extended to straight. Nell was rubbing Eamon's back on the part of the spine she reckoned to be closest to his lungs.

"There's my big brave boy," she cooed. "The less sobbin' there is, the more breathin' there'll be. How can we make it better? I know—we'll have simmering hot water and eucalyptus ready at the stove for as long as the hot weather lasts. There'll be no waitin' to get you breathing again."

When Nell isn't caring for my children, thought Rory, *she is thinking of ways of caring for 'em better. Never was a man so lucky as to have a wife like Nell.*

"I'm off to have a scrub, love," said Rory softly.

Nell didn't look up. Rory walked toward the door.

"Dinner'll be a little late tonight," she called out after him.

Money, loans, and cranky bankers, mused Rory, as he shuffled off to the washroom, *aren't important in the grand scheme of things.*

A step at a time, that was the way to keep their marriage stable. So, nothing at all would be said to Nell until he next heard from Mr. Withers.

* * * * *

Chapter 7
Capitulation
December 1922

Rory was sullen at Sunday lunch. Displeasure hung over the table like the heat of a midsummer day. Eamon sat up tall in his chair and ate without speaking. Polly, already fed, was strapped into her high chair next to Nell and was chewing on a crust of bread. Daisy tapped a chicken leg with a knife to see if it would break.

Nell interrupted.

"Daisy, leave the bone alone. Do you want me to cut the chicken into smaller pieces for you?"

"No, thank you, Mum."

Daisy turned her attention to prodding peas.

Rory looked at Nell as if to accuse her and then spoke.

"So, when exactly was it that you asked Father O'Kelly about this?" he asked.

"I told you, Rory, I just said a few words to him after Mass a couple of months back."

"I said that *we* could have a talk with him after Mass and that we weren't to be making a big deal of it."

Rory didn't raise his voice. It was the absence of meal table banter that set the tension.

"You were surrounded by men talking about your business," said Nell. "I couldn't just go up to you and drag you out of there. That would have been making a fuss."

For Nell, Rory's discovery of her little deceit was untimely. By now, three receipts had failed to show, and the loan was supposed to be paid out. She had planned to challenge Rory again. But he kept her at a distance with evasion.

"It's probably new bank policy," Rory had said, a week or so ago, behind the veil of a newspaper spread across his face. "Why waste money on a paper receipt when a check stub does the trick?"

But Nell was not convinced.

She glanced sideways at Daisy and Eamon. They were paying no attention and continued eating.

Rory addressed again the issue of the moment.

"What do you call having a meeting after Mass the Sunday after next so that we can all discuss the labor we can contribute to a new school building? I'd call that a big deal."

He didn't look at Nell and returned to his meal.

"Rory," said Nell, lifting her tone just enough for Rory to hear but for the children not to notice. "There is no harm done. Father O'Kelly had already started thinking about another school, and the Bishop has agreed to fund the building. Why, or who suggested it, isn't going to become anyone's business."

"Not if it all goes well, it won't," mumbled Rory.

He looked out the windows of the side veranda toward the heat simmering above the fields. A spray of purple Jacaranda petals slipped past in the gust of a breeze, the last of the season's flowers.

"What sort of a man are you making of me, Nell?" said Rory, eventually. "Sneakin' past me, showing me up to our priest."

"The sort of man who'd lend his wife the liberty to do the best she can for his children."

The tautness in his face then fled. His voice relaxed to gentle.

"You might have told me," said Rory. "You could have mentioned that you'd spoken to him about building a school. You said you'd asked him about getting Eamon some books."

"I did, then we just sort of drifted into the subject of schooling generally, and I pointed out how many children out here were being home schooled. It was as simple as that."

Nell stood to collect their plates. Rory's reaction had been more than temperate. A lot of husbands would have scolded a wife for speaking in private with a priest.

Rory turned to Eamon and smiled.

"Did you hear that, lad?" he said. "You'll be readin' and writin' like a gentleman before you know it."

Eamon giggled, and Daisy was quick to join in.

"Mum, have I eaten enough veg?" asked Daisy. "It's time for pud now, isn't it?"

Nell made a quick inspection of her plate. Daisy had gone as far into the meal as they would get her.

"That it is, Daisy Burke," she said. "That it is."

* * * * *

Father O'Kelly was at home in the presbytery. The affray after Mass had rattled him, and he needed a cup of tea.

Barry Walsh and Marcus Moloney had been close to coming to blows. And they would have if he hadn't intervened. Barry and Thellie lost their eldest boy in the Great War, shot in the chest mid-battle in Turkey, all for the sake of Empire. He died in a field hospital, and the army didn't say he hadn't suffered. Diarmuid Ryan Walsh was one of the ten names on the memorial plaque they had placed in their new Town park.

Moloney was gloating, again, and had garnered all the attention.

"Collins is gone. Out of the way. It's time for Ireland to take back control and form a Republic across the island."

And Barry Walsh had snapped.

"You don't bring that here," bellowed Walsh, waving a quivering finger that threatened to bend into a fist. "Why in the bloody hell do you think our lads fought and died? So that we can live out here in the way that we do and *not like that*."

"What about the Irish at home? Your bloody British Empire isn't doing much for my brothers and sisters, or for anyone else in the parish with family stuck in it," retorted Moloney.

"This *is* our home," said Walsh hotly. "*This* is our home."

O'Kelly shuffled over to the stove, recalling how he'd defused it.

"You will both be barred from church for a month if this behavior is ever repeated."

The tap water battered the kettle's tiny base. He placed it on the stove and noticed movement out the window. O'Kelly smiled. The Lord had delivered him some light relief. The aristocrats were out.

The kangaroos still astounded him. With lean paws hanging and long legs bent to a steadying angle, they occupied the countryside, vertically, in the manner of men. Ever genteel, they loped through the bushland when feeding, then folded elegantly to rest on knolls of grass they had selected beneath the trees. But once disturbed, they would dash away, and faster than the four-legged animals by far, on two strong legs alone.

Was there another creature, wondered O'Kelly, *on God's blessed earth that was ever at all like them?*

O'Kelly was tiring of the problems in Ireland. With water boiled, he returned to the table and reverted to the needs of the parish. His immediate concern was where to put the new school they were planning to build in the country.

Whatever decision he made, it had to be fair. He had drawn a sketch of the western end of the parish. A mile and a half was the furthest the children could be expected to walk. A few of the families out that way had ponies, but he couldn't be seen to be preferring anyone. The school must be accessible to all. He scoured the map for a location.

There were two possibilities, both of which would require modest extensions off the road, and both more or less central to most of the children's homes. But that was all he could tell from studying a map. He decided to hitch his sulky to his horse and ride out to make an inspection.

He noticed as he drove that the wheat crops of the west were ever more prevalent. Wedged between the cattle country of the coast and the endless flatlands of the interior, the settlers here had started by farming livestock. In the beginning, no one had thought of planting anything. Now, every flat piece of land broad enough to sustain a crop of wheat was packed with high, creamy stalks. Their peaks rippled in the breeze. The cattle had kept their place by grazing on the hilly lands between them.

There was one site near the river and another on the flatlands that was better by way of location. But the children loved to swim, and O'Kelly wanted the schoolhouse to be as much a place where they were happy to gather as a place of formal learning.

He parked the sulky and walked along the grassy bank. Still breaks slowed the river's flow. The children would quickly transform them into swimming holes. Trees with wide branches hung overhead, from which a rope would surely be attached for swinging into the water. He had never known this particular reach of the river to break its banks, so there was little danger of flooding. Despite the longer walk for a few of the families, it looked like the better option.

Across the river, smoke was rising. He couldn't see a fire; it was obscured by a wall of bark, which leaned against pieces of broken branches that had been pushed into the ground like tent poles. The structure sat at the bottom of the knoll, so O'Kelly couldn't see its foundation. Then, from the left, he could see the top half of a figure of a man walking up the slope. The body of a small aristocrat, stained red at its haunches, was slung across the back of his shoulders. It was positioned behind the Aboriginal man's neck. His arms looped over the top of the dangling corpse, securing it like a carried log. He rolled the kangaroo down to the ground where it would have fallen near the fire.

There is another reason to put the school there.

He knew them well enough. They wouldn't dare come near, but they would watch from afar. Inviting their children to join the whites in school was out of the question. It wasn't provided for in the law of the state. But the Aboriginals would see the settlers' children coming and going. They would wonder what they did all day in the building, observe them playing outside from a distance, and understand that they were happy.

Then, he would follow Reilly's lead and start providing the Aboriginals with food and perhaps combine it with a lesson or two for their children. They would build a little bridge of stone in the shallows, and gradually venture across it. Please God, the children of both races would even begin to play. Now, there was a plan to build their trust and bring settlers and Aboriginals together.

Efforts like that would save their lives. They might not even have to move to a mission.

* * * * *

"Charlotte," said Nell, "would you happen to know what the legal value of a receipt is, and how it differs from a check stub?"

It was Tuesday afternoon in the second week of December. On the grassy bank of Charlotte Noonan's pond, half a dozen children fed a family of ducks near the rushes at its edge. Eamon was handing out fragments of dried bread from a crumpled paper bag. The gathering of girls surrounding him, Daisy Burke and Charlotte's four daughters, snatched at the morsels, then ran back to the pond to toss the bread across it. To their right and up a hill, Nell sat on a rug next to Polly, who was drifting off to sleep. Charlotte was extracting cups, plates, a thermos, and cake from a picnic basket for their afternoon tea.

"Well," said Charlotte, "I'm not a man of commerce, but I've plenty of common sense. From what I can gather, a check stub is proof of payment, and a receipt is proof that the person receiving it accepts it. It's a fine distinction, but nonetheless a difference."

"That's what I thought," said Nell.

"So, why do you ask?"

Charlotte sat cross-legged on the rug.

"It's just that we stopped getting receipts from the bank for our loan repayments at the end of the winter. It doesn't matter in the sense that we completed the whole thing last week with the last installment, and we have all the check stubs. But I haven't felt able to update our books, and I was wondering why the bank stopped supplying receipts."

"I don't know," said Charlotte. "There could be any number of reasons for that. Have you asked Rory to chase them?"

"Of course, I have," said Nell, "but he just fobs me off. Says we are so close to the end that it doesn't matter, and that they'll send us a letter closing the whole thing off when we're done. Which is now."

"So, what's the problem?" asked Charlotte.

"To be honest, I'm not actually sure, but something's just not quite right. And so far, there has been no letter."

Heat haze tarpaulined above the pond as the two women watched their children.

"Nell," said Charlotte tentatively, "I agree this is all a little odd. Is it that you have some sort of doubt that the bank hasn't received the repayments at all?"

Nell smiled. She could always count on Charlotte to pin point her troubles with precision.

"No. Rory is not the type of man to go off and squander money in secret. But I started to worry because around the same time the receipts stopped coming, Rory became sort of quiet and unsociable, and even a bit short-tempered. I'd never seen him like it. But then he came back to normal, around the beginning of spring. I just wish, I suppose, that he thought it was as strange as I do that we've stopped getting receipts from the bank."

Charlotte unscrewed the thermos and commenced filling their cups.

"If it's not an indiscreet question, can I ask if you ever told Rory about your inheritance—let him know that one day, money will be less of a problem than it is now?"

Nell was a little taken aback by the sudden change of subject. She took a moment to answer.

"No, I haven't."

"Nell!"

"Not with the moodiness he's shown, and now I might have missed the boat. Rory will worry about how this affects my brothers. Once he knows we are to get a fifth of what they view as theirs, he might try and stop me accepting it. Honor among men and all that. And I have to wait in any event until Jacaranda Ridge is sound—not just unburdened by loans, but sure of bearing profit into the future."

"So, is it still only you and Hector who know you are to have a fifth of his estate?" asked Charlotte.

"Well, yes," said Nell. "And now Da's setting up a trust so he can start buying our children shares come New Year. He's just written to me and asked me to post the documentation to him at Ballycallan proving our loan to the bank is paid out before he takes the plans for the children any further. I've just written back to put him off for a bit, explained that I didn't want Rory chased over it with all he has on his plate."

Charlotte sighed, then passed Nell a saucer and teacup.

"Nell," said Charlotte. "Who are you married to, Hector or Rory?"

Nell hid a little behind her tea.

"I am ashamed you have to ask," said Nell.

"If I were you, I'd not bother Rory about the slow arrival of the receipts. No news is good news. And I would stop letting your father in on anything to do with your marriage, whether it concerns money or otherwise. You are doing the right thing in pushing your father back. Accept his money for the sake of the children, but you and Rory should control it, as man and wife."

Nell sipped at her tea without speaking. Best not to mention to her the further mystery of a loan contract that had lost its place in her filing. She didn't want her neighbor to think she was a meddling, worrisome wife.

"Now, here," said Charlotte. "Take a piece of this cake. It came out of the oven this morning."

* * * * *

Archibald Withers played the ace of spades, but tetchily.

The drawing room in the modest home of the Reverend Ian Parker had none of the ordinary luxuries of the Protestant middle class.

There was no wooden sideboard in which to display porcelain imported from home, and from which the wife of a respectable vicar might be expected to serve decent tea. There were no heavy curtains to barricade the sun, only a pastel band of homemade drapes that encouraged in the light. And a soft cushioned sofa stood in the place of a standard feature of the better salons, an upholstered settee carefully reserved for the benefit of guests.

The Parkers possessed only one set of furnishing that Withers considered appropriate: a mahogany bridge table and four polished chairs. Otherwise, the Parker home was barely fit for a visit.

Withers won another trick and gathered up the cards. It wasn't Parker's home that irritated him the most. It was his bald informality. Withers glanced discreetly toward the unruly shelves of a book-lined wall and the trail of half-read tomes that languished on the sofa. Beneath a mask of civility, Withers was utterly mortified.

She didn't even tidy, thought Withers, of Parker's perfectly idle wife, *before greeting their banker for a Sunday hand of bridge.*

Withers coughed, clearing the film that was gathering in his throat. Some of the Anglicans, and even their leaders, were as lame and unruly as the Catholics, as lame and useless as that blaggard Rory Burke.

"Well, Archie, you're on a winning streak today," Parker said jovially. "If you were a betting man, I'd send you off to the races."

If only you knew, thought Withers, pulling in his bottom lip. No luck at all in what was important—finishing off the blacks. Burke's precocious decline to participate in his carefully crafted plan had left everything in abeyance. The bugger had dared to call his bluff, and Withers didn't like it.

"Rather more skill than luck, Reverend. And please do be a gent and acknowledge the talents of your good lady wife. Mastery in bridge takes a team of two, and I couldn't be winning without her."

"Indeed, Archie, indeed. But how could I do so without ignoring the progress of my promising eldest?" said Parker, smiling across the table at his daughter. "She is learning at a pace, wouldn't you say?"

"Indeed, that is so, Reverend. Indeed."

Withers glanced, disinterestedly, at the plain teenage girl to his right.

All four were seated by the broad drawing room window. All three Parkers enjoyed the warmth of the sun ebbing through it. Withers mopped his brow with a handkerchief and wished he were spared it.

Parker took a count of the division of tricks, gathered the cards, and shuffled them.

"I shouldn't complain. My luck's not so bad," added Parker, dealing another hand. "I had some news from down Port

Town way on Friday that will bring us all good cheer. I'll be announcing it to everyone at church once a few more details are settled. But Archie, I know you'll keep my confidence if I share it with you now."

Withers looked up, attentively, and stopped arranging his cards.

"Do tell, Reverend," replied Withers. "I'm all ears."

"Well, I've persuaded the Bishop to release us funds— significant funds. And all to be put to the most pressing of our causes—the redemption of the Aboriginals!"

Parker played an ace of hearts as Withers' own heart pounded. He laid his cards face down on the table. Parker had fired a salvo.

"I'm sorry, Reverend—funds for what? Has this been discussed at parish council?" said Withers, coldly.

"I've raised it in general terms many times—many a time. You know my views on this. It's our Christian duty to bring them in and see to their salvation. And finally, it seems, we'll be able to do just that."

"Reverend, with respect, a general discussion is insufficient to support the sensitive question of funding."

Withers' mood was darkening in inverse proportion to the intensifying midday light.

"Well, I can share that with you now. As a first step, we're to build them a mission. Not too far from Town—somewhere on the Crown lands just to our west. The Bishop is confident that with his links to the government, we will secure permission to build it."

"And what exactly," said Withers, "will occur in this *mission*."

"Calm down, Archie, old boy. Calm down. I know we've not always seen eye to eye on this, but it will simply become their home. It's going to take some time, perhaps a number of years. But it's been done elsewhere, so we can just as well do it up here."

"Do what? If I may say, it ill becomes you to speak in riddles."

"Entice them in with food and shelter," replied Parker cheerily. "Once they've spent some time with us at the mission, and learned our ways, we can progress to their integration. It's in the epistle of James, Archie—chapters one and four, if I remember correctly. Be a *doer* of His word and judge not your brethren. We must be *active*, Archie, in converting them to our ways. *Active*."

Withers believed he may well faint.

"I am sorry, Reverend Parker. What precisely do you mean by *integration*?"

"Have the Aboriginals join our Christian community! Mrs. Parker and I have seen all of it happen with our very own eyes in other parts of the country. With time and patience, their men are capable of excellent work on farms. They're particularly good with cattle and horses. Some of them might even be trained up into the rural trades. And the women can be taught to do just as well in all aspects of domestic service. Isn't that right, darling?" said Parker, turning to his wife.

"That is just so, Ian, it really is. Their women keep homes beautifully."

"And we'll need more servants as the Town continues to prosper under the sterling—if you would permit me to say, Archie—stewardship of the bank," added Parker.

Withers clutched the arms of his chair, containing coursing rage. For the moment, he was surrounded, engulfed in the waxing of the well-meaninged weak, whom he would have routed by now if it weren't for *Rory Edmund Burke*.

"Come now, Archie, pick up your hand. We can talk all this through over lunch."

Withers let go and complied, wordlessly. He might be down, but he wasn't out. What a good decision it had been, not to post his little fish the receipts he doubtlessly craved. Rory Burke wasn't off the hook, and it was time to reel him in.

* * * * *

The meeting had started out smoothly enough. It was late Sunday morning, after Mass. There were plenty of willing hands and just enough talent. It was more of an extended picnic of the families of the western farms than a meeting.

The townsfolk had gone home for Sunday lunch. Their children already attended school in Town. O'Kelly was able to speak in private to the parishioners who were to benefit from the country school, save for the inevitable presence of Mr. Roddy O'Doherty and Dr. Dunne. They were all gathered under the churchyard's low and shady tree, beneath an umbrella of foliage giving away that the tree had been imported.

"Yes, Father, I could offer every second Sunday afternoon over a couple of months to help with the building," one of them said.

And the others all chimed in.

"The men will need lunch. I can put together a roster and organize the ladies to see to it," added one of the women.

Billy Murphy didn't hesitate.

"Father, I can draw up plans that anyone could follow. I'll oversee the work myself, and we can craft our planks from the local hardwood. That just leaves some sheets of iron to buy for the roofing, nails, and anything special needed by the schoolhouse, like a blackboard and slates."

"Have you ever built a school, Mr. Murphy?" asked O'Kelly. A slither of sponge cake hung off the priest's fork. A fly buzzed around it.

"No, Father, I haven't, but it won't be unlike a church. It'll be smaller, and with an entrance for hanging coats and bags, but I can use the same basic plan."

All twelve of the children were there, the younger ones leaning on their fathers' shoulders or nestling in their mothers' laps, while the older ones threw stones to see who's went the farthest. Ordinarily, they would take no notice of grown-up talk and hive off into their games after Mass. But today, they stayed nearby. The plans were about their school.

O'Kelly was sitting near the center, pleased with the progress of the meeting, when Dave Noonan objected.

"We are not building it there, Father—no bloody way," he said. "It might be near the river, so the kiddies could swim, but there are blackfellas campin' not a couple hundred yards away on the other side of it."

The map that had drawn Dave Noonan's attention was placed in the middle of the gathering. O'Kelly had marked the reach in the river where he wanted to build the school with a large red X.

Rory looked at Dave. He knew he would only speak up like that if it were true. Rory had noticed the blackfellas there, but a good while back. There was no way he was ever going to kill them, but that didn't mean they were to be anywhere near a school to be attended by his kids.

"Father, I think that's right," said Rory. "I've seen 'em up there as well."

Roddy O'Doherty was positioned discreetly at the outer edge of the circle. He took a step forward, caught the eye of O'Kelly, and glared at him.

"We can clear them off ourselves, Father," offered Noonan. "They're camping, anyway, in a top spot for fishin'."

Then, Dr. Dunne shuffled forward.

"And I, of course, worry about disease. They should never be allowed so near us."

O'Kelly managed to arrest his shoulders before they drooped.

What am I to do with these so-called Christians!

"Oh," said O'Kelly. "What a pity. I didn't realize."

O'Doherty took a small step backward.

Then, the muttering of the men was broken by the voice of a woman.

"Father, I am not sure the spot you proposed is a bad idea at all. It would suit us. It's the shortest walk for Eamon from Jacaranda Ridge. I'm thinking of his breathing."

Nothing was said by anyone. All that could be heard was the wind, the birds, and the hum of the bush.

Nell looked around to hardening faces, but Rory's had fallen to ash. O'Doherty again took a small step forward, and Rory moved to defuse the embarrassment.

"My wife's mistaken, Father. We've no real need for the school to go near our home. She's forgotten that I'll be teaching Eamon to ride once the weather chills. He'll be able to travel by pony."

Nell looked at Rory, confused, then fearful. Charlotte shook her head discretely, but enough so that Nell could see, and Dave jumped to Rory's aid.

"Father, have you considered this?" said Noonan. "There's another place a little more central to all the homes and which is already partially grassed."

"Where is that?" asked O'Kelly.

Noonan crouched by the map.

"Here, Father. It sits squarely in the middle of the farms, and there's not a blackfella anywhere in sight."

Barry Walsh interjected.

"I'm still worried about that part of the riverbank where the blackfellas are camping, and where we *won't* be having a school. What about getting them off it, Father?"

O'Kelly had to think quickly. He had to stop the meeting from descending into an attack on the people he most wanted to protect.

"That's a matter for the Town Council, Mr. Walsh. My only concern is our school."

Nell went into retreat. She pulled Polly up from her lap to standing and moved closer to the map.

"Father, my husband is right," said Nell, quietly. "That spot, the one in the middle, looks the fairest. It's a long walk for no one."

"It suits us, too," added Murphy.

O'Kelly wanted the subject closed before any more talk took alight. O'Doherty might weigh in at any moment to support clearing the Aboriginals from their camp.

"Well, that's settled then. A fine school on the vacant lands at the center of the farms, and by now, we've all earned our lunch."

O'Kelly hastened the meeting to its end by folding his map and standing.

* * * * *

Withers bashed at the typewriter keys so that they threatened to break from their metal.

He had to get this right. Parker was not to prevail.

He had been up since well before dawn. Under cover of the milky light of very early morning, Withers charged by foot up the hill on which sat the Protector's pad-locked shed.

He was back at the bank by half past eight. The correspondence had to be written, in private, before the bank opened at ten.

But the plan went close to turning awry, as Withers had always feared it might if his own hands were sullied. Richard stopped at his door at a quarter past nine. It had slipped Withers' mind that it was the Monday of the month on which Richard started early.

"Good morning, sir," he said. "I hope I am not prying, but I heard a bit of commotion. Do you need to be working so hard, and at this hour?"

Withers stopped bashing at the typewriter.

"Oh, Richard, yes, good morning. I'm catching up on what turned out to be a slightly idle week."

"I see," said Richard. "Sir, I don't wish to speak out of turn, but there is a white mark—a smudge of some kind—traversing the left corner of your forehead."

Withers touched his brow.

"What was that, Richard?" said Withers, feigning confusion.

"There is a white mark, sir, just where I said," remarked Richard. "Oh, and my goodness, sir, there is one on your lapel, at the top on the right as well."

Withers reached for his handkerchief.

"Oh, dear. Thank you, Richard. I was out at the Protector's shed in the early hours this morning, the one he keeps on bank land, just doing a check on his supplies—flour, other imperishable goods, that sort of thing. It was a hike, all right, to get to it, so I fear I am a little disheveled."

"Very good, sir," replied Richard. "I'll return for tea at eleven."

Withers resumed working as soon as the door clicked shut. Forgery hadn't been offered as a subject of study at Withers' exclusive school. Classics and Maths, English and History had carried him to the path of commerce. But times were desperate, and a bit of harmless deception of the lower classes was a means more than justified by ends.

Withers ripped the document from the typewriter rollers, produced without error on letterhead. There wasn't a reason for anyone to doubt it had been sent from the head office in the City.

Withers ground his teeth as he read the words he had chosen to fool Rory Burke, on a letter dated the previous Monday.

Dear Mr. Withers,   *11ᵗʰ December 1922*

We were in the process of spot-checking a loan extended by your branch in December of 1916 to one Rory Edmund Burke. It was due to come to an end in November of this year, but we have received no repayments since July.

Moreover, we have come across an irregularity of a serious nature. The land titles registry reveals that Mr. Burke misled the bank on the size of his landholding. He has signed to the effect that he is the owner of one hundred and eighty-five acres of freehold land, but the state records reveal that he holds only one hundred and fifty-five. In other words, the agreement appears to be based on fraudulent misrepresentation of a more than trivial nature.

As you know, both the bank and the state courts take a dim view of matters of this kind. That being so, please transfer Mr. Burke's file to the head office in the City, along with anything you may have to add yourself on how this situation came about. We will then consider the avenues of redress that are available to us under the law, including referral of the file to the state prosecutor of crime and the institution of a civil action for damages against Mr. Rory Edmund Burke.

Yours sincerely,

Frederick Adams
State Managing Director

Withers loosened his tie. Imagine the Town if Parker had his way!

The thought of it was choking. Their clean Christian community would be crawling—literally crawling—with Parker's do-gooders from the south. Parker's Christians would take the Bible, distort its teachings, and deploy it in support of the philosophies of the weak, common humanity, equality among brethren, and the supposed equal value of every human soul, irrespective of race.

If he hadn't been a gentleman, he'd have spat on the floor. The blacks would end up living in the confines of *his beautiful Town*.

Withers read the letter again. It was convincing and would do the trick if accompanied by theatrics. Withers slipped it into an unmarked envelope and put it in the top desk drawer. He picked up the telephone. He didn't want to speak to Richard again face to face.

"I want you to keep an eye out for one of our customers. When Mr. Rory Burke next comes in, send him in to me. And if I am in a meeting with someone, come in and interrupt me. It's important that I speak to him on next sighting."

* * * * *

Nell spun the pot of drawing tea[62] in the hope that she would find a way out, that the circle made by dragging its handle would release her from a bind.

But it didn't.

It couldn't be delayed any longer. Nell had received her da's letter on Friday and taken the week-end to reflect. But she hadn't a choice. His message was blunt and firm, and she had to do something before showing up at Ballycallan at Christmas.

You are to bring those documents with you. I mean it, Nell. No proof of a paid out loan means no acquisition of shares.

Despite everything that Charlotte had said, Nell had no choice but to raise it with Rory, again.

But she knew to do it gently.

Nell opened a packet of shop-bought biscuits, a luxury for morning tea to tender Rory up. The missing receipts had to be gathered, and Rory was the only man who could do it.

Eamon was in his bedroom. The door was closed, and he was reading. Daisy played hopscotch outside, beneath a wilting haze of purple petals, the Jacaranda tree having lumbered, like all of them, from spring into the summer. Polly sat in her high chair near Nell.

Nell glanced through a newspaper as she waited for Rory at the table. Hector's timing couldn't have been worse.

Rory's face had broadened and brightened, his moods had flattened to even, and he was downright chipper when it came to sharing his thoughts.

Just last week, he'd held her in bed and cooed about their prospects.

---

[62] Steeping tea

"You know what, Nell? It doesn't even matter that cream is failing out our way. By next quarter's end, we will be doing well from corn and pigs alone. I reckon we might as well switch them cows from dairying to grazing, and take the easy profit from beef, although it takes a little time."

Nell looked out the window and watched Daisy hop on one leg as steadily as many walk on two. As Daisy turned to take the return trajectory, there was a creak at the back screen door.

Da understands the world of commerce, thought Nell. *He's right. We have to have those documents.*

"Flamin' roos,[63]" said Rory. "I can fence that top paddock as much as I like, but the buggers'll still jump over it."

Rory ambled toward the table.

"Shop-bought biscuits," he said. "What's the occasion?"

"No real occasion," replied Nell. "I just thought that we might enjoy a bit of luxury a little more often now that we can."

"Hmph. I suppose you're right. As long as we don't go eating away our profits."

Nell broached the subject while pouring Rory's tea.

"Speaking of profits, Rory. I was hoping to have the books inked in before we head off for Christmas—you know, tie off the record for good. But we still haven't had a letter from the bank closing off the loan, and the last three receipts are still missing."

Rory sat up straight in his chair.

"What?"

"I mean, when you go into Town this afternoon, could you pop into the bank and ask about it? The receipts don't matter so much if we have the letter. It's just that I'm itchin' to complete the books, and I don't feel I can without it."

---

[63] Kangaroos.

Nell retreated toward the stove, ostensibly to get water from the kettle.

"You just can't give it up, can you, Nell?"

She stopped in her tracks and turned around.

"What?"

"You can't leave it—I mean, leave it to me to decide what's best for us, as a husband and a man."

"That's not it, Rory. Not at all. It's just for the sake of our books."

"So why did you speak out yesterday about where to put the school when you hadn't spoken to me? You embarrassed the livin' daylights out of us, Nell. Takin' a stand on where to put the school that was different from everyone else. It was unreal. Siding with the blackfellas in the presence and hearing of Roddy O'Doherty. You risked shamin' the whole bloody family."

Nell stood at the stove with color draining.

He's been stewing on that overnight, thought Nell, *he said nothing about this after the meeting!*

"I didn't side with anyone," she cried. "It was about what was best for Eamon."

Rory stomped toward the door.

"And why not tell the whole bloody world you've defied Dr. Dunne and treat Eamon with eucalyptus? That'd really set the cat among the pigeons."

"It didn't ever occur to me, Rory, that you had a quibble about how we treat Eamon."

Rory snatched his hat off its peg.

"I'll drop in a word, Nell, when I'm at the bank this afternoon, provided I've the time. But after that, the subject's closed. The bank's been good to us and seen us right. I'm not makin' a fuss over paper."

Nell ran after Rory and called out after him from the back stairs of the house. Daisy carried on hopping, oblivious

"I'm not questioning how you make decisions for us," she cried, "it's more about being *responsible.*"

Rory kept on walking away, as if he heard only the birds.

Oh, why won't you argue back Rory? Give me a better reason, please, so we can get this all sorted out.

Once back at the kitchen table, Nell had only Polly for company. She reached for the teapot. Although half full, it felt heavy.

And how am I going to deal with Da?

* * * * *

"Mr. Withers, sir, we are in luck. Mr. Rory Burke has come by today, and he has been kind enough to step in. Should I have Mrs. Evans bring in tea?"

Richard popped his head in the door.

"That won't be necessary, Richard," said Withers, curtly. "My business with Mr. Burke will be brief."

"Very good, sir," said Richard. "I'll leave you to it."

Rory shuffled from one leg to the other as he stood in Withers' doorway. The sun scored a rectangle of light in the middle of Withers' desk. It cordoned off the fateful spot where he would meet the error of his ways.

Withers stared at him, coldly.

There you were, thinking you got away with it, you smug piece of Irish shit.

"Close the door and get over here."

Withers didn't offer a seat, opened the drawer, and put the envelope prepared that morning in the middle of the oblong.

"Open it."

Rory's hands trembled as he read.

"Mr. Burke, have you ever heard of the word *diplomacy*? It's a master art of we, the members of the moneyed class. Do you have an idea, Mr. Rory *Edmund* Burke, of what it means to be *diplomatic*?"

Rory shook his head.

"You see, Mr. Burke, this is the art I have been practicing with you. But sadly, to date, I have failed, and look where we've both landed."

Rory took a small step to the side. He wanted to run away.

"The letter, sir," he said quietly, "from your head office in the City. It says you have received no repayments from us since July, but all of them have been made. We've the check stubs to prove it. I came by today, sir, to chase up the paperwork to confirm the end of our loan."

"Ah, Mr. Burke, that's what I mean by diplomacy. It's simple, really. I didn't send on your repayments to the City, or issue a receipt, as I had no wish to waive the rights of the bank. I was just so certain—so very, very certain—that we would come to an agreement via the route of diplomacy, so that the matter would be kept out of court. As it transpires, I was right to protect our interests."

Withers reached into his waistcoat pocket and tossed a key on ring and chain across the desk. It slid to within Rory's reach.

"All is not lost. Fortunately for you, I have taken the initiative. What was required was a change of *strategy*."

Rory dropped the letter back onto the desk, numbed.

Withers snarled.

"I've bagged the bloody flour myself, at considerable personal risk, and laced it with whatever I saw fit. The Protector does not know, and will never know, that the flour has been tainted."

Rory moved to sit.

Withers barked.

"You are to stand until you are offered a chair."

Rory froze.

"I telephoned the Protector this morning and let him know that I would arrange a man to make a food drop for him soon, very soon. Deliver the flour to the wretched blacks, and the prosecution will never take place. You will keep Jacaranda Ridge. I will manage the head office with *diplomacy*, Mr. Burke, and take the blame myself for the inaccurate assessment of the size of your run. But if you don't do as I say, you're done. Your farm will be gone, you will face a jail term, and *I* will move on with clear conscience."

He opened a drawer and pulled out a map folded to the size of a handkerchief and flicked it across the desk.

"This is where the buggers live. It's the Protector's map."

Withers retrieved the bogus correspondence from where Rory had dropped it on the desk and put it back in the drawer.

"Make the delivery tomorrow. Now, get out."

Rory picked up the key and the map, put them into his shirt pocket, and left.

* * * * *

Nell marched like a trooper across the baking plain that ran to the Noonans' farmhouse. Polly was on her hip and Eamon held her hand, while Daisy ran in front of her, unencumbered.

"Mum, slow up. My chest is hurting," cried Eamon.

"Eamon, love, if you can keep up with me, we'll be at the Noonans' sooner rather than later. We'll get you a little lie-down and have you breathing in no time."

"Just a little slower, Mum. It's hurting. Will you steam me with the eucalyptus oil when we make it to the Noonans'?"

Nell stopped. Daisy had sped ahead. The three remaining Burkes were stationary in the center of an open field, grass scorched to yellow, soil parched to powder. Eamon sat on the ground, cross-legged. He cupped his hands around the base of his face and coughed. Nell plopped Polly next to him, her little head covered by a cotton hat. Nell thanked the Lord that Eamon wasn't hacking and wheezing. It was just the standard splutter of her poor boy's early summer discomfort. If it had been any worse, she would never have set out.

"No, I won't, Eamon, and you know the eucalyptus oil is our secret. It will be all right, love. We're almost there."

Nell put her hands on her hips and looked around. It was the baldness of everything that bit in the pit of her stomach. There was barely an incline, not a trace of a curve, and green leaves were nowhere to be seen. Even the clouds were gone, defeated by the heat, and it was only half past ten.

When things turned bad and Nell couldn't go home to Ballycallan, she made her way to Charlotte's.

"Charlotte, I'm at my wits' end with him. I really am," said Nell, once the children were out of earshot and she was settled in Charlotte's kitchen.

"We've had our disagreements in the past, and on the odd occasion, he's even shouted at me. But I've never seen him go into a flying rage in the way he did last night."

"Tell me the latest."

"When we were getting ready for bed, he mentioned a daft plan. Announced he was going out bush today to look for a cow that has strayed."

"My goodness, Nell, you are a chancer. I never press Dave about work."

"So, do you never ask him, Charlotte, about where he's working and why?"

"Not at all. That's a taboo. We are lucky, Nell, that we are allowed to do the book-keeping. Most husbands don't even permit that. And in any event, what's so daft about bringing in a cow?"

"We lost her three months ago. He had a good look at the time and couldn't find a trace of her and gave up."

"So why does he think he can find her now?"

"I've no idea, Charlotte. But when I asked about that, he flew up into a fit, ran fair across to the other side of the bedroom and shouted like a madman. It's a miracle he didn't wake the children. Ranted that I was a meddler who didn't know her place, that I didn't even trust him with money. It finished with him snatching a blanket and sleeping on the settee."

"Well, there's obviously more to this than a stray heifer. What else has been happening?" asked Charlotte.

Nell looked outside through a high and wide window of Charlotte's scrubbed-to-gleaming modern kitchen. Daisy was skipping rope. Eamon watched from Charlotte's back stairs, knees pressed to his chin, with Polly sitting nearby in one of Charlotte's baby baskets. The elder Noonan girls counted as Daisy carried on, jump after energetic jump.

Nell knew where the tension lay.

"Me and Rory had a scrap over morning tea yesterday before he headed into Town. I had to ask him to pick up the paperwork over the loan. I know you told me a couple of weeks ago to leave Rory be, but Da replied to my last letter by digging in his heels. No loan documents mean no shares. Because of Da's latest salvo, I had to ask. Rory reacted by turning on me and said that I'd embarrassed him by speaking out of turn over the building of the school, and even questioned how I treat Eamon's condition. Said I didn't respect his ability to do what was best for us."

"So you had two fights yesterday?" asked Charlotte.

"Yes," said Nell, quietly.

The water on the stove came to the boil. Charlotte got up, poured it into the teapot, then put it in the middle of the table.

"Nell, what did I say to you when we last had a chat? And now you tell me you may as well have kicked your husband in the private parts."

Nell blushed.

"I know, but what else could I have done?"

"Well, a full faith disclosure is something that springs to mind. Like telling him at last that your father has you over a barrel with an inheritance."

"I can't do that, Charlotte—not at the moment. Rory would explode."

Charlotte sighed, got up, and poured the tea.

"So, did he bring the receipts back home with him?"

"No, he didn't," said Nell. "It was as if I never asked."

Charlotte returned to her chair at the end of the table.

"Nell, what I see here is an accumulation of things. I saw the way you were at the meeting we had about the school. And you did, Nell. You spoke without consulting Rory first. You should have known what that would do to a husband's pride, and in front of all your neighbors. At the same time, you've been what I would term as nagging him about financial matters— something else that isn't women's business—and you've capped it all off by questioning him when he wants to recover one of your lost herd. I am not defending his behavior, Nell, but I can see why he is angry."

Nell stirred her remorse into her tea.

"I know you're right," she said, "but what do I do about my da?"

"Can you call in help from one of your brothers to get him to back off?"

"No, I can't. Now they are all married, I write to their wives, so they've drifted from me a little."

"Then I'd tell your father again at Christmas that there has simply been some sort of delay with the administration of the loan. As for you, Nell, I'd be reminding myself of my duties as a wife. Poor Rory, with a man like your father to compete with. Don't do it again. Don't undermine Rory, or you'll finish up one of the loneliest wives in the west-lands. Mark my words."

Nell fiddled with her teacup. She had to learn to navigate the precipice between her birth family and the one she'd made with Rory with a lot more tact and grace.

"Follow my advice, Nell, and Rory will come good," said Charlotte. "Your husband will come good."

* * * * *

Rory Burke was chopping wood after returning from the cream run early. His axe bit hard into the thicket of bark. Its splinters sprayed into ever bigger bursts as the axe struck harder and harder. The last dying blooms of the Jacaranda tree hung above his head and scattered at his feet, as if a halo was crumbling against a backdrop of blue.

"Blacks, blacks, bloody blacks," he cried, reefing the axe from the ravaged timber before unleashing another assault.

Perspiration shimmered on Rory's lanky limbs while high in the trees a still cockatoo kept guard.

What was there left for an honest man to do? You could work to the bone, save all you had, and this bastard of a place would still get ya. Fires, floods, and windstorm. All his life, he'd fought like a lion, but ended up ever wrong-footed.

Who had caused Eamon's asthma? The blacks. Who had tried to nick Sean's cattle, curse their only source of water, and knock down their home by pointin' the bloody bone? The blacks. Whose side was taken by his not-so-obedient wife when it came to selecting a place for the school? That of the blacks. And what stood in the way of all he'd worked for, so he could stand up tall among the men of the land, free of loans and pressure from banks?

The bloody rotten, filthy, blacks.

Rory threw the axe aside, panting. It skidded across a morbid mix of dusty dirt and dying purple petals.

And now he might end up in jail.

Why in the world did we all leave Ireland?

Rory kicked at the ground, still panting.

Forsook our families, abandoned our homes, and left lush fields that might have fed us.

"For a better life," shouted Rory, retrieving the axe. "A better bloody life than the one I've got, not hardship, pain, and grind."

Rory resumed chopping furiously.

But that life would be over soon, and for good. It didn't matter where Father O'Kelly built the bloody school, because the blacks were as good as dead. He would do exactly as Mr. Withers asked and deliver the buggers a present, a little gift for Christmas, and today.

A small consignment of problem-solving sacks of poisoned flour.

* * * * *

The silence hanging in the Burke family drawing room was as heavy as the humidity.

Fatigue has aggravated Rory's ill-humor, thought Nell, as she got on with her sewing. *He took most the day away looking for that cow and, now, he's completely exhausted.*

They would be back at Ballycallan soon to feast the birth of our Lord. Ordinarily, Nell's spirits would be on the soar at the thought of heading home, despite the three day journey. But Christmas this year would be complex.

She stitched a button onto one of Rory's shirts but with one eye on her children.

Nell let Daisy and Eamon play at Rory's feet, hoping it might soften him. Her plan backfired within minutes. Daisy struck a nerve.

"Daddy, can me and Eamon go play with the pickaninnies if we see 'em again in the bush?"

Nell looked up at Rory. He ignored her and stared at Daisy.

"What are you saying to me, Daisy Burke?" asked Rory.

"Why can't we swim with the pickanninies, Daddy? They splash and laugh just like us. And I want to touch their skin."

Eamon was throwing a small, dried-up pork knuckle in the air, then scooping up the other jacks left on the floor in sweeps. He coughed between turns.

Nell stopped sewing.

"Daisy, love, where did you see the pickanninies?" she asked gently.

"We seen 'em up the river one day. They are the skinniest kids I ever saw."

"And were there any grown-ups with them?"

"No, Mum," replied Daisy. "Just some kids. Three, I think, and all boys."

Rory touched Eamon's leg with his foot.

"Lad," he said, "is this right?"

Eamon stopped his game and turned toward his mother. She was as serene as his father was angry.

"Yes, it is, Dad. I seen 'em as well."

"Why have I not heard of this before? I've told you not to go near them blackfellas," said Rory.

Eamon gripped the jack.

"We didn't, Dad, I promise. They were swimmin' in the river one day when me and Daisy were there skipping stones. Then we ran off back home once we seen 'em."

"And have you seen them again, lad?" asked Rory.

"No, Dad, never. I promise."

Then suddenly, Eamon blew up.

"Dad, I never even spoke to 'em! Never ever said a word and stopped Daisy from doing the same!"

He threw the jacks across the floor.

Rory stood up and shouted.

"By God, you backchat me and you'll end up with the strap! And you hide from me, lad, where you've been and what you've done, you'll play at home and nowhere else."

"Rory, he's a boy," snapped Nell. "He doesn't remember every bit of detail of his day the way we do. Aboriginal children played on Ballycallan when I was a girl. They never did us harm."

Nell's words struck her husband like the blow of a metal rod. He sat back down.

"His breathing's been buggered since September, Nell. *September*. He's never had it that early and, now, we find out he's been exposed to the bloody blacks."

Nell spoke through gritted teeth.

"Rory, what *are* you driving at?" she said.

"Maybe it's as Dr. Dunne always said," said Rory hotly. "Them bloody blacks go around cursing the whites. And look where we are with Eamon. He's gettin' worse, not better."

"Is it true, Mum?" cried Eamon. "Are the black people making me ill?"

"Rory," said Nell. "Let's discuss this *later*."

The children looked at one another, bewildered. It was the first time they had ever heard raised voices between their parents.

"We won't do it again, Daddy. I promise that we won't," said Daisy.

"It's all right, Daisy," said Nell. "It wouldn't be the end of the world if you did."

Rory walked out and left it to Nell to put the children to bed. He knew full well that there wasn't a chance the Aboriginals would be seen again.

* * * * *

It wasn't turning out like an ordinary Christmas—not as Nell would have liked it.

All the McTiernans were up at sunrise to go to Christmas Mass. Two of Nell's brothers, Brendan and Robert, were home that year at Ballycallan rather than at their in-laws. Violet managed to find beds for everyone, no matter how many of her brood returned.

And Christmas Mass at the Port Town cathedral was no ordinary service. It was a society event. Suits, hats, and colorful fabrics populated the gardens of the churchyard.

The cathedral itself was made of stone. And not just any old stone. Blocks of granite, grooved out into waves, softened the high church walls. A cemented pathway ran up to its entry from a fully bitumened street. Fifteen-foot doors required a hefty push before the cathedral could be entered. And the sun lit up its stained-glass windows as the Christmas worshippers filed in.

Please God, prayed Nell, as the service commenced, *get me out of this fix with Da.*

Trouble descended just after Mass. The congregation were gathered in the cathedral gardens. It was a hot day, but not unbearably so. Banks of roses—red, white, and pink—all nestled comfortably on a silky lawn, were unwilted by the heat. The cathedral bell had just stopped ringing. A small crowd collected within the gardens around a young and passionate priest. He was from the City and said the Mass because the parish priest was away.

He was more or less continuing his sermon. It had been about Aboriginal people.

"They have souls as worthy as mine and yours," he said, to the slowly growing gathering.

"But, Father, that can't be right," interjected a parishioner. "Some of them live like animals."

"Too right," added another. "May as well shoot 'em like roos."

At that, the young priest exploded.

"No! No! No! Killing is forbidden under the sixth commandment of God and the law of this state. Anyone who breaks this commandment is condemned to eternal damnation. You hear me—ETERNAL DAMNATION."

And Rory Burke passed out.

He was caught before he hit the ground by a parishioner bigger than he.

"Oh my goodness!" cried one woman.

"Is he conscious?" asked another.

"Oh no," cried Nell.

She rushed forward from the outer ring of women but was beaten to Rory's side by her brothers. They were standing closer to him. Brendan loosened Rory's collar and tie.

"Could we have a little space, please?" he said. "Rob, can you fetch a cushion from one of the sulkies for his head? Rory, mate, can you hear me? You out cold or are you just havin' a bit of a spell?"

Rory recovered within a minute or so, just after Robert sped back with the cushion.

"You all right, mate?" said Brendan. "You gave us a bit of a fright."

A doctor pushed forward, parting the crowd.

"See if he can be helped up," said the doctor.

Robert and Brendan obliged.

"Struthe, what happened?" said Rory.

The doctor examined his eyes, took his pulse and temperature. He gave quiet counsel after finishing.

"I would say, at this stage, that it was all down to the heat. Your eyes are clear and active, and your speech seems normal. But there's to be no exertion today, and I'm to be called if this happens again."

On the road back to Ballycallan, Nell tried to mop Rory's brow.

"That's enough," said Rory.

He pushed her hand away.

"It was just a simple turn."

Nell put her hankie back in her purse and shut it brusquely. Her husband had left her with nothing to do but watch the emerald paddocks roll by.

* * * * *

Hector and Violet's homestead at Ballycallan ran the length of a velvet hill, in the cautiously regal style of the settlers who'd come with little and done well. A freshly painted open veranda skirted all four of its sides, decorated with curls of iron at corners where its supporting poles met the roof.

On a side veranda, the McTiernan women began preparing Christmas lunch. Nell worked with her sisters-in-law, Doris and Peggy. They were chopping vegetables outside in the breeze. Inside, Violet tended to the roasting of a large leg of pork, along with a couple of farm-killed chickens.

Nell was able to mask her exhaustion and smile as she sliced up parsnips. She kept an eye on her precious boy and her rambunctious girl as they played in the rainforest nearby. They were keeping her from wits' end.

"Rory, you must tell me," she had said, in a whisper when they reached the steps of the homestead, "why you are so tensed up. If you can't share your troubles with your own wife, then who on earth is there that you can?"

Rory was quick to turn his back and look toward the hills.

"Leave it, will you, Nell?" he said. "I'm buggered—that's all. And a bit of peace and quiet while we're here on holiday would be just the ticket."

The children ran in and out of the rainforest. From the veranda, Nell saw Eamon on a rock at its edge, commanding his cousins like a ringmaster.

"It's Pete's turn to come up and touch the lucky stone. Then, whoever gets touched by Pete is dead for ten seconds."

He was standing with a stick in his hand.

"But it's my turn, isn't it?" cried Daisy.

"No, it isn't," said Eamon. "You're to come in after Pete."

Violet came out onto the veranda—a slender woman, clear-skinned and boney-cheeked, her grey hair pulled back into a bun.

"Doris, once you are done with the spuds, can you see that the carrots are peeled? Peggy, I might need you to help me in the kitchen in a bit, once I've had a spell. A round of dishes need cleaning before serve-up."

"Violet, I'm not sure this is enough pumpkin? My kids love it," said Peggy.

"Mine as well," added Doris. "I think we should probably double what we have."

Everyone is trying, thought Nell, *doing their best to carry on as normal, not to let Rory's turn, and his detached behavior, blemish their Christmas Day.*

Nell emptied a chopping board piled with sliced parsnips into an empty pot. She glanced again toward the forest. Her children could still be heard and Daisy's form vaguely made out, ducking in and out of the ramble of trees.

Nell turned back toward the table in search of more vegetables to chop. Hector appeared in the doorway. His hands were pressed against each side of its frame as his stocky body leaned forward. White-bearded and bald, he filled the space with the confidence of the achieved. He caught Nell's eye, when the others weren't looking, and tilted his head toward his study. It was at the far end of the veranda.

Nell sighed.

Here cometh the inevitable call.

"Ma, I'm just popping off to check on Polly before lunch. She's just about due to wake."

"All right, dear," said Violet. "But when you're done, can you come back and help us? Once the veg are boiled, we won't be far from serve-up."

"Of course, Ma."

Nell untied her apron and set off down the corridor.

* * * * *

The door of her father's study was ajar, so she pushed it. The grin of a jovial grandfather had, by then, been hidden away. It was replaced by something few women saw: the determined regard of a businessman. Hector sat on an armchair just by his desk. One hand lay upon his stomach. The other rubbed his chin.

She closed the door behind her.

"All right, Nell, I've done as you asked and let this lie until now. I've not raised the question of the loan with Rory. But you had better tell me what's up."

Hector wasn't the sort of man to commence his dealings with small talk.

Nell settled, gingerly, on her father's settee.

I wish I wasn't here.

"I've nothing to say, Da. No explanation or a suggestion of what to do. We've not been sent any kind of document acknowledging that the loan is paid out."

"So, no letter and short three receipts?" asked Hector.

"That's right," said Nell, softly. "You know, Da, there's not a lot I can do, and Rory says we're not to press the bank over something as trivial as paper."

Hector let his hand drop from his stomach.

"Bloody hell, Nell. He's an honest fella, but he needs to toughen up. You're at the mercy of the bank, you know, until they sign you off."

"Da, as far as I can see, our financial worries are over. I can't go into the bank without turning heads, and I'd probably be ignored if I did. And I have told Rory a hundred times to sign everything in duplicate and bring it straight home. He hands me all the post unopened, and we've not heard a peep from the bank since winter. But at the same time, they've given us no trouble. So as far as Rory's concerned, our debt to them is over."

"So, why's he getting around like a cove who's lost all he had?" asked Hector. "Even before that fainting spell today, I could barely interest him in a beer with your brothers, and he's hardly said boo to a goose. Robert's already had a word with me, and he reckons we should take him back to the doctor."

Nell rested her heavy to aching head on her hand.

"He's been like that off and on over the last six months. Just when I think he's come back to normal, he seems to drift off again. I've spoken out of turn a couple of times—once in front of the other men and in his presence and once to Father O'Kelly in his absence, but which he found out about anyway. I've racked my brain, and I can't think of anything else."

"That's not enough to explain his behavior. Nell, love, the bottom line is that money might have been spent at the races for all you know. This can't go on any longer."

Nell's voice gained in volume.

"Da, what you've said is wrong and unfair. Rory is as honest as the day is long and barely spends a cent on himself."

Hector played his trump card.

"He still doesn't know, does he love, that you are going to one day inherit?"

Nell sat deeper into Hector's settee, as if that was where she'd been pushed. Sorrow wrought of relief mixed with shame had to settle before she could answer.

"No," said Nell softly, "he doesn't."

"Good!" replied Hector. "You're to get him to chase the bank come New Year. You hear me? You must have something to prove to the law that you've met your obligations. And once you have it, you're to send it to me, and I'll return it by course of post. It's as I said in my letter. I can't go ahead and buy the shares for the children without it. And I can't let you part with money for investments unless I know you're free from debt."

Nell stared at the floor. She was out of arguments.

Hector stood up.

"If I haven't had the documents by the end of January, I'm coming up for a visit, and I'll go to the bank with him myself. And as for his membership to the Pastoralists' Club, I'm not taking him in for his first club dinner until all of this is cleared up."

Violet called out from the kitchen.

"Nell, where are you? We're exposing the meal. Can you come and give us a hand?"

"And if he puts up even the slightest resistance," added Hector, "I expect you to take my side."

Nell sighed.

Fact is, I wouldn't be able to get us out of this if I didn't have Da behind me.

"Very well, Da," said Nell. "I'll make Rory go into the bank as soon as we get home. But for now, I had better get back to the others before he sees that I'm gone."

* * * * *

CHAPTER 8
REDEMPTION
January 1923

Rory Burke was heading out bush, hoping to find a miracle.

It was early Saturday morning, in the second week of January, during the longest of all his summers. Nell and his children were all still sleeping. The sun was tinting a mystical sky from oily black to gray-blue. Birdsong began to chime, while the animals made their morning retreat back into the depths of the scrub.

Rory left a note for Nell in the kitchen.

Gone for a ride.

He slung the saddle across the horse's back, then yanked its straps into place. Since just before Christmas, he'd felt hollowed out, and it was only getting worse.

After this life, am I headed for hell?

He crossed himself and mounted.

It had been easy at the time, thought Rory, as his horse trampled through the bush.

The bags of flour had been mostly small, a little awkward to carry in saddlebags but nothing he couldn't handle. And the campsites of the blackfellas stood out, as clear to a bushman as the Hotel Imperial in the main street of the Town. They were located in clearings and skirted either by rock or by river, with the remains of a fire somewhere near the clearing's middle.

That was a few weeks ago. As far as he knew, there hadn't been a storm, a fire, or other intervention that might have saved his soul, that would have consigned the poisoned flour to oblivion before the blackfellas were able to eat it.

The chances they didn't take it are slim.

Rory rode ever less steadily as he revisited each of the campsites. From the base of the mountain to the reach in the river, he dismounted a half-dozen times, then scoured the clearings so close to the ground that he might have been looking for gold. He kicked at the site of each of his sins, the unholy dirt where the sacks no longer lay. All of them were gone, lifted no doubt by a hungry blackfella who was, by now, at peace and with the Lord along with everyone in his family.

At the sixth site, Rory slipped, then recovered, then staggered back to his horse. He wasn't able to get back on, as if life had left his legs. But he managed to walk her, one empty limb following the other. The midsummer heat crept beneath his shirt in time with the strengthening sun.

"They're not fully human, lad. They're savages. And it's down to us to turn a profit from all this land that they've been wastin'."

Sean's words rang through Rory's head like the church bells of the Port Town cathedral. He was twelve years old, and Sean was ramming wooden posts he'd hacked out of trees into the uncooperative earth. He was claiming another paddock from the wasteland.

"All this land, lad, growing nothing but scrub and gum trees. And now, we are here by the will of God. It's the *will of God* that it's cultivated."

Young Rory Burke listened to Sean, all right. But all he had wanted was to go home to Hannah.

Rory reached the riverbank. He found a rock on which to rest. The water was still, and willow trees shaded each side of the river. His own children came here to skip stones and swim, to enjoy the calm and the shade. Rory had gone there to weep for himself and to pray for the souls of the blacks.

With knees pulled up to his trembling chin, Rory rested his head on his arms. What else could he have done? The only answer was nothing. He was bound by his duties as a man: feed his family and honor the work begun by Sean. But the only way open to doing just that lay in killin' Aboriginals. Rory knew he would be respected in this earthly life, by family, church, and community, but he'd hold the secret all alone that he was destined to burn in hell.

Rory lifted his head. The world was blurred by a wall of tears. He'd be going to hell, all right, and no amount of going to confession would fix it. Rory dabbed his sodden eyes with the sleeve of his cotton shirt. It had been hand-sewn with love by his own Nell Burke, his lady wife who deserved so much more than he would ever be able to provide.

Rory blinked, rubbed his eyes, then blinked again. The film of fluid between him and the river was lifting.

And he couldn't believe what he saw.

A score of dark-skinned men and, at least, a dozen women drifted toward the willows then sat by the river. Their children were so swift in their charge to the water that Rory couldn't count them. They were all as thin as a human could be, but as alive as the birds in the trees. This was no mirage. It was a miracle. The sound of breaking water as the little ones splashed in proved it.

Rory crossed himself, leapt to his feet, and bolted toward his horse. He needed to talk to Father.

* * * * *

The brush buffed briskly across the leather of Archibald Withers' shoes. The state of a gentleman's footwear reflected the condition of his soul. A scratch or a smear was a judgment of its bearer: idle, inattentive, and flawed.

He dropped the brush and polishing rag back into a well-worn pouch. Standing by the window of his top-floor flat, Withers scowled and pondered.

Why in the bloody hell weren't they dying?

He looked down the length of the Town main street. Protestant families were beginning to gather. Some passed in and out of just-opened-for-business shops. Others chatted in neat little groups, attired in quality clothing. The Catholic hordes would follow, much later, once they had managed to get out of bed. And the tone of the Town would suddenly be lowered by ill-disciplined laughter and movement in packs. Withers took in the civility of the view while he could.

It was uncanny, thought Withers, as he watched the activity beneath him.

In his last three forays into the countryside, one in the week after Christmas and two made in the New Year, he'd seen more of the blacks than ever—loitering by the side of the road, wandering across white men's paddocks as if they owned them, and gathering behind the butter factory, scratching like animals at disused cream cans.

It was the opposite of all he had hoped. It was as if the buggers had been breeding. Over three weeks had passed since their supposed termination. Something must have gone wrong.

Neither thorough tidying of his pokey flat nor reflection while reading the newspaper yielded any answers. Then, Withers put on his shoes, grabbed his hat, and descended the stairs. As he stepped onto the floorboards of the south side of the street, he bumped, by chance, into Richard.

"My goodness," said Withers. "Good day. How timely. Would you have a moment for a word?"

"Good day, sir," replied Richard. "Of course. I've several minutes to spare."

Withers settled his clerk into a shadowy doorway and launched an interrogation.

"Sir, I can assure you, I watched Mr. Burke with my very own eyes," said Richard.

"Richard, are you sure—I mean, absolutely sure? The blacks needed that food. The poor wretches are starving. I made a promise to the Protector that I'd see to it that that flour was delivered before Christmas. Was the work properly done?"

"Mr. Withers, sir, if I may say again, from what I saw he did the job. It's as I reported before Christmas. At eleven o'clock on December 18th, Mr. Burke unlocked the shed, loaded bags of what appeared to be flour on each side of his horse, came back down the hill, and wandered off into the bush. I followed him myself as far as the river. He dropped a small sack by a smoldering fire, stabbed a hole in it, shoved it under a rock, then moved on into the interior. That's when I lost sight of him."

"And did you check the shed afterward? Was it completely empty?"

"Yes I did sir. And yes, it was. There were a couple of broken shelves and a pile of old bricks, half a dozen or so sealed tins, an empty unmarked bottle. But nothing aside from that and the flour bin, which was almost empty. Nothing at all. And no sacks of flour."

Withers scanned Richard's face for the trace of a lie.

There was none.

Richard was beginning to feel uncomfortable, jammed as he was in a darkened corner by Withers' lanky frame.

"Mr. Withers, sir, could I beg the indulgence of a question? Why are you asking again? Has someone suggested that Mr. Burke lied and took the flour for himself or simply failed to deliver it?"

Withers sensed the peril of potential for gossip. He stepped back to let Richard out.

"No, that's not it, Richard. That's not it at all," said Withers. He straightened his tie.

"It's just that I can see that the natives still want for nourishment, scavenging and such for food scraps. It's a difficult sight for a Christian to bear, and I promised the Protector I would help. Now, run along, Richard, and I'll see you at the office at ten sharp Monday morning."

"Ah, sir," said Richard. "I'll see you before then. At church tomorrow at nine."

"Yes, of course, Richard. And good day."

The clamor of Saturday morning commerce was growing. As Withers strolled, black-suited and bowler-hatted, he was calmed by the busy shops to his left and the bustling open street to his right. Then Rory Burke sped by on horseback, as if teasing him with timing.

"I hope you fall off and break your neck, you useless Irish peasant," muttered Withers. "I released you a little too soon."

Withers moved like a lord surveying his manor, drawing up an inventory as he went: haberdashery, bookstore, tailor, and barber. All this fine work, the civilizing work of the bank, would be carried on and expanded. His own naïve church might throw up obstacles, but this work would not be routed. Archibald Withers would see to it or be damned.

* * * * *

John O'Kelly savored the peace of a quiet Saturday morning. The rest of the Town would be out and about, peering in shop windows, stopping and thinking about what could be purchased and what could not, of what could be reaped without risking depletion of their profits from the land.

But he was still taking time to recover.

He was settled on his front veranda, leafing through a book of watercolors. He had painted the pictures himself as a much younger man. *The Forests of Glendalough* was his favorite, and he lingered on the image.

Dogged tufts of foliage gathered between the trees. Some of the leaves were as light as petals, while others were hardy and serrated. In this youthful depiction of the natural world, the forest canopy fell in fragments, carried on the current of soft-blown winds and enlivened to the color of lime by an obstinate afternoon sun.

You wouldn't credit it, thought O'Kelly, *that a country like Ireland as blessed by the riches of nature could be just as burdened by the wars of man.*

But from all he had read, and by the grace of God, it appeared to be coming to an end, and the Free State seemed destined to prevail.

O'Kelly turned the page and looked up. There was someone riding up Presbytery Hill at a gallop. Rory Burke got off his horse, tethered it to a tree, and ran up the veranda steps.

"Mr. Burke, what a surprise," said O'Kelly, standing to greet him. "What's the matter?"

"Father, I've seen a miracle," stammered Rory. "The miracle you asked me to pray for in confession before Christmas. It's happened. The blackfellas are alive. They are all still alive!"

O'Kelly put a hand on Rory's shoulder.

"Mr. Burke, wait here on the veranda. I'll boil the kettle and make a fresh pot of tea. Take a seat while I fetch it."

Ten minutes later, and by the witness of a row of white wood gum trees that ran all the way to the road, Rory told O'Kelly all.

"I prayed as hard as I could, Father, just as you said, from the day I came to confession, the day after I committed the evil deed and the day before we left for the coast. I said as many Hail Marys and Our Fathers as I could ever remember offering to try and stop the blacks from dying. And today, I checked myself, set out first thing this morning. We got back from Ballycallan Thursday night. The poisoned flour's nowhere in sight, taken by someone, but not by blackfellas."

"How do you know?" asked Father O'Kelly, dryly.

"Because there's a whole mob of 'em gathered down by the river where the willow trees are hung, a whole flaming tribe of 'em, and all of 'em fit and swimming," said Rory, excitedly.

"Father," added Rory, after gulping at his tea. "Do you think that none of them might have died? Do you think God intervened over Christmas so that the flour was taken away? Angels, a storm, or another act of God of some kind?"

Father O'Kelly edged his chair backward to secure a bit of distance. He needed to work his parishioner into place and complete an important lesson.

"Do you see this mark on my forehead, Mr. Burke," said O'Kelly.

"Yes, I do, Father," replied Rory. "Did you have an accident or somethin'?"

"And this painful scratch on my elbow. Have you noticed that?"

"Now you mention it, Father, I do," replied Rory.

O'Kelly leaned forward to strike.

"I have racked my brain, Mr. Burke—really racked my brain—to work out what part of that terrible day in the week before Christmas had been the worst. Was it the shock of hearing, in the sacrament of confession, that our trusted Town banker had been plotting to kill? Or had the dismay been worse, the brutal, ugly, infinite dismay of hearing that a decent Catholic—an ordinary man like you *who I have known and liked all his life*—could be swindled and bullied into helping?"

Rory swallowed hard. Ecstasy was being drowned by shame.

"The truth is, Mr. Burke," continued O'Kelly, "that I injured my head when stumbling at the stables. I fell face down, ground into the dirt under the weight of a saddle, something I'd not lifted for many a year. But with the power of prayer, I achieved the impossible—the physical capacities to straddle a horse having left me many years hence. But I managed it—eight mounts and as many dismounts once I found the campsites you described. And this mark on my elbow—this *painful* gash on my elbow—was sustained as I fell, once more, on the rocks at the river, tossing the poison I'd found into its current."

Rory bit his bottom lip to stop it from quivering.

"So, it was you, Father, who took away the flour," he mumbled.

"Yes, it was," said O'Kelly, leaning back in his chair.

"I removed them the day you told me what you'd done. By which I mean the day after the delivery. All six of the sacks were full, untouched, exactly where you said you had left them. The Aboriginal people are safe."

Rory pulled out his handkerchief and wiped away a tear.

"I don't know what I can do to thank you, Father," he said softly.

"I do," replied O'Kelly curtly. "It is as I said to you in December during confession. Your penance is not yet over."

"Remind me again, Father?" said Rory.

"You are to tell me, Mr. Burke, and immediately, if you ever hear of anyone planning to harm Aboriginal people, be it a member of our parish, a Protestant like Mr. Withers, or anyone else. You understand, Mr. Burke? You are to tell me *everything*."

"Yes, of course, Father. I will, no risk."

O'Kelly finished his tea, stood, and pulled a wooden cross from the wall.

"And hang this cross somewhere where you'll see it often, just as a reminder. You break the terms of your penance and the forgiveness of our Lord will be spent."

Rory took the cross without speaking and put it in his satchel.

"I expect your family might be wondering where you are. Have you told them you are here?"

"No, Father, I haven't."

Rory reached for his hat on the seat just by him.

"Good. It's best kept that way. I am sure you have, in any event, some affairs to attend to in Town. And say a prayer of thanksgiving to the Lord for his mercy as you ride."

When Rory left, O'Kelly closed the presbytery door by leaning against it with his back. The grandfather clock at the end of the hallway struck twelve.

Withers is an animal! I should have kept him closer.

He placed his palms against the door and closed his tearing eyes.

You're a man alone, John O'Kelly, fighting a war within your own community.

A short-term victory might have been his, but how to make it endure?

Could he speak with Reverend Parker about Archibald Withers, and would he be believed? But he barely knew the Anglican vicar; sectarianism kept them apart. And the government Protector of Aboriginal people was so close to Roddy O'Doherty as to be useless; a word, in that direction wouldn't work. And to cap it off, Mr. Burke had told all in the sacrament of confession. He could never breach its seal.

It would take much more than the help of the Lord to keep the Aboriginal people from harm. They needed the protection of the rule of law. So, O'Kelly resolved to speak to the Bishop about getting the Town a policeman.

* * * * *

"Rory, you frightened the daylights out of me, you really did."

Nell, in a nightie, sat in front of the dresser, brushing her black hair to silky. She watched her husband in the mirror. Rory sat on the side of their four-post bed, slowly removing his socks.

"It was like I said this morning, love. I wanted to get to the saddler in Town before the crowds and have a bit of a ride in the bush."

"Well, you might have said so in your note. You've been so quiet and contrary lately, I thought you might have taken leave of your senses."

Nell had already worked out how to prevent a visit from her father. She had found an excuse for Mr. Withers to come and visit Jacaranda Ridge. Then, she would ask herself about the missing receipts and the letter closing out the loan.

But she had to do it soon.

Nell swung around and studied her husband. He was unbuttoning his shirt, in the way of the Rory Burke of old. He pushed the shirt from his back and shoulders with a smooth and easy shrug, then reclined to flat on his back. Rory stared at their tinny roof, its wooden cross beams and sheets of iron, his hands clasped behind his head.

The peak of the roof disappeared from view, rising beyond the reach of the lamps.

For Nell, Rory was looking at the excuse she had selected, and carefully, to entice a visit from Mr. Withers. Why not seek another small loan to plaster in the ceiling? If they invited Mr. Withers to Jacaranda Ridge, he could see how the funds would be used. Then, she might be able to find out more about those wretched missing receipts.

But Nell, for now, wanted to know why Rory had relaxed.

"Rory," said Nell gently.

"Yes, love?"

"Did you find something special when you went for a ride today—something that freed you of your troubles?"

Rory rolled over toward his wife.

"Not really. But I've got this."

He reached into his trouser pocket and produced a crumpled envelope.

"Picked this up on the post run yesterday. Forgot to give it to you. It's a document from the bank you've been asking about ending the loan and the three missing receipts. Moloney said it arrived at the post office just before Christmas, after we'd left for Ballycallan."

Nell took the letter out of the envelope and read all of its words—every delightful, liberating word. With a stunted gasp of extreme relief and a pounding heart, she put it and the receipts in her dressing table drawer, closing it quickly, then turned back toward Rory, casually.

"That was strange, wasn't it, Rory?" said Nell. "It's taken the bank six months to catch up on our correspondence."

Rory reclined, again, to laying on his back.

"Reckon they forgot about us. I'm sure Mr. Withers has bigger fish to fry."

Nell went to the long bowl on the sideboard. She poured water into it from an adjacent pitcher and took her time to wash her hands.

I can't believe my eyes, she thought. *Was there nothing to this all along?*

Nell let the water ripple around her fingers. This terrible chapter of blue moods and moroseness, had it finally come to an end? Had she made matters worse, blown it out of proportion, and created a problem herself?

Rory then showed that his turn to good humor was part of a general trend. He showed interest again in his family.

"Love," he said, still looking skyward. "I don't really want to turn up at this working bee by myself tomorrow. It's a chance for the kids to gather and play as much as getting that school built. Could I just take Daisy? She'll be missing out if she stops at home."

The knot in Nell's stomach began loosening.

"But that means leaving your son at home, and Daisy will come back with tales of all he's missed!"

"Well, perhaps we could all go, just once, and we can both watch Eamon so he doesn't run himself ragged. He was good as gold at Christmas, keeping out of the running part of the games with his cousins. And the bit of the season that gives him grief is pretty much over."

"Rory, you know I want us all to join in, but we can't right now. It's too cruel to make him sit out in front of all the other boys. It's different from playing with his family."

Rory smiled and let it be.

As they settled into bed Nell curled her body along the length of Rory's. A dammed-up stream of feeling was returning to its natural flow.

But when Rory began snoring, she leapt out of bed. The same instinct to protect that had triggered her attack on the Jacaranda tree in 1915 spurred her to check for herself.

I have to see if the signatures match.

Nell picked up the not-quite-extinguished candle sitting by her bed. She went back to her dressing table, pulled its drawer open, and took out the letter and receipts.

She padded down the corridor to the drawing room.

My Rory has a heart of gold and is a little too quick to trust. Has someone in that bank abused it, taken our money and given Rory fakes?

Nell checked her records, relieved and perplexed. Withers' signature was distinctive and was the same on the loan contract as on the letter bringing it to an end. And the three receipts bore the same stamp marked on all the others she'd filed. It was unmistakably that of the bank.

So, what has this been all about?

But she may as well have asked the night why it turned to day. It had all unfolded beyond her reach in a domain reserved to men.

Nell went back to bed.

Better to ponder the parts of this, she thought, *that I am actually able to see.*

For sure, there was a pattern to the last six months. When Rory felt he wasn't providing, he retreated into himself: sulky, distant, and even cold. But when he stood as an equal with the other men of the land and was on top of his dealings with the bank, he reverted to his regular self.

Perhaps Charlotte had read everything correctly? If I paid better attention to being a dutiful wife, would it be better for us all?

And had the absence of paperwork completing the loan worried Rory as much as she?

In the solitude hollowed by the cathedral of night, the crux of it all became clear. Her father had treated her just like a son, but the fact remained that she wasn't. And Da was to be kept from Rory's finances; her inheritance was no license to its access. She would send the receipts to Ballycallan, no risk, in the post out Monday morning but only to stop her da from visiting Jacaranda Ridge.

There were frontiers set between man and wife that were there for a marriage to prosper. Nell kissed the middle of her husband's back as he tumbled more deeply into sleep. There was much for them to be thankful for. The black side of the ledger surpassed the red,[64] all her children would be going to school, and her Rory had finally come good.

* * * * *

---

[64] To be in the red means to be in loss (as above, origin in the color of the ink to show money going out).

Part III - Holy Days
(1928–1929)

~⦿~

CHAPTER 9
ASPIRATIONS
September 1928

Every beloved wooden thing inside John O'Kelly's fully wooden church was smothered in spiritless gloss.

It might as well have been a different building from the church erected in 1885. He remembered the laying of floorboards on wide wooden stilts, the filling in of open squares with rough timber walls and plain but precious glass, and the delivery of the statue of the Virgin Mary to the right of the altar as a gift from the Bishop to mark their fortieth year. It was opposite the figure of Jesus, to the left, which had been presented to the church to celebrate its first.

Now, the frayed planks of wood that made up the church walls were obscured by layers of paint, and every pew had been lacquered by a tradesman who had moved up from the south. And the floorboards were drenched in medium brown, in keeping with the fashions of the City.

For John O'Kelly, all of this meant distance; distance between his parishioners and the land from which they lived. The mark of man was trumpeting over the footprint of God.

But the song of native birds still managed to seep in. They were as natural to O'Kelly now as the scents of the air. Long ago, before coming to Australia, he hadn't heard a bird screech at the pitch of a crying child or occupy the sky with tones ranging from the rhythm of laughter to the snapping of sticks. Ubiquitous by day, they beat at the back of all sounds made by men.

There was much in these days referred to as "boom" that perturbed Father O'Kelly. With prosperity came vanity, opportunity fostered greed, and the rapid onset of wealth bred nothing but contempt for the poor.

He lifted one tired knee, maneuvering his body from the position of prayer to sitting on a pew. His strength had been drained in direct proportion to a significant loss in weight. All movement had been slowed to more than half by the invisible bulk of old age.

O'Kelly was cold, but not due to the weather. It was the soulless chamber that had once been *his* church, and a deadening sense of failure, that was chilling his spirit and sapping his strength. He asked the Lord for forgiveness. In this twilight year, aged seventy-six, he was compiling an inventory—a life lived well in the service of the Lord was marred by a pair of failings.

He had lost his church to Father Anlon Sheehan, and the interests of the wealthy had prevailed.

Mr. O'Doherty had been insistent and Father Sheehan supportive. Once upon a time, a ghost gum[65] afforded depth and dignity to the twenty-foot window behind the altar. But the O'Doherty family had wanted to share their riches through the gift of a stained-glass window, so the clear glass had to go.

The new window bore down on Father O'Kelly like a stage clown at the Port Town Show. There were so many gaudy shapes, so little thought put into how they should be arranged, and such intense clash of color, that it bullied his eyes into slits.

---

[65] A tall and majestic looking type of eucalyptus tree with white wood.

It was ever there to remind him of the rise of the rich. The church had sent Father Anlon Sheehan to care for him, and Sheehan had taken care of the wealthy.

O'Kelly remembered a less than ideal start.

"Father O'Kelly, it's an honor, and I mean sincerely an absolute honor, to share my first parish with a priest as distinguished as you."

"Distinction is not a quality that I would say befits me," O'Kelly had replied, on a summer day two years earlier. "But I will take it in the spirit in which it was meant."

They were strolling together from a platform at the new Town train station.

"Well, all I can hope to do is duplicate your work in building up the parish. There are some fine families here now, Father O'Kelly—some really renowned and very fine families indeed. And I'm looking forward to working with all of them and moving the parish forward."

O'Kelly moved on swiftly to what he viewed to be important.

"And what would you say about the Aboriginal people, Father Sheehan? Where do they fit in?"

Sheehan stopped still on the station platform.

"To be honest, Father, I've not given it much thought. Best not to interfere, I would suggest, and leave their fate to God."

O'Kelly's gut tightened at the memory of it—how a spray of sweat had appeared on his brow as if he'd been spat on the head by the devil.

The only saving grace, thought O'Kelly, *is that mad man Archibald Withers hasn't moved, again, against them.*

O'Kelly fired a shot across the banker's bow in February of 1923.

"How fortunate I set aside that plan to fund our ailing farmers," O'Kelly had said, when he ran into Withers in the street, "so what we have can now be diverted elsewhere."

"Do tell, Father," replied Withers, "are there others in the parish in need?"

"As a matter of fact, there are. I will need the resources to seek legal advice if they are persecuted or maimed. Here, I speak of our Aboriginal people, God's first inhabitants of this land."

So, he had told the Bishop that he would not move. He might have entered old age, but he would never quit the parish to fester to death in a home for the elderly in the south and abandon the Aboriginals. That meant Father John O'Kelly and the not-long-ordained Father Anlon Sheehan shared a parish and a home, but little else.

O'Kelly lowered his head, partly to pray but also to shield his eyes from the assault of color in the window. He was asking the Lord to bless him with the virtue of fraternal tolerance, when a hand pushed lightly on his shoulder.

"John," said Sheehan. "Please come. You've been here for more than two hours. I heard you shuffle out at first light. Mrs. Phillpot is serving breakfast."

O'Kelly smiled at Sheehan. He was not to see how he felt. "Have I really? Oh dear. Of course, I'll come, Anlon, if you would be kind enough to lend an arm to help me stand."

* * * * *

The annual church fete was about a month away. Nell was at work in the kitchen, depleting Rory's only bottle of fine Scotch whiskey. It was an annual ritual, in which an inch of liquor was blended through the jumble of nuts and flour, butter, and fruit she had dried herself that would soon become a cake. It was donated every year by the Burke family for the raffle. Her right forearm rose into muscular curves as it pushed a wooden spoon through the dough.

Nell kept beating. She turned away from the window giving out to the Jacaranda tree and toward the table behind her. Eleven-year-old Daisy sped into the kitchen from the corridor with Polly, aged seven, and four-year-old Patrick not far behind, swept along on a gale of giggles.

"Daisy Burke, I told you—you were to watch your baby sister for the first half hour when you came home from school. For goodness' sake, you're the eldest girl. Have you left her on the veranda?"

Nell put the bowl on the table and her hands on her hips.

"Yes, Ma," said Daisy, shooting past her mother toward the back door.

Before it could close behind Daisy, Polly grabbed it, hurtling down the stairs in pursuit. Patrick trailed her. Nell watched out of the window as her middle three continued the chase by circling the Jacaranda tree. Its hefty branches, adorned with clusters of pregnant buds, reached up to infinity blue.

Suddenly, Daisy disappeared. Seconds later, her head reappeared from behind a branch a third of the way up the Jacaranda tree. She had scaled it from the back, even though she knew she was not allowed to climb higher than the lowest of its branches.

Nell snapped the window open.

"Daisy Burke, if you don't get down now, you'll be in bed by seven with no pud and no story."

"Watch me, Mum."

Emboldened by the speed of her ascent, Daisy leapt. She landed, squarely, legs bent to perfect angles, fists punching straight as a die high.

Nell shook her head, wiped her hands on her apron, and went out to the side veranda to check on Grace Margaret Burke.

The baby signaled her hunger with a cry. Nell opened her blouse and settled on a sofa to nurse her. She was thankful for the four-year pause that had come between Grace and Patrick. Not that each child wasn't a blessing, but they had five to feed now, aged thirteen and under, since Eamon's birthday in March.

Yet, Nell hadn't lost sight of their great good fortune. There was still plenty of room for all of them. Grace slept in the room with her and Rory, leaving the boys' and girls' rooms sleeping only two children each. If Eamon left for boarding school in the Port Town after Christmas, Patrick would be left in a room of his own, a bit like a little prince.

From the side veranda, Nell could see they were in the honey of their lives. She and Rory had started out like a pair of fragile saplings, all alone and at the mercy of the winds. Now, the Burkes were like a well-built house: broad-based, solid, and safe.

Rory's corn crops stood firm and lush and promised a bumper yield. Up to the left, she could just catch a glimpse of one of the sloping paddocks on which they kept their cattle. The move to grazing from dairy farming had doubled their profits. And Rory had been one of the first western farmers to produce bacon and pork from a piggery, so he was nearly able to name his price.

The struggles and strains of their early marriage were like a bad and distant dream. Even Da had seen fit to pay a compliment when he and Ma came to visit at Easter.

"I know it's boom time for everyone, love, but you and Rory have done wonders with this place. I don't think I can make a single suggestion for bettering the profit you're getting from the land," said Hector to Nell in private.

"I appreciate the thought, Da, but you can direct your compliments to Rory. It's mostly been done by his hand, even if we planned it together."

But Hector hadn't done as Nell had asked.

I have to somehow get Da to come around, thought Nell, as she continued feeding Grace, *and share the truth with everyone about the content of his will.*

Nell kissed her baby on the forehead. If she were to secure what was rightfully hers, it had to be done in steps.

"This situation is no good, Da," Nell had said, on a freezing night in 1924 by the fireplace at Ballycallan. "I don't want Rory left in the dark over my fifth of the run. I'd tell him myself except I fear what he'd say — we're not to accept it until you've told my brothers that their quarter is going to be a fifth. Otherwise, he'll feel like a thief! Da, could you please put the boys in the know,[66] for me?"

Then, Hector surprised her with a blunt rebuke and withheld what she had needed.

"Have you ever heard, Nell, of not rockin' the boat?" he said. "Or that sleeping dogs should be left to lie? Taking the lid off that can of worms while I'm still living and breathing could well end in worse than tears, and you and Rory with nothing."

And whenever she asked Hector to reconsider, he simply wouldn't discuss it.

---

[66] To inform someone of something important of which they are unaware.

"Do you not think that your aging da is owed a turbulence-free retirement? I've given your kids a start in life with a little set of shares, and you a slice of Ballycallan. Isn't that enough?"

Nell sighed.

Da and I at least both see that this is tricky and delicate.

She hadn't a choice but to bide her time—for the right moment to compel Da to act. But, so far, that was yet to materialize, and it wasn't even on the horizon.

In the face of an imponderable, Nell drifted back to the concerns of the day. Was Eamon to go to senior school or prepare for, one day, running Jacaranda Ridge? And could Daisy be enticed into taking an interest in the art of keeping house?

Nell had looked at it every which way and couldn't find a solution. Could Eamon's departure from home be avoided or had she no choice but to let him go?

"Nell," Rory had said, the last time the subject was raised, "it comes down to one thing or the other. We finish him up and he learns the farmer's trade with me, or he leaves home and prepares for a profession."

It was late at night, and they were in the kitchen. A shawl of wintery evening gave Nell the courage to suggest the unthinkable.

"You know, Rory, the bus for that new government secondary school in Town will be stopping near us just down the road."

"So, what's that to us?"

"I don't know," said Nell. "It's just a shame, in a way, that the church doesn't encourage it for the Catholic children as well. It's a bit sad that all of our bright boys have to be sent away to the Port Town to board."

"Nell, you know I don't like the thought of him leaving either, but you can't be serious about makin' him take his schooling with the non-Catholics? He'd be out all on his own."

"I'm not," Nell had replied innocently. "I'm just saying it's a shame, that's all."

Baby Grace finished feeding, and Nell wiped her mouth. She knew she wasn't being sensible and, perhaps, not even fair. For goodness' sake, it had been her idea to get the primary school for the country children built in the first place! Without it, Eamon would have had almost no chance of moving on to secondary education. But they were all so precious, all five of her children. Could she bear to let Eamon go?

Daisy popped her head onto the veranda.

"Mum, me and Tommy Walsh wanna go play by the river and build a cubby-house. Can we go, Mum, can we go?"

"Daisy, your da will be back soon to take Tommy back to his grandma's. Why don't you go over to the Noonans' and play with the girls over there before we sit down to dinner?"

"Because dolls are boring," retorted Daisy.

"Daisy, they are not. They are lovely and exactly the sort of thing a young lady should be interested in."

"I'm gonna race Tommy to the river. See ya."

And Nell's eldest girl shot off.

Nell put Grace back in her bassinet, a smile playing around her mouth. She knew she couldn't object, not with any sincerity. She had been just like Daisy at that age.

But there was one big difference between her and Daisy. Nell's father hadn't been Rory.

* * * * *

Archibald Withers studied a table laid by his wife for afternoon tea.

He had become the bank's regional manager for the whole of the northwest, Leader of the Town Council, and chairman of the Chamber of Commerce. The boom transformed his ambitions, and no one was more surprised than him. A will to run the west-lands had crept up in stages, propelled by each surge in its wealth.

The Town had been joined to the statewide railway for just over two years. This, combined with the prolonged peace, attracted more merchants and tradesmen. The services available in the region were close to those offered in the Port Town. They were becoming a center of commerce.

Returning home to England, or the City, would mean climbing a ladder made by other men. By staying where he was, he could scale his own. This was where he would leave his mark.

The lace that covered the circular table was knitted by Millicent Withers. He leaned forward and touched it. The stitching was as firm as its pattern was intricate. She was thorough, was Millie—thorough and dependable. What a good decision he had made in asking her to wed. A lady once known as Millicent Brown, hand-picked from the Anglican community, now followed him in step. He'd a wife who, so far, gave no cause for trouble and who never let him down. Marriage into one of the wealthy families of the land, in the spring of 1926, was the honor of his life.

She was in the kitchen, making their tea and arranging a plate of fresh-out-of-the-oven biscuits. Withers looked out toward their garden through the curve of imported French windows. They gave out onto rows of roses, alternating between red and white.

I am glad, thought Withers, *that she pressed to set up what is becoming a family tradition.*

If he were ever constrained to work into the evening, he was to come home for afternoon tea. It kept them together as man and wife, even when he was deluged in work. Millie, he mused, was quickly maturing into a wife of trustworthy judgment.

She pushed open the drawing room door.

"Butternut snaps today," she said brightly, "and a date loaf to go with it. I baked it this morning—something heavy to keep you going at the bank past seven."

"That's perfect, darling," said Withers. "Let me take the tray."

He put it on the table and picked up the teapot to pour.

"Millicent, darling," he said. "When is the vicar due back from the mission?"

"Not for another fortnight."

She reached for her cup.

"Have you already grown tired of Sunday Bible group?"

"Not at all, Millie, not at all. Mr. Jones is doing a fine job with the text Reverend Parker assigned us. But I want to find out what's going on out at Parker's blasted mission."

"I know it's not ideal," said Millie. "But he can't be everywhere at once. He'll be here for the whole of Advent. That's the more important time of the year."

Withers stirred his tea.

"It's just that it has all been so terribly disappointing. Back in 1925, I thought I had him routed. Once I lost the battle on having the mission built at all but won the war of persuading the church to erect it a couple of days ride away, I felt able to give up resisting it. He bleated like a beaten lamb over the blacks living nowhere near us. But once he'd accepted it, I thought they'd be packed off in no time—cleared well out of the Town."

"And why do you think they haven't been?"

Millie passed him a biscuit.

"I don't know," said Withers. "But I have my suspicions. Either he's not trying hard enough, or they are simply being stubborn. The black men of this country aren't known for their gratitude for the charity of the whites and the great good fortune bestowed on them by the civilizing mission of the churches."

"That's certainly so," said Millie. "But my impression of Reverend Parker is that he would be slow to use a firm hand."

Withers looked at his wife across his teacup as her fork slid into her cake.

Well done, Archie. You selected the perfect mate.

"The sooner he gets all the natives off the land, the better," said Withers. "Things can't go on as they are. They are spoiling the drive into Town."

And I've been distracted for far too long, thought Withers, *by the unexpected boom. What's more, that impotent old priest O'Kelly is in a position no more to translate idle threat into action.*

Millie reassured him.

"It's all God's work, darling, but it's going to take time," said Millie. "We're just going to have to do our best of a Sunday in the meantime. But I do hate to see you disappointed."

"Disappointed I am indeed, my dear," said Withers. "But, perhaps, our Reverend can be chivvied along. It would be good to have him back."

* * * * *

Eamon was doing his afternoon chore in the pigpen. Most lads his age were assigned two jobs a day—one for the early morning and one toward the late afternoon. Dr. Dunne limited Eamon's to the second of these on account of his breathing. His wheezing remained chronic in late spring and early summer only, but it was a long way short of cured. So, Eamon did not rise in the small hours with Rory. He was not to be exhausted before school, but he joined his father in the afternoon to help out with the pigs.

"Son, make sure they get every drop of that feed. Some sat wastin' in the bottom of the pail yesterday," said Rory, as he swept sawdust from the floor.

"I will, Dad," replied Eamon.

Eamon shook an upturned bucket above the feeding trays.

Rory pushed the last of the sawdust to the side of the pigpen. It collected in mounds against the wall. He leaned the broom against it and tipped his hat back so it sat high on his brow. Now was as good a time as any to probe Eamon on whether he held any love for the land.

Could a way be found to make it the work of his life?

Rory joined Eamon at the fence.

"Do you enjoy your chores, son? I mean, on the way home from school, do you think about how glad you'll be to get out and spend some time on the land?"

"It's all right," said Eamon. "So much the better because it comes with your company."

Eamon placed the bucket by his feet and stepped onto the lower of the rungs dividing him and Rory from the pigs. He leaned over the fence. He wanted to watch the battle to feed.

"How would you be then if I wasn't here?" asked Rory, tentatively. "If you had to take care of Jacaranda Ridge yourself?"

"That'd be all right. Be a bit boring without you," said Eamon. "How would I cope with the work during the warm months?"

Eamon cupped his hands to make a rest for his chin.

"We could get you in some help, son—pay laborers, I mean—for the couple of months of the year when you can't work the land yourself. We've established the farm in profit, and I can't see it sliding back."

Eamon watched with detached fascination as pig snouts jostled and pushed in the trough. They were sucking and chugging at the slop they were fed as if it were nectar.

"I'm not sure I always want to live this far away from Town," said Eamon. "I don't know. Some of the lads at school say that life on the land's too hard—better off thinking about easier jobs with the banks or the government."

Part of Rory's soul deflated. Eamon was growing up into a townie, all right. But Jacaranda Ridge was their family property, and it had to be worked by one of his sons once he retired.

"You know, son, your grandfather scratched Jacaranda Ridge out of almost nothing. Before he came along, half of it was going to waste at the hands of the blacks. Nothing is more important than this work carrying on once I'm too old to do it."

"Daisy'd be better at that than me, Dad," said Eamon with a grin. "She'd work so hard that she'd have us dining with the O'Dohertys in no time."

"Well, Daisy'll be marrying one day and taking care of her own family. It'll be down to either you or Pat to take responsibility for all we've worked for."

This was all new territory for Rory. Of his eldest children, he'd one, a boy, who was already a teenager and whose future had to be planned, and another, a girl not far behind him. But neither of them was going to be easy—Eamon, because he probably couldn't be put into the ordinary role of the eldest son and carry on with the family farm, and Daisy, because she resisted every attempt to come off the land to learn how to keep house.

"Eamon, if you want that sort of life—that sort of desk job life—we'll have to get you more education. You reckon you could cope boarding down Port Town way? Or you might be able to live with your grandparents at Ballycallan and go to secondary school as a day boy?"

Rory watched Eamon and felt he knew what he was thinking. Could he bear leaving Nell? Could Eamon give up the hot cocoa that he shared with his mother every Thursday evening when his da went over to the Noonans' to play cards with the men? Was Eamon ready to abandon her comfort in the warm months, when his lungs gave way and all of them worried that he would not be able to breathe?

Rory watched the pigs. They were burying their snouts in the trough. Asthma didn't seem to be an illness suffered by them.

"I'll have to wait and see what the other boys decide," said Eamon, eventually. "I wouldn't want to go and live down Port Town way on my own."

Rory looked at Eamon's profile. He was showing signs of becoming a man, trying to work out where he should be and what he was ready for. But Rory rejoiced, albeit to himself. His boy Eamon had choice—*choice*—just like the wealthy folk from the vast runs further west. He could reckon through for himself what to do with his life. And it was all by the grace of the work of Sean and Hannah, and him and Nell. Rory put his hand on his fine lad's shoulder.

"Son, I'm going down to the workshop. Once you've cleared up, you're done for the day."

"Thanks, Dad," said Eamon, and stepped off the fence to complete his chores.

* * * * *

The new bank was the Town's first concrete building.

The timber structure of Withers' early trading had been dismantled and replaced in 1924 with an imposing monolith. Its two stories were coated in cream and finished at its edges in ruby red, dandifying the main street like a splendid pendant. The corners where the outer walls met were blunted to oblique by curves, in keeping with modern design. Steps made of slate rose from the street toward enormous double doors. They were lacquered in gold, and each of them was etched to the height of a man's head with depictions of wheat stalks, slender leaves scratched lightly around them.

Withers' enormous office was in the middle of the top floor, and both his desk and the room that housed it had trebled in size. Almost every item in the room was shiny, from floorboards to tables, walnut cabinets and chairs, and the black marble bust of the bank's long-dead founder. It sat in the middle of the far back wall, opposite Withers' new work post. The king remained hung, in dignified portrait, above the enormous desk.

A double brick wall, facing the street, housed a vast pane of glass. It was handily appended on each interior side by a narrow supporting wall. From there, Withers could watch the goings on down in the street without fear of being seen.

But his idyllic view of the perfection of commerce was blighted. Some of them were loitering at each pristine end of his beautiful, soon-to-be-bitumen, Town main street.

Lazy bloody blacks.

"I will clear you off if it kills me," muttered Withers, into brightening morning light.

He turned to the map of the region lying open on his desk. It was fully updated, given to him by the natives' Protector during his winter visit. The banker backed his chair to the window and studied it.

How he admired the intricacy of the Imperial cartographer's record. Everything was marked. Every river, every stream, every undulation, from each bare skerrick of a hill to mountains, and every suggestion of a gathering of dwellings fit to be called a town. With his own red pencil, Withers circled the missions set up in his region for the salvation of the blacks. The shelters in the bush in which many of them still lived had been marked by the Protector, a few weeks before, in blue.

It was going to be easier than Withers thought: Presbyterian sixty miles to the southwest, Lutheran due west fifty-five miles, Church of England due south seventy miles, Roman Catholic southeast seventy-five miles, and Baptist due east fifty miles. They formed a helpful arc, and there was a railway station seventy miles to the south of the Town, at a village called Purgatory Creek. From there, all missions could be accessed by road.

He pulled on the handle of the left-hand drawer. It obliged by gliding toward him. The carefully laid out tools of his trade were ready. Pens with gold nibs, inkwells, pencils, rubbers, sharpeners, rulers and slide ruler, magnifying glass, binoculars, and a slim silver-tipped compass.

He picked out the compass and allowed its tip to drop on the post office, spiking that repellant Republican who masqueraded as a postmaster. Withers twisted its ribbed steel tip so the pencil encircled the Town to a diameter of a hundred miles.

Once I am done, the white man will be protected by a sphere of the civilized of over one hundred glorious miles!

This was more of a buffer than he had hoped for.

He put down the compass and walked to the window. He looked out of it, pondering.

A forceful word was required with the Town's delinquent policeman.

Sergeant Brian O'Keefe was a burly man with an unfortunate passion for whiskey. But he was unencumbered by commitment to wife or children and held no firmly felt beliefs.

He had been in the Town for almost five years and had proven contempt for principles. Prosecute crimes committed against the poor? Not likely. Turn a blind eye to a first offender? Only if connected to power and money.

And he had already displayed unerring vigilance in punishing the blacks.

"Why, that is excellent, Sergeant O'Keefe. Really excellent," Withers had said when he first came by for advice. "The black man is bound to comply with our laws. If he thieves, he must be jailed. This is a matter which has been overlooked that can be corrected now you are here."

But far too few of them have been caught so far, thought Withers, *with one of their filthy hands in the cream can.*

How many men could he muster to move them out, and where could they be stored in the interim? He didn't want it turned into an exhibition. Could O'Keefe see to their transfer over the Christmas to New Year holiday, when most of the townsfolk were at the seaside? He would assure O'Keefe that both the Chamber of Commerce and the Council would commend him for his work once the task was complete.

There is only one way to deal with a fellow like O'Keefe, thought Withers. *Play it crude.*

He wasn't going to beat around the bush. Simply tell him what's in it, irresistibly, for him, then command him to shut his trap. O'Keefe was so poorly thought of, he simply wouldn't be believed if he ever decided to squeal.

What's more, O'Keefe was a Roman Catholic. He could provide leverage with that group of townsfolk that might otherwise elude him.

As for the Anglicans, he would deal with them via Parker. They shouldn't pose a problem. Escalation in effort toward the blacks' redemption, during the holy days of Christmas, was likely to appeal. But how it was presented was crucial, given Parker's endless waxing about "humanity" and "dignity".

Dust kicked up with every passing motor vehicle and horse-drawn cart. There had been little rain of late, and it was becoming a white light of a day. He squinted, trying to follow the Town's machinations beyond a rising screen of desiccated soil. It persisted on dry days, almost seditiously, as if attempting to enmesh the settlers into the parchment of the land.

Withers gasped.

My goodness, Mr. Rory Burke is entering Christopher Miller's jewelry store. Whatever he is buying, it can't be from Miller's top shelf!

He had done well enough in the boom, but not so well that he could be buying jewels for his wretch of a wife.

What a timely reminder, thought Withers.

The lily-livered bugger had avoided him, assiduously, since the summer of 1922. He came into the bank only once a fortnight and only ever dealt with a teller.

"Speaking of squealing," muttered Withers, as he leaned closer to the window, "did you go crying off to Father O'Kelly in 1923?"

At minimum, Burke was a bloody liar, but his come uppance would keep. He was untrustworthy, and was to be excluded from the just demise to which the blacks would be subjected at Christmas.

Withers' thoughts were disrupted, again, but this time by something that pleased him. Reverend Parker drove into Town. From the state of his sulky, and the exhausted demeanor of his horse, Withers guessed he was returning from the mission.

There was a knock at the door.

"Come in," said Withers, still looking out at the street.

"Mr. Withers, sir, I have today's mail. Is there anything yet to go out?"

Richard placed the letters on the desk.

"Not quite, Richard, but please sit down. I am going to draft a note for delivery later today."

From the right-hand drawer, Withers took out watermarked paper, and from the left, a gold-tipped pen. The inkwell on his desk brimmed in blue. He wrote:

Dear Reverend Parker,   *27ᵗʰ September 1928*

I was delighted to notice, by chance, your return through the main street of our Town today. May I be one of the first of our congregation to wish you a very welcome home.

Mr. Jones has done a marvelous job with the Sunday Bible group. However, I am sure I am not alone in saying we are delighted that the full service will resume in the lead-up to the birthday of our Lord.

I was wondering if you would give me the pleasure of tea at the bank one afternoon at your earliest convenience, once you are settled back in at home.

Yours ever,

Archibald Withers Esq.

He folded the note into an envelope. He addressed it to "The Reverend Ian Parker: by hand" and passed it over to Richard.

"See to it that this is dropped at the Vicar's home during the course of the day. And I am unavailable for farm visits for the next fortnight."

"Yes sir," said Richard, and left.

* * * * *

Nell watched the sphere of warming milk that occupied a black iron pan. Clinging, it was, to the flats of tepid, as if loath to come to the boil. Then, a skirt of bubbles broke its film and ran around the edges. Nell grabbed the handle with a well-gloved hand and poured its hot fluid into cups.

Eamon sat at Rory's seat at the family kitchen table. It was an unwritten privilege of a Thursday evening. When Rory was at Dave's playing cards with the men, Eamon could assume his place.

"Must add cocoa to the shopping list," said Nell. "There's just enough here for a full cup each, but there will be no second dibs tonight."

"I won't be wanting another, Mum," said Eamon. "Jimmy Murphy lost a round of marbles when we were playing outside at lunchtime. Silly bugger bet me a stick of chocolate, and I ate the lot after dinner."

Nell handed her son his drink.

"Eamon, you should have saved some of it, and you know that I don't like you betting. You boys should be playing just for pleasure and not to take things from one another."

"Best to tell that to Jimmy, Mum," said Eamon. "He's always up for a wager."

The buzz of unstoppable western insects was uncut by four walls and a roof. The kitchen floated on the hum of the night, as mother and son meandered into talk of the plans to be made for next year.

"You know, Eamon, I've counted 'em up, and you've something to be proud of. It's twenty-three months since your father and I had to have words about you losing your temper."

Eamon stirred his cocoa, breaking the gathering film.

"You mean, when Dad clean bowled me in the Noonans' yard and I kicked the stumps for six?[67]"

"That was it," said Nell with a hint of a smile. "And we made you spend the rest of the day at home."

Eamon put his spoon to the table and the delicious liquid to his lips. If the truth be known, it frightened him, what he called the dragon, and he hoped himself it was gone—a surge of rage that came from nowhere and pushed his body to a shudder.

Nell noticed Eamon's mood dipping a little and steered him back to the table.

"So, when you boys aren't gambling, do you speak much about the future? We're just a few months from the end of school, so there's a lot to be sorted out."

Eamon put his cup back down and thought about what to say. They were like a tag team of some sort, his mother and his father, and worked as a perfect pair. One knew exactly where to start again where the other had left off. Had his dad told his mum about their talk up in the pigsty? Eamon presumed that it would have been so and proceeded as if he had.

---

[67] Literal meaning is to hit a ball in the air over the outer boundary of a cricket field, scoring six runs. It is often used as a metaphor for driving something a long way.

"You know, Mum," he said, "I don't mind the land, but I'm not sure it's the life for me. But I'm not wrapped either about going down south for years to a boarding school."

Nell looked into her lovely son's face, his reticence visible in the gaslight.

"What is it, Eamon?" asked Nell gently. "I'm not surprised you don't want the land. I've never felt it drew you. But have you really had enough of study and books, or is it just that you want to stay here?"

Eamon ran a finger along the rim of his cup.

"Mum, did you ever realize that when I was a small boy, I was frightened to fall asleep?"

Nell frowned and put down her cup.

"You were what?"

"Mostly frightened to go off to sleep—scared that while I wasn't awake, my lungs would seize, and I'd stop breathing—maybe never wake up."

Nell put her hand in front of her mouth and managed to hide her shock. She'd coddled him, rocked him, rubbed his back, and waited until all seemed calm. But now, it seemed she hadn't relieved all the grief Eamon had suffered.

"No, I didn't, Eamon," said Nell softly. "But I can see why you felt as you did."

How Nell wanted to go sit by her first-born son, put an arm around his drooping shoulder, and provide a mother's comfort. But Eamon was on the verge of becoming a man, and the time for mothering had passed.

Eamon looked up from his drink.

"Mum, this problem I've got—my difficult breathing when the weather turns warm—do you think they'll ever find a cure?"

Nell's eyes teared a little and her throat needed a clear.

She coughed.

"I don't know, Eamon," said Nell quietly. "One day, I would hope, but perhaps not soon. Dr. Dunne says you might grow out of it, so let's hope that's not far off."

Nell poked with a spoon at the chocolate sediment gathering at the base of her cup. Eamon didn't deserve this cross. Nell kept praying he'd be rewarded one day with perfectly good health, but that was yet to be granted.

"Do you think, Mum, if I went to the Port Town school, there would be someone there to help me—someone to get me through the worst and make sure I can carry on breathing?"

Nell leaned forward.

"There is one thing I am able to promise you, Eamon. Your father and I won't be letting you go unless the care you need is there."

"And what will we do if it isn't?"

"Let's cross that bridge when we come to it, but there's no chance in the world that your father and I would ever send you off to harm's way."

Then, Nell let Eamon lead the discussion, sharing thoughts on the subjects he might study. But all the while, the tempting alternative kicked around the back of her mind. That secondary school being built by the government might yet hold the answer.

* * * * *

CHAPTER 10
STRATEGIES
October 1928

For the most part, it looked like a jumble of junk.

Rory strolled along a row of trestles, disappointed. He was looking for a watch for Eamon—a gift to be passed from father to son and paid for only by him. The new ones he'd looked at in Mr. Miller's store were beyond the funds in his smokes tin. But there wasn't a secondhand watch on offer at the Catholic church fete.

The Catholics turned out once a year to sell what no longer served them. Thirty percent of the takings went to the church, and the sellers pocketed the rest. The churchyard was abuzz with potential buyers, but so much of it was rubbish that the takings would be slim. There were used shoe brushes, battered belts, and faded ties—all laid out neatly on pressed cotton sheets, to the end of fetching tuppence, thruppence, or the high price of a shilling. Rory thanked God that the Burkes belonged in the band of families donating something for raffle rather than folk who advertised their need.

The shade beneath the stairs leading up to the sacristy beckoned him. Rory ambled toward it.

Oh well, he thought, as he rolled a cigarette and squatted in the cool. *This isn't the last of my tobacco until Christmas after all.*

There was no point now in using his smokes money. If Eamon were to be presented with a watch, it would have to be new and paid for out of family funds. He'd return to Christopher Miller's and buy it, once the news had been broken to Nell.

Eamon was going to board at the Port Town school. It was the only option they had.

Rory looked at his eldest son in the gaming corner. He was playing cards with three other lads under a moleskin tarpaulin. There was no sign yet of a cough or a wheeze. The spring was late and wasn't yet upon them. Rory could hear the youngsters engaged in the manly art of betting through a game of poker played with cards and shells.

"I'll raise you two on that," one of the boys said.

"Well, I'll see you," replied Eamon.

Then, he scooped up his winnings.

"You gotta get up early in the morning to put one over a Burke!" cried Eamon jubilantly.

Rory drew long and slow from his cigarette. Eamon wasn't a farmer, with or without asthma. He wasn't even an outdoors type. Rory had never once seen him run out onto the land, not even in winter, nor had he ever objected to being kept from the farm in the morning on the orders of Dr. Dunne. It was just as Eamon had said. The land wasn't the attraction for him. It was the spending of time with his da. Eamon lacked the drive he would need to keep the farm in profit.

Rory looked around the churchyard. Some of the parishioners took tea beneath the thick fan of foliage made by the low and shady tree in the middle of it, and where his children's school had been planned. Rory reckoned that the Burkes were doing better than most. They weren't in the league of the craftsmen like the Murphys and would never do as well as the farmers from the big runs further west. But they were miles ahead of the Town's newcomers, the salaried workers, and the small-time traders. There was no shame in being a Burke.

And his son Eamon was good enough, all right, for the Port Town school for boys. The time had come for the Burke family to produce a man of learning.

Up to Rory's right, in a thicket of scrub, he heard something rustle. And then, by a rock that was surrounded by bushes, a pair of jet-black heads popped up. The fine hairs on the back of Rory's neck bristled and God snatched away his breath. The Aboriginal boys right before his eyes could not have been more than ten. By the grace of God, he hadn't killed them in 1922.

Rory remembered what he would have done before his brush with the gates of hell. He'd have walked towards them, waved his arms, and shooed them back into the bush. They had to be stopped from piercing the film between the world of the whites and their own. But now, Rory blanked the Aboriginals out—he'd walk across the other side of the road when they huddled by the curbside. It was all too raw, still too close, to that terrible, lonely summer.

Nell's voice could be heard above the rabble. She carried her Christmas cake in a basket with the ease of the long-accepted Rory's good girl, Polly, sat next to Grace in her bassinet by the trunk of the low and shady tree. Polly was reading a book. Patrick followed his mother, circling her skirt like an erratic planet. He ran off every now and then to pull on the leg of a trouser or the hem of a skirt of someone other than his mother and then shot back to hide behind Nell.

"Yes, that's right, Thell. The whiskey I used this year has come all the way from Europe. Rory finished the bottle that was brewed in the City a couple of months ago. So, I bought him a new one from Scotland by post. I ordered it in the catalogue."

"So, Nell, if we win your Christmas cake this year, we'll be eating fruit soaked in whiskey from the other side of the world?"

"Too right you will. Too right."

"Well, in that case, the Walshes will have three tickets, please. No, you can make that four."

What a difference, thought Rory, *that row of numbers inked in black in our ledger make to the way we live.*

The black ink had trebled when compared with November of 1922, when they paid out their loan. Back then, the Burkes had teetered at the cusp of ruin, and Rory vowed they would never return there.

He looked up and watched the birds flying above. Some swooped, others fluttered from branch to leafy branch, pitting the foliage with dashes and darts. How would Nell take it once he told her that Eamon was to go away to board? Rory knew full well what it meant; subjecting Nell to something never suffered by Hannah, splitting her from her first-born son as he started to become a man. There might be a row, and tears, no risk, but she'd come around in the end. There was one thing Rory could be sure of in his wife; what was best for their children came first.

"Hey, Rory, getter over here," called Dave Noonan from the other side of the churchyard. "There's an advert here for a saddle. You're lookin' to buy one, aren't you?"

Rory walked toward the notice board. It was almost two o'clock and just about time for a beer.

"G'day, Dave," said Rory, as he scanned the scrabble of notes. "Too right I am, but where is it?"

"You a blind man?" said Dave. "It's there, bang in the center. Being sold by our own Billy Murphy."

"Good-O," said Rory. "I'll ask him about it when I next see him. We headed to the Imperial? I reckon we've put in enough of an appearance here."

"Agreed," replied Dave. "Just lemme go and tell Charlotte. She's out the front selling toffee apples."

Dave jogged off. Rory lingered over the adverts. There was plenty to sell, all right—stuff too big to be laid out on trestles. Then, his attention was caught by a notice in the corner.

> *Dance Classes with Madame La Bonne. European-trained expert in all forms of dance offers preparatory classes for girls and young ladies. Small groups and one-on-one tuition available. Be the belle of the ball and not a wallflower! For all enquiries, come to 52 Renforth St. Classes commence soon!*

"There's something to think about," muttered Rory.

Miss Daisy Burke was nowhere to be seen and was probably off climbing trees. Learning to dance might be just the thing to help ease her off the land. But, first, he would deal with persuading Nell into position over Eamon.

* * * * *

Nell brushed crumbs of cake and biscuit off a linen tablecloth. She held it up, gave it shake, and folded it into the basket that had carried the Christmas cake. The winner had claimed it just an hour before. One of the townies had the lucky ticket and left the fete happy that her Christmas table would be bettered by country cooking. Nell felt sorry for all of them—the folk who didn't live off the land. They passed their existence in homes like boxes, then earned their way by working in another.

Across the all-but-empty churchyard, Nell could see her two parish priests. They were seated in the middle of a bench under the low and shady tree. The midspring night was gliding in gracefully, rather than falling like a platform with its supports kicked away, as it did in winter.

I had better move in now, thought Nell, *before Father Sheehan takes in Father O'Kelly for an early evening meal.*

Most of the congregation had returned to their homes. Charlotte had found a quiet spot on the presbytery veranda and was counting the takings and minding Grace, while her own girls played nearby. Nell's other children had gone to the Walshes. So, she had both priests to herself.

"Can I rest with you a little, Father? My Rory will be back from the pub in no time to pick me up, but my legs are a little weary."

She sat at the end of the bench.

"That comes as no surprise, Mrs. Burke," said O'Kelly.

He leaned forward on his cane toward her.

"You worked the churchyard today like the best of the bookies[68] at the races."

"How much was raised this year?" asked Father Sheehan.

"Charlotte's still counting the takings of the day, but she's already tallied the raffle. Three and six,[69] she said it came to. Double the funds from the Burke Christmas cake last year."

"Well done," said Sheehan. "The more we can help ourselves in the parish without going to the Bishop, the better."

"The parishioners here are always willing to do their bit, Father," said Nell. "And the Bishop's got more than enough on his plate, what with the boarding school in the Port Town to

---

[68] People who run a business taking bets.
[69] Three shillings and sixpence.

fund, as it seems to be growing and growing. Have you any idea of the number of boys committed to attending it next year?"

O'Kelly replied swiftly. He wanted to cut off Father Sheehan, who had parted his lips to speak.

"Seven hundred and fifty-eight, twelve of which hail from this parish," the old priest said proudly.

"That many already?" said Nell. "And only five years since it opened its doors."

"Five and a half to be exact, Mrs. Burke," said Sheehan. "And what a success it's been."

"That's our next big decision," said Nell. She sat back deeper into the bench. "Whether Eamon's to join Rory on the land or head off to the Port Town to board."

"He's a fine boy, and bright enough to matriculate,[70] according to Mr. Geharty," said O'Kelly. "And he's not a lenient schoolmaster. So, will he be going south with the other boarders, or is he more a type for the land?"

Nell moved her basket from her lap to the ground and smoothed the wrinkles in her skirt.

"If the truth be known, Father, he's not. It's early days yet, and he's only just short of five years of age, but our land's more likely to be worked by Pat when Rory retires. He's full of energy, has no breathing problems, and loves the outdoors. But the worry over the Port Town school for Eamon is its distance. I'm dreading having him so far from home, what with his asthma to think of."

"There's nothing to be concerned with on that front," chimed in Sheehan. "There is an excellent nurse at the Port Town school and an infirmary. Eamon will be in safe hands."

---

[70] To graduate from high school.

Nell teetered on the edge of a precipice. Could she stop herself from crossing, again, a boundary that a wife should never breach? The answer was that she couldn't, not after what Eamon had said at cocoa.

"I don't doubt that, Father," said Nell. "But it will be so much harder for Eamon, coping on his own. It's a shame, in a way, that we can't send him along to the new government secondary school here in Town."

A wedge of silence that fell from nowhere stopped the conversation dead. Sheehan ran a hand, exasperated, through a shock of his golden-blond locks, and even the square of his jaw seemed to stiffen.

"But Mrs. Burke," he said, "it is, for all intents and purposes, a *Protestant* school. Surely, you are not advocating the mixing of our children with a community of non-Catholics in the adolescent years? The church must do its duty and guide the boys to manhood!"

Nell stammered out an answer.

"No, not at all, Father—that wasn't my meaning at all. I simply meant that a Protestant family in our position wouldn't have the same dilemma. And I was just thinking that we could perhaps teach our boys the scripture at a Sunday school if some of them attended the government facility here."

O'Kelly rested his cane on the side of the bench and took Nell's trembling hand. The smooth of his voice oozed into the chill in the air like warm water replenishing a bath.

"You're a blessed woman, Mrs. Burke, and the thought you have shared wasn't sinful. I can only imagine the pain of a mother bidding farewell to a first-born child who hasn't had perfect health. But you're not to overreact. He will be cared for well down Port Town way. There's no chance Eamon will be neglected."

Rory drove his sulky into the gate of the churchyard. Nell reached for her basket and stood.

"Thank you, Father, you've given me comfort. And I've just seen my Rory come to fetch me. Good day, Father Sheehan. Good day, Father O'Kelly."

"Good day, Mrs. Burke," replied the priests in unison.

"And safe travels," added Father O'Kelly.

* * * * *

"The greatest difficulty lies in preventing them from running away. They are fleet of foot and are still able to speak in impenetrable languages."

The Reverend Ian Parker was at the bank for afternoon tea, as had been requested by Withers. He was relieved, and a little surprised, to find a sympathetic ear in his local banker. It wasn't completely in character for Withers to be sensitive to the challenges confronting his mission.

Parker wondered.

Has marriage started to better him?

Parker sat opposite the banker, who was seated at his desk.

"To where do they run?" asked Withers. "After all, surely the mission provides them with all they need?"

"I have seen to it that it does. They live in clean, if humble, dwellings. There is an infirmary, a chapel, and I even have plans for a playing field on which they might learn the games of white men," replied Parker. "But they sometimes get together in packs, in what seem to be family or language groupings, and disappear back into the bush. Some of the shelters supplied by the Protector out there are still standing, and they set up camp in those. Or they simply make their own."

Parker reached for one of Millicent's home-baked biscuits.

"Please do help yourself, Reverend," said Withers hastily. "So, do they never abscond alone?"

"Almost never. We tend to pick them up in groups, then keep them together as much as possible. There's no other way. It would be cruel to break them up. And it's better to work on their conversion to Christianity in familial units. They almost never come in individually either."

"Indeed, Reverend, it would be callous to separate them, and I can see the wisdom in a collective approach to their redemption. Please, let me pour you more tea."

Withers was playing for time. He might have just learned something significant.

"Don't mind if I do," said Parker.

"So, Reverend, what you are saying is that the poor wretches who *are* alone, who have somehow been split from their clan, are far less likely to abscond?"

Parker nodded.

"Indeed, that's right," he replied. "The church becomes their home. Archie, do forgive me, but while I am delighted by your turn toward an interest in our missionary work, I am rather wondering where all this is headed?"

"And you are right to do so," replied Withers, smugly. "Reverend, it's just that I have been thinking—perhaps, we in the broader community could be doing more to help you in pursuit of the work of God."

"Archie, I am always open, and indeed grateful, for any offers of help," said Parker.

Withers pushed on.

"You know, I do these home visits in the countryside. It's an essential part of my work, making sure that all of the bank's customers are satisfied. And I can attest to the fact that despite your Christian efforts, there are many camps of natives still dotted around our region, and one as close as the river that flows through the western edge of the Town. May I show you? I've a map that's been marked up by the Protector."

Withers didn't wait for an answer and pulled the map from his middle drawer. He opened it on the desk.

"Here. The poor wretches are probably still scattered in approximately half a dozen groupings within about nine miles of the Town."

Withers turned the map so Parker could see it.

"Slightly more than I would have expected," said Parker.

"But my guess, after what you have said, is that some of these are returns who have failed to settle in the missions," said Withers.

"Of course," conceded Parker.

The vicar began to worry. Withers was entering territory in which he might do more harm than good.

"But Archie, we have the added problem in our region of the distrust they have in the whites, which is probably why they won't settle in the missions. Something to do with that early incident involving the O'Doherty family—two of the sons dying in suspicious circumstances. Perhaps they have gotten wind of the fact they are still blamed for it by the whites. A more likely reason for absconding, I would say."

Withers cocked a doubting eyebrow. Parker squirmed a little in his chair.

"There's not much we can do for the moment, Archie," said Parker.

He put down his tea.

"Despite everything, our little Anglican mission is almost full of people from the lands further south, and the missionaries are struggling to maintain order. We can tolerate some expansion, but only prudently."

"But Reverend, this is where I say we have been short-sighted," persisted Withers. "As you can also see from the map, there are four other missions in addition to ours in the region—one Catholic, one Presbyterian, one Baptist, and one Lutheran. If we work together, we could have all the natives settled in civilized quarters within a few short weeks."

Parker pulled on his beard.

"Who precisely might 'we' be?"

"We the community, and we all the religions. I am speaking now as Leader of the Council. Have you considered, for example, enlisting the help of Sergeant O'Keefe and some of his men and distributing the native families among the churches?"

"I can't say I had," replied Parker, dryly.

Now, his good humor was waning. He would never cross a man of Withers' standing, but handing Aboriginals over to faiths in which he did not believe was where he drew a line. And as important as Sergeant O'Keefe might be to the Town, Parker had not taken to him. Their rotund, burnt-orange, officer of the law was too fond of drink and too reliant on bullying for his liking.

Withers sensed he was losing Parker—realized he had failed to anticipate resistance. He had been too abrupt, moved forward too quickly, and irritated him.

Withers tacked back.

"Good gracious, I have lost all sense of time. We are only minutes away from my four-thirty appointment."

"I must be away in any event," said Parker. "I owe time at home after all these weeks away."

Withers saw Parker to the teeming street. At the doorway, he watched his vicar drive off and worked out how to get him on side.

All I need do is surround you, Parker. You haven't the spine to resist a pack.

He turned and handed Richard the outbound post for the morning. The top letter was addressed "by hand" to Sergeant Brian O'Keefe.

* * * * *

"Polly, keep quiet. You'll wake them up and spoil everything."

Polly was giggling. Patrick had drawn the shape of a red ball. It was supposed to be Father Christmas. He wouldn't be traveling down anyone's chimney if he were really that size.

"I can't help it if Pat's drawings are stupid," whispered Polly.

"Don't you call me stupid," little Pat hit back. "And who said you were such a smarty?"

"Shut up," hushed Eamon. "It's supposed to be a surprise."

Daisy was the mastermind. She had found an old kerosene lamp under the desk in Rory's workshop—one that her parents wouldn't miss. She concealed it behind the bedroom cupboard, along with a set of spare matches from the kitchen. The children met in the girls' room just after midnight, when their parents were sure to be asleep. Each of them planned to make them a Christmas card. They would then be hidden and, later, Eamon would carry them in his satchel on their way to Ballycallan.

It had been easy to keep it from Nell. Daisy took colored pencils, paper, glue, and scissors from the play-box on the side veranda. The only people who ever looked into it were the children. She hid them in the space beneath the floor and the bottom of the girls' chest of drawers.

"How 'bout this?" Polly whispered, as she held up a picture drawn on her knees on their bedroom floor.

"That's lovely, Polly—four perfect reindeer. How did you learn to draw so well?" asked Daisy.

"From a book at school. I traced them, then I added the shapes," replied Polly proudly.

"My Father Christmas isn't so bad, is it Eamon?" asked Patrick.

His brother held it up to the light.

"I wouldn't say that was so terrible at all," said Eamon. "It's at least as good as mine."

Patrick beamed.

"Daisy, what are you drawing?" asked Polly.

Polly was curled up next to her big sister. Daisy had managed to start her own drawing now the little ones were done.

"It's a Christmas tree. With big green leaves, a star, and snow falling all around it."

"Does it always snow in the North Pole, even in summer?" asked Patrick.

Eamon and Daisy looked at one another. Neither was sure how to explain it.

"It's not summer in the North Pole. It's coming into winter," said Eamon.

"How can it be winter?"

Pat's cherubic face contorted.

"Well, because the seasons aren't the same in all parts of the world. We have summer from December to February, but in the North Pole, it's winter."

"That's sad," said Pat. "That means they can't go to the beach for Christmas holidays."

"Well, not everybody can," said Eamon. "Not everyone is as lucky as us."

Just then, there was a muted thud as the lamp hit the floor. It fell from a low wooden stool.

"You idiot, Pat," said Eamon, grabbing the lamp quickly. "You knocked it over when you stood up."

"Why is everyone picking on me?" said Pat. "It's not fair."

"We are not picking on you, " said Eamon. "I just don't want a fire started."

Daisy took command. She didn't want the secret project sprung by a stroll down the hallway from her parents.

"Shhh. Come on everybody," whispered Daisy. "We're done. Help me clean up. But do it *quietly* so we don't wake them up."

* * * * *

Rory and Nell lay in bed and smiled. Grace slept in her crib beside them, while the insects rattled through the still of a cool spring night.

"They won't burn the house down, will they, love?" asked Rory.

"I checked the old lamp, Rory. It's as safe as any of them," replied Nell.

"Bit early this year, aren't they?" said Rory. "Plannin' for Christmas in October?"

"Thellie's just been teaching the kids how to make gift cards. Ours, I guess, are a bit quicker off the mark than the rest."

The candles lit in their marital bedroom had almost burnt to their base. Rory slipped back into his own thoughts as the beat of the night drew him in. His kids had so much more than he and his sisters in childhood. The two beds in which the six Burke children had slept were shoved up one end of the shack. There had been no closed-off room in which Rory and his sisters could play. So, for them, games had always occurred outside, and in daylight, their adventures driven by whatever they could find in the scrub.

And it occurred to Nell, as she listened, how little her children had in comparison with her and her brothers. The Christmas of the year in which she turned ten, they were gifted a kit for painting in oil and an easel to go with it. None of Nell's four brothers, or she, had much of a talent for painting. But Da was determined his brood would enjoy all the amusements of the coast's upper-class.

That easel, thought Nell, *sat outside forever and was barely ever touched.*

Eventually, her mother took up painting, gracing the vista of Ballycallan with evidence of a creative presence.

And her parents' rambling homestead had more nooks and crannies to encourage indoor play than any child could wish for. But her kids had only their bedrooms and the verandas, the drawing room being off-limits to play without the supervision of an adult.

A homestead was what Jacaranda Ridge needed. If the boom carried on, they might put it on the rise in the terrain that Nell had selected when Eamon was an infant. And it was timely now for another reason. Rory would need all the help he could get, including the aid of an eldest son, if only to fetch and carry. Eamon couldn't help them put up a homestead if he were boarding down at the Port Town.

And if that doesn't work out, thought Nell, *the Burke family homestead could be funded, eventually, from my share of Ballycallan.*

"Rory," said Nell. "Do you think it might be time to start thinking about building a new house? We'll likely be blessed with more children than the five we already have. Could we fit it in, Rory, do you think, building ourselves a homestead with running the farm?"

"Dunno, love," said Rory. "Hadn't crossed my mind. The problem is time and helpers. I can't neglect the farm, love, and I've no spare time. If we paid Billy Murphy to do it, that'd wipe out a lot of our savings."

Nell rolled closer to Rory and stroked his chest.

"I guess if Eamon were here, he'd be able to lend a hand. If we waited, that is, until we were clear of the months in which he gets ill."

Rory was about to return Nell's caress but stopped. That morning he had given Eamon's application for enrollment in the Port Town school to Father Sheehan. He had planned to let Nell know as soon as the subject was raised. But now a glut in his throat and a heaviness of tongue held him back.

"Nell, love," he said tentatively. "I think you have to let go of this idea that Eamon will be around forever. He's becoming a grown man. We're to let him decide for himself what his future will bring. If the Port Town school will have him, we can't stop him from goin' off to study."

Nell stopped stroking and sat upright so she could see Rory's face.

"I'm not talking about taking his future off him. There's plenty of future for him here. Our area's booming. It's just a bit barmy that we have to send him all the way down south if he's to get more education when there's a brand-new school right here."

Rory sat up as well, so he could see his wife. He loved her for her dash of the wild, but all this grasping at keeping Eamon at home had to be batted away.

"Nell," he said gently, "that government secondary school may as well be on Mars. No Burke child will ever set foot in it. It's for the church to see our children right when it comes to education."

The last of the candles lighting their bedroom went out. They both lay back down, so Rory didn't see the film of fluid that had started to lacquer Nell's eyes. She closed them to prevent the onset of tears and nestled at Rory's shoulder. A lonely wish to reverse the inevitable was yet to be extinguished.

What this calls for, thought Nell, *before I declare the battle lost, is a bit of a chat with Charlotte.*

* * * * *

A body can bulge in many ways, and Sergeant Brian O'Keefe managed all of them. The purple ripples cracking across his nose betrayed the blight in his smaller blood vessels. The pockmarks turning inward, and the white-capped nodules pushing out, were the result of long-term crowding in skin never thoroughly scrubbed. His gritty mop of hair, the color of unwashed carrots, leapt ungainly from a colossal head, contracting that day only because he was capped for duty. And his greasy shirt was pulled tightly around a tub of a torso kept upright, precariously, on spindle legs.

Birdy the black-tracker was sweeping the reception area of the Town's police station. O'Keefe, with an ink pad, worked through a pile of papers at the counter. He smoked as he stamped his way through them.

Birdy had been with the sergeant for roughly a dozen changes of season. O'Keefe had come across him in the bushland, with an injured leg and a badly bruised arm, but with no one around to help him. It had never even occurred to O'Keefe to ask the black man what had happened.

O'Keefe looked the fit but scrawny fellow up and down and saw he was well made. He might have stumbled into just what he needed. With food, water, and some fitful draws on police-issue tobacco, he tempted the little bloke onto the back of his saddle. Birdy, he had called him from that day forward, like a sparrow with a broken wing.

"Stables need a sweep, boss?" asked Birdy, leaning on his broom.

"Not a bad idea, Birdy. Cup of tea would be nice first," replied O'Keefe.

"Sure thing, boss," said the black-tracker, quickly.

Just then, Richard arrived. He ignored Birdy. For him, the Aboriginal man was but an oily smear against a chalk-white wall. The bank clerk removed his cap out of respect for the sergeant, and Birdy left the room via the tradesman's door at the rear.

"Morning, Sarge. Paperwork keeping you off the streets?" asked Richard, cheekily.

"At least for the next little while, but it'll be done soon," mumbled O'Keefe.

"I have a letter for you from Mr. Withers. I trust it will bring a happy note to your morning," said Richard, grinning.

"No doubt it will," replied O'Keefe.

He grabbed the letter.

"And good day to you, Sergeant," said Richard, skipping back out to the street.

"What in the bloody hell does he want?" muttered O'Keefe.

Dear Sergeant O'Keefe,   *9ᵗʰ October 1928*

I trust this letter finds you well.

I am writing to you in my capacity as Leader of the Council. I was hoping you would be so kind as to come by the bank. There are some matters of community concern that I would like to discuss, and with respect to which I am hopeful of being able to assist.

I look forward to seeing you either Thursday or Friday, whichever suits you best. An appointment will not be necessary.

Kind regards,
Archibald Withers Esq.
Leader of the Council

"That'll be Monday, at the earliest," mumbled O'Keefe. "The later, the better."

Birdy returned with tea in hand for the sergeant and nothing for himself.

"What's up, boss?" asked Birdy.

O'Keefe folded the letter into his pocket.

"Nothing just yet. All quiet on the home front—at least, for now."

They were in private, so Birdy sat on the bench opposite the reception counter, cross-legged, his back pushed straight against the wall.

"Those stables cleaning themselves, Birdy?" asked O'Keefe curtly.

"Sorry, boss?"

"The stables—the feckin' stables. You were gonna give 'em a sweep for me."

Birdy grabbed the broom.

"No worries, boss. Too right. I'll sweep 'em proper clean."

O'Keefe watched as Birdy skedaddled.

I'm not keeping you on for your brains, Birdy, thought O'Keefe. *You can bank on that.*

* * * * *

John O'Kelly sat on his front veranda at lunchtime on a Sunday. It had rained all morning, but the sun was breaking through the clouds and mopping the sky with its might.

From a comfortable armchair, O'Kelly delighted in the spectacle unfolding before him. It was sent by God in the guise of weather. In Australia, the will of the Lord pushed and shoved the elements at the pace of a farce or a drama. He remembered God's will as more temperate in Ireland. When compared with a humid Australian day, nature's force at home merely simpered.

Father Sheehan was away, taking lunch at the O'Doherty homestead. This was an increasingly frequent occurrence, one made possible by the purchase of a presbytery motor vehicle. It had been bought by the church for the use of "the priests". Father Sheehan had managed to persuade the Bishop that he needed it to care for an old man. But it hadn't changed life for O'Kelly a jot. He was far too advanced in years to learn to drive it himself, and a tad fearful in any case of combustion driven engines.

And when it came to dining with the O'Doherty family, O'Kelly wasn't always included. The days when O'Doherty would come to the presbytery had been relegated to the past.

"Anlon," O'Kelly had asked, that morning over breakfast. "Why can't Mr. O'Doherty come here?"

"I'm a little embarrassed by the hospitality we can offer, when compared with his on their run."

"But that is not the point," O'Kelly had said. "It is for the parishioners to respect the church and not the other way round."

Sheehan's response verged on terse.

"If you think Mr. O'Doherty intended disrespect by not asking you to join us, I can put your mind at ease. I'm sure it's the distance and that's all, since it's such a long drive to his run. If parish business comes up in the course of the meal, I'll fill you in when I get back."

O'Kelly played with the remains of his lunch as a breeze stroked the open veranda. Mrs. Phillpot's excellent Sunday roast was sadly going to waste.

The acquisition of a housekeeper who knew how to cook was a far more welcome development. But how could he work up a passion for food when there were people in his parish still scratching for it?

Fifty years, thought O'Kelly, as he prodded at prime roast beef.

In almost fifty years, he'd made no progress with the Aboriginal people. Once upon a time, they would occasionally come to the presbytery looking for food. But when Sheehan had showed up, even that stopped, their trust not extending to a stranger.

Father Reilly had tried to help; O'Kelly's only ally had done all he could to help persuade the Aboriginals off the land, before Riley moved to the Port Town in 1926. He'd made half a dozen forays north, with Bibles, trinkets, pictures, and provisions to help lure them south to his mission.

But nothing ever worked.

And as for securing a policeman to protect them, that had failed to meet his hopes. What they got from the government in Sergeant O'Keefe was an idle drunk in disguise, who was quick to arrest Aboriginal people for the tiniest breach of the law.

Mrs. Phillpot walked onto the veranda.

"My goodness, you've crossed your knife and fork halfway into that meal. Is my cooking losing its magic?"

"Not at all, dear lady. The food is delicious. It's just that I'd too much cake at morning tea after mass."

"Well, let me clear it away and put it in the icebox. Perhaps you'll have an appetite for it afterward."

O'Kelly closed his eyes, let his head tilt back, and dozed off.

How different it all might have been. He dreamed into his long-cherished hopes. He saw Aboriginal women sharing their knowledge of the land with smiling settler wives, of them finding food in the scrubland together, their children playing along the river, oblivious to the difference in skin color. And working men, European and Aboriginal, building the structures, physical and social, of a new community, and from the wisdom of both worlds.

And nobody was plotting to kill.

* * * * *

The checkered blanket draped by Charlotte Noonan's pond held the remains of a family picnic. Traces of chicken, beetroot, carrot, and bean were smeared on a scatter of plates. Rory, Dave, Eamon, and Pat were a stone's throw away. They played cricket on the flatland. Eamon kept the wicket on account of hot weather, and little Pat the field.

Meanwhile, Daisy, Polly, and the four Noonan girls giggled and chased each other by the far side of the pond. The charcoal black trunks of burnt out trees in the middle of the water split the view from the rug, under an arc of empty sky.

Nell put Grace back in her bassinet and began cleaning up. She was just in time. Charlotte walked up the incline and with a basket carrying their pud. She was a little short of breath.

"Fresh out of the icebox," said Charlotte, as she knelt to open the basket. "Heaven knows how we coped without them."

"Too right," said Nell. "Everything was made fresh and then eaten immediately before it was spoiled by the heat. It was like a race against the sun."

A stringy bag slipped from Charlotte's shoulder and spilled apples across the blanket. They were green and gleaming.

"Aren't your trees doing well, Charlotte? I've not seen such a lovely set of apples since the last Port Town Show."

"I know, Nell. And they're delicious too. Our apple tree must have been blessed by our Lord. Go on. Take one."

The "tock" of Dave's new leather cricket ball on Rory's willow-wood bat filled the break in conversation. Rory hit the ball for four[71] and Pat was on the chase. Nell picked up an apple and rolled it from hand to hand. Charlotte had provided the opening Nell sought through a casual mention of God.

"The ways of our Lord, Charlotte, they're mysterious, all right. Sometimes, we're showered with blessings, and sometimes deprived a little bit cruelly of what we feel is our due."

Charlotte was placing a cake in the middle of the blanket. She frowned, sat back on her haunches, and looked toward Nell.

"Whatever do you mean by that, Nell? From what I can see, we are enjoying times in which we want for nothing—except, perhaps, a spot more of rain."

Nell rubbed the apple on a pleat of her skirt.

"Well," she said, "I was just thinking of that school—the new government secondary school that's about to open in Town. On the one hand, God has blessed us with a place of higher learning for the kiddies but, with the other, taken

---

[71] To hit a ball along the ground to the outer boundary of a cricket field, thereby scoring four runs.

it from the Catholics. I mean, don't you think it's a shame, Charlotte, that our bright boys and any of the girls who want to go on to teach have to board somewhere down south? After all, we've paid for that school with our taxes."

Charlotte sliced the cake.

"I suppose that's one way of looking at it," said Charlotte. "But there's nothing to be done. The Protestants have their way of doing things and we have ours, and the church is seeing to it that ours carry on."

Nell tossed the apple a couple of inches into the air.

"Have you ever thought though," she said, "that it's all a little strange. I mean, Catholics have been able to achieve so much more here than in Ireland. We own so much of the land, Irish families run some of the biggest Australian businesses, and there's never been a quibble about our participation in Parliament, whether it be federal or state. I just don't see why the church insists that our kiddies should be kept from theirs."

Charlotte smiled. The thing that drew her most to Nell was her gumption and the stealth with which she deployed it.

"This is about Eamon, isn't it, Nell?"

Nell stopped tossing the apple. You had to get up early in the morning to put anything past Charlotte.

She nodded, slowly.

"Nell, you have touched on one of the hottest subjects there is. How unlike you! As you say, we all do so well out here, so why upset what's working? For goodness sake, I'd add that you and I can even vote in Australia. And thanks to the church, our boys are on an equal footing with the Protestants when it comes to entering the professions. Start putting them in mixed secondary schools or putting our boys at the mercy of the state, then all these efforts might dissolve, and quickly. They are taking care of us, Nell—the church, that is. But I agree, it's a shame that the only way it can be done is by sending them away to board."

Nell looked over to the surface of the pond. It jittered in the sweep of a breeze.

"Well, that's not what Father Sheehan and Father O'Kelly said when I asked them last week," she said.

"What?" asked Charlotte sharply.

"When I asked them about our boys going to the state school here and getting their religious education of a Sunday. They didn't mention anything about a lack of faith in the education provided by the state."

Charlotte folded her arms.

"Oh my goodness, Nell, what exactly did you say?"

"Nothing really—nothing more than I have just said. Just that I couldn't understand why our boys couldn't attend the new government secondary school, and that we could see to the boys' religious education within the church."

"And nothing more than that?"

"No," replied Nell, morosely.

The invisible belt restraining Nell's will pulled tight. The same constraint of social convention that had stopped her probing Rory, back in 1923, on the sudden presentation of proof that their loan was finally paid out.

Charlotte handed Nell a slice of cake, then sat back on her haunches.

"Nell, for reasons that I don't need to go into, nobody understands the depth of the divide between us and the Protestants more than me. And I can imagine, Nell, the pain entailed in having to send a child away because that is what is best for them. But if you raise this subject again, *especially before the priests*, they'll wonder about your senses and perhaps if you might be losing them."

Rory hit the ball for six runs into the air, declared out because it landed in the pond. Everybody cheered, and Dave Noonan laughed. He could well afford to replace the new ball with another.

"My goodness," said Charlotte. "I'm experiencing déjà vu. Which friend of mine got herself tied in knots by meddling where she oughtn't over her husband's dealings with the bank? Hmm. Who might that have been? And my goodness, that turned out to be *really* something to worry about, didn't it!"

Nell signaled resignation with a grimace. They had run into the wall, again, another of the no-go areas for women and the sacrosanct province of the men. It was for Rory and the priests to decide Eamon's future; a wall that Charlotte wouldn't help her scale.

"Well, that's a subject closed," said Charlotte. "And thank goodness nothing more was said."

* * * * *

Father O'Kelly was awakened by footsteps—familiar, leather-bound footsteps ascending the presbytery stairs. He opened his eyes slowly.

Father Sheehan was returning.

"John, I hope I haven't disturbed you," he said. "I'd have crept if I knew you were sleeping."

O'Kelly suppressed a surge of displeasure and recovered his manners.

"Not a bother, Anlon. I nodded off into a nap after lunch. What time is it?"

"It's almost five o'clock."

Sheehan took a seat nearby.

"My word, that's more than a nap. Rather the mark of a lazy man," said O'Kelly. "So, tell me about your lunch."

"Nothing out of the ordinary. The main topic of conversation was enrollments in the Port Town school, seeing as they close next week. There are four more boys applying this year. Roddy's youngest boy Andrew among them, plus the three already accepted. So as a community, we're moving ahead."

"Does that four include Eamon Burke?" asked O'Kelly.

"Indeed, it does," said Sheehan. "His application for enrollment came in last week. All the boys have excellent records and will have recommendations from Mr. Geharty. He's a respected school master, so I can't see any of them being turned down. I expect we will hear fairly soon."

Sheehan took a moment before continuing.

"John," he said. "I don't wish to sound uncharitable, but isn't the mother a little on the odd side? I mean that woman, Mrs. Burke. Surely, she wasn't suggesting last Saturday at the church fete that our boys should be educated with the Protestants? That new government school is not the place to be rearing Catholic gentlemen."

"Bull-headed, I would say," replied O'Kelly. "And a little too unafraid to speak her own mind. But what you heard at the church fete was a last throw of the dice from a mother not wishing to part with a son. Nothing more than that."

"Are you sure? I mean, should I perhaps be thinking of taking one of the better women aside to have a word with her? She came close to insulting the church."

O'Kelly sighed. He pulled on the arms of his soft, cushioned chair so that he could sit up straighter and higher.

"Anlon," he said dryly. "I wouldn't profess to have much to teach you about running a parish. But there is one early lesson to be learned. Make a wave only in the event of absolute necessity. Mrs. Burke's casual remarks fall so far short of that threshold that it cannot even be measured."

The shadows of dusk stretched across the churchyard. They were as long as the gulf in the outlook on life that ran between the two priests. A tint of yellow caressed the rooftops of the Town main street. It sprinkled into off-shoot streets that were turning into suburbs. All of it could be seen from Presbytery Hill; a civil, God-fearing community, carved as if by a miracle into a tired and ancient land.

Sheehan searched for a change of subject that would take them to common ground.

"Oh," he said, "there is one more thing that came up over lunch. There might be some progress on a subject close to your heart. Mr. O'Doherty said he'd met with Mr. Withers at the bank. Withers floated the idea with him of having a meeting of some sort, convened by the Council, to talk about the missions."

"He what?" exclaimed O'Kelly.

The young priest frowned.

"Oh. I thought you would be pleased. It is apparently early days yet, but the Council is prepared to help bring the remaining blacks in so they are not left to perish. So, an informal gathering is being mooted of all concerned. That would include Mr. Withers for the Council, me apparently for the Catholic mission, and the Protestant clergy of the Town."

"Anlon," said O'Kelly through gritted teeth. "You are to keep me informed of every development on this subject, each and every one. Is that clear? I am to be involved in *everything*, including any meeting."

O'Kelly was trembling because his soul had been scratched. "Of course, John, I will. Of course."

An emotional old man, thought Sheehan, *has to be calmed down.*

"But you're not to let yourself fret. With a bit of luck, it might be the end of a problem we could do without. All the Aboriginals might finally be transferred out. I told Mr. O'Doherty that there is plenty of space at the Catholic mission. Now, come along. It's getting chilly. Let's move into the drawing room to read."

O'Kelly stood with the help of Sheehan's arm.

This is not something I can afford to let lie, thought O'Kelly. *What on earth is Withers up to?*

* * * * *

An hour before his employment permitted entry to the Hotel Imperial, Sergeant Brian O'Keefe, on Monday, tottered through the Town's main street, capped and spot-cleaned. He was on his way to the bank to see His Eminence, Archibald Withers.

The street was chaotic. There were more motorized vehicles than horses these days, whether drawing carriages or carrying men in saddles. When O'Keefe arrived in the Town, in 1923, he could stride down its center with every beast commanded by man faltering in his wake. But the machines were different. Liberated by anonymity and haughty in their might, they departed from a pre-planned passage for each other, but no one else. O'Keefe joined the other townsmen making their way on the footpath, secure under the protection of shop awnings.

Outside Withers' office, O'Keefe removed his cap, then spat on his hand, presaging a final attempt to remove a grease stain.

Withers responded to a spiritless knock.

"Come in."

"Mr. Withers, sir, I received your note," said O'Keefe. "I came as soon as I could."

Withers let his tardiness lie.

"And very kind of you to do so. Please, have a seat. I won't detain you long. I know how busy you are."

The Sergeant took his place. He searched for something to say to say in return but Withers barged on.

"It has been brought to my attention that the churches need help in clearing off the remaining blacks. As Leader of the Council, I am asking whether you might be able to help them out."

"I'm glad to do what I can, Mr. Withers, but I have duties and orders to follow within the confines of the force."

O'Keefe sensed the burden of additional work and was doing his best to avoid it.

Withers continued, unperturbed.

"Sergeant O'Keefe, I am aware that you have two large cells in the police station. Is there anywhere else in which prisoners could be stored if you had, say, up to seventy of them?"

"Heaven forbid that I would need to, but there is a large basement beneath the building. It would be as safe as any cell."

"Excellent!" exclaimed Withers. "And is there a generous number of men whose services you can secure at reasonable rates to deal with any situation which requires emergency labor?"

"Yes, sir, there are. I can safely say that I am able to command the obedience of the locals."

O'Keefe began to worry about Withers' lack of small talk in opening the meeting.

Withers stood up, produced his pencil-marked map from the drawer, and spun it toward O'Keefe. His voice skipped with excitement.

"I have made a study. There are about half a dozen camps of blacks within nine miles of the Town, but some of them considerably nearer. It's difficult to tell, but they are likely to number sixty to seventy. I have spoken to Reverend Parker, briefly, and had a word with Mr. Roddy O'Doherty as well. The idea is to clear them off early in the morning of December twenty-sixth, gather them all at the police station for the purposes of compiling an inventory, then ship them off together by rail in the late afternoon here, to Purgatory Creek. It's the railway station nearest to all the missions. Provided all the faiths agree, the blacks can then be shared among them, after transfer by cattle truck."

O'Keefe scratched his head.

"I am yet to have discussions with your Roman Catholic priest. How are you with him? His name is Sheehan, isn't it?"

"It is, sir," replied O'Keefe. "He is relatively new to the parish. So, on the one hand, he will be open to any advice I might be able to provide about local affairs. On the other, Father O'Kelly, although retired and very elderly, might also give him counsel."

O'Kelly is so bloody old now, thought Withers, *I can simply run over him.*

O'Keefe cleared his throat.

"Sir, I can see the wisdom in what you are planning, but I fear that we are over-stretched already at the station, and I am not sure how we would round them all up. And we will have to make an exception for my black-tracker Birdy. I will need him to stay on."

O'Keefe was ducking and dodging as quickly as his cerebral functions were able. Meanwhile, the banker was fuming.

The only reason you have been able to keep a black-tracker at all, is because he helps you find black thieves.

Withers knocked over an empty inkwell as he sprung to his feet, enraged.

"Damn it, man, I said all of them. Every godless last one of them is to go."

Withers was shaking.

"They come back like those bloody hunting sticks you still see them throwing. Well, this time, they are going to be put away for good. We cannot live encircled by vermin."

Withers collapsed into his chair, panting.

"What are they frightened of?" he barked.

"Fire and bullets," said O'Keefe, quietly.

"Well then, that's how you bloody well do it. On the 8th of November, I will be convening a meeting of all the clergymen at the Town Hall. You and I need to converse again in private before that meeting takes place."

"Yes, sir," mumbled O'Keefe.

Then, Withers unleashed a proposal impossible to refuse.

"If the natives do not return after we clear them off, you will have a long-term loan at absurdly low interest, which will enable you to buy your own house and live in it for the rest of your days. The bank will simply recover the capital sum from the sale of it after your death. You will also be given a lump sum payment that I will organize from local sources. As for your men, they will be paid generously out of Council funds and with support from private donors. Beat the living crap out of the bastards if you have to, but you are to move the filth of this region into the missions. Now, get out, get on with organizing it, and keep your mouth shut about the money."

O'Keefe stood up and shuffled out without speaking. On the strength of a promise like that, he would think of a way of getting by without Birdy.

* * * * *

Rory Burke was chopping wood under the Jacaranda tree in full bloom.

A hemisphere of purple, the prodigy of petals, framed Rory's movements as he worked. The axe rose and fell, then rose and fell, in the dry of midday heat. It warmed and slowed up everything.

Rory thought of Hannah, Sean, and marriage, as he dismembered the timber with disinterest on the gravelly grass between the Jacaranda tree and his house.

Rory wanted the wood broken up and stored ahead of the lash of summer storms. He approached the task from within a void of will that was draining his strength.

But it afforded him space to reflect.

The choke that had seized the back of his tongue over Eamon's enrolment was repeating in his thoughts. The letter had arrived in the post that morning. Eamon was accepted to the Port Town school.

A moment that should have been a source for joy had been tarnished by the fog of guilt.

Damn lies, tricks, and intermittent distance—failings copper-fastened to his marriage to Nell were clasping as tightly as ever. Lodge Eamon's enrollment papers and don't tell Nell; spend an entire marriage paying off some paddocks so that nobody knows but Dave and not Nell; and, go out and nearly murder a mob of blackfellas and forever keep it to yourself.

Secrecy was something he wanted no more. The boom had ferried him and his family to the dreams of Hannah and Sean. A profit-bearing farm, educated kids, choice on the work from which they would live and respectable social standing. But his marriage to Nell still wasn't graced with the blessing that united his parents—honesty, openness, and trust.

Rory remembered overhearing his parents on a baking summer night. He couldn't sleep and was aged no more than nine. He lay awake at the far end of the shack.

Hannah's voice was strained to harsh. He could barely tell it was hers.

"You're not to shoot them, Sean," Hannah had said. "God knows how many of them there are living out there, and they might retaliate with spears."

"Well, what in the bloody hell am I supposed to do with 'em? They're stealing our cows, and the only cove here to impose law and order is me."

"Well then, that's what you do. You educate them with punishment and show them you *are* the law. You show them out in the clear light of day what happens if they thieve."

Rory pulled the axe from the wood lethargically. He raised its head, again, then gravity propelled it groundward. He'd done as Sean never would have. When confronted with a dilemma about dealing with the blacks, he'd kept his wife out of the picture.

And it had started with those acres and Dave.

High in the trees, the foliage rustled, liberating a small flock of crows. Rory looked up. They streaked ebony dots across the scoop of blue suspended above the land.

"There'll be no stoning of crows out here," thought Rory. "They skitter too high in the sky."

Rory resumed chopping. How could he have foreseen it? When he'd done as Dave had wished and kept their deal a secret, it triggered a chain reaction, widening the cavern in his marriage.

But the time had come to close it.

Splinters began to fly again as Rory picked up the pace. Before he moved to repair his marriage, he'd ask Father O'Kelly where to start.

* * * * *

CHAPTER 11
INSTIGATION
November 1928

Nell tidied the little table between the comfortable seats on her back veranda in the last month of spring. Peggy, her sister-in-law, strolled toward her across the tufty grass of the yard. She held a mop in one hand, a tin bucket in the other. It swung because it was empty. The sky behind her lay drenched to the horizon in the deepest of heavenly blue.

"Now, Peggy, that's what I call timing," said Nell. "I've just finished cleaning the roof gutters."

Peggy plodded a little back up the same stairs that she had skipped down earlier that morning.

"That old shack has been swept and scrubbed back to its former glory," she said.

Peggy fell into a wide armchair.

"It's too good a building to be somebody's workshop. Are you sure that's how best to use it?"

Nell thought the same herself, but Peggy hadn't seen what the shack was replacing. She sat in the armchair next to her.

"I'd have taken you to Rory's current workshop if I were sure I could get the door open. I don't believe he's thrown a thing away since the two of us were married. It will be a longer walk for him over that hill, but he'll be able to move once he's in it."

"How did you get on with the roof?" asked Peggy. "I don't know how you cope with the height."

She wiped her handkerchief across her brow.

"Work is work as far as I'm concerned," said Nell, leaning back into her armchair. "I hardly notice where I am when I'm in the middle of my chores."

"So, you weren't distracted by the view up there? That Jacaranda tree must be magnificent when looked down on from a height."

Midmorning sunlight had turned each petal-rim pink so that its bursts of mauve were aglow.

"It's fuller and brighter than any spring that's passed since I came here as Rory's wife."

Little birds flittered across the tree's twisting branches, while an early start to full-pelt[72] spring cleaning eased toward morning tea.

"You know," said Nell, "I've got a bit of an attack of the guilts. This is the second year in a row that you and Brendan have come and helped us with the spring harvest. Rory and I haven't made the gesture for you in coming up to three years."

"Goodness, Nell, think nothing of it. With all of our brood aged over ten, it's not hard to get away. They are all billeting[73] with friends. You can think about returning the favor to us when your little ones are older."

"We can probably do something before then. You're to let me know when we can."

Peggy put her handkerchief away.

"Now you mention it, there might be something. If Rory can get away for a bit before Christmas, we could use another pair of hands."

"How so?" asked Nell.

Peggy kept looking at the tree.

---

[72] To go about doing something quickly and intensely.

[73] To be staying full board with an associate.

"Now that Hector is getting on, we've started thinking about life once he's gone. None of the boys want to sell Ballycallan and divide the profits between them, but nor do they want to work it in quarters."

Nell gulped.

My brothers have already started planning!

"Four small farms mightn't support each of the families," added Peggy. "So, consolidation is the idea. On all four boundaries of Ballycallan, there are good-sized profitable runs. If they were each owned by a McTiernan son, then Hector's run could be added to all of them."

Nell's mind was racing, as if chasing a bus that had already departed and was setting out on its way.

"A farm bordering Ballycallan has come up for sale, and Brendan plans to buy it. He made an offer just last week. If it's accepted, we'll sell up and move. So, if Rory could spare a couple of days to help ready our farm for sale, both of us will be thankful."

"Why, that's wonderful," said Nell, flatly.

"Just think of it, Nell. If we can pull it off, we'll be known far and wide as the McTiernans of the near northeast. Ballycallan would become a station,[74] but one located on lush coastal land!"

Drawn into the haze of mauve before her, Nell tried to make sense of her feelings.

Had she been a terrible sister and a downright treacherous wife? Had concealing her share of Ballycallan been a fatal, unfixable mistake? Or was it Da who had been wrong, all along, in trying to slip a daughter a slice of his run in the first place?

---

[74] A very large farm, usually in the interior of Australia, on land more dry than lush.

"Are you all right, Nell?" asked Peggy. "You've gone a little quiet. I thought that you would be pleased."

If Da is going to do this, thought Nell, *he's to sort it out this side of the grave and not leave it to me once he's gone.*

"Of course, I am," said Nell. "But just out of interest, does Da know about all this? I mean that my other brothers hope to join up with you at home if the right land comes up for sale?"

"Not yet," said Peggy. "It's a bit delicate, telling someone you've made plans for what's to happen once they are dead. If the right moment surfaces in the Christmas holidays, Brendan will speak with Hector then. Right now, he thinks me and Brendan just want to be closer to Ballycallan."

I don't even know if it's legal, thought Nell, *for a daughter to be willed land over sons.*

"That would seem to be a good time to raise it," said Nell. "A bit awkward to do it before then. And give me a shout when you need Rory up north. We'll organize ourselves so he can leave."

Nell got up to put on the kettle.

I had better write to Da.

* * * * *

Father O'Kelly waited for Rory on the presbytery's back veranda. Mrs. Phillpot was in Town running household errands while Father Sheehan was visiting the sick. None of it was an accident. The two planned absences dictated the timing of his meeting with Rory Burke.

"Tuesday afternoon would fit me well," the old priest had said on Sunday. "A quiet word now is out of the question. The women are about to start serving morning tea."

"I can come into Town for this and that on Tuesday, Father, no risk."

O'Kelly listened out for a visitor.

This and that, he mused.

Whatever it was that Mr. Burke wanted to speak of was likely being hidden from his wife.

The front door creaked, and footsteps followed from one end of the corridor to another. Mr. Burke had seen his note.

"Good day, Father," said Rory. "I assume I'm not intruding by letting myself in. I've just now read your message."

O'Kelly reached for his cane and stood at the speed of the dignified advancing in years.

"Not at all, Mr. Burke, not at all. You have saved an old man from what has sadly become a lengthy voyage down the hallway. Please take a seat just there by the railing, where I can enjoy the comfort of your company."

As O'Kelly sat down, he reviewed his goals. He was doing his all not to descend into fretting, but he had to find out what was brewing. Was there a chance Mr. Burke had asked to see him to report harm being planned to Aboriginals?

I tied him tight enough, thought O'Kelly, *in 1923, to a promise to tell me all. To divulge any secret that had come from anyone entailing a plan to hurt them.*

And Mr. Burke hadn't sought his counsel in years.

Please God, he is coming to help.

"Father, thanks for letting me come by. I guess I should tell you what it's all about. I wanted some advice on dealing with Nell and enriching the bonds of our marriage."

Disappointment heaved through the old priest's being, but he was able to disguise it.

"Why, I'm surprised to hear that, Mr. Burke," said O'Kelly. "You, Mrs. Burke, and your lovely children are a picture of family happiness. Whatever more could you want aside from what you have already—a blossoming west-lands family?"

Rory looked at the floorboards and took his time to reply.

"Honesty, Father, and openness. A wife with whom I share my woes, along with all my victories."

O'Kelly gazed across the presbytery yard. It had been blighted by the onset of order. Father Sheehan's vegetable patch was shoving symmetry into ancient land, sending the pleasure it once gave him to the heavens.

"And that is not the case to date?" asked O'Kelly.

Rory shook his head.

"No, Father, it isn't. I applied to enrol Eamon in the Port Town school and haven't found a way to tell Nell he's been accepted. I convinced myself that I needed to do it alone just to keep the peace. But that's not the truth."

O'Kelly went into tactical pause. There was nothing to be gained in letting Mr. Burke know his wife had told him she wanted Eamon home.

"Then, what is the truth, Mr. Burke? Why do you think this is?"

Rory looked toward the floorboards, again.

"In fifteen years, I've managed to thread a string of little lies. That's what it is that unsettles us as a couple. She still doesn't know Dave owns those top paddocks—even though they will soon be paid out. And she certainly doesn't know about the sacks of poisoned flour that I delivered to the blackfellas back in 1922 and how close I came to murder. And when it comes to dealing with our children, I struggle to get through to her, about everything."

O'Kelly snatched at the thin of a chance to open a channel for information.

"So, you never said a word to her, Mr. Burke, about Mr. Withers' terrible plot?"

Rory sat up a little straighter.

"No, Father, I didn't."

O'Kelly leaned forward.

"And since then, there's be nothing at all? I mean, you've made no plans at all to harm the Aboriginals, or heard of any either?"

Rory frowned. He didn't really want to talk any further about what his banker had tried to force him to do.

"My goodness, no, Father. I'm a man of my word, and now I give the blackfellas wide berth."

O'Kelly allowed the cry of a passing galah[75] to hover between him and Rory. Mr. Burke wasn't a liar, but nor could he be classed as brave.

Would he have the courage to share Withers' aims in calling this meeting even if he knew what they were?

"And did you keep that cross, Mr. Burke—the one I gave you to remind you of your Christian duty to fill me in on any schemes you hear of concerning Aboriginals?"

"That I certainly did, Father," said Rory. "It hangs to this day in my workshop, just above my bench."

O'Kelly lowered his voice.

"There is nothing more serious—nothing that comes close—to breaking the command not to kill. Any foul intentions to defy this command must be immediately reported to me."

Rory was perplexed.

"I know that, Father," said Rory. "But I came here today to talk about my wife."

Father O'Kelly leaned back in his chair. Nell was the only parishioner who had been on his side in 1922 when they

---

[75] A small Australian bird (cockatoo).

debated the location of their school. The idea of building it near Aboriginal people hadn't bothered her a jot. And if she wasn't blessed with the courage of Mary, she wouldn't have tried to get Eamon matriculated in the Town. All that added up to a long shot at help. If she ever got wind of some despicable plot, she'd be the one to speak out.

It was worth a try.

"It seems to me that you need, Mr. Burke, to communicate more openly with your wife. Tell me again, Mr. Burke. When will you own these toxic paddocks, the ones that ended you in strife with Mr. Withers?"

"In a matter of weeks," said Rory.

"Well, why not celebrate it?" said O'Kelly.

"And how can I do that, Father?" asked Rory.

"Select a time and place at which you can take your wife aside, very soon, perhaps for a picnic or some other treat. Tell all then—about the grief the land caused you in your dealings with Withers, including your brush with mortal sin. And while you are at it, you may as well ask if she's heard of any other scheme like it. A clearing of the decks might change the pattern of your marriage and purge it of deceit."

Rory swallowed hard. The paddocks he could manage, but could he really let Nell in on the fact that he had once attempted murder?

Father O'Kelly repeated himself, to make sure Rory obeyed.

"Share your thoughts and ideas with your wife—about everything, Mr. Burke. She may surprise you with her willingness to listen and her capacity for forgiveness. The gulf between you might close."

Rory brushed the top of his worn felt hat, then put it on his head.

"You are right, Father, as always," said Rory. "I will choose a special setting for a private word and find a way to tell her everything. Don't get up, Father. I will walk myself to the door."

O'Kelly turned and watched Rory meander into the shadow of the corridor. That low-slung swagger had barely altered since he was a boy.

* * * * *

Rory was in the workshop chiseling. At Christmas, each of his children received a toy left by Father Christmas. The Burke children were like all the others and passed through childhood without questioning the origin of their gifts, although Eamon and Daisy, by now, knew. Their source in Rory's carpentry and Nell's paintwork remained a secret until childhood's end.

For Eamon, there would be a varnished pencil box, and Daisy was to be gifted her own cooking bowl made of turned wood with a spoon to match it—just like her mother's but smaller. Polly would delight in a pony head crafted in timber, with painted eyes, a nose, and mouth, mounted on a stick. With this, she could frolic in the yard and imagine she were part of the world of the big girls with real ponies. Patrick would receive a Shanghai that would be the envy of all the boys, but on the promise that it would be used only in the pursuit of birds and insects or hitting fixed targets on walls. And for Grace, there would be a rattle filled with small stones, washed by Nell before they were sealed in a cylinder made by Rory, then decorated with colorful swirls.

It would all have to be packed into a box, tacked shut, and then hidden under a blanket for the Christmas journey to Ballycallan.

Nell slipped into the workshop and sat on a bench behind Rory. She watched him quietly as he worked on Eamon's pencil box.

"There's no other way is there, Rory?" she said. "Eamon's heading to boarding school, isn't he?"

Rory stopped working, put down his wood file, and turned around in his chair.

Well, stone the crows,[76] thought Rory, *I didn't expect that.*

"Didn't hear you come in, love. But, now you mention it, there isn't. The acceptance came at the end of October, last week. Eamon's not a man of the land, but he's a head for figures and more. We'll be doing him right if we send him on to matriculate. Father Sheehan says other local boys are going, so he'll be as happy as Larry once he's there."

Rory arched his shoulders slightly, waiting for Nell to object.

He needn't have worried. She asked about something else.

"When were you talking to Father Sheehan about this?"

Charlotte's warning of the consequences of her small but serious indiscretion repeated in Nell's mind.

She began to perspire.

"When I gave him Eamon's enrollment a couple of weeks back. He reckoned it was for the best."

"And did Father say anything else?" asked Nell.

"About the school? No, he didn't. Said he had to get on— late for something or other."

Nell exhaled. Praise be. Rory knew nothing about her not-so-quiet word with the priests about the government school and sending Eamon there instead.

---

[76] Early twentieth century expression of surprise.

Rory turned back to his work.

Strange, he thought. *All that worry about how she'd react, and she let it go straight through to the keeper.*[77]

Rory selected a light hammer from the wall and tapped nails into Polly's horse head.

Nell picked up the object sitting next to her.

"Rory, Daisy's bowl is beautiful. It's a shame, in a way, it's not going to a little girl who's ready to use it."

"Wouldn't worry too much about that, love," said Rory as he kept working. "Daisy'll be in the house with you before we know it."

"Why do you think that?"

Rory drew strength from his win over Eamon. Time to move on to Daisy, and do just as Father O'Kelly had said and share his plans with his wife.

"Well, I saw somethin' at the church fete that might help interest her in starting to behave like a lady. Did you hear about that Madame La Bonne who's moved into Town? She's French, I think. Offerin' dance classes. I reckon if we could get Daisy into somethin' like that, it might divert her energy, and get her onto a grown-up path for a girl instead of chargin' around the bush."

"She's offering what?" asked Nell.

"Madame La Bonne's teaching girls to dance. Daisy'll be old enough for the dances before we know it, so we may as well start preparing. And I'm not sendin' her out into adult life unless she's learnt how to keep a house. So, I reckon dance classes first, home duties next."

---

[77] To let something drop without objection. Origin in the game of cricket, in which the batter chooses not to hit a ball and lets the wicket-keeper catch it.

Nell dropped down from the bench.

"Rory, she'll come around," said Nell. "Children always do. Once she sees she's out of step with the other girls, she'll ask me about running a household."

"Can't see that happening anytime soon," replied Rory. "Bein' out of step's never worried her before."

"She hasn't had to grow up before. You'll see. She'll be in the kitchen with me every night before dinner when the time is right. And before too long, she'll be making your shirts for you instead of me. But I'm not sure we should be rushing off to pay someone to teach her to dance, not yet."

Rory stopped working but didn't turn around. Nell had closed her mind to a good idea just because it had come from him. So much for the hope she was softening.

"I'd better start making our dinner," she said.

Nell navigated past Rory's collection of junk as she walked toward the doorway. She stopped in it and turned back toward him before leaving.

"Be sure all the presents are put on the top ledge and out of reach of the children. I'd not put it past Daisy to go clambering up the shelves and work out for herself who's getting what."

"As good as done, love," mumbled Rory.

He kept tapping nails.

Not quite the right moment, thought Rory, *to see if my lady wife is up for a date with her husband to hear all he has to confess.*

* * * * *

Authority was imposed by a column of flags.

They bore down on the audience gathered in the drafty Town Hall: two Imperial, one at each end of the podium and, in the middle, the flag of the state and one of the federation. Their yellow council banner furled out above Withers' combed and lacquered head. He stood at the lectern like a general directing his men. The gathering of the earnestly concerned was being herded toward the one, intractable solution.

"The situation is as follows, gentlemen. I have long had the greatest admiration for your individual missionary endeavors, and as Leader of the Town Council, I have taken the view that the time is past due for the Town to do its part."

The Council's stenographer sat to one side of the stage and was taking meticulous notes. Sergeant O'Keefe sat at the other. The suspense of guessing what was to come next fastened the clergymen's attention to the stage.

"But I cannot be seen to be favoring one church over another."

Father O'Kelly looked around the room as discreetly as he could. He was searching for an ally. The Protector of the Aboriginals sat behind Withers. He was clearly in the know and on Withers' side. Was it possible to garner support from one of the Protestant preachers? They were all there: Reverend Parker of the Church of England, Petersen the Lutheran pastor, the Presbyterian McLoughlin, and the new man of God of the Baptists, Dr. Thomas.

Was help from Father Sheehan, sitting behind him, completely out of the question? At the rear of the Town Hall, in a huddle of others, Mr. Roddy O'Doherty and Dr. Dunne sat together.

Then, Reverend Parker stood up.

"Mr. Withers, I do not wish to denigrate what you seek to achieve. But there is a question here of expertise. Dealing with the Aboriginal man requires a delicate hand. I wonder if it is really a realm in which the Council is best involved?"

O'Kelly was about to stand to join him, when Withers shot back, unrelenting.

"The Council will collect the blacks as part of our duty to tidy and protect the Town. It is then for the churches to step in and divide them between the missions. I would suggest, if I may, that descent into an inter-denominational squabble among the clergy would jar in the eyes of your respective congregations. Made up equally, I might add, of my constituents."

Withers turned the page of his speech.

"The fact is, gentlemen," he said, "that they are a threat to public health."

O'Kelly tried to catch Parker's eye, but the vicar was watching the stage.

O'Kelly rubbed his forehead, massaging regret. He had always liked the look of Parker—a quiet family man—but with him, he had missed a trick. If he had followed up on Mrs. Burke's hint that their boys might be schooled with the Protestants, he'd have had reason to contact Parker. He would have had just cause to break the sectarian divide and inquire about the state school. That would have been the moment to build a bridge into the topic of Aboriginal welfare.

"But I wish to take the opportunity to make one matter perfectly clear," continued Withers. "You have my personal assurance that due respect will be paid to tribal and family groups. These will not be ruptured in any way at all, and kin will remain with kin. They will be treated with compassion."

A barrage of Protestant words and phrases then rattled through O'Kelly's head. Withers said it was time for action, to grasp the nettle, to rid the Town of a menace, and assist the churches in marching the blacks to redemption. Shillyshallying had been costly to one and to all, and the Council was duty-bound to take action.

"Are there any questions?"

Parker and Thomas exchanged a whisper, but neither was moved to object.

At least the Protestants speak to each other, thought O'Kelly, *when pushed to it by the occasion.*

O'Kelly stood, gingerly, with the help of his cane, and stared at Withers coldly.

"I would like to know about the wishes of the Aboriginal people. Who has met with them? And how can you be certain of their willingness to come in?"

Wither's ignored him, glanced at Sergeant O'Keefe, and nodded.

He sprang to his feet.

"My word, Father, you have raised the very point I neglected to address in my introduction. With my black-tracker, Birdy, I have visited their camps so that they have come to know us well. They view us as friends, so we can transfer them safely from the squalor in which they currently reside more as guides than predators."

O'Kelly looked around, again, for a hint of resistance. It didn't emerge, and he resumed his seat, despondent.

If there were ever a man who couldn't be trusted, it was their own, alcoholic, Sergeant O'Keefe.

Blessed Virgin Mary, prayed O'Kelly, *deliver me the wisdom, at this dawning eleventh hour, to stop whatever Mr. Withers is planning.*

There was a creak, then a shuffle, from the back of the room. All heads turned as Roddy O'Doherty stood.

"Mr. Withers, sir, may I take the opportunity, and I believe I can speak on behalf of all the pastoralists, to congratulate you on this excellent initiative."

O'Doherty stopped speaking, profiting from the power of pause.

"We, as a community, have allowed this distressing situation to go on for too long, and I know Dr. Dunne, who is sitting beside me, agrees. It will be my honor to propose the motion at the very next meeting of the Town Council, with acknowledgment of the contribution of our Leader."

Dr. Dunne stood up next to him.

"And I will be delighted, of course, to second it."

O'Kelly slumped and leaned on his stick. Withers beamed and closed his folder.

"Very kind of you to say, Mr. O'Doherty," said Withers. "And with that, I draw this meeting to a close."

* * * * *

Rory dismounted and set off for Nell's kitchen beneath a purple burst of flowers. He still wasn't sure if he'd made the right decision. Wristwatch or pocket watch? Plated in silver or gold? He held the watch box nestled in his pocket, knowing he was about to find out.

He removed his muddy boots at the veranda. Through the window, he saw Nell walking into the kitchen. She picked up a bowl on the kitchen table and examined it. With the children nowhere in sight, Rory whipped inside.

"A wristwatch is all the fashion," said Rory, sitting in his socks at the table. "And better for a lad than a watch he's to keep in his pocket."

"How does it stay on?" asked Nell, as she poured the mixture into a cake tin.

"There's a tiny buckle at the end of the band," said Rory. "And it closes behind the wrist just like a belt, and just as safe. Mr. Miller showed me in the shop."

"And it didn't cost more than ten shillings?" asked Nell.

She put on her kitchen gloves, opened the oven door, and slid the cake inside.

"No, love, it didn't. It was even a little less," replied Rory.

"All right. Let me take a look at it before I wrap it. I hope it's smart. We don't want the lads at the school from the big runs to be shaming Eamon over his timepiece."

Rory pulled the watch box from the pocket of his trousers. He opened the lid, slowly, and gave the box to Nell. She drew it closer and let her feelings settle. This was a watch befitting the best of their young Catholic men.

I would stop this if I could, thought Nell, *but there is nothing that can be done.*

"Rory, it's perfect, plated in gold and all. I'll wrap it in no time. Dinner will be on the table in about half an hour when I'm done baking Eamon's sponge."

Rory kissed his wife on the forehead.

"Just enough time for a country gent to take his bath. And I'm glad, love, that you like it."

A little while later, their children gathered around the side veranda table: Eamon, Daisy, Polly, Patrick, and baby Grace in her high chair. All hatted in cardboard and blowing paper whistles that folded out to a length of half a foot, they reveled in the festivity. With lollies on the table, it was just like one of the seven dinners a year that marked a Burke family birthday.

Patrick looked at Eamon with awe.

"Eamon, will there be little boys at your school as well?"

"No, Patrick, there won't. I'll be one of the littlest of them all."

Eamon spoke a little wearily. The weather had turned warm, and he had been wheezing most of the day.

"And will you bring us all lollies and chocolates back from the big shops in the Port Town?" asked Polly.

"If Dad sends me some pocket money, that's where I'll spend it," replied Eamon.

"And will you write to us with all your stories?" chimed in Daisy.

"I will, but you have to listen to Mum or Dad when they read them out to you."

"Do you really want to leave us, Eamon?" asked Daisy.

"It's not that I'll be leaving you. I'm just away in the term times for school. And I do want to go now. There will be a group of us lads from the Town."

Rory and Nell entered from the door of their bedroom. They took their places at the table, Rory at one end, Nell at the other, with Eamon sitting by Rory. He held the lovingly wrapped gift in his hand and spoke.

"It's a happy day for all of us. It's thirteen years and eight months since Eamon Lawrence Burke came into the world. And he's now on his way to becoming a man. As you know, we've not long since received news saying he's been accepted into the Port Town school. Son, your Ma and I wanted to say how proud we are. So, we brought you this gift to take with you on your studies."

Rory held out his laborer's hand to shake that of his scholarly son. Tears welled in Rory's eyes at the breadth of his first son's smile and the firmness of his grip.

"Go on, Eamon, open it," said Nell.

She coughed behind a handkerchief, daintily.

"Open it, Eamon, open it," the children called out.

With wrapping paper peeled away, he prized open the box.

"Dad, it's a watch. A grown-up man's watch!"

"That it is, lad," said Rory, as his son leapt to embrace him.

He ran to Nell to do the same from behind her, at the far end of the table. She clasped the arms in which her boy engulfed her.

"Keep it for Sunday best now, till you go off to school. But you can wear it at Ballycallan on Christmas day."

"I will, Ma, and thanks."

* * * * *

"John, I don't see that there is any other way. From what you have said, we have done all we can. If we can't persuade them to come off the land, I can't see the harm in the help being offered by the Council."

They were in the presbytery drawing room, a bit more than a week after Withers' speech.

"What, Anlon? I am sorry," said O'Kelly, surfacing from a book.

"The proposal, John—the project outlined by Mr. Withers and Sergeant O'Keefe at the meeting in the Town Hall. It would seem to be best for all."

O'Kelly said nothing. He looked out the window, longingly, at the bushland, for a flicker of movement. It was to no avail. The kangaroos would not be joining them.

"John, you have been awfully quiet of late," said Sheehan. "Could I beg the indulgence of some insight into your troubles? I am your friend. Perhaps I can help."

Father O'Kelly poured himself some water from the pitcher sitting beside him. He didn't offer any to Sheehan, who was sitting on the sofa.

He drank a mouthful of it, then spoke.

"Withers tried to murder them," said O'Kelly, bluntly.

"What? Who has tried to murder whom?" asked Sheehan, incredulously.

O'Kelly closed the book, put it in his lap, and looked Sheehan in the eye.

"The Aboriginal people. Withers tried to kill them a few years back with a consignment of poisoned flour. I managed to get wind of it and dumped all of it in the river myself before it could be eaten. Withers is not a man to be trusted with the welfare of Aboriginal people."

Sheehan was shocked to breathless.

"But Mr. Withers is such a gentleman. I can't imagine him ever attempting to do such a thing. And besides, how would he have done it?"

"For goodness' sake, Anlon, will you *listen!*" snapped O'Kelly. "I said, *Withers tried to murder them.* He managed to dupe one of the local farmers into finding them and poisoning them."

"All right, I *am* listening. Who? Who was going to help him and how did you find all this out?"

"Never mind who or how I know," replied O'Kelly, "but do I look like a liar?"

"I'm not suggesting that for a second. But what is it that can be done? The plan to move the natives out to the missions is already fixed."

O'Kelly was scanning the weaving wall of bushland on the other side of the window. Where were they, God's creatures, when help was needed to stiffen his resolve? The flapping of a crow on a crown of high scrubland carried with it too little succor.

"Would you help me, Anlon, with whatever I asked—with whatever would bring me comfort?"

"Of course, John."

The young priest leaned forward.

"Then we are to go to see Sergeant O'Keefe, together—when he is not at the drink, that is—to give him a friendly reminder. That dignity, charity and, above all, humanity are at the heart of God's teachings. That under the commandments of our Lord, we are to love our neighbors. So, if distress is visited on the Aboriginal people, he will commit a mortal sin and be judged in the eyes of our Lord."

Sheehan crossed his legs and scratched his head. This was a proposal for the church to involve itself, and directly, with the affairs of the state. Father O'Kelly had to be checked.

"John," said Sheehan, "I concede that Sergeant O'Keefe isn't the most observant Catholic, and his liking for drink is unfortunate. But my impression is that he's fairly harmless. He manages to get to Mass every now and then, and I just can't see a trained man of the law doing anything to flout it. Isn't it best just to leave him be?"

O'Kelly stood up, leaning on his cane.

"A just man falling down before the wicked is as a fountain troubled with the foot and a corrupted spring," he said.

"I'm sorry, John?"

"I said, a just man falling down before the wicked is as a fountain troubled with the foot and a corrupted spring. It's *Proverbs,* Chapter twenty-five verse twenty-six."

"So, what's that to do with Sergeant O'Keefe? Please don't speak in riddles."

O'Kelly put his hand on Sheehan's shoulder and squeezed it. Both were surprised at its strength.

"A gentle reminder, Father Sheehan. There is no higher law than the law of our Lord, and it is *we* who are his policemen."

O'Kelly looked at Sheehan with a mix of compassion and muffled disgust. Sheehan's lack of experience was caving in to the force of O'Kelly's conviction.

"Anlon," added O'Kelly. "Can you imagine how awkward it would be if something went awry on the way to the Catholic mission and the Bishop started asking us questions? Think about it. What a pickle would we both be in if he ever got wind that we left the Aboriginals in the hands of a drunk and someone ended up getting hurt or killed. Don't you think, Anlon, that it would be for the best if we took protective measures?"

"Of course," said Sheehan, nervously. "I'll pass by the police station on Monday and see if a meeting can be arranged."

* * * * *

Nell's hands were clasped beneath her chin as she prepared what she would say.

The last thing we need is a row over Daisy, when one is perched on the horizon over Da's will.

Hector had replied to the letter Nell sent after Peggy shared her brothers' plans. He was coming for a visit to Ballycallan, and soon.

Polly sat at the other end of the kitchen table, where Rory had the previous night. The little girl was stirring salad cream, engrossed in what she was doing.

"Mum, can I add the little cap of vinegar yet?" asked Polly.

"Not just yet, love—in a few more minutes. We need to be sure that the egg yolks and mustard are properly mixed in."

"Will you tell Dad that it was me that made this and not Daisy?" asked Polly.

"Of course, I will Poll. But he'll probably work it out himself now that she's gone running out on the land to look for him."

329

The exchange with Rory of the night before across the length of the same kitchen table was as heavy as this one was light.

"Every Saturday morning, Nell, when we come back in from Town—no exceptions. Daisy is to stay in with you and help prepare lunch. The others can come out on to the land."

"Well, good luck with that," said Nell. "Am I to tether her to the stove like an animal? Because that's what it will take."

"Love, you could make a bit of effort. Show her that what you do is interestin'. We'll never get her in if you don't."

"All right," said Nell. "But I'll never get her to stay if she's alone with me and Grace. I'll keep Polly in to help as well, and you can go on to the land with the boys."

Nell watched Polly as she kept stirring the salad cream. The cold meats were cut, the salads made, and their pud stored away in the icebox. Nell wished the morning had gone to plan, that she was sitting opposite Daisy and not Polly, and that her first-born girl was as content as her second to help prepare the midday meal.

It had all gone pear-shaped after Rory left the house and Daisy rebelled.

"Why can't I go with Dad?" she had cried, her body stretched across the table. "I can run almost as fast as Eamon, and I'm as good at diggin' and fencin' as well."

She pushed aside the cookbook lying next to her.

"Daisy, it's not a question of being fair. I need you to help me here. And you have to learn to cook. You'll be rearing your own family one day."

"Not till I'm a grown-up, and that's ages away."

"Daisy, love, it isn't really. How will you manage to find a husband if you've no idea how to feed him?"

"Well, you can teach me once I find him."

"It doesn't quite work that way. You need to know before. And anyway, the boys aren't doing anything interesting. They're just patching that hole on the roof of the piggery."

With that, Daisy had sat up, lively and alert.

"They're what?" she asked.

"I meant, it's not as if they've gone out herding cattle or cropping corn. They are just fixing the piggery."

"But Mum, it was me that cut them patches of iron for Dad and painted 'em. And now you're tellin' me that it's Eamon that's gonna finish the job and not me? It's not fair, Mum, it's not fair."

Daisy had launched herself across the kitchen table, again, and sobbed.

"All right, young lady," said Nell. "But only for this week so you can finish that chore and let your da know that's why once you're up there. But next week, you're to stop in with me and Polly. No excuses, no turns, no tears."

And Daisy was gone in a second.

Her chair still sat at an angle at the table, like a gate someone forgot to close. Nell stood up, pushed it back into place, and inspected Polly's salad cream.

"Looks from here that you're finished," said Nell.

Polly gave up the bowl like the dream child that she was.

"That's perfect," said Nell. "You can pop in the vinegar, give it another good stir, then it's ready to be served."

Nell turned around and saw Rory at the door, dripping sweat and disappointment.

"Poll, can you go out on the front veranda and keep an eye on Grace? She'll be waking soon for a feed."

"All right, Mum," said Polly.

Rory took off his hat and walked toward his chair. Nell returned to hers at the table's other end.

She addressed her husband head on.

"Rory, I'm sorry, I couldn't get her to settle. Did Daisy explain it to you? Once she found out there was a job she started at the piggery that was being finished by the boys, I couldn't interest her in the kitchen. Rory, what do you think? Can't we leave all this until the New Year and let her enjoy the summer, especially if it's her last as a girl?"

Rory sighed.

"In a way, that's not the point, love. The point is you're not listening to *me*."

Nell spoke, softly but firmly.

"Daisy's my problem, and turning her into a suitable wife is my duty, not yours. She's in her last year of schooling next year. We can leave her education in the domestic arts until then."

Rory let the kitchen clock tick for a good ten seconds. Time cooled the simmer between him and his wife, but not his resolve for a result.

"All right," he said, getting up from the table. "But she's to have had enough learning to cook us a meal by Easter."

"That she will have no risk," replied Nell. "And I'm serving up in ten minutes."

Nell walked over to the cutlery draw to prepare setting the table. Rory ambled out.

One battle won with a minimum of fuss, thought Nell, *am not so hopeful it will be the same for the next.*

* * * * *

Beer was the best tonic a man could have against the descent of summer's heat. Dave and Rory sat at the bar of the Hotel Imperial, their hats sitting toward the back of their heads so that dampened foreheads could breathe.

Some thirty years back, two skinny lads with skin as fair as the sun was bright would sit in a style that was not dissimilar on rickety wooden stools. Back then, they would lean on the balustrade of the Burke shack veranda, each clutching a glass of bubbling liquid of a dusty summer day.

"You boys sip at that creaming soda and don't gulp it," Hannah Burke would say. "We've one bottle only for all the summer, so you're to drink it as the treat that it is."

Rory looked over his beer at Dave. In many respects, his friend hadn't changed. Dave was the larrikin,[78] Rory more proper. Dave was an extrovert, while Rory wanted to know a cove before he spoke too much himself. Dave lived life with a shrug of the shoulder—a fib here, a deception there, never seemed to bother him, particularly if it kept the peace.

But Rory wasn't comfortable with lies.

Still, the boys had been inseparable. Dave had kept nothing from Rory, and Rory nothing from Dave.

Rory remembered how he'd saved Dave's skin for stealing lollies from his mother.

"I've been nicking a few here and a few there from that jar Ma's collecting for lent. Now, she says she's gonna count 'em all before she gives it up for raffle."

"So, how you gonna get found out?" asked young Rory.

"I just seen that she's been making a note of how many she's put in each week."

---

[78] A high spirited and mischievous person.

"So how many have you taken?"

"Only five, I reckon. One a week from the beginning of Lent."

So, Rory pulled from beneath his bed his stash of hard-boiled lollies. He gave five of them to Dave.

That's exactly how I got myself into this mess, thought Rory. *Respecting Dave's need for deception.*

"What date are we due down Port Town way to get that land register changed?" asked Rory.

Dave wiped a dribble of beer from his chin.

"January fourth," said Dave. "Can't do it any earlier. We're not even heading down to the Port Town until the twenty-eighth of December. Got a job to do up here first."

"What sort of job is that?"

Dave reached for his beer and wondered what to say. Could Rory be brought in, or was he too much of a sissy? Would he be risking good wages from Roddy O'Doherty if he told him what he was up to?

No. Best to keep it to himself.

"Nothin' that interestin'," said Dave, as he put his beer down on the bar. "Just a small job a little way to the south. Have to slip away from Charlotte and the girls for a day and a night Boxing morning."

Rory's ears pricked up at a giveaway phrase: "nothin' interestin'." Dave deployed it whenever somethin' dodgy was being kept close to his chest. Rory pondered whether to ask him more, then decided to let it go.

At the moment, I have neither time nor will to be rescuing Dave from folly.

"That suits me," said Rory. "We're not due to leave the coast to come home until January seventh."

Dave ordered another round. It was filled by the barman in seconds.

"You don't have to be there, mate, at the land registry, I mean. It's for me to sign over, not for you to accept."

"No, I'll come along, just for the entertainment. You know, Dave, I've made up my mind about something—something that's been bothering me for a while. But I need to let you in on it before I have a word with Nell."

"So, what's it about?" asked Dave. "Nell find out you've been joining us for the odd game or two-up[79] of a Saturday afternoon?"

"No," said Rory. "That wouldn't likely bother her anyway. It's actually about that land."

"How so?"

"It's simple, Dave. January fourth is also our fifteenth wedding anniversary. After we're done at the land registry, I'm takin' Nell to dinner at the Pastoralists' Club, and I'm gonna tell her what we did back in 1913 so that I had enough land to marry her."

Dave stopped on his way to taking a swig and put his beer back on the bar.

"What do you mean you're gonna tell her?"

"I'm gonna tell her that I never had a hundred and eighty-five acres when we married and that I only had a hundred and fifty-five. That me and you cooked up a deal to get me closer to the around two hundred acres Hector had wanted, and that I've been slipping you payments for the whole of our marriage. That's what I'm gonna tell her."

---

[79] A gambling game involving betting on the outcome of the toss of coins.

"Christ, mate, you give me the willies when you get all righteous and worried. What's the flamin' point to that? And it might be easy for you to get Nell to swallow, but Charlotte'll give me a grillin' over why I kept it from her."

"The point is that I should have told Nell once we were wed. I hated it, Dave—every sneaky payment that I've ever slipped you in cash—keeping a little tranche of family money to myself and then passing it on to yours. I want a few things changed between me and Nell, and it's startin' with those acres."

Dave studied the froth topping his beer, calculating how to resist.

"All right," he said, as he pushed down his hat. "But don't rush anything either. It was fifteen flamin' years ago. I'll say nothing to Charlotte until we meet come New Year, and you are to let me know when you tell Nell."

* * * * *

Hector McTiernan blinked away exhaustion deepened sleep. Then, with eyes wide open and laying flat on his back, he was gradually able to focus. A delicate cone of meshed material hung grandly above his head, its point pinned to a white wooden ceiling. A mosquito net was a permanent fixture of Nell's side veranda bed. It reminded him of where he was.

I know full well that I have not been fair, thought Hector, as he stared at the breeze nudged netting, *and now it's all come to a head.*

Back in the beginning, it had seemed so simple. He didn't want Nell left out.

It just struck me as being completely unfair, mused Hector, *for Nell to inherit nothing. And when I promised her a share of Ballycallan, I had to keep it from the boys.*

336

Some of their mates were among Nell's suitors, and she wasn't to fall for a gold digger.

Hector grabbed at his boots from under the bed and sat up to put them on. He tightened the laces with rough tugs.

But then, you realized, you silly old bugger, how the community might react.

The constraints of doing anything different were clear on a recent visit to the City. On a business trip, a department store beckoned him in from the pavement. The broad wooden counter in the men's wear section he'd approached with trepidation. A fedora hat, cut in velvet no less, suited a handsome fella like him. But Hector closed his wallet without taking out money and handed the purchase back.

Not the bloody thing done up Port Town way, thought Hector, *to go posin' in the latest fashion.*

"And it's not the done thing either," whispered Hector, on Nell's side veranda, "for a daughter to be willed land over sons."

What will happen once the community finds out Ballycallan is part owned by a sheila?[80]

Would suppliers still sell them what they needed to run it, and would its produce hold its value?

The horizon that morning, thin and straight as a campfire pan, cooked an egg yolk of a sunrise.

It's gonna be a scorcher today, thought Hector, *and maybe in more ways than one.*

He looked at his watch. It was a half past six. Rory by now would be out on the land and the children probably still sleeping.

---

[80] Slang for *woman.*

Hector shuffled down to the kitchen doorway, rubbing his eyes as he went.

"Everyone gone or still in bed?" asked Hector, as he stood at the kitchen's threshold.

"Yes, Da," said Nell, turning around toward him, "the kids won't be up 'til seven."

Hector seated himself in Rory's chair at the end of the kitchen table.

Nell said nothing, brought the teapot from the stove, and began pouring from it for her father.

"Yes, love," said Hector, as if by the by, "it's all perfectly legal. It's the moral part I'm yet to square."

Nell put down the teapot, pulled out a chair from the table and dropped into it, heavily.

There's no time to discuss this in niceties.

Her da was finally granting permission for her to talk about the will. He hadn't mentioned it when he replied to the letter she had sent after Peggy and Brendan's visit. He'd simply said she was to sit tight and wait until he came up to Jacaranda Ridge. It would be a quick overnight on his way up to Brendan's to help him with the sale.

"That's what I've been saying all along, Da. If a fifth of Ballycallan will one day be mine, you have to help me explain it to the others. The boys, all the wives, and Rory."

Hector grimaced, took a sip of his tea, then returned his cup to its saucer. He laid his hands flat on the table.

There were two ways this could go.

"The first thing is you are not to worry. My solicitor says one hundred percent my will complies with the law. And provided I'm not of unsound mind, no one can say what I leave you isn't yours."

"That's all well and good," said Nell. "But it's as I said when I wrote. The boys are planning what they are going to do when the farm is split *four ways*. Selling land now and moving families so they can build a bloody station."

"They can, Nell," said Hector. "The only thing of which they are not aware is that they will have to buy your share."

Nell stood up, suddenly, and went to the window. Purple petals flew from the Jacaranda tree, caught by a passing breeze. She turned back toward the table, just as quickly.

"Why have you abandoned me over this," said Nell. "I'd have been better off never knowing."

"Well, in hindsight, I'd have to agree."

"Right then," said Nell, resolutely. "This is how I see it. Could you please go back and see your solicitor before Brendan has a chance to talk to you? Just change the date of the bloody will to some date near to now. Then gather us around when we are home at Christmas and explain what's going to happen. And I never, ever, want Rory to find out I knew that land was mine."

Hector winced and stroked his beard. Nell had no clue about commerce.

"Nell, love, my solicitor will think I'm potty," said Hector, "if I go to the bother of redrawing the will and make no change to it but the date."

"Well, for God's sake, Da, then think of something. Alter who'll get some of the horses."

Then, Nell did as she had throughout childhood. Folded her arms and turned her back in a pose excluding compromise.

Hector picked up his cup of tea and cast the first option aside. If he called a meeting and shared the truth to all, it would end as he'd always feared. In dispute, disappointment, and discord. Nell's hot temperament was too much of a risk and the boys might give it back to her in spades.[81]

"I can't do that Nell," said Hector quietly, "but there is something that I can do."

Nell kept her back to him, lost in the tree, biting her bottom lip.

Why is it always so extremely hard, thought Nell, *to garner support and respect.*

"I've written a letter to all the boys and will file it with the will. It explains to them why I've done as I have, and that it's to be kept a family secret. Play it cool, and you will have your land, with no loss of love from your brothers. News like this shared in the wake of my death is more likely to be accepted. Emotion and loss bind people together. It trumps the greed that can tear them apart."

Nell turned around, cheeks flushed red. Hector stood to close the subject.

"Gotta get on now, love," said Hector gently. "I'm going for a wash."

* * * * *

---

[81] To respond way more forcefully to a challenge or attack from another.

CHAPTER 12
CRUCIFIXION
December 1928

Father O'Kelly was praying at dawn, on a pristine Christmas Eve morning. A golden thread stretched across the base of a rapidly dying night. He watched it thin to nothing and the blue of the sky enrich.

So far, he'd received no intelligence. Neither Mr. Burke nor anyone else had spoken to him of Archibald Withers and what lay in store for the Aboriginals.

You should have discouraged him, thought O'Kelly, *from delaying that dinner with his wife.*

"I've selected January fourth, Father," Rory had said, when asked about it in the churchyard, "exactly fifteen years since the day we wed. I couldn't think of a better time to clear the secrets burdening our marriage."

Father O'Kelly was kneeling on the presbytery's back veranda and struggling to concentrate. An event that took place toward the beginning of his priesthood, and one that occurred that month, were colliding in his mind.

He thought all the way back to a summer day in 1881.

The scrub had been coarse and sharp. He pulled his hat to the sockets of his eyes, his back bowed into an arc of respect. His horse was plodding through the heat. Her splendid legs had sprung sprightly off the soft plains of Ireland but seized up on the rough of Australian country.

Young John O'Kelly reached an opening in the bushland and gasped.

They were at a distance of a couple of hundred yards. A terrorized black woman ran for her life from a rabid white man on horseback. The crack of his whip on the far side of the clearing pumped at O'Kelly's heart and pulled in his heels. He charged his horse toward them.

The white man jammed her into a corner of trees and tall scrub.

"Yield!" cried O'Kelly. "Yield!"

She ran to her right, and the horseman reeled, just as hard, blocking her as she went. He cracked his whip again, so she spun to her left, the rims of her eyes shining like white light before he blocked her on that side as well. With her arms outstretched and her hands splayed open, she grabbed at the branches she was able to reach, only to let go as he cracked so close to her naked back, she might have thought she were already dead.

The horseman turned around, threw a glance at O'Kelly, then turned back toward the woman.

And shot her.

The horseman sped away as O'Kelly roared with rage. He had been startled, perhaps, by the small white oblong resting at O'Kelly's neck—the unmistakable mark of a priest.

The horseman had a pistol. He had had a pistol, but O'Kelly didn't see it.

And my charge toward him might have prompted the attack.

Back on the veranda on Christmas Eve of 1928, O'Kelly wept into his hands.

"Help me, God, please help me. I have done nothing but fail the first people of this land."

The second of his regrets occurred that month. The meeting between him, Father Sheehan, and Sergeant O'Keefe had done nothing to quell his fears.

"Look here, Sergeant," Sheehan had said, when the policeman finally agreed to meet them. "It's not the role of the church to interfere with the police force—to tell you how to do your job. But it's just that we're a little unsure. How many meetings have there been with the Aboriginal people—to befriend them, I mean? It's not that we are prying, Sergeant. It's just that we'd like to know more."

It had all taken place in the police station foyer. Father O'Kelly sat on the end of the bench near the entrance. Birdy had been allowed to stay there, exceptionally, despite the presence of visitors. He sat on its farthest end. O'Kelly's attempt to tip his hat to him foundered. Birdy wouldn't look at him.

Sheehan stood at the counter, opposite O'Keefe. The priests were not invited into O'Keefe's private office, offered tea, or even a chair. O'Keefe was as immovable as the soaring cliffs of the Town's quarry.

"My word, Father, too many to count," said O'Keefe. "We go out into the bush every Monday—me and Birdy, that is. Check on 'em, and give 'em a food drop if the Protector has been in. And it's Birdy here that goes in for a chat. Isn't that right, Birdy?"

The black man nodded and grinned.

Sheehan looked at O'Kelly, and O'Kelly scowled back. The policeman had to be pressed.

"If I may say," Father Sheehan coughed and continued, "it's all a little surprising. Were you aware that Father O'Kelly has been trying to bring them in for years? I don't want to detract from your achievements, Sergeant. It's just that we were wondering how it was managed?"

O'Keefe then put the priests in their place.

"May I suggest, Father Sheehan, that you address your concerns to Mr. Roddy O'Doherty? It was he who moved the motion through Town Council. What has been agreed cannot be undone. You should be addressing your concerns to him."

O'Kelly leaned forward to tug Sheehan's sleeve. The young priest sensed his desperation and took a step to the side to avoid it.

"Of course, Sergeant," said Sheehan. "And I hope you will be able to excuse me. Now you mention it, you are right—it completely slipped my mind. I should have approached Mr. O'Doherty at the outset."

And so, it was that an old priest's resolve was sucked away to nothing. Overwhelmed by the tide of deals sealed in secret and the crushing weight of power.

On the presbytery back veranda, O'Kelly looked up from worn wooden floor boards and dried his eyes with a hanky. The remains of the night had peeled away, releasing a porcelain sky.

"Almost nothing," he muttered, "has changed."

O'Kelly stood, aided by his cane, and shuffled back to his room. He wanted to check that everything he needed was packed in his swag.[82] His train heading south would be pulling into Town in no time.

* * * * *

The Burke family entered Ballycallan just before nightfall on December twenty-fourth. The children made the six-foot drop from Rory's long cart the moment the wheels ceased turning. All the Burke children, save for baby Grace, ran to Poppa and

---

[82] Small bag carrying essentials when travelling in the bush.

Nan. They knew there would be sweeties and treats waiting inside, and an extra creamy pud after dinner.

Ballycallan had three times the land of Jacaranda Ridge. And Hector employed men, some black, mostly white. Not many men; nonetheless, he was of the employer class in the near northeast. He had jobs for four stockmen—two black, two white. They met the void in labor caused by the departure of Nell and her brothers, and the onset of Hector's old age.

"Because they're half the price, and if you treat 'em right, they'll do a job as good as any white man," Hector would say, when challenged about the presence of Aboriginals on his run. "And they won't shoot through[83] at the first tiny sign of tuppence extra pay elsewhere."

Once the greetings were over, the Burke children raced off to the old blacksmith's workshop. They all took turns at pumping on Hector's long-dormant bellows. That evening, they scrapped over who would get to sleep on Nan's veranda. On it, there were two large beds, walled in by white nets that kept the mosquitoes at bay while letting in the sounds of the night.

And the homestead at Ballycallan had been renovated from the riches earned in the boom. All the floorboards were covered by handwoven rugs. White lace draped over each of Violet's polished tables, and pictures painted by a professional artist hung on the dining room walls. The kitchen sparkled in copper with the smartest of cooking implements, while the Burkes' kitchen up north remained monotonous in its reliance on pitch-black steel.

---

[83] To leave suddenly, without explanation, and with no mention of future whereabouts.

Every part of Ballycallan bore the touch of a tradesman. All its windows sheltered beneath painted awnings, while those in the Burke home were still shielded by bark that Rory had stripped from trees.

The next day, after Christmas Mass, the children tore up the hill to play in the bushland behind the back veranda. But this was subject to rules. They were never to lose sight of the house.

The women collected in the kitchen. Violet, Nell, and all four of her sisters-in-law—Doris, Posie, Peggy, and Nonie—took morning tea before preparing Christmas lunch.

"Nell, your girls are growing ever more gorgeous," said Nonie, as she sliced a piece of sponge cake. "In a few years, you and Rory'll be pickin' and choosin' from suitors."

"They've the gift of good looks, all right, but that doesn't make them any less of a handful," replied Nell.

She was sitting at the far side of Violet's enormous kitchen table and could see outside into the rainforest.

"It's a blessing when they're that active," chimed in Posie. "My eldest is no farm girl. Kieran and I tried to get her out onto the land, but she's got not a jot of interest in it."

"She'll be a Port Town bride then?" asked Nell.

"It looks that way, all right," replied Posie.

"It doesn't look that way for Daisy," said Nell. "She'll be a woman of the land like her ma, no risk."

Nell looked out again beyond the kitchen door. It had been wet down south, and the rainforest running by the homestead seemed to breathe. Leaves the size of wheat sacks hung from trees as high as windmills. Nell let herself drift, for a moment, into its sound and smells.

On his visit to Jacaranda Ridge, Da shut that window for discussing the will as quickly as he opened it.

"So, when are you and Rory going for this fancy dinner?" asked Doris. "The Pastoralists' Club has a restaurant as fine as any in the City."

Nell blinked at being brought back in.

"On the fourth of January, our fifteenth anniversary. Rory says he wants it to be special."

"Well, that it certainly will be," said Peggy. "My goodness, fifteen years *is* a milestone."

Nell prized a mouthful of cake with a fork from her plate. *Sure is.*

That was when she would share the news—the enormous, hidden, festering news. A whole fifth of Ballycallan would someday go to her. She would persuade Rory herself it wasn't wrong to accept it, assure him it was legal, then get on to her da about telling her brothers before their plans went any further.

And please God, Da's wishes will stick, and that land will one day be mine.

The men gathered on the front veranda. Brendan, Robert, Kieran, and Travis—all had their turn at home that year for Christmas rather than with the parents of their wives.

It had been organized by Brendan. Sometime over the holidays, Hector would hear about their vision for Ballycallan.

"Now we live down here," said Brendan, "I see that moving cattle by motorized vehicle hasn't taken over completely."

He took a beer from the icebox.

"It'll be cheaper, no fear, but I can't see the cattle taking to it," said Robert. "I'm not sure how we'd herd them in, and they'll be unsettled by the rough of the ride."

"Don't know about that," said Kieran. "That new road into the Port Town is as flat as a gin's[84] heel. Be a smooth ride for a bullock."

They talked on. The sun dawdled to twelve o'clock.

"De Valera's down, but not out," said Hector. "Got himself and a party of his own into the Dail.[85] He'll be chippin' on till there's a Republic in Ireland—so your uncle writes from County Killkenny."

He took a long gulp from a beer bottle.

His sons rallied to show interest, but it was mostly just to humor him. Mustering enthusiasm for the politics of a country they could only hear and read about wasn't easy, even when it was part of the events of the world. For Hector, it also meant talk of the lives of brothers and sisters, cousins and friends, whom he would never be able to forget.

"He won't manage it, Da," said Travis.

"It's a crazy idea," added Robert. "The Republic of somewhere out in the Atlantic Ocean. The English will never agree to it, and they'll never get it by fightin' 'em."

Hector drank despondently. He actually had to persuade his own sons of the need for a Republic in Ireland, and Rory didn't even want to discuss it.

Rory leaned against the veranda rail. Behind him, deep green hills flowed like waves to where the horizon met the sea. He allowed the conversation to unravel without contributing but remembered Hector and Sean at his wedding. They sang songs of revolution, cursed the oppression at home, and toasted each other as landowners here. In this country too, there were limits, all right, on what a Catholic could be. But Rory knew

---

[84] Obscene term for an *Aboriginal woman.*
[85] Irish Parliament

they amounted to nothing when compared to the barriers in Ireland.

Any strife in Australia's been all of my own making, thought Rory, *as my wife will hear on January fourth, in a private dining booth at the Port Town Pastoralists' Club.*

"Hector, can you come inside and start carving?" called Violet. "We're almost ready to eat."

* * * * *

The grandfather clock ticked coolly. The street had fallen silent. The Christmas Day traffic of townsfolk returning from morning church services had finished, and lunch, in most homes, was underway. But it hadn't yet started in the Withers household. Millicent still wasn't out of bed, and Archibald was beginning to worry.

She is going to have to get up soon, he thought, as he carved the chicken at the empty dining room table.

He had carried it in from the kitchen after cooking it in the oven himself. It was annoying to find her sleeping, still, when he returned home from church.

He handled the embarrassment well in the face of the inevitable queries.

"How many months gone is she, Mr. Withers?" one of the ladies had asked.

"Between two and three, I believe," he replied. "Although I leave such matters to Millicent and her nurse."

"It will pass, Mr. Withers," someone else offered. "I know it's a great worry for you, and the sickness that can come in the early months of pregnancy is just terrible. But in a few weeks, she should be just about back to normal."

He never enjoyed the obligatory after-service chat in the churchyard. But it was excruciating when he had to field questions of such delicacy. If Millicent had managed to attend the service, it all could have been avoided.

And he had been subjected to children. The number of them the Anglican community were producing appalled him. Some of the families were so large, they might as well have been Roman Catholic. It was partly Reverend Parker's fault. He had set a terrible example. If he counted correctly, Parker had already sired seven himself. Children shrieked, chattered, and ran in the churchyard like poor-house urchins. Ordinarily, he and Millicent would stay for an acceptably polite quarter of an hour. The questions about her health that Christmas Day had detained him longer, and alone.

Irritated, worried, and angry, he eased the last piece of overcooked chicken from its carcass. Then, he paced the length of the dining room, trying to work out what to do.

He stopped, pulled back the curtain, and peered out the window. Tomorrow, in the late afternoon, and provided that idiot of a police sergeant obeyed his orders, the blacks would be marched through the street en route from the lock-up to the train station. The journey would take them, inevitably, past his own home. There wasn't a way out of it. After reflection, Withers adhered to his original position. Come the twenty-sixth, he and Millicent were to be gone, no matter what.

O'Keefe was a bloody fool and met his limits quickly. Should anything go awry, there was a better than even chance that he would come knocking on his door, asking what to do. O'Keefe might even embroil him in exposure to elements of the transfer that had to remain concealed. It was too risky. He and Millie could not stay in Town. Putting himself at Sergeant O'Keefe's disposal was out of the question.

She walked in, gingerly, still pale but with color rising.

"Millie, darling," said Withers, and rushed to take her hand. "You look so much better."

"I wish I felt better. Did you pass my apologies to Reverend Parker?"

"Of course," replied Withers. "Everyone understood and wished you a quick recovery. And now I can see you are achieving it."

"Not as quickly as I would like," said Millicent gloomily.

She took her place at the table.

"My love, I have failed you as a wife. I saw the vegetables all prepared in the kitchen, and now I see you have roasted the chicken yourself. Archie, what an unlucky man you are, wedded to a woman who cannot even manage to present a Christmas lunch!"

"I will not hear that talk in our home. What sort of a husband would force his expecting wife out of her sick-bed on the holiest of God's days? And now, it will be my pleasure to serve you. Let me fetch the veg."

In the kitchen, Withers mulled through how to get her moving. The lake-side cottage was booked from four o'clock on the twenty-sixth at a village to the east. They had planned to reach it after a long day tomorrow on the road in the sulky. But that was the sticking point. She had been ill every morning for the last fortnight, and far too ill to travel. The subject of whether to travel tomorrow would inevitably surface over lunch. She would likely suggest they should stay at home rather than spend the holidays away.

He cursed himself for not having thought of it earlier.

He scooped the potatoes into a serving bowl and plotted out the journey. As they tumbled across the porcelain, he realized something. In the past two weeks, when all this had started, she had been as well in the afternoons as she had been ill in the morning. She had, he had noticed, reorganized her day so that chores and duties took place more toward its end than the beginning. Now, it was obvious. He could easily alter the timing of their trip. He carried the tray to the dining room and resolved to say nothing until Millie raised the subject herself.

It played out just as Withers expected.

"Archie," said Millicent, as she unfolded her napkin. "About our holiday. I know it will be an unforgivable waste, and the cottage came at the full holiday rate, but I cannot see that I will be fit to travel in the morning."

"I know, my love. I have observed the pattern of your day, and the trouble you have had in starting it. That's why I have decided that you shall have your holiday, regardless."

"How so?"

"Because my lady deserves only the best, and my lady shall have her cure by water. We shall leave today, once we have cleared up and packed, and stay in a suite at the traveler's rest tonight. That will leave us a half-day journey on the twenty-sixth that we can take in the afternoon once you are better so we will be by the lake before nightfall."

Millicent beamed.

"Archie, you are a gem—a gem of a man and a gent."

"Perhaps, my love," Withers replied. "But if that is so, I am a gem who has been paired with a diamond."

* * * * *

The veranda tables at Ballycallan were divided into major and minor. The twelve adults were seated like royalty at the large one. It was covered in lace to their knees. The meal was arranged around roses cut from the flower bed kept by Violet. Trays piled high with the meats of chicken, turkey, and pig, all surrounded with fresh veg, were passed from one plate to the next, with every one of them bearing a regal stamp on the back. And a blessing encircled them. It was a mild summer day. The hills exhaled, glimmering in green. They rejoiced in the gift of freedom from the heat and danced their way to the horizon.

The lower table, in uncovered wood, was longer and set out places for the eighteen McTiernan grandchildren. Tinsel hung in loops at its edges, tacked with tiny nails by Hector's hammer and arranged by Violet's hand. The plates for the meals of McTiernan children and teenagers were filled by their mothers before being returned to the table. Their meal was as quick as the adults' was slow. They rushed to resume their games.

"Last one to the smithy shop's a rotten egg," cried Daisy, the second she finished eating.

"The only rotten egg's gonna be you, Daisy," shot back a cousin, and they all scampered off.

"You steady on there, Eamon Burke," Nell called out. "You run yourself sick, and there'll be no holiday for any of us."

"I won't, Mum," he replied.

But then Eamon stopped, turned around, and strolled over to join the adults. He had reached the age at which he could elect to sit at their table, a least for dessert. He fondled his wristwatch and listened to the grown-ups talk.

"Mum, this caramel tart is unbeatable," said Brendan. "No disrespect to you, darl," he said to Peggy. "There must be something in the dairy products of Ballycallan."

"You've not gotten that right," replied Peggy. "It's not in the cream—it's your mother's talent and skill that makes the difference."

"Well, I'm going to be the first to jump in for seconds," said Hector. "Nell, can you pass me the plate?"

Nell did as she was asked and transferred the tart to her father, diagonally across the table. She managed to do so without looking at him, but so the others didn't notice.

Behind the house, Daisy led the pack of marauding, well-fed children. She was astride the pole lathed by Rory, capped with a horsehead made of wood, that had been meant as a gift for Polly. She touched the old smithy shop wall, then reeled back to run down Nan's hill again, going faster.

Just after she set off, she stopped in her tracks, her brown eyes widened by surprise.

A lizard stood before her. Not an ordinary lizard, but a beast the length of her own lanky legs, and as tall at its head as a doggie.

Daisy was not one for turning and squealed with delight. As the frightened reptile thrashed its way back into the bush, Daisy chased it down a track, left hand gripping the pole, right hand beating its end with a stick she imagined to be a whip. The lizard charged ever deeper into the bushland. Daisy followed it determinedly.

Eventually, it slipped into a crack between a cluster of rocks and disappeared. Pleased with the chase, Daisy stopped, wiped her brow, and turned to head back to Nan's. But the familiar form of the roof of the long back veranda was gone.

At first, she frolicked on, remembering she had slipped into a gully. If she went back to its end, she would see Nan's iron roof poking above the scrub. But there, she met only the base of another low hill. Then, she remembered something else. She had darted over that hill at full flight when chasing the giant lizard. She would see Nan's veranda once she scaled it to the top. Instead, the short hike upward led to a plain of ruddy, uncut scrub.

Daisy flung the horse to the ground and broke into a run that sent her further into the bush, screaming, "Mum! Dad!"

Back at the homestead, it was half an hour before the other children noticed she was gone.

It was another four before the adults came to realize that they wouldn't find her before nightfall.

* * * * *

O'Keefe had to tip his hat to Withers. He marveled, by his campfire on the evening of December twenty-fifth, on how Withers had handled that Town Hall meeting.

Born to authority were the words that sprang to his mind. O'Keefe had taken none too small a pleasure in watching the holy men squirm, unaccustomed as they were to each other's company. As for the visit to the station from the Catholic brethren, one pansy priest and the other a decrepit, they were never going to put him off. There was too much money at stake.

"Put the feckin' fire out, Birdy. Time we got some shut-eye."

And so it was that Sergeant Brian O'Keefe went on horseback to meet up, that Boxing Day morning, with the men he had stationed at an Aboriginal camp about seven miles to the south of the Town.

O'Keefe kept one eye on the passing bushland and the other one on Birdy who walked by him as they traveled.

"Better move in before the sky starts singing, boss," said Birdy, as they began to approach the camp. "Blackfellas'll be up with the sun."

"All understood, Birdy," said O'Keefe.

It was to be executed during the hour of the night that was lightened by the touch of the day, when the animals of the dark were still lively, twitching but content in the weak morning light.

They reached journey's end.

"You blokes ready?" O'Keefe murmured as he dismounted.

"Too right, Sarge," one man whispered.

Three hatted heads nodded.

"Good," said O'Keefe.

He opened his satchel and pulled out three pistols and tossed one of them to each man.

"Christ, mate," one of them said, "Mr. O'Doherty didn't say anything about guns."

"And he didn't say anything to me about pansies when he told me who he'd designated to help at this camp."

The men shoved the guns behind their waist belts.

"Any one of these coons bolts, you shoot 'em, or you blow them luscious wages Mr. O'Doherty's agreed to pay you. And don't forget who's the law out here. *Me.* Now get on with it."

First, there would be fire. If the blacks could not be entrapped with fences, O'Keefe had planned, then the fear of God could be put into them to stop them running away. The humpy was squared off at a distance of thirty feet, four stakes were put in place, each with a high burning stick flickering in red and flashes of blue. The three men crept forward, one with rope and all with pistols. They could see the Aboriginals were sleeping. They retreated, a little, stopping once the flames were about ten feet to their rear. One of them blasted shots into the ground.

Twenty or so yet-to-be-saved souls stirred with a start.

One man moved to the far side of the humpy. A second round was shot.

They could hear them speaking to each other but understood nothing.

O'Keefe boomed.

"Come out, we won't hurt you. You dash out into the scrub, we'll shoot you dead, and if we miss, we'll set the bush alight."

O'Keefe could just make them out, all dressed sparsely in calico rags. Embraces fueled by fear gathered them together. Meanwhile, the muscles of the white men relaxed, freeing their caught breath. If there were spears to fight back with, they would likely have already been thrown, and there was no sign of any bolters.

O'Keefe fired another shot groundward. Then, all was still in the humpy. He went forward, stopping at its edge.

The Aboriginals gawked at O'Keefe's enormous stomach. It was the shape of that of a pregnant woman. The leanest of the men waved his arms, then pointed toward the hills. He cried out repeatedly. O'Keefe understood only the scatter of words said in English.

"Go back! Go away! Little children crying!"

"You can keep your heathen language to yourself," said O'Keefe. "You speak to me, then you do so in the King's English in complete feckin' sentences. Come on. We are moving you out of this dirt into clean Christian digs. Now, get goin'."

O'Keefe prodded the air with his pistol.

The Aboriginal people stumbled out.

All necklaced in rope that ran uninterrupted from the first in line to the last, all twenty were marched seven miles to the Town police station. Some of the women carried children on their hips. Birdy strutted by their side, stick in hand, content to flick a weakening blackfella's leg. At the station, O'Keefe was buoyed by the sight of a plan falling into place. Four further chains of about fifteen native souls a piece were already behind bars, herded in by others of his men.

"The mob we've brought in can go in the cellar," he said.

"Can fix that, boss," replied Birdy.

Invective launched lividly from deep in Birdy's throat. O'Keefe didn't understand a word of it, but the terrified twenty descended the stairs without speaking.

* * * * *

On Christmas night, Hector and Violet gathered their eighteen grandchildren at their enormous kitchen table, nine on one side of it, nine on the other. Violet had assembled each one an evening meal made up of leftovers from Christmas lunch and was finishing serving up. Hector sat at the table's head, with Eamon by his side.

Nell, numbed by shock, watched from a pitch-black veranda.

"You want to go out with the men tomorrow, Eamon," Hector asked gently.

Eamon sighed.

"Of course, Pop. But I'm not much of a bushman. I might do more harm than good."

"I'll go", said cousin Pete, "since I'm the eldest grandchild." They were barely touching their food.

"How are we going to find Daisy?" another cousin asked meekly from the far end of the table.

"We'll have her back in the morning," said Violet, as she sat down at the table. "Your uncles will gather help, and we'll bring her back in."

"Why can't they go now?" asked Patrick, looking up at Hector.

Patrick was leaning his head on the small of one of his hands. With the other, he moved his food around the plate with a fork in slow circles.

"We can't find her in the dark, Pat. Your uncles and da would only get lost as well, and we still wouldn't have her back. It's the bushman's law. Searches can only go on in daylight," explained Hector.

"Where will she sleep?" said Pat.

"She'll have a lovely sleep under a tree," replied Hector. "Or she'll have found a little cave and will curl up on a big flat rock."

"We have to find my sister," said Polly. "I'm too little to be Mum's big girl."

With that, Nell ran down the corridor to her girlhood room and flung herself on the bed. Her sisters-in-law heard, from the homestead salon, the distress of rapidly moving feet. They followed her into the muggy lamplight of the bedroom.

"It's a mild summer night, Nell," said Posie. "The poor little mite'll be scared out of her wits, but she'll not suffer in this weather."

"And there's not been a dingo seen in these parts for twenty years," added Doris. "There's nothing out there that could attack her. And all the Aboriginals here are either missioned off or working on farms."

"Or she might have been bitten by a snake, fallen down a hole, or run off a cliff," cried Nell from a dampening pillow.

Eventually, she sat up.

"We couldn't get her off the land," blubbered Nell. "And now it's taken her."

"You don't know that, Nell," said Nonie. "She can't have gone that far. We'll find her in the morning."

"Where's Rory?" asked Nell.

"I think he's on the front veranda with all the men bar Hector," said Peggy.

Nell went to find him. The McTiernan brothers and Rory Burke were standing over a map on a table, working on Daisy's rescue. Nell stopped and watched from a distance, in the shadows, leaning her head against a veranda pole.

They were planning to blanket the bush.

"There's a a whole mess of properties within three miles of here," said Robert, "and I reckon about twenty fit men living on them."

"Well, we should all set out as soon as there's light and get as many as we can to help," said Travis.

"I'll go over to the McDougals'," said Kieran. "I saw Bill McDougal only yesterday."

"And I'll take the Fitzgibbons'," said Travis. "All six of their men are home. Saw them at the pub a few days back."

"All right," said Robert, "that leaves me, Brendan, and Rory. Rory, seein' as you've met the Martin family on the other side of the road, I'm sending you over there."

Rory was hanging on to the side of the table, barely able to stand.

I am not even the family member in command, thought Rory, *when it comes to finding my daughter.*

"I am going out to look for her at first light," mumbled Rory.

"You're what?" asked Travis.

"I am going out to find my daughter," said Rory more firmly, "as soon as there is light."

"Steady up, mate," said Robert. "I know you're upset, but Ned Kelly's robbin' this coach.[86] The countryside around Ballycallan isn't something you know much about. It's best to leave the lead of the search to us."

Rory raised his voice.

"My daughter, my responsibility, so we do it as *I* say."

Nell moved forward from out of the shadows. She touched Rory's elbow and whispered.

"They're just trying to help, Rory. We grew up here and know the terrain and its people."

Rory turned to face his wife, having taken what she had said as against him.

"Jesus Christ, Nell, I told you we needed to get Daisy to them dance classes at Madame La Bonne's. That girl's as wild as a mountain brumby,[87] and now we've gone and lost her."

Rory pushed past Nell and started pacing the veranda. Her brothers looked at each other, confused.

"Madame what?" asked Nell, her hands on her hips. "How in the bloody hell can you be talking about dance classes at a time like this?"

"You don't even bloody remember, do you, Nell?" shot back Rory. "I tried to tell you a couple of months back in the workshop. Gotta redirect Daisy's energy into something more

---

[86] I am in charge. Ned Kelly was a famous Australian bush ranger (outlaw).
[87] A free-roaming wild horse.

ladylike and disciplined. If you'd bloody well listened to me instead of stompin' off, we might not have lost her."

Rory sat on a nearby settee and put his head in one of his hands, while a reservoir storing disdain for constraint burst inside his wife.

"How bloody dare you, Rory, turn around and try and blame me when the girl I've reared goes missing. I would have thought that I might be left one patch, one tiny little patch, where I can be left to make the decisions."

Rory looked up, amazed, as Nell barreled on.

"It's not bloody easy, Rory. I had no control over a house falling down and even less of a hand in how to fix it. Giving up the next stage of my son's development because it's the men who have to decide is about as cruel as something can be. And how about the months of anguish and worry when you turned into Mr. erratically Strange and Moody when we were waiting for receipts from the bank? And what did I have to do? Swallow it. Swallow what was happening and say nothing, and that applies to *everything*. So, don't ask me, Rory, if it gets down to pointing the finger, about the marks I give *you* as a husband."

Rory sprung to his feet.

"Well, at least I *am* a husband Nell, and not half-attached to a meddling father to the exclusion of *you*."

Rory glanced to his left. There was Hector, standing in the doorway, with eyes flashed open to bulging.

Silence spasmed for what felt like forever. It even quelled the flutter of the fruit bats. Then, Rory snatched a freestanding night lamp sitting on the veranda railing.

"I'm going out to look for her now."

Bolted, Rory did, down the stairs, across the lawn, and up the hill to the track in the bushland behind Ballycallan's homestead.

Nell ran after him, screaming his name, but Brendan caught up with her, and quickly. He tackled her to the grass and held her down. His cowboy hat flew off as he fell.

"Sorry, Nell, can't let you go. Two McTiernans lost in the bush is already two too many."

Nell wept unconsolably on her brother's shoulder. Eruption ejected the truth.

"That's the heart of all our troubles," sobbed Nell. "We are all supposed to be Burkes."

* * * * *

A filthy freight train rocked and shuddered, tilting carriages bereft of windows every random way. Black hands slammed against their metal walls, and voices wailed. O'Keefe stood in the middle of one of the cars and fired a shot clear through the roof. Twenty Aboriginals scurried toward a corner, fearing for their lives.

The ropes in which the five groups had been gathered remained in-tact. Withers was emphatic when he met O'Keefe, in private, just before Christmas.

"Now, remember. You are to effect their transfer from the police station to the railway before nightfall, at five o'clock on December twenty-sixth, after an inventory is taken at said police station of how many of them we've cleared. Do you understand?"

"Yes, sir, but I could just as well transfer them in the morning as soon as they are moved in from the scrub. There is a train at nine o'clock."

"Sergeant, if this is to go well, you are to do exactly as I say. Tell me, who will be awake at eight o'clock Boxing morning to see that our native brethren were indeed moved out, roped together on a clan by clan basis?"

"I should imagine, nobody."

"Precisely! They are to be put in the cargo cars of the train that departs at six in the evening, one clan per car, still roped. A wait at the station will guarantee an additional source of witness."

So, come the late afternoon of December twenty-sixth, O'Keefe put five human columns on show. They lurched through the Town's main street, just on the stroke of five. Withers was right. The promenade yielded the assurance of twitching curtains, despite the post-Christmas exodus to the coast.

And O'Keefe obeyed the rest of Withers' orders.

"You are to do nothing, and I mean absolutely nothing, to depart from the plan approved by the clergy until well after nightfall. By that, I mean the other end of the rail journey."

"Of course not, Mr. Withers, sir. Under no circumstance at all."

"But if you fail to split and mix them, they will most certainly return. If any single one of them is ever sighted again within fifty miles of the Town, the bank will suspend your loan. They are to be disbanded and mixed under the cover of distance and darkness."

The shroud O'Keefe needed to collect his prize descended at Purgatory Creek.

Ten headlights paired on five cattle trucks lit up the night at its train station. A score of strongmen pulled from the region's farms were primed and raring to go. They charged from the vehicles to meet the train.

In the black of the night, women screamed. Some bit, and the men threw bony fists at enormous jaws and walls of muscular stomach. Heels were dragged across a car park made of rough-edged rocks. Feet were split and stained the ground red.

They were being torn apart.

"Cut the rope, then toss two from each column into each separate vehicle," bellowed O'Keefe to the men.

"Then, do the same again, but make sure you chuck the next two, then the next two, into a different vehicle. I want the heads of these black bastards put well into a spin."

Birdy was confused.

Boss is moving out these blackfellas tough, he thought. *I could have led 'em easy into the vehicles if he'd have left 'em in the ropes.*

"Then slam the feckin' door and lock it proper when you're done," cried O'Keefe.

He charged to the cab of each truck, shouting commands at the drivers as he thrust a map into each of their hands.

"You to the Presbyterian," he said. "Your mob to the Catholics," he shouted at the next. "This lot to the Lutherans. And you, cart 'em off to Anglican land."

O'Keefe ran to the back of the last of the vehicles. It was destined for the mission of the Baptists.

"Birdy, get over here. I need you to tell 'em that if they try to bolt, we'll feckin' shoot their black arses. Don't wanna risk that they're not just pretendin' they don't understand English."

"Yes, boss, but they not all my language."

"Just get over here and fecking try," cried O'Keefe, his blood coursing.

Birdy stood at the rear of the truck for the Baptists, its back doors open, its cargo whimpering. O'Keefe positioned himself behind Birdy. He had barely uttered a word when O'Keefe's familiar hands grabbed him, one on his neck, the other beneath his crotch. He hurled Birdy into the back of the truck.

As the door slammed shut behind him, Birdy scrambled.

"Boss!" he cried, thumping on the truck's iron doors.

"What's going on, boss? Gotta help you at the station, boss. Still can help you like a woman, boss. Boss! Boss!"

The engine had already started. The vehicle was moving on.

Sergeant O'Keefe, breathless, looked toward the gaslit station at Purgatory Creek. Could he be sure his acts would be verified so that Mr. Withers paid him his due?

He needn't have worried. Roddy O'Doherty was unmistakable. Tall, broad, and ample of girth, he saw all from the train station's porch. And O'Doherty wasn't alone. Dave Noonan sat close by him, blowing smoke rings, blithely, into the night.

Birdy sat, stunned, on the floor of the truck as the vehicle shuddered on. Just the night before, O'Keefe had pushed his face against the police station wall once his men had been paid and gone home. Rammed, Birdy had been, deeper and rougher than ever before. In Town, he had heard some of the whitefellas snigger when their women weren't around and call him "Bend Over Birdy." Boss would always take care of him, he reckoned, if he just kept up "Bend Over Birdy."

As Birdy lay crumpled on the police station floor, O'Keefe panted and found the solution—the hidden whorehouses of the Port Town. O'Keefe could dispense with Birdy's satin arse after all. With the cash parts of his prize, he could join the other gentlemen in the whorehouses. The railway had brought them closer, and he could travel to the Port Town more frequently. Therein lay the answer. He needn't take a risk over Birdy.

* * * * *

Christmas of 1928 was afflicted by two deaths and tempered by one salvation.

By the time they reached the Baptist mission, Birdy had been beaten to witless. The missionaries lifted him from a hook for the hanging of cow carcass, and on which he had been impaled. He was rushed to the infirmary, but all too late. His head was smashed in several places, his face split and torn. The nurses hadn't expected to find a pulse and didn't. So, there departed the sole independent witness to the Dispersal at Purgatory Creek.

This group of natives was particularly savage, O'Doherty explained when the clergymen later asked. They had all behaved perfectly until it came to moving them from the train to the cattle trucks. There, they had attacked, without warning, the farmers who had given up their time in the holidays to help the churches with the transfer. They even turned on one of their own, and viciously, when the white man wasn't there to supervise.

The farmers had carried on as best they could during the melee, but it was no longer clear which blacks were from where, so they were bundled off more randomly than planned.

In such circumstances, the clergymen might think themselves fortunate, O'Doherty went on, to receive any new souls at all.

Only Parker was perturbed. He knew Dr. Thomas reasonably well and resolved to find out more. *How could the black-tracker have ended up dead?* He also planned to raise his concerns with Withers when they next played family bridge.

But come New Year, Millicent and Archie left quickly after church of a Sunday, on account of her health, and didn't go out again socially until April. By then, Parker had thought better of it. It might appear ungrateful. Best to move on.

And how Mr. Withers was impressing the Anglicans. Since the summer of 1928, and the news he was to become a father, he was so much more calm and measured. No one ever picked up a connection with the Dispersal and the disappearance of the Town's Aboriginals.

For the Burkes, that Christmas was long remembered and passed into family folklore.

On December twenty-sixth, Hector, got up first and wandered out onto the veranda. It was going to be another cloudless day. The yellow-crested whites soared low along the length of the horizon, their wings brushing lightly at the sky. It was tinted with enough sunlight to silence the insects, but too little to push the birds into song.

Hector put on his boots. As he did, he spotted a familiar, sloping black stick of a figure crossing his long lawn.

It was Jock the stockman.

"Jock," said Hector, in a whisper.

His voice carried, unobstructed, in the nascent day.

"Jock, what are you doing here?"

Jock turned, strolled up the incline toward Hector, and stopped just short of the homestead.

"I come back early, Mr. Hector," he said softly. "Bit of trouble up at Mum's country. Can I stay in stockmans' digs at the bottom of the run, Mr. Hector? Bit of work to be done down there anyway."

Jock turned away. Whitefellas rarely asked about spats[88] within Aboriginal families, but Jock wanted to be sure his boss didn't.

"Not a problem, Jock, but don't worry about the work until after the holidays. There's a bit of trouble here as well."

"What trouble, Mr. Hector?"

"One of my granddaughters has gone missing. She's been out in the bush all night. And I should have tied down my son-in-law to stop him from going lookin' for her. I didn't, so he bolted off and has now gone missing as well. We're about to restart the search."

"Where did you lose the little girl, Mr. Hector?"

"We are not sure, but probably in the uncut scrub between here and Patterson's cliff. If she had run down to the road or across a paddock, we'd have seen her."

"Lemme take a look," said Jock. "See if I can find her tracks."

Hector looked at his watch. It was just after five. There was just enough light to enable Jock to work, and there was not yet a stir from anyone.

"Don't worry about my son-in-law's tracks for the moment. He's a bushman and can better cope."

Hector left a note for the others.

Gone out early.

Go and get the neighbors.

Back soon. Don't worry.

Hector

"Come on, Jock. Let's go."

On Christmas Day, the heavy boots of Rory Burke and five McTiernan men ransacked the bush. They had all but

---

[88] Arguments.

obliterated the delicate markings of Daisy's path. But Jock just managed to make out where it started. Soon, a trail emerged.

By a quarter past six, Nell cradled Rory on the back veranda at Ballycallan while her brothers gathered the neighbors. Rory's nighttime search had ended just minutes before, when he stumbled back in from the bush. He hadn't gone far. The lamp went out not long after he left, having exhausted all its fuel.

Nell watched the sky with Rory's head in her lap. The pallor of dawn would soon be replaced by the brilliance of a day unblemished by the dash of clouds.

She picked up where she and Rory had left off, but lovingly.

"I stayed connected to Da for the sake of our family," said Nell softly, "not because I wanted to block you out. He's left me land, Rory, a fifth of all this, so I had to keep him placated."

Rory sat up and blinked.

"He's what?"

"His will divides the estate into five and not four, but the only people who know are him and me. I didn't ever tell you because I thought you'd object, and I didn't want to hurt your pride."

Rory removed his arm from around Nell's shoulder and looked up into the scrub.

So that was how Hector stuck his ore in.

And that was the cause of the cavern.

"Your brothers don't know?"

"No, not yet. Da wants it left until the will is open. He's written them a letter that's filed with it."

Rory shook his head, up and down, and side to side, as if trying to clear out cob-webs.

He spoke once his mind had steadied.

"So, the only reason was to save my feelings? The only thing that made you reach the conclusion that was somethin' you couldn't confide in me?"

Rory prayed a little as he waited for her answer.

Please God that the love of my life didn't think I couldn't provide for our family.

Nell took in a deep breath.

"There were so many things I didn't understand when I moved out to the west-lands but that I just had to accept. From little things like bans on eucalyptus oil and strange tales about Aboriginals to having to live in an unsound house. None of it made me feel safe. I couldn't work the land anymore in the way I had down here because I had become somebody's wife, and I felt awkward about asking even the most sensible questions because that somehow made me a nag."

Nell wrapped her arms around her knees.

"I tried to learn to obey; to accept my duties without flinching. But, sometimes, I thought I would choke."

God what a woman gives up, thought Nell, *once she decides to marry.*

Rory didn't understand what Nell was quite driving at but felt the bitterness weighting her words. She turned and looked at him.

"I know it was wrong, very wrong, and I'm sorry. But that fifth of Ballycallan is mine. It's *mine*! For God's sake, I earned it. And I was never going to make the slightest move that might risk me never getting it, no matter who I fell in love with."

And every excuse I ever made for keeping Da's will secret, thought Nell, *was a poor attempt at self-justification.*

Rory kissed his wife on the forehead then held her as tight as could be. With his head resting on the crown of her head, just where it lay in 1915 after she attacked the Jacaranda tree, Rory confronted his own truth.

She's a right to know why I drew away from her for about half of 1922, and how the thirty acres I didn't own came back to haunt us all.

What courage left in Rory's sallied soul readied him to confess.

Then, there was a rustle in the scrubland. Nell and Rory looked up to the top of the hill and tore off toward it.

The unmistakable form of Hector McTiernan emerged from the bush in slow strides. He carried Daisy securely, who was crying in his arms, while Jock walked tall by his side.

Daisy clung to Nell's neck when Hector handed her over. Soon, it was impossible to tell whose tears ran more fully, Daisy's or her mother's.

Nell rushed back to the homestead, her skirt bustling. She wanted Daisy inside.

"Rory," said Hector, as he set out to follow her. "There's someone here who you might like to thank?"

Rory wiped his eyes with the end of his shirt sleeve and turned to look at Jock. The words of gratitude he wanted to speak were somehow trapped in his mouth. Rory had never been so close to an Aboriginal man. The nearest he'd probably ever been to Aboriginals was the mob he saw in January of 1923, at the willowy reach in the river near Jacaranda Ridge, and whom he had almost poisoned.

"He won't bite, Rory," said Hector dryly.

Rory managed an awkward smile as Jock unleashed a stunning grin. His quivering hand was extended to Jock's, then diverted to his pocket. Rory dropped a shilling into Jock's long palm, then shot off to be with Nell.

You didn't go out trying to kill blackfellas back in 1922, thought Rory, as he ran down the hill, *you went out trying to kill people!*

Now, there was no way in the world Nell could know the truth.

A black man has saved a Burke life!

Sleeping dogs would be allowed to lie, and his revolting secret was his punishment. And that applied to all of it. Admitting to fibs about who owned what land on the Noonan–Burke boundary was a slippery slope toward having to tell his wife that her husband once attempted murder.

And she thought she'd committed a mortal sin by not mentioning that inheritance!

They had Daisy back. That was all that mattered, and Nell had closed the cavern. And it had been all along about somethin' simple—a hunk of Ballycallan.

Rory stopped at the homestead's back veranda and sat on the bottom step, panting. He would leave it to Dave to transfer those paddocks, come January, but it would be forever kept from their wives. And the Burkes would pack up and head home to Jacaranda Ridge and celebrate New Year as a family.

I don't want to spend the holidays with my in-laws after everything that's happened.

Throughout the three-day journey, Eamon and his mother swapped places. The teenager sat up on the front board of the long cart by Rory; a handkerchief touched by the oil of the elderberry helped him whenever he wheezed. Nell stayed in the back with the rest of her children, close to Daisy all the way. But she was able to rejoice in her own liberation. Hector elected to set her free on the evening of the day Jock found Daisy.

Hector chose his moment within a swamp of feeling, just as he'd described in Nell's kitchen. But he didn't need to wait until his own demise and the reading of a letter in his will. The near loss of Daisy pulled the McTiernans together, and Nell's brothers were told all in his study.

"I just couldn't bear to let my little girl go," said Hector, in brittle voice his sons had never heard. "I couldn't bear to leave her all alone to fate at the distance of the west-lands."

Nell's brothers promised their father they would respect his decision, one he persuaded them to be just, as Violet held his hand. A fifth of Ballycallan was willed to Nell, and it would be up to them to either buy her out or divide the profits into fifths. And over handshakes, backslaps, and brandy balloons, the McTiernans sealed a family secret.

The Burkes reached home on New Year's Eve and parked by the Jacaranda tree. When the long cart stopped, Nell found herself seated at the cuts she chopped into the bark; the trio of incisions made by a frightened young mother when Eamon was an infant. She ran her fingers across them. That Christmas, Nell McTiernan was left down south at Ballycallan, and the woman returning to her home at Jacaranda Ridge was Mrs. Rory Burke.

* * * * *

The second death of Christmas 1928 touched many more than the first.

Father O'Kelly told Father Sheehan that he would spend Christmas with Father Reilly, who had just returned from several months in Ireland. He would take the train south to the Port Town on the morning of December twenty-fourth and return home on December twenty-ninth. Anlon Sheehan drove John O'Kelly to the Town railway station and wished him a blessed and happy Christmas. They would meet again, in the early New Year, when Father Sheehan returned from the City.

O'Kelly didn't tell him. He didn't tell Sheehan that his profound distrust of both Withers and O'Keefe had only come to deepen. He never let on that he had been praying every day since Withers' wretched Town Hall meeting, asking the Lord to guide him. Sergeant O'Keefe, he was fully aware, would do nothing to stop violence or even killing. And O'Kelly never confided, never to anyone, that in the week before Christmas, God had answered his prayers and told him what to do.

Someone had to warn them.

So, he packed his swag on the evening of December twenty-third, but not to prepare to visit Father Reilly. He boarded the train at the Town railway station on Christmas Eve morning, but got off at a stop eight miles to the south.

From there, O'Kelly set off on foot, cane in hand, swag on his back, and walked deep into the bush toward a place where he knew they once camped. With God's help, he would find some Aboriginal people, persuade them to tell all the others, and to flee.

Merciful Lord, the old priest prayed, as he cut through the hardy scrub, *you have left me with one unfinished task—a burden which I am yet to complete, and for which I ask your help. Grant me your favor, oh merciful Lord, by showing me the path to souls yet to be saved so they are alert to the danger ahead.*

As O'Kelly walked, he wondered why he was left with this last-ditch effort. Then, as if answered by the Lord himself, his thoughts drifted toward his own error.

Had he ever stood up to Roddy O'Doherty—pulled rank and told him that God's wrath would strike if his disdain for Aboriginals persisted? Had he ever been willing to resist the Bishop, with his distaste for conflict with the state, and challenge the Protector on his dereliction of duty, both to the government and Aboriginal people alike? And had he ever had the fortitude—*had he ever even tried*—to educate the ignorance out of his own parishioners, so they would embrace all the Aboriginals had to offer rather than moving them on, repeatedly, wherever and whenever felt by them to be remotely in the way?

And what about Rory Burke, Archibald Withers, and their disgusting, murderous plot? He'd dealt with it with no more than a wag of a finger, as if Burke were a naughty child.

"I should have reported the pair of them," bellowed O'Kelly, "to the Port Town police, and immediately, for an act of attempted mass murder!"

The truth was he had failed to cultivate allies and lacked the strength of character to lead.

For that would have taken the courage of Luther, and Martin Luther he certainly wasn't.

O'Kelly began to sob.

I am sorry, Mother. I am sorry, Father. I abandoned you to no end. I promised your son would do you proud, and all I have done is fail. Keeping the Irish in Australia within God's Kingdom in their treatment of one and other was the least our Lord would expect. I fled on a promise to bring His word, His light and, above all, His love to the first people of this land. I succeeded only in breaking your hearts.

He stammered into speech.

"Bless me, Father, for I have sinned…"

That prayerful walk was the last ever taken in John O'Kelly's life, and this tearful confession his final. The old priest fell, when a bloody rupture flooded his brain and cast away his spirit. A Bible was found lying at his heart, tucked inside the pocket of a battered black coat, while the delicate cross he had held in his hand was released into the limitless bush.

* * * * *

Made in the USA
Monee, IL
06 July 2021